✎§ PARZIVAL ?❧

PARZIVAL

BY

Wolfram von Eschenbach

TRANSLATED AND WITH AN INTRODUCTION BY

Helen M. Mustard & Charles E. Passage

VINTAGE BOOKS

A Division of Random House

NEW YORK

CONTENTS

INTRODUCTION

1. WOLFRAM'S POEM

THE SCOPE OF *Parzival* is greater than that of any medieval literary work except Dante's *Divine Comedy,* and in his way Wolfram encompasses as much of human experience as does the Italian poet. His two spheres, the Arthurian circle and the Grail circle, include most of the important aspects of human existence, worldly and spiritual. So broad is the canvas Wolfram paints and so many and diverse are the highly individualized characters he portrays, that there is room for almost every possible human situation. We find the world of childhood in the young Parzival and in the charming Obilot and her playmate Clauditte; the man's world of battles and tournaments, strife against the enemy and unswerving loyalty to friends and kinsmen; the woman's world of joy and sorrow in the love for husband and children; a sense for cruelty and suffering in human life in such scenes as Sigune and the dead Schianatulander or in Herzeloyde's grief at the loss of Gahmuret; the quest for something beyond human existence in Parzival's long search for the Grail; and the whole concept of a dedicated society, serving the Grail and representing a sphere spiritually exalted above the normal realm of life.

Interestingly enough, Wolfram seems less medieval and more modern than Dante. He has his roots firmly in the medieval world, to be sure. In *Parzival* we truly see knighthood flowering and displaying its greatest ideals, the bravery and courtesy of the men, the gentleness and modesty of the women, the respect for Arthur's world of knightly virtues, and the reverence for the sphere of the Grail and all that it represents. But one also sees much that is almost modern in tone, and one marvels that this medieval poet could so transcend his own tradition. The inner development of the hero, the first story showing such a development in Western European literature, strikes a modern note. So too does the relationship between the sexes. In the traditional medieval romances, love was usually an extra-marital experience. In Wolfram love and marriage are synonymous, an almost unbelievable anomaly for the chivalric age. Where there is an extra-marital relationship, it is either deliberately light in tone, as in the Gawan-Antikonie episode, or it is associated with punishment and suffering, as in the relationship between Anfortas and Orgeluse. The ideal relationship, and one which Wolfram treats with great understanding and tenderness, is love in marriage. To be sure, Wolfram had a predecessor who was also interested in the problem of marriage, Hartmann von Aue, but whereas Hartmann is most interested in the effect which marriage may have on the man's pursuit of knighthood, Wolfram treats the theme much more profoundly in its meaning to both men and women.

Still another way in which Wolfram goes beyond the traditional medieval world is in his treatment of the Grail theme. There is here no trace of dualism or of asceticism. The Grail circle is set off, but not separated from Arthur's world. The Lord of the Grail may marry and have children. The knights of the Grail practice the calling of knighthood, and they may even leave the Grail castle for long periods to become lord of a land left without a ruler, and marry in that land, and have children. The women in the service of the Grail are always free to leave and marry, though their children are then expected to return to the Grail. Parzival is urged by Trevrizent to continue in the practice of knighthood even while searching for the Grail. The two worlds, the Grail world and the world of knighthood, are constantly mingling. It is clear that Wolfram is affirming the goodness and meaningfulness of life in this world and that the Grail sphere is not set in opposition to life itself, but is simply the other side of the scales, another aspect of human existence.

Last but not least, Wolfram's portraits of children strike one as particularly modern. No other medieval author, indeed, perhaps no author before the nineteenth century, has shown such keen and sympathetic insight into the mind of a child. The boy Parzival, little Obilot, and the child Loherangrin are real and unforgettable children.

In spite of its scope Wolfram made his *Parzival* into a meticulously structured work, far more carefully and artistically patterned than any work from his contemporaries. It is divided into sixteen "Books," each of which is subdivided into units of thirty lines each. These divisions were very likely made by Wolfram himself, since most of the manuscripts agree in this respect. Each book is of course a unit, and even the small sections of thirty lines for long stretches form individual paragraph-like units. Professor Springer has shown in a recent article with what mathematical preciseness these units are arranged in relation to the core of the work, Book ix. Discounting the first 108 sections, the Gahmuret prelude (probably a late addition to the work), there are 324 sections (109-432) before and 324 sections (503-826) after Book ix, which itself numbers exactly 70 sections.

This careful external structure is paralleled by an inner structure just as meaningful. Space does not permit a detailed analysis here, but the thoughtful reader will discover for himself the nice balance which Wolfram keeps between Grail circle and Arthurian circle, between their two chief representatives, Parzival and Gawan; will note how the main thread of work is never completely forgotten even when Gawan is in the foreground, how significant brief scenes can be for the structure of the work as a whole—for example, the scenes with Sigune—and how many interesting parallels between Grail and Arthurian worlds are woven into the poem—for instance, the Castle of Wonders as a parallel to Munsalvaesche.

2. GENERAL BACKGROUND

The heroic oral poetry of the ancient Germanic peoples, which survived in Iceland and was there committed to writing, disappeared gradually from among the continental Germans in the course of the Middle Ages, and for a long time no adequate substitute took its place. Heathen gods and heathen manners were honored in those poems, and the Church could not approve of either, much less foster their preservation in writing. Thus the numerous German dialects came to be represented during their "old" period, roughly from 500 A.D. to 1000 A.D., almost exclusively by utilitarian and devotional works, and no secular literature worthy of the name was created.

In adjacent France, however, the rapidly emerging French language had already become the vehicle of the remarkable *Song of Roland* by approximately the year 1100, and a large quantity of heroic poetry, the "chansons de geste," used the same literary idiom throughout the twelfth century, always with ecclesiastical approval because of the Christian subject matter. In Germany the eleventh century witnessed those extensive linguistic changes that transformed the German dialects from their "old" into their "middle" forms, which are delimited, roughly speaking, by the dates 1000 to 1500. It was in the Rhine valley and in the southern or "high" area of the country, and in a cluster of dialects often, though not quite correctly, referred to collectively as Middle High German, that poets around the mid-twelfth century began to translate and adapt recent French works, thereby preparing the way for a significant secular literature in Germany.

Around 1150 also, French poets, in addition to topics of the "chansons de geste," turned to subjects drawn from classical antiquity, such as the unknown Norman poet's *Roman d'Eneas,* or to themes drawn from a Celtic source, such as the lost version of a Tristan narrative known as the *Estoire.* By 1180 German poets, with a marked advance in sophistication over their prior efforts, worked from these newer models. From this decade we have Eilhart von

Oberg's *Tristrant und Isalde* and Heinrich von Veldeke's *Eneit*. By this time French poetry had witnessed a fresh development, for since perhaps 1160 the celebrated innovator, Chrétien de Troyes, had been producing narrative poems of the type known as Arthurian romances. Again the German poets followed suit, and in the 1190's Hartmann von Aue translated, or, more properly speaking, adapted Chrétien's *Erec* in a poetic idiom which his contemporaries found a marvel of lucidity and charm. Probably just at the turn of the century he similarly adapted Chrétien's *Yvain* (German: *Iwein*), while in the interval between he had added two works on quasi-religious themes: *Gregorius,* adapted from a French poem called *La Vie du Pape Grégoire,* and *Poor Henry* (*Der arme Heinrich*), from more complex sources. These four narratives, together with his lyric poems, established Hartmann as a fine poet in his own right, equal to the best the French could offer, and as the harbinger of German poets who were about to surpass the French altogether. The order of the day was now Arthurian romance and Chrétien was the admired master of that genre. The German version of his semi-Arthurian *Cligès* is lost. If his pious non-Arthurian *Guillaume d'Angleterre* (of disputed authorship) was not translated, and if his Lancelot poem was neglected in favor of the paler, independently derived Swiss *Lanzelet,* his 9234-line fragment of a romance of Perceval, *Li Contes del Graal,* engaged the attention of Wolfram von Eschenbach, a younger contemporary of Hartmann's. On this theme Wolfram composed his *Parzival,* a chivalric romance of 24,810 lines in rhymed couplets, which may stand as the noblest literary achievement of the Middle Ages, with the sole exception of Dante's *Divine Comedy.*

Two other works flank it on either side. First, the great version of *Tristan* by Gottfried von Strassburg, and second, the fine compendium in which an unknown Austrian poet brought together the ancient Germanic stories about Siegfried and Kriemhild and made of them the continuous verse narrative called *The Song of the Nibelungs.* Still other poems, of a second magnitude, cluster around these major works, while contemporaneous with all of them stand the great numbers of lyric poems of those German troubadours who in their own language were termed *Minnesinger* and whose prince was Walther von der Vogelweide.

Walther outlived all his famous poet-contemporaries and with his death, in approximately 1230, the glorious summertime of medieval German literature closed. It had been a great age, and personalities and events in Germany, as in Western Europe generally, had matched these artistic accomplishments. The sequence of rulers of the Hohenstauffen family, who since 1138 had commanded the German world as Holy Roman Emperors, had themselves been poets, warriors, crusaders, visionaries. Frederick Barbarossa had, in fact, perished in 1190 while on a Crusade in the Near East. The fabulous Frederick II, temporarily deprived of his heritage, was crowned King of Sicily as a four-year-old boy in 1198, at just about the time *Parzival* was begun. The years 1211-1212, when *Parzival* must have been finished or very nearly finished, saw Frederick's election as Emperor and his adventurous return to his fatherland to claim his patrimony against enemies. His coronation in 1215 at Charlemagne's capital of Aix-la-Chapelle (Aachen) occurred very near the end of Wolfram's life. Frederick's "conquest" of Jerusalem was to follow. His vision of a restored secular empire of the Caesars had meanwhile been countered by the vision of Pope Innocent III, who desired a religious empire with the Popes as the new Caesars, and Innocent III was possibly the ablest and keenest of all Popes. His Papacy from 1198 to 1216 almost exactly coincided with Wolfram's poetic career. In the same period Saint Francis of Assisi (1182-1226) was already engaged in that life and teaching which still touch men's hearts. France was being ruled by the capable hand of Philip Augustus (1180-1223); his successor was to be Saint Louis. England had the romantic Richard the Lion-Heart for its king from 1189 to 1199, and thereafter witnessed the troubled reign of King John, from whom rebellious nobles wrested the Magna Charta of rights in 1215. In town after town across Western Europe the great cathedrals were being built, and everywhere the fervor of the Crusades could be felt.

By the time of the death of Walther von der Vogelweide, sinister political portents were beginning to be observed for the German Empire. Fortune still smiled on Frederick II in 1230, though he was already deeply committed to his fateful clash with the Papacy. By 1240 fortune began to avert her face from him. He died in 1250, personally betrayed by trusted friends and with his grand Caesarian vision unrealized. The Empire then plunged into the dismal interregnum from which the Hapsburgs were ultimately to restore it and give it a different orientation. Even before Frederick's death the Pope had fled Rome lest the Emperor's armies should take the city and make him prisoner, and had found refuge in the Papal enclave city of Lyons, an unwelcome guest amid surrounding French territory. The action foreshadowed the grim Papal schism to come and the "Babylonian captivity" in Avignon. Interregnum and Avignon together spelled the end of the high Middle Ages. To say that medieval German literature died in 1230 with Walther, or even in 1250 with Frederick, would be unfair. But it declined ever more rapidly, and by 1300 it was a withered forest in which few or no birds sang.

During those years of decline more than one minor poet derived inspiration from Wolfram's works and from *Parzival* in particular. The preservation of seventeen complete manuscripts of his major poem and of more than fifty others in fragmentary form indicates how widely known it was. In 1477, when the art of printing was still in its infancy, *Parzival* was republished in printed form. With the Reformation forty years thereafter, however, it passed into eclipse along with all other medieval German books. For the next three centuries it was to be known only to scholars, though it was never to be totally forgotten as *The Song of the Nibelungs* was. To North German Protestant intellectuals, all those monuments to the Catholic era were unwelcome, while South German Catholics, as a bulwark against heretical content, chose most often to confine themselves to Latin. The protracted religious strife in Central Europe was hostile to literature in any case, and throughout Western Europe the new Renaissance spirit indiscriminately scorned everything that was medieval. But the compelling reason for the neglect was social in nature. That older literature had been almost exclusively composed by knights, about knights and ladies, for knights and ladies. And knighthood, once admirable, was now an anachronism and an absurdity, as *Don Quixote* testified.

The latter eighteenth century saw the exhumation of these books by antiquarians motivated by curiosity and by incipient nationalism. The men of the Age of Enlightenment saw nothing of value in them, but the Romanticists around 1800 were to espouse their cause with enthusiasm. The enthusiasm led to gross misinterpretations, but it also led to textual study and investigation of the historical background, and the sober scholarship of nineteenth-century critics cannot fail to command admiration and gratitude. The less sober public, on the other hand, too frequently forced these works to stand as patriotic monuments or as monuments of edification chaste and unmarred by the crass problems of the day. Thus Wagner's *Parsifal,* splendid as it may be musically, is, as a literary work, a pretentiously moralizing opera libretto, wholly alien in spirit to the work it professes to dramatize.

The language embodying this admirable literature continues to be a barrier to appreciation and understanding, and even native Germans find themselves dependent upon translations into the modern idiom. Where a speaker of modern English may, with a little effort and good will, read Chaucer's latter fourteenth-century English, which is the lineal ancestor of his own speech, Wolfram's Middle High German is a century and a half further removed in time and only a collateral ancestor of contemporary German. Yet those twelfth- and thirteenth-century dialects of South Germany—Alemannic, Franconian, Austro-Bavarian, etc.—are not insuperable obstacles. *The Song of the Nibelungs* yields its meaning after very brief study; with a little effort Gottfried and Hartmann may be read for pleasure, though not parsed in each detail; the charm of the lyric poets may be felt even if occasional passages remain obscure. But then the confident reader takes up *Parzival* and is plunged into dismay. He follows the external action more or less, but the copious vocabulary and the uncommonly difficult grammar ultimately defeat him and he abandons the book. The difficulty may be approximately described as a combination of Chaucerian archaism with Robert Browning's complexity of diction.

Over and above the work itself there are still the normal and legitimate questions any interested reader will ask: How does it happen that the "Grail" is neither "Holy" nor a chalice, but a kind of green stone? Who was this "Kyot" by whom the author repeatedly asserts that he heard the story of Parzival told? How much of the story was Wolfram's invention? Where did the original story come from? Where, geographically, is the action supposed to take place? What of these outlandish names of persons and places in which the author takes such delight? Some readers will surely wonder what the author meant by his statement that "he didn't know a single alphabet letter," and still others will puzzle at the insistence upon "Anjou" in a German poet's work, especially in connection with the Grail.

To none of these questions, alas, can brief and certain answers be supplied. Tantalizing mystery besets every side of this poem, and the literature of proposed solutions is vast indeed—and mutually contradictory. The problems themselves are fascinating. In fact, there is a real danger of becoming so involved in them that the work of art itself becomes obscured. Yet a summary of the principal problems and of their known or hypothetical solutions is indispensable, although the poem itself will warm the heart and delight the fancy well enough whether or not these problems are ever solved.

3. The Author

Specific information about the author is scarce and arrived at chiefly from inference. He must have been born around 1170 and must have begun *Parzival* around 1197 or 1198. The first six books of the poem patently constitute a unit and at the end of Book vi the author speaks as though he were winded from prolonged effort. Continuation of his narrative is made contingent upon the approval of an unnamed lady. Presumably an interval ensued before he resumed his story, and quite probably the first six books were circulated among readers as a more or less self-contained work. An imitator named Wirnt von Grafenberg has a poem entitled *Wigalois* which shows the distinct influence of *Parzival,* but only from Books i through vi. The puzzling Introduction, perhaps as far as 3,25, may well have been added at a later time to parry hostile critics; likewise the oddly intrusive "self-defense" at the end of Book ii.

In Book vii (379,18-19) there is mention of the fact that "Erfurt vineyards *still* show the marks of the same disaster," namely of being trampled down by horses; the reference must be to the siege of Erfurt by King Philip in 1203. The Margravine of Heitstein referred to, in past tense, in Book viii (404,1-2) must be Elizabeth von Vohburg, a sister of King Ludwig i of Wittelsbach; she died in 1204. Allusion to the conquest of Constantinople by the Crusaders in 1204 seems to be the basis for the remark in Book xi (563,8-9): "When Greece was the way it was when they found the treasures there." Beyond these *points d'appui* there are no definitely ascertainable dates. The opening lines of Book xv may suggest another interval between periods of composition. As for the conclusion, all that can be said is that *Parzival* was completed before the author began work on his poem *Willehalm,* since lines 4,20-24, of the latter speak of the mixed reception accorded to *Parzival,* and the ensuing text repeatedly alludes to characters and situations in the previous poem.

The nine extant books of *Willehalm* deal with legends surrounding an actual personage, Count William of Toulouse, who, after heroic battle against the Saracens in 793 and valiant support of Charlemagne's son, Louis the Pious, retired to a monastery and ended his days as a saintly monk. At 393,30 there is mention of the splendor of Emperor Otto's coronation in Rome in 1209; at another point there is mention of a siege weapon called a *dribock,* first known to have been used in Germany in 1212. If, as has been suggested, the theme was appropriate only for a time when a Crusade was being preached, the only suitable event would be the Crusade proclaimed by Frederick II at the moment of his coronation in Aix in 1215. Somewhere, then, between 1209 and 1215 lie the termination of *Parzival* and the undertaking of *Willehalm*.

Eight or nine lyric poems are also recorded under Wolfram's name. Two fragments of another romance have been preserved under the title of *Titurel,* simply because that proper name occurs in the opening line, though a more appropriate title would be *Schianatulander and Sigune.* The subject matter is closely meshed with *Parzival,* while the complex stanza pattern allies the work with the lyric poems. Scholars are divided as to whether the work should be seen as a forestudy to *Parzival* or as a sequel to it.

Willehalm, which was undertaken at the desire of Landgrave Hermann of Thuringia, was never finished. The Landgrave is mentioned in an aside, at 417,22-26; he died in 1217, but his death is not implied in the poem. (Stanza 82a of *Titurel,* which does refer to his death, is spurious.) The conclusion is, therefore, that Wolfram either discontinued his poem upon the death of his patron or that he himself died at about the same time. In any case, there is small likelihood of Wolfram's having lived beyond 1220.

Of several towns named Eschenbach, the one associated with the poet was unquestionably the little hamlet near Ansbach which since 1918 has been officially designated "Wolfram's Eschenbach." Located in 1200 within the fluctuating borders of the Duchy of Swabia, it was on the very edge of Bavarian territory, and early in Book III of *Parzival* (121,7) the poet says "we Bavarians," probably because of family origins. At least three references are made in the course of the poem to features that could come only from intimate acquaintance with the locality: the doughnuts of Trühendingen (modern Wassertrüdningen, just south of Eschenbach), Abenberg Castle just east of the town, and the Mardi Gras battles staged by merchants' wives in Tolnstein (modern Dollnstein) also near Eschenbach.

That Wolfram was a knight and extremely proud of his status, however poor he may have been money-wise, is evident to any reader of his poem. Incidental references to place names throughout his works indicate a familiarity with Bavaria and the central German province of Thuringia; place names beyond these limits are probably from hearsay, such as Aachen, the Rhone river, the painters of Cologne and Maastricht, and the like. Trevrizent's itinerary in Book IX may duplicate a journey of the author's as far as Cilli in modern Yugoslavia, though the point is dubious. Poor knight that he was, it was natural that Wolfram should take service with one nobleman or another. The reference in Book IV (184,4) to "my lord the Count of Wertheim" may indicate an actual master; or again, it may indicate nothing more than that such a nobleman was host or guest at a recitation of Book IV. In the course of the first Grail scene (230,12) the poet says that "such huge fires no one has ever seen before or since here in Wildenberg." The location is in dispute, but it may well have been the great manor house of the Lords of Durne in the Odenwald south of Frankfurt-am-Main. Elusive as these identifications may be, it is certain that Wolfram spent considerable time at the court of Landgrave Hermann at the famous Wartburg near Erfurt. There he enjoyed the patronage of that Maecenas-like nobleman, who later furnished him with the French source for *Willehalm*. There he encountered a mixed array of courtiers and met Walther von der Vogelweide, as 297,16-25 indicates. There, too, legend was to make him compete in the singing contest which Wagner makes the subject of the second act of *Tannhäuser*. It is dubious that Wolfram ever met Tannhäuser, who was a real person, but it is sure that he was in real life very little like the pious baritone named Wolfram who sings the aria to the Evening Star. Melancholy resignation to celibacy like that baritone's goes quite contrary to the impression we receive from the personal allusions made in *Parzival*.

4. "Ine kan decheinen buochstap"

With the question of Wolfram's learning we come to a crucial, unsolved, and probably unsolvable question. The language used in the often-cited passage at the end of Book II seems plain enough:

> ". . . if anyone requests me to do so [continue the story], let him not consider it as a book. I don't know a single letter of the alphabet."

The latter sentence: *"ine kan decheinen buochstap,"* would seem to mean, very plainly, "I don't know how to read or write." One school of critics denies emphatically that an illiterate could have composed *Parzival,* and they explain the words by saying either that Wolfram meant he knew no Latin, or that, tongue in cheek, he was scoffing at the pretentiousness of Hartmann von Aue, whose *Poor Henry* begins:

> *"Ein ritter sô gelêret was,*
> *daz er an den buochen las*
> *swaz er dar an geschriben vant:*
> *der was Hartman genant,*
> *dienstman was er zOuwe."* [1]

It is true that Hartmann was learned, and that Wolfram seems to evince a certain antagonism toward him in more than one reference; it is true that Gottfried von Strassburg was learned, that he was a disciple of Hartmann's, and that in *Tristan* he makes disparaging remarks about an unnamed poet who can be no other than Wolfram. All of which tends to support interpretation of that sentence as a comic overstatement of "small French and less Latin," or as a rhetorical declaration, for comic effect, of the opposite of the obvious truth. On the other hand, all the numerous references to the source work involve expressions like "as

[1] "There was a knight so learned that he read in books whatever he found written in them. His name was Hartmann and he was a vassal at Aue."

the story *says*," "as I *heard* it told." Wolfram does not use the words "I read" or any words that could be interpreted to signify reading. Of Kyot, however, he expressly and pointedly says that *he* read the original story. As for Wolfram's knowledge of French, he remarks in *Willehalm* (237,3ff.):

> "To take quarters is called *loger* [*Herbergen ist lo-schiern genant*], that much of the language I have learned. A loutish Champagnois could do much better at French than I, the way I speak French."

Again the claim is only to a speaking knowledge of the language, not to a reading knowledge.

Folklore researchers in all areas of the world agree as to the prodigious quantities of verse committed to memory by singers and reciters in illiterate milieux, and in the face of such evidence there is the possibility that Wolfram composed orally. His extensive knowledge of the works of antecedent and contemporary German poets presents no difficulty, since they would have been recited orally, just as *Parzival* was obviously intended to be. The incidental lore in which he delights could also have been acquired by word of mouth. In fact, his distortion of names would find a plausible explanation in such a process.

Carrying this theory to its logical end, Kyot or an intermediary would have had to read aloud to Wolfram from a manuscript, publicly or privately, or would have had to narrate in prose summary the total contents of the sixteen-book *Parzival*. The illiterate author would then have had to retain all that information while he worked out his poem over a period of years, and would finally have had to dictate the total work, in sections presumably, to one or more scribes. The French *book* source for *Willehalm* would have been read aloud to the poet. Composition of such lengthy works on such a basis, especially by a peregrinating poet, so baffles the modern mind that one quickly returns to the "no Latin" theory, or to the "anti-Hartmann sneer" theory, or to the "out-and-out spoof" theory. Then, just as one has comfortably settled for one or the other of these, he is brought up short by the lines in *Willehalm* (2,19-22):

> *"swaz an den buochen stêt geschriben,*
> *des bin ich künstelôs beliben.*
> *niht anders ich gelêret bin:*
> *wan hân ich kunst, die gît mir sin."* [2]

The words surely echo Hartmann's words, but Wolfram insists, apparently, on his own illiteracy.

There the problem hangs in mid-air. Nor does stylistic analysis aid in a solution. The involutions—and they are manifold—could be the result of oral improvisation; they could equally well be, along with the occasional startling treatment of metaphor, the hallmark of a unique mind. Oral improvisations could, of course, be read back to the poet later for improvement. Yet, would it not rather be a *writing* poet who would produce so many passages of precisely thirty or sixty lines, the column-length of a manuscript page? Witness the "self-defense" at the end of Book ii, the lists of conquered knights in Book xv, the catalogue of jewels in Book xvi—to take only the more conspicuous examples. A *writer* once embarked on some enumeration or digression might well fill out his column or page before resuming his main discourse. Still, the poem reads like an oral work. The scenes, the pauses, the transitions, and above all the asides, convey the impression of oral delivery caught, as it were, by an agile taker of shorthand. Gradually we form a concept of Wolfram, not as a poet or author, but as a public reciter and entertainer who delivered his recitations for sheer love of the story and for the glorification of the knightly class. Sometimes, as in the Parzival-Feirefiz duel in Book xv, he seems to have conjured his characters to life just a few feet away and to be in actual anguish as to the outcome of the fight. By his intense empathy, by skillful modulations of his voice as he took the different roles, he may have given his audiences the equivalent of a theatrical experience. But whether he did so with or without the benefit of his *a b c*'s remains a question without an answer.

---

[2] "Whatever in books stands written, of that I have remained unskilled. I have not been taught otherwise: if I have skill, intelligence gives it to me."

5. KYOT

There is no longer any doubt among scholars that Chrétien was Wolfram's main source, but the question as to other sources still remains, and Wolfram does not help to clarify the issue by his puzzling references to a certain Kyot as his master. Chrétien's romance, *Li Contes del Graal,* composed a literary generation before Wolfram, begins, after a brief introduction, with the child Parzival in the wilderness, that is, with Wolfram's Book III. Then with far greater brevity, with many characters unnamed, and different in hundreds of small details as well as in ideas, it follows the story outline up to a point roughly equivalent to manuscript page 645, or two-thirds of the way through Book XIII. There it breaks off, at line 9234, in the middle of a sentence. Chrétien therefore is not the source for Wolfram's first two books, nor for the conclusion of the poem in the last three books.

Six times in the course of the work Wolfram refers to Kyot as his source in addition to Chrétien, and from these references a scholarly controversy arose which is still raging to this day. The first reference to Kyot is in Book VIII, 416, where Wolfram describes Kyot as either *l'enchanteur* or *le chanteur,* either a magician or a singer, depending on how one interprets the word "laschantiure" in the original. Scholars do not agree on which is the preferable translation. Philological evidence seems to point to *l'enchanteur;* however, *le chanteur* fits the general context better:

> Kyot was called *l'enchanteur* [or *le chanteur*] and his skill would not allow him to do other than sing and recite so that many are still made glad thereby. Kyot is a Provençal who saw this tale of Parzival written in heathen language [i.e., in Arabic]. Whatever he told of it in French, I, if I am not weak in my wits, am telling further in German.

In the longest of the Kyot references, beginning Book IX, 453, Wolfram tells more about Kyot. He says that he has refused to answer people's questions concerning the Grail because "Kyot asked me to keep it secret." Kyot, the well-known master, he says, found the first source of the Grail story, discarded, and in heathen writing, in Toledo, and having learned the *a b c*'s of heathen in order to decipher the manuscript, "Kyot the wise master" (455), then took to studying all the Latin books to find a people worthy of being the keepers of the Grail, and in the process read the chronicles of Britain, France, and Ireland, among others, before he discovered that the appropriate country for his purposes was Anjou. Wolfram even names here Kyot's source, a heathen by the name of Flegetanis, described as a learned scholar who set down in heathen writing the tale Kyot took such pains to read.

The last important mention of Kyot comes at the end of *Parzival*, where Wolfram says:

> "*Ob von Troys meister Cristjân*
> *disem maere hât unreht getân,*
> *daz mac wol zürnen Kyôt,*
> *der uns diu rehten maere enbôt.*
> *endehaft giht der Provenzâl,*
> *wie Herzeloyden kint den grâl*
> *erwarp, als im daz gordent was,*
> *do in verworhte Anfortas.*
> *von Provenz in tiuschiu lant*
> *diu rehten maere uns sint gesant,*
> *und dirre âventiur endes zil.*
> *niht mêr dâ von nu sprechen wil*
> *ich Wolfram von Eschenbach,*
> *wan als dort der meister sprach.*" [3]

The word "endehaft," translated here as "correctly," may mean "precisely," "correctly," or possibly "all the way to the end." This would then appear to be a criticism of Chrétien's

[3] "If Master Chrétien de Troyes did not do justice to this story, that may well irk Kyot, who furnished us the right story. The Provençal correctly tells how Herzeloyde's child won the Grail, as he was destined to do, when Anfortas had forfeited it. From Provence to Germany the true facts were sent to us, as well as this adventure's final conclusion. I, Wolfram von Eschenbach, shall tell no more of it now than the master told there."

poem for its fragmentary form or its "incorrectness," and seems to indicate that Kyot had furnished Wolfram with a complete and "accurate" version.

The composite data offer a rather bizarre personage: a Provençal poet, who wrote the story of Parzival in French, who was called *l'enchanteur* or *le chanteur* and was for a time in Toledo, Spain, the headquarters of magicians, who knew Arabic and Latin and read widely in history books, and who, to judge by the sentence "Kyot asked me to keep it secret," came to Germany and personally transmitted his subject matter to Wolfram.

No such scholar-poet is known to history, however Wolfram may call him "well known," nor is there any trace of a Provençal poem on the Parzival theme, or any such French poem. The name "Kyot" represents north French "Guiot," English "Guy"; the proper Provençal form would be "Guizot." With Wolfram's fancifulness in regard to names well in their minds, scholars looked with considerable anticipation to the Old French poet Guiot de Provins—Provins being a town just southeast of Paris—who wrote around the year 1200. Apart from some songs, however, no work of his is known except a satirical poem entitled *La Bible,* the contents of which do not remotely suggest a man interested in the Parzival theme.

Nineteenth-century students of *Parzival* took Wolfram at his word and assumed that Kyot existed and that his work and memory had perished, and a persistent but unrewarded search began for evidence of Kyot's existence. More recently scholars tend to regard Kyot as a tongue-in-cheek fiction of Wolfram's. Yet the argument between the two schools of thought continues.

Those who believe there was a Kyot argue that it is unthinkable that Wolfram should not have had some major source for the Gahmuret prelude and for the conclusion of the work, since medieval writers always worked from sources. They maintain that the consistency of the total work points to some well-integrated source, probably French and perhaps from southern France because of the southern landscape which would have been unfamiliar to Wolfram, a source which is unfortunately unknown but whose existence should not be doubted simply because it has never been discovered.

Those who do not believe there was a Kyot do not deny that Wolfram probably had sources other than Chrétien, but they agree with the recent studies by Rachbauer, Fourquet, and Mergell which show that there is no room for any main source other than Chrétien. They also argue that Wolfram's account of Kyot is obviously too fantastic to be credible. Among other things, Kyot comes from Provence but writes in French; he is called a *chanteur,* that is, a lyric poet, but Wolfram maintains that he wrote a long narrative poem. The tale of Kyot's source, so this argument runs, is so completely incredible that few scholars have ever taken this "information" seriously. Furthermore, it would have been characteristic of Wolfram, with his keen sense of humor, to play a joke on his audience and readers, perhaps also on his poet contemporaries, some of whom, like Hartmann von Aue, boasted of their own book learning as an indication of their poetic ability. Another argument against the existence of a Kyot is Wolfram's *Willehalm.* The Old French source for this work is known, and there is no Kyot to confuse the issue; yet Wolfram's poem shows the same differences in form and in ideas, when compared with the source, as the differences between his *Parzival* and Chrétien's.

More important for the reader than dwelling on this probably insoluble problem of sources is the realization of Wolfram's poetic achievement. Any comparison with his known sources only points up his great gifts as a writer, the astonishing imaginativeness and ingenuity with which he could expand and alter his source to suit his own artistic purposes. No other German medieval poet shows as much originality and individuality in the treatment of his sources as does Wolfram.

6. ANJOU

With Anjou the reader finds himself confronted by a new problem. If his interests have lain with France, he may correctly identify the word as the name of a pre-1789 province almost exactly congruent with the modern department of Maine-et-Loire, located at the base of the Breton peninsula, with the city of Angers as its capital. It is four hundred miles from any point where Wolfram is known to have been. In the Middle Ages, Anjou was an ancient and powerful state, having been successively the land of the Gallic Andes, the Roman *civitas* of the Andecavi, a Frankish *comitatus,* and since the ninth century the possession of the counts descended from Fulk the Red. In 1129 Matilda (Maude), granddaughter of William the Conqueror of England, married Count Geoffrey Plantagenet of Anjou, who became the father of Henry II of England and the grandfather of Richard the Lion-Heart and King John. Thus, though Anjou was never a kingdom as Wolfram says it was, Count Geoffrey's offspring were kings of England in Wolfram's day and their descendants in turn constituted the royal line of England for centuries thereafter. Angevin territory on the continent, moreover, had been greatly expanded between 1100 and 1150, so that it was a veritable empire that Geoffrey added to the Anglo-Norman crown.

Miss Weston devotes an appendix of her 1894 translation of *Parzival* to a table of parallels between actual Angevin history and tradition and the alleged Angevin history interwoven into Wolfram's poem. These parallels may be pressed even further.

If we tentatively equate Herzeloyde with Matilda, some curious likenesses become at once apparent. Matilda, the widow of Holy Roman Emperor Henry V, as Herzeloyde was the widow of King Castis, was heiress, through her father and grandfather, to the two lands of Normandy and England, as Herzeloyde was heiress, through Castis, of the two lands "Waleis" and "Norgals." A second marriage, both in history and fiction, added Anjou as a third realm.

Machinations of Matilda's cousins, Stephen and Theobald, Counts of Blois, deprived her son Henry of his lands, just as the brothers Lehelin and Orilus deprived Parzival of *his* rightful heritage. Upon the death of Stephen on December 19, 1154, Henry did come into his rights and was recognized as King Henry II of England, Duke of Normandy, and Count of Anjou; restitution of Gahmuret's lost lands are indicated in Book XVI as lying beyond the limits of the poem, but Kardeiz will definitely regain them.

Count Geoffrey Plantagenet, on the other hand, shows little resemblance to Gahmuret except in so far as he was the able warrior-ruler, known as "the Handsome," who married the widow, heiress to two lands.

Count Geoffrey's grandfather, Fulk IV, however, found himself in 1060 the dispossessed younger son of the Count of Gâtinais (= Gandin?) and Ermengarde, Countess of Anjou, his elder brother Geoffrey III, "the Bearded," having, like Galoes, inherited everything. Unlike Gahmuret, Fulk IV did not go abroad and magnanimously give his brother a clear field. He stayed at home, content at first with a small assignment of land and wealth, but soon rebelled against his brother, took him prisoner, and made himself ruler in his stead. He ruled from 1068 to 1109.

Count Geoffrey's father, Fulk V, "the Young," ruled from 1109 to 1129, and then at age thirty-seven turned Anjou over to Geoffrey and himself went to the Holy Land, married Melisinda, daughter of the King of Jerusalem, and succeeded to the kingship there in 1131. His sons, Baldwin III and Amalric I, both ruled in the East. Thus Count Geoffrey had, not one, but two half brothers who were Eastern kings, though neither is reported to have been speckled black and white like Feirefiz.

Gahmuret, therefore, bears traits of three successive Angevin rulers, and the suggestion has been made that one of Wolfram's sources, particularly for Books I and II, may have been an oral or written account of the history of Anjou. Such an account, if it existed, might be expected to concern itself primarily with the Angevin rulers themselves and only secondarily with Matilda and her enemies, Stephen and

Theobald. Therewith would be explained the relatively minor roles accorded in the poem to Herzeloyde and the brothers Lehelin and Orilus. It hardly needs to be said that Henry II of England (1154-1189), who in the parallel genealogical tables would correspond to Parzival, bears no resemblance to the hero of the poem, but some scholars do tend to find resemblances between Parzival and Henry's son, Richard the Lion-Hearted, whose reign from 1189 to 1199 overlaps the inception of Wolfram's poem. The reign, from 1199-1216, of Richard's brother, the ill-reputed King John, almost exactly coincides with the poem's composition.

But in what way could these foreign monarchs be of concern to Wolfram? By the marriage of Matilda, the sister of Richard and John, to Henry the Lion, Duke of Brunswick, the Angevins became the supporters of the Guelf party in Germany, and there is good reason to believe that Wolfram was a pro-Hohenstauffen Ghibelline and therefore should have been *anti*-Angevin. Clearly, these Angevins were not his Angevins. His Angevins were long ago, primarily in the period from 1060 to 1160, and their all too human lives had mellowed into story.

Interestingly enough, it was in Wolfram's early manhood that Angevin luck and Angevin power suffered a grave reversal in trying to seize the Celtic-French province of Brittany. The Bretons had been displeased when their Duchess, Constance, married into the Angevin family, but they loyally supported her son, Duke Arthur, when he came to rule in 1194. Surrounded by Angevin territory as they were, they sensed that their independence was menaced. When King John came to the throne in 1199, he made it clear that he intended to control his nephew, Duke Arthur. Soon after, the Bretons found support in the nobles of Anjou itself, as well as in those of adjoining Maine and Touraine. The four provinces defied King John, recognized Arthur of Brittany as their joint King, and concurred in Arthur's decision to declare himself a vassal of Philip Augustus, King of France. War ensued in 1202, and Arthur was captured by John and murdered in 1203. The intervention by Philip Augustus led to European involvement, with the French victory at Bouvines in 1214 bringing Anjou, Brittany, and other western provinces under the control of Paris. Thus we have the striking coincidence that just at the time when Wolfram was bringing the simple Parzival to Arthur's court in Nantes (Book III), there was in actual fact a "King" Arthur ruling in Brittany.

As for Nantes, that Breton city just over the border from Anjou had repeatedly been claimed by Angevin counts and more than once had been fought for. Miss Weston sees a partial explanation of the puzzling episode of Ither and the spilled wine by reference to Angevin tradition. Ither, red-haired like many of the historical counts of Anjou, is portrayed in the poem as having come to Nantes to issue some challenge to King Arthur. The seized goblet was one of those ritual gestures of medieval times indicating such a challenge; that some of the wine spilled on Queen Ginover was, however, an unfortunate accident. Again, the story is marked with apparently pro-Anjou feelings, for Ither, who should be a villain, is represented as more than a match for Arthur and all his knights combined. Ginover mourns his death at Parzival's hands in terms that seem excessive for her husband's opponent, and ultimately we learn that Ither is Parzival's kinsman and hence an Angevin.

None of this information, however, provides the slightest clue as to why Wolfram should have been interested in the Angevins and their story in the first place, or why he should through the length of his poem have glorified an alien ruling house. He must, we theorize, have been recapitulating a French, and specifically Angevin, source story; "Kyot the Provençal" must, we imagine, have been really "Guiot the Angevin." But if he was, then why on earth should Wolfram assert the contrary?

7. ARTHUR

Parzival is, by definition, an "Arthurian romance," a tale about King Arthur, yet the astonishing fact remains that neither this nor any other such romance, for all the homage paid his name, really deals with the famous monarch as a primary figure. Honored he is in these narratives, but he stands neither in the background nor in the foreground of their canvases. Benevolent but curiously inactive for so renowned a warrior, he occupies rather the middle ground, leaving the forefront of the action and the principal interest to his knights.

His own provenience is obscure and complex. Tradition puts his lifetime in the decades just before and just after 500 A.D. and makes him a Christian Briton fighting encroachments of the pagan English. If so, he would have spoken a Brythonic Celtic language of which no records exist and which was the predecessor of historical Welsh. He would have looked back upon a Britain, Brythonic in population since prehistoric times, briefly invaded by Julius Caesar in 55 B.C. but Romanized only since the successful invasion of 43 A.D., officially Christian along with the rest of the Empire since 313, abandoned by the imperial legions in 410, and thereafter invaded by the heathen Germanic tribes of the Angles, Saxons, and Jutes. He would have been responsible for halting these tribes around 500 by force of arms at the edge of Salisbury Plain in Wessex, from which limit in southern Britain their invasion did not proceed northward for another half century. (An Arthur in northern Britain at this date is highly improbable, though often claimed.)

About 540 the historian Gildas speaks of such a British victory in his *Liber de excidio et conquestu Britanniae,* but he names the hero Ambrosius Aurelianus and locates the site at an unidentifiable Mt. Badon. In a venerable Welsh poem known as the *Gododdin* around 600 we read of a certain warrior that he fought with great power, "though he was not Arthur." It is, however, not certain that this passage is not an interpolation of a later date. Still, in the decades on both sides of the year 600 at least five Britons were christened "Arthur," a fact which suggests commemoration of a national hero. More explicit statements appear no earlier than c. 800 in the Latin *Historia Brittonum* of the priest Nennius (Nynniaw) of South Wales. If this book is a mixture of fact and fiction compiled from Gildas and various sources, it seems nonetheless to record long-standing traditions when it mentions Arthur by name, terms him, not a "king," but a *dux bellorum*—a leader of armies—and lists his twelve victories over the Angles and Saxons. And if these battle localities cannot all be identified, their wide dispersal across the map conveys the impression that Arthur's fame was extensive. As of 955 approximately, the *Annales Cambriae* (*Annals of Wales*) assign the Battle of Badon to the year 516, and to the year 537 the Battle of Camlann "in which Arthur and Medraut fell." Juxtaposed with other information, both dates seem to be a dozen years or so too late.

Meanwhile folklore had been reshaping the image of Arthur. Nennius' *Historia* already contained a description of a stone which retained the footprint of Arthur's dog, made while the hero was hunting the boar Troit. The boar hunt itself is related in the story *Kulhwch and Olwen*. In the manuscript anthology known as the Black Book of Carmarthen there is a poem (No. xxxi) that is both obscure and hard to date, but it shows Arthur in the company of other heroes: Cai (i.e., Keie), Bedwyr, Mabon son of Modron, and Manawydan son of Llyr, the last two of whom are traceable to ancient Celtic divinities of the sun and of the sea respectively. Monsters and witches are their opponents, as well as human armies, and the geography has to be expanded at least to Edinburgh in Scotland in order to encompass their feats. The pre-Norman poem *The Spoils of Annwfn* portrays Arthur and fellow heroes on a voyage to the underworld (Annwfn).

In *Kulhwch and Olwen,* the seventh story in the *Mabinogion,* we have a full-fledged tale about Arthur and his mighty exploits. If the final written form of the *Mabinogion* anthology must be dated after 1300, experts agree that this particular story had attained its present form before 1100; a century or two must be allowed for its evolution. The ninth-century Nennius knew at least the gist of its boar-hunt sequence. Here Arthur is addressed as "sovereign prince of this Island." His court is at Kelliwic in Cornwall. He summons vassals from France, Brittany, and Nor mandy to fight for him. When Kulhwch invokes his aid in the name of his warriors, the invocation fills more than six pages! A few of the names invoked will reappear in the romances, but for the most part these heroes never transcended the confines of Welsh folklore, and none of them is "knightly" in the continental sense.

After 1100 reports of Arthur multiply extravagantly. In 1113 the servant of certain traveling canons provoked a near-riot in Cornwall by denying a Cornishman's statement that King Arthur had never died. In 1125 William of Malmesbury, an Anglo-Norman, wrote of Arthur as a Breton hero for whom the Celtic inhabitants of Brittany made fabulous claims. The same author reported the discovery of Walwen's (i.e., Gawain's) tomb in southwestern Wales. A troubadour elegy from Provence in 1137 has the line: "Like Arthur I shall be lost forever." Around 1110 sculptors carved Arthurian scenes on the archivolt of the cathedral of Modena in Italy, labeling the figures with names which, though of Welsh origin, can be shown to be Latinizations of Breton forms. Italian documents of 1114 and 1125 are signed by actual persons named Artusius; a Walwanus is named in a Paduan charter of 1136. In 1165 a mosaic pavement, depicting a king astride a goat and bearing the legend "Rex Arturus," was placed in the cathedral of Otranto in the extreme south of Italy. Contemporary Welsh legends, meanwhile, show him as a ludicrous figure who comes off second-best in contests with saints. Possibly the clergy sought to offset popular reverence for him. He is also heard of as a king of the dwarfs, as a dweller at the Antipodes, as a mighty warrior tarrying in the blessed western Isle of Avalon, whence he will return in time of peril to save his people. A report from Sicily around 1211 makes his tarrying place a palace inside of Mt. Etna.

Welsh legends of the most disparate sort, themselves infused early with Irish elements, had, by 1100, passed through the hands of Cornish and of continental Breton intermediaries to the lands of Romance speech, including Norman England. Strategically situated and bilingual Brittany was the important channel of transmission. Each transmission was oral and of the process not a single written text remains to testify in any of these languages. Against such a background, however, and not *ex nihilo*, was composed the famous Latin *Historia regum Britanniae* (*History of the Kings of Britain*) of Geoffrey of Monmouth around 1135.

Geoffrey was the Ossian-MacPherson of his day by virtue of an immensely successful book which claimed to be true history and which was, in fact, in considerable part fiction. Born at or near Monmouth in southeastern Wales, of Celtic parentage—whether Welsh or Breton is a point still argued—he spent most of his life in Anglo-Norman Oxford, which was still not far from where Celtic and English idioms converged. To glorify the British people in the face of the English, the Anglo-Normans, and the French and to off-set the sparse and unfavorable reports of them in the records of those other nations, he amplified the statements of Gildas and of Nennius with matter drawn from oral traditions and, apparently, from his own fertile imagination as well, to trace an illustrious line of British kings from Brutus, great-grandson of Aeneas, down through the centuries. Among their numbers stand Cymbeline and King Lear. Ninety-first of this royal line is Arthur, to whom is devoted the last third, roughly, of the total work. Arthur is not only King, but Emperor, having conquered all of "the Island" as well as Ireland, Iceland, Norway, and Gaul. He has defied Rome itself and is on his way to Italy and the final conquest when the treachery of his nephew Modred requires his return home. Fighting against Modred and the Anglo-Saxons enlisted by the latter, Arthur receives mortal wounds in the great battle by the river Camel in Cornwall. The year is 542 A.D.

Twenty years after Geoffrey, in 1155, the Anglo-Norman Master Wace turned this Latin history into a French poem, where, among other newly added details, there is the first mention of the Round Table. Within another five years or so, Chrétien de Troyes, court poet to Countess Marie of Champagne, composed our oldest preserved Arthurian romance, *Erec*.

8. THE PERCEVAL SAGA

Nineteenth-century scholars found themselves baffled in their attempts to account for the subject matter of Chrétien's romances. His only known predecessors were Geoffrey and Wace, yet his stories were clearly independent of these sources, while details sometimes agreed, sometimes disagreed with those two works. Chrétien, it was reasoned, must have invented his plots. Twentieth-century scholars have reversed this lame judgment on the basis of the mass of evidence for the lost oral traditions partially described above. It is now certain that Chrétien and his contemporary, Marie de France, drew upon Celtic stories known to them through bilingual Breton minstrels who narrated their tales in French prose. In the opening lines of *Erec* Chrétien vaunts the superiority of his written verse romance over those tales spoiled in the telling by persons who earn a living by recitations. Some written French sources, however, must also have existed. In his Perceval romance, *Li Contes del Graal,* Chrétien states explicitly that he has worked from the book (*li livres*) lent him by Count Philip of Flanders. The fact that Count Philip's book is lost is no reason to doubt that it existed. New, superior versions of a story regularly led to the discarding of older versions. The vast extension of Chrétien's unfinished Perceval story by at least four subsequent authors seems, on the other hand, to be independent of Count Philip's book. The second of these continuators (anonymous, until recently called Wauchier de Denain) twice says he is abridging the contents of a vast *conte* by the story-teller Bleheris, whose name, in various forms, is mentioned by other persons of the twelfth century. Both oral and written material *of equal antiquity* must have served the writers who prolong the line of Perceval tales in various languages through the thirteenth and fourteenth centuries, for the scenarios and characters of these tales are often demonstrably Welsh in origin. Yet no Welsh story of Perceval is preserved or known prior to the prose romance of *Peredur* in the *Mabinogion*. Although our total *Mabinogion* manuscript is later than 1300, a manuscript fragment of this particular Welsh prose romance is dated around 1225, which date is, disappointingly enough, later than Wolfram's *Parzival* and long after Chrétien's Perceval tale. *Peredur* is on the one hand primitive in quality and on the other hand unquestionably influenced by continental notions of chivalry. Its testimony for early stages of the legend's evolution must therefore be heard with much caution.

This late Welsh version calls its hero Peredur, which is an ancient Welsh name. Chrétien called his own hero Perceval; we do not know why. Wolfram's form "Parzival" may represent his own pronunciation of "Perceval," while his etymology in Book III (140): *perce à val*—"pierce through the middle"—is unconvincing but may repeat an independent French source. Chrétien attempted no etymology, and scholars have produced no conclusive one. It would be plausible that "Peredur" was the Welsh story-teller's restitution of the hero's native name, just as he restored "Owein" where the French wrote "Yvain." On the other hand, where the French wrote "Erec" (from Breton: Guerec), he substituted, not the probable Welsh original "Gwri" or "Gware," but the name of a Cornish hero, Gereint.

Nevertheless Perceval, whether originally called Peredur or otherwise, was Welsh-evolved and evidence points to northwest Wales as his place of origin. From the local tribe known to the Romans as the Venedotes came the Latin regional name of Venedotia or Guenedocia and the Welsh regional name of Gwynedd. Its capital was the Roman fortress city of Segontium on the narrow strait that divides the island of Anglesey from the mainland, and which, in the Welsh form of Caer Seiont or Caer Seint, still exhibited imposing ruins in the Middle Ages. After Roman withdrawal in the late fourth century the area was seized by Goidels (Irish), but these settlers were soon displaced or absorbed by Brythons (Welsh) from the narrow waist of Britain north of there, led by a chieftain named Cunedda. From the latter descended the kings of Gwynedd, whose fortunes varied greatly but who were frequently the most powerful rulers in all Wales. The mixture of Irish and Welsh populations at that stage offers one of many opportunities for the infusion of Irish elements into our story. Details of Perceval's childhood, for example, bear striking resemblance to the childhood feats of the Irish heroes Cuchulainn and Finn. There is, moreover, reason to think that these Irish motifs, before they were ever attributed to Perceval, were worked into the biography of the Welsh hero Pryderi, which is known to us only in the much altered form found in the first four stories of the *Mabinogion*. The adventure of the Waste Land once fell to Pryderi, as the story *Manawydan son of Llyr* shows, and that same story also contains the motif of the Siege Perilous which is connected with Perceval in the continuations of Chrétien's poem. Thus, in a way not entirely clear, portions of the Perceval saga appear to have first been elaborated as portions of the Pryderi saga. One wonders whether the transference was in any way connected with the fact that Pryderi's story was localized in Dyved, southwest Wales, while Perceval's was localized in Gwynedd.

If the political borders of Gwynedd fluctuated, two areas remained consistently under the control of its kings: the large and fertile island of Anglesey, which fed the people in times of war, and mountainous Snowdonia across the strait on the mainland, which offered a formidable barrier to any invader from the east or south. The Welsh term the region Eryri ("abode of eagles") and its highest peak, Mt. Snowdon itself, Yr Wyddfa. "Snowdon," a name now restricted to the peak, was the Anglo-Saxon name (Snaudun, Snaudon) for the whole range. One of Chrétien's continuators makes the hero say: *"A Sinadon la fu jo nes."* (At Sinadon was I born.) In Manuscript H of Chrétien's own text, Perceval, addressing the first knights he has ever seen, points to the wooded mountainside and says that there lie *li destroit de Scaudone* —"the mountain passes of Snowdon." The first quotation may be ambiguous inasmuch as "Sinadon" (in various spellings) often meant in the romances *"la cité de Sinadon en Gales,"* a term applied to the ruins of Caer Seint and the new town of Carnarvon rising beside them. But the second quotation is clearly rural, and those rugged mountain valleys, which were difficult of access and more than once provided retreat in time of war, could well have given protective seclusion to the hero's widowed and grief-stricken mother In one manuscript (R) of Chretien's work her retreat is described as a "deserted and solitary forest"—*la gaste forest soltaine*—and it is very likely that Wolfram, who seems to have used a copy of this manuscript, misunderstood the rare form *soltaine* and so called her retreat "Soltane." Extraordinarily heavy rainfall is the plague of the Welsh mountains, with Snowdonia, hardest beset of all, receiving ninety inches annually. It is interesting that Parzival, astonished at the bountiful lands of Gurnemanz, remarks to himself in Book III (162): "My mother's people don't know how to farm. Their crops don't grow this tall, any that she has them sow there in the forest. She always gets too much rain."

In the French language the Welsh regional name Gwynedd was approximated in the spelling Goinnet, and then replaced by Norgals, i.e., North Wales. Herzeloyde is Queen of Norgals, as well as of Waleis, i.e., Wales. Further, R. S. Loomis has shown how the medieval writing of Goinnet as Goiñet led, through confusion of one superior bar for double *n* with another superior bar for the syllable *er,* to scribal misreading as Gomoret, which is still a country in Chrétien's tale, and ultimately to Gahmuret, the name of Parzival's father.

Finally, the hero of the saga doubtless owes something to a historical warrior named Peredur, whom Geoffrey of Monmouth terms "lord of the men of Gwynedd" (*dux Venedotorum*), and who died c. 580 A.D.

9. PEREDUR

The Welsh prose romance, *Peredur,* is disappointingly vague as to geography, as are its companion pieces dealing with Erec and with Gereint (Yvain), but in striking contrast to the geographical realism of the other eight tales in the *Mabinogion.* It begins: "Earl Efrawg [= York!] held an earldom in the North, and seven sons had he." (The historical Peredur was one of the seven sons of Eliffer.) The father and six brothers, it is succinctly stated, perished in battle, and the widowed Countess then took her infant seventh son and fled to a wilderness with women, boys, and meek folk, so that this one child at least might never know of war. For thirty-six paragraphs of rapid narration, and without names for most of the characters, the story runs through episodes that parallel Wolfram's Books III to VI. Here, in occasionally shifted order, are the equivalents of Herzeloyde, Karnachkarnanz, Jeschute, Orilus, Ither, Keie, Antenor, Cunneware, Iwanet, Gurnemanz, Anfortas, Sigune, Condwiramurs, Kingrun, Clamidê, Segramors, and Gawan.

In the "Anfortas" passage Peredur is sitting in converse with his host when a great spear streaming blood is carried through the hall. At sight of it all persons present set up a great lamentation; the man, however, "did not tell Peredur what that was, nor did he ask it of him." A short interval ensues, and then fresh lamentation breaks out at the sight of "two maidens coming in, and a great salver between them, and a man's head on the salver, and blood in profusion around the head." The Welsh word here translated as "salver" is *dyscyl,* which, as shall appear in the section next following here, was the semantic equivalent of Old French *graal,* i.e., "grail." What little clarification the Welsh tale has to offer for these mysterious matters is postponed until the end of the story.

At paragraph 34 we have the scene of the blood-drops on the snow; paragraph 35 reports the defeat of "Segramors" and the directly ensuing defeat of Cei (Keie), over whose prostrate body Peredur rides twenty-one times before releasing him to the surgeons. Paragraph 36 brings the courteous Gwalchmei (Gawan) together with the hero. In other words, we are well into Wolfram's Book VI. Then, from paragraph 37 through paragraph 63, there follows a whole series of adventures that have no parallel in either Chrétien or Wolfram. They include one adventure of Arthur's, Peredur's unlucky love-suit to Angharad Golden-hand, and his companionship with Edlym Red-sword, an Earl "from Eastern parts." For a time Peredur adventures in a valley full of tents and windmills, with the astonishing result that he goes to live with the Empress of Constantinople and rules for four-teen years "as the story tells!"

Suddenly we are brought back to Arthur at paragraph 64. The King is at Caer Llion on Usk, "a main court of his," with four heroes about him: Owein (Yvain), Gwalchmei (Gawan), Hywel (Howell), and Peredur Longspear. Clearly, a batch of alternate adventures has been awkwardly in-serted, for at paragraph 64 the story stands where it stood at paragraph 36 and we are still within Wolfram's Book VI. Now there arrives the loathly maiden messenger, the equiv-alent of Wolfram's Cundrie. Gwalchmei accepts her chal-lenge to deliver a maiden besieged in a castle, while Peredur receives her curse for having witnessed the lamentation in the hall of the Lame King without inquiring its cause. She mentions only the blood-streaming spear, without so much as a word about the "grail" and its severed human head swim-ming in blood. "By my faith," exclaims the hero, "I will not sleep in peace till I know the story and the meaning of the spear. . . ." Gwalchmei and Peredur then leave Arthur's court on their respective quests.

Directly thereafter, paragraphs 66-68 recount the Anti-konie adventure of Wolfram's Book VIII, with no hint of the Obie-Obilot story of Book VII. Paragraph 69 says that Peredur has meanwhile "wandered the Island" without find-ing the object of his search. Just then he encounters a priest who blames him for bearing arms on Good Friday, and in the space of two paragraphs we have the parallel of the Trevrizent passage of Book IX. When he leaves the priest on the third day he is searching for the Castle of Wonders.

By paragraph 75 Peredur, not Gwalchmei, has come to the Castle of Wonders and there undergoes a series of adven-tures which bear no or very little resemblance to those under-gone by Gawan in Books X and XI of the German poem. Nor is there any parallel whatsoever for the complex events of Wolfram's Books XII through XV.

At paragraph 81 Peredur arrives on foot at a castle where he finds his own lost horse tethered beside Gwalchmei's. Within are sitting Gwalchmei himself and the Lame King. A "yellow-haired youth" now explains that he has, in a series of transformations, sometimes male, sometimes female, encountered Peredur in various of the latter's adventures. For his actions he begs Peredur's forgiveness, then concludes:

> "And the head was thy cousin's, and it was the witches of Caer Loyw that had slain him. And 'twas they that lamed thy uncle. And thy cousin am I, and it is prophesied that thou wilt avenge that."

The final paragraph 82 describes how Peredur and Gwalchmei in a horrendous battle slew all the witches of Caer Loyw (i.e., Gloucester). "And thus it is told of the Castle of Wonders," the story concludes.

The Welsh tale has a wild charm of its own, but it is no match for Chrétien's *Perceval*, much less for Wolfram's masterwork. Its composer was surely unaware of the latter, and he seems to have been unaware of the former. Belief now tends toward some sort of cousin-relationship between *Peredur* and *Perceval*, with some French version anterior to Chrétien's and lost to us to account for the chivalric and French-derived component in the Welsh redaction, but with additions to the latter and with some restitutions to it from oral Welsh tradition.

We may, however, look upon *Peredur* as standing closer than any other surviving version to the Welsh prototype as the latter must have existed around 1150, before Chrétien took it up. Its contents testify to several points: 1. the episodes of Wolfram's Books III through VI were already "canonical" in the saga, though their precise order might vary; 2. after the entry of the loathly maiden messenger the narrative was to divide into alternating Peredur adventures and Gwalchmei adventures; 3. beyond this bifurcation point tradition was much less settled as to what was to be included and excluded, or even as to which adventures belonged to which one of the pair of heroes; 4. Peredur's final exploit was in some way connected with the king in whose hall the "grail" had been seen, though in *Peredur* the exploit has to do with vengeance, not with healing; 5. the hero had been brought into conjunction with Arthur. We can further discern what wider study confirms, that

Gwalchmei (Gawan) was already being dislodged by the folklore process from his position of pre-eminence as warrior-hero to make room for Peredur, but that epic degeneration had not reduced him to the quasi-villainous level where we find him in some later French romances. Chrétien, around 1180, treats him with dignity, and Wolfram, just after the turn of the century, makes him noble but subordinates him morally and poetically to Parzival.

10. THE GRAIL

In northeastern Wales, not far from the English border, rises the high, ruin-crowned hill of Dinas Bran which dominates the picturesque valley of the River Dee. The hill and surrounding country were once rich in lore, as the place names testify, about Bran, son of the Celtic sea-god Llyr. When Christianity denied Bran's godhood, folklore transformed him into an inland king who owned treasures and who sometimes fished from a boat in the river. One treasure was a drinking horn (Welsh: *corn*): "the drink and the food that one asked for, one received in it when one desired." A second treasure must also once have been his, even if the late Welsh list of the Thirteen Treasures of Britain assigns it to the historical sixth-century King Rhydderch of Strathclyde, —else why should it turn up in the French romances as a possession of King Bron? This second treasure was a platter (Welsh: *dyscyl*): "whatever food one wished thereon was instantly obtained." The word *dyscyl* was, as has been mentioned, the semantic equivalent of Old French *graal,* and around 1240 the writer Helinandus defined *graal* as "a broad and slightly deep dish" (*scutella lata et aliquantulum profunda*). Thus, according to Professor Loomis, while *corn* was properly rendered into Old French, in the nominative case, as *cors, dyscyl* was also properly rendered as *graal.* That Chrétien had in mind a platter seems apparent when he makes the hermit uncle of the hero say that the golden, gem-studded *graal* which Perceval had seen in the mysterious ceremony, contained neither a pike nor a lamprey nor a salmon; oddly and significantly it contained, rather, a single mass-wafer (*oiste*), and it was being carried to the Fisher King's bed-ridden father, who for fifteen years had been miraculously sustained by no other food.

From these facts and from much supporting evidence, R. S. Loomis concludes that the magic platter of Rhydderch had, in French, become first "a grail" and then "the Grail," whereas its companion talisman, the horn, by virtue of a fateful homonym in Old French—*cors* in the sense of "horn" and *cors* in the sense of "body"—had become the "body of Christ" (*corpus Christi*), i.e., the mass-wafer. Continentals were in any case, he points out, unfamiliar with drinking horns; a blast horn in such a context made little sense to them; and the whole episode seemed so awesome and sacred that only the Eucharist suited the circumstances. Thus a semantic blunder led ultimately to the creation of the supremely poetic symbol of the Middle Ages, the Holy Grail.

Centuries earlier, perhaps before these objects ever came into the possession of Bran, the horn and the platter served food and drink inexhaustibly in the halls of the Irish gods, as may be seen from ancient Irish tales called "Adventures" (*echtrai*). To those immortal banqueters the talismans were presented by Ériu, the divine personification of Ireland, who bore alternate aspects, a radiant summer aspect and a hideous winter one, whence came two separate characters in the romances: the beauteous maiden who bore the Grail and the loathly damsel who served the Grail as messenger. The *echtrai* also recount visits by mortals to those halls of the gods, and in that motif lies the ultimate foundation of our story. Such, in extremest brevity, is Professor Loomis' reconstruction of the Grail story's evolution.

Grave objections, moreover, confront those who would have the Grail holy and Christian from the outset and no wise pagan: the Grail of the romances is found in a castle, not in a church; a king, not a priest, is its keeper; a female carries it, contrary to all church usages relative to the Eucharist; the Holy Grail does not appear in literature or in art prior to Chrétien's time; nor did the Church ever recognize the Holy Grail as a valid Christian relic.

But if Chrétien conceived of the Grail as a platter of a size to hold a pike, a lamprey, or a salmon, his successors did not agree. The mysterious object raised questions, and where a modern might ask: "What is it?" the medieval mind asked: "What must it have been?" No sacred object was conceivable outside of Christianity; therefore the search was for a known Christian relic with which it could be identified. Early in the mass of material which prolongs Chrétien's poem from line 9234, where he broke off, to beyond 60,000 lines, there is an anonymous insertion in the First Continuation where the writer asserts a specific Christian origin for the Grail. It was, he says, the vessel which Joseph of Arimathea caused to be made and which he set at the foot of the Cross to catch the blood dripping from the dying Christ. The notion was derived, not from the canonical Gospels, but from the fourth-century apocryphal *Gospel of Nicodemus.* By 1202 probably, and not later than 1212, the Burgundian poet Robert de Boron, in a work usually called *Joseph d'Arimathie,* claimed that the Grail was indeed Joseph's Crucifixion cup, but it was also the very chalice used by Christ Himself in the institution of the Eucharist at the Last Supper. Both the anonymous writer and Robert go on to relate how the relic was brought westward, and Robert is at pains to equate Joseph's companion, Bron, with the Biblical "Hebron" of Numbers 3:31. We directly recognize Bron as the Welsh King Bran of Dinas Bran and the many treasures, and Professor Loomis astutely notes that both Joseph of Arimathea and King Bran were keepers of the *cors,* in radically different senses of that word.

Conceptions of the Grail continued to vary among the French writers of the first half of the thirteenth century. The prose romance of *Perlesvaus* (before 1212) explicitly identifies it as the Crucifixion cup, with no mention of the Last Supper relic, but goes on to present scenes where it undergoes mystical changes. Gawain sees it assume three successive forms: a chalice *in the Grail,* a child, and a crucified man with a spear in his side; Perceval beholds it in a fivefold transformation. The prose *Lancelot* (1215-1230) terms it the "Sankgreal" (*sang réal*—"royal blood"), but does not specify what sort of object it is. The *Queste del Saint Graal*, prose sequel to *Lancelot*, elevates the Grail to the equivalent of the Beatific Vision. Mystically and awesomely it floats into Arthur's hall, inspiring the knights to vow themselves to its quest. Later, Galahad, son of Lancelot, beholds Christ Himself emerge from the Grail to declare: "This is the holy dish wherein I ate the lamb on Sher-Thursday." The declaration is quoted in the fifteenth-century English with which Malory freely translated the French source. Tennyson, in the nineteenth century, accepted Malory's conception of the Grail as the Last Supper relic, and Wagner, for all that he drew materials for his opera *Parsifal* from Wolfram, made the same identification.

In the poem of *Parzival*, however, the Grail is none of the things so far mentioned, but a stone, apparently a kind of super-jewel surpassing in its powers the virtues of all other gems. Whence Wolfram derived such a concept is unknown.

Squarely in the middle of Book IX (467-468)—which itself has a mathematically exact centrality in the total work—the question of the Grail is broached between the hero and the hermit uncle. The latter's reply (469-470), contains almost all that we learn about the mysterious object:—it has two names, "lapsit exillis" and "the Grail"; by its power the phoenix kindles its death-flame from which that bird rises into new life; no one, be he however ill, can die within a week after beholding the Grail; old age and physical decay, save for grey hair, are suspended in beholders; its greatest power derives from a small white wafer deposited upon it every Good Friday by a dove from heaven; it produces food and drink in any quantity for its company; to that chaste company boys and girls are summoned, and other momentous commands are issued, by messages which appear around its edge—in Wolfram's arresting phrase: *von karacten ein epitafium*—and these letters vanish as soon as they have been read. The strange statement added by Trevrizent (471), making a connection between the neutral angels and the Grail, is even more strangely revoked by him in Book XVI (798) and need not detain us here. Taking these points collectively, we may say that Wolfram's conception of the Grail limits itself to elements which are either inoffensively secular or of such a genuine religious quality as could not possibly be taken for sacrilegious.

Many details of Wolfram's Grail castle and Grail ceremony are unique with him. Unique too are the "templars" who guard his Grail. At the time of *Parzival*'s composition the actual Knights Templars were in mid-course between the founding of their Order in 1119 and its spectacular extinction in 1312. Organized to protect pilgrims to Jerusalem, they had gained the powerful support of St. Bernard of Clairvaux in 1127, and by 1150 were already possessors of huge land grants, extraordinary privileges, and the admiration of all Christendom. As international financiers and bankers, they guaranteed safe transit of valuables and of persons from point to point, and their network of military posts extended from Armenia to Ireland. Wolfram's templars reflect the historical Templars, but are specialized for fiction by their dove emblem on garments and horses and by particular rules established in their headquarters at Munsalvaesche.

11. The Geography of the Poem

Not the least puzzling factor in *Parzival* is its geography, which confronts the reader at every step with an astonishing mixture of known and utterly unknown names. "Where in the world are we?" one may well ask.

The poem opens with a journey of Gahmuret, the hero's father, to the Orient; it closes with a journey of Feirefiz, the hero's half brother, to the distant East. No other Perceval romance contains a parallel to either character or to either journey, but even if research were to discover literary sources for them, there would still be no mistaking the fact that Wolfram intentionally conferred upon his story an extension in space that was the widest conceivable in his era. Not only do the two journeys admirably frame the total action, but we observe that the furthest reaches of the world come to know and revere the Angevin family. Knighthood, too, is practiced everywhere, and by stressing that point the hero pays high tribute to his own cherished social class. At the close of the poem Feirefiz is reported to be spreading Christianity through far-off India, and in the mention of that fact the poet pays reverent tribute to his cherished faith.

Gahmuret, as landless younger son, travels to Asia to enter the service of the "Baruch of Baldac," whose realistic counterpart should be the Khalif of Baghdad. From there he goes to Alexandria and Babylon (Cairo) in Africa and subsequently to the land of Belacane, where all the inhabitants are black Moors. Her kingdom must also be in Africa, for tradition had always claimed Africa as the homeland of Negroes. Book II brings Gahmuret briefly to Spain and thence to French-speaking areas of Europe. The significance of all this is made clear in Book IX, 496, when Trevrizent, speaking of his own knightly travels, says that he had fought "in the three parts of the earth, in Europe and in Asia and in far-off Africa." Hence Gahmuret also establishes his fame as a knight in "all three parts of the earth." Since at least the time of Herodotus (IV, 42) those three names had comprised the triple division of the world's total known land-mass.

Early in Book II Gahmuret lands at Seville (Sibilje), which is still a port town fifty miles up the tidal Guadalquivir, whence he proceeds inland to Toledo (Dolet). Either Wolfram or his source knew that Toledo *was* inland. When Gahmuret discovers that his cousin, King Kaylet, is not at home, he follows him to the tournament at Kanvoleiz in the land of "Waleis." With his arrival there, maps suddenly fail us. His journey has been overland, the people speak French, and the vegetation is subtropical. We, with our modern erudition, realize that "Waleis" should have been Wales; Chrétien spoke of Wales (Gales) and called his hero "Perceval the Welshman" (Perceval li gallois); but to Wolfram it was the region of almost identical name northeast of Paris and known to us as Valois. The region had never had any particular distinction as an independent political entity, and long before 1200 it had been absorbed into the Kingdom of France. The great fortress castle of La Ferté Milon dominated the landscape, but it would be rash indeed to equate it with "Kanvoleis." Nor is there any subtropical vegetation there.

To the tournament come knights from Hainaut (Hanouwe) and Brabant, actual provinces of Belgium to the north. Knights also come from Gascony (Gascane), Aragon (Arragun), and Portugal (Portegal), actual regions to the south, as well as from unidentified lands. The city would seem to be a central point for champions from all nations of Western Europe. We must, therefore, assume a French language territory somewhat differently shaped from the way our maps represent it, flatter perhaps, to bring Valois south into olive country and yet allow for a focal location of Kanvoleis relative to Western European countries. Such is Wolfram's "Wales," about which there is nothing Celtic.

Within French language territory also—we hope to the west—lies King Arthur's land of "Bertane" with its capital city of Nantes. Nantes is very real, and "Bertane" is clearly Brittany. The tradition of the romances, moreover, located in Brittany the Forest of Broceliande, which Wolfram terms Prizljan. But here the significant Breton details cease, and available evidence shows the majority of remaining geographical features to be Welsh. In taking over the Welsh tales, in which, to judge by the *Mabinogion,* place names were copious and precise, the Bretons suppressed and garbled names unfamiliar to them and occasionally substituted names from their own native region. Nantes might be such a substitution, possibly, in this case, for an original Caer Seint. The transmission process occasioned that striking oddity of Arthurian romance in general, the fact that the existence of the British Channel is often ignored. Brittany in France (Britannia minor—Little Britain) becomes one with the Island of Britain (Britannia major—Great Britain), and a man may ride horseback from Nantes to Karidoel, which is Anglo-Norman Carduel or Cardoile and modern Carlisle on the English-Scotch border. Rightly, then, Arthur is King of Britain, "the Island" as it is regularly termed in the *Mabinogion,* which is to say the nostalgic dream of a Celtic realm without the intrusion of Englishmen.

The events now constituting Wolfram's Books III and IV were originally disposed about a perfectly realistic landscape in Gwynedd, northwestern Wales, in rugged Snowdonia "above," i.e., west of, the River Conway. Munsalvaesche was, in the saga, the hill of Dinas Bran overlooking the River Dee in northeastern Wales, which, with political fluctuations, belonged now to Gwynedd, now to Powys. The word Dinas Bran has been made to double as a city designation, another capital of King Arthur's, in Chrétien's Dinasdaron and Wolfram's Dianazdrun. South Wales, on the other hand, appears in our text as Destrigleis, a distortion of Chrétien's Destregales. The latter equals Welsh Deheubarth, literally "right part [of Wales]," which was explicitly Latinized by Giraldus Cambrensis as "Dextralis Pars (Sudwalliae)." Erec, as King of Destrigleis, has his capital at Karnant, Chrétien's Carnant or Caruent, which is the ancient Roman administrative town of Venta Silurum and modern Caerwent. Rivalry was age-old between these two regions of North and South. In a great arc to the east of both lies England, which the Welsh call Lloegr—the Logrois, Logres, and Löver of the romances. Wolfram takes Löver to be a country but seems to consider Logrois to be a castle with its dependencies. There is partial evidence to suggest that Book VII of our poem was once localized in Cornwall and Book VIII in marsh-surrounded Glastonbury, the "Isle of Avalon," and there is a tradition, too complex to set forth here, which placed the Castle of Wonders at Gloucester, where the peninsula containing those regions adjoins the southeastern corner of Wales. With the jointure of North Welsh Perceval traditions and South Welsh and Cornish Gawan traditions, there seems to have been a partial and unrealistic fusion of the respective geographies.

Many place-name identifications for *Parzival* remain unknown or tentative, but the terrain must be seen as originally Welsh, overlaid with incongruous additions that are properly Breton, and finally invested with subtropical features which suggest a recasting of the entire story, prior to Wolfram, by a man from the south—from Provence perhaps. In this connection it is well to recall that "Provence" was a term that applied to the entire southern third of France, from the Alps to the Atlantic, the area of the *langue d'oc* as opposed to the area of the *langue d'oïl,* and not merely the old "Provincia" in the southeast corner adjoining Italy. In fact, the standard Old Provençal of the troubadours was the dialect of Limousin, and the province of Limousin is contiguous with Poitou. These subtropical features, which cannot be Welsh, Breton, or German, offer one of the chief arguments for "Kyot," whose very existence some serious scholars deny outright.

Our poet, however, accepted the composite geography of the tradition as he found it and manipulated the details for his own good artistic reasons. His total landscape seems to be bisected by the River Plimizoel. From one side of this stream extend diversified lands which may be generally designated as Arthur's, while from the other side stretch mountain and forest regions which are under the control of the Grail. On Joflanze meadow beside this stream Arthur twice establishes his splendid camp, but he seems not to advance beyond these waters. Near Joflanze Orilus has his smaller camp; near Joflanze Parzival beholds the blood-drops on the snow; at Joflanze itself Parzival receives Cundrie's curse at the end of Book vi and her blessing at the end of Book xv; to the site of the blood-drops on the snow Condwiramurs advances with her retainers from Brobarz to be met by her husband and escorted to Munsalvaesche; from Joflanze Parzival withdraws finally in one direction at the end of the poem to go to the Grail, while Gawan and Arthur retire from there in the opposite direction to go, respectively, to the Castle of Wonders and to Camelot. Out of the confused data of tradition Wolfram created a purely poetic geography which is consistent, symbolically meaningful, and artistically admirable.

12. THE TIME ANALYSIS OF THE POEM

Consistent, symbolically meaningful, and artistically admirable also is the time analysis which Wolfram created for his poem out of the disparate elements of tradition. In an article of 1938, Professor Hermann Weigand contrasted the vague, implausible time sequence of Chrétien's version with the minute exactitude which Wolfram bestows upon his narrative. Six years' time accounts for the total work, and the line of development arches from a first Pentecost when Parzival is made a knight in name to a seventh Pentecost when he becomes truly a knight in spirit. Within this six-year period no specific date is ever mentioned, yet twice the author introduces such elaborate time calculations that one is led to believe he intended the reader to compute his schedule of events. Professor Weigand discovered a close-reasoned calendar, slightly expanded here, which offers important information for the understanding of the total poem. One starting date must be assumed, and Professor Weigand began with the snowy Good Friday of Book IX, arbitrarily selecting the earliest Good Friday possible by the church calendar, March 20. The resulting calculations are here presented in the poem's own chronology.

After the preparatory story of Gahmuret in Books I and II, Book III comes to Parzival himself, and in brief but vivid summary we see him grow from a small boy into a youth. On an April morning he sets out to find King Arthur and become a knight. From that point the almost continuous action of Books III and IV occupies twenty-four days, including the interval the hero spends with Gurnemanz. The sequence ends to all intents and purposes with Clamidê's arrival at Dianazdrun, where Arthur is celebrating Pentecost (216). The luckless encounter with Jeschute occurred on the second day of this sequence, and at its conclusion the author remarked (139) that the lady's banishment from her husband's bed was to last for "more than a year." It is September 18 when Parzival next encounters her in Book V and vindicates her honor, swearing his oath to that effect upon the reliquary at Trevrizent's hermitage (271). Some fifteen months have therefore elapsed, and those months Parzival spent in happy union with his wife Condwiramurs in Pelrapeire. The significant interval is only very vaguely indicated by the closing lines of Book IV (222-223).

It is on September 17 that Parzival takes leave of Condwiramurs at the end of Book IV. Book V opens with the extraordinary ride that brought him by evening of the same day to the Grail castle. On the 18th he leaves Munsalvaesche, is denounced by Sigune, reconciles Orilus and Jeschute, pledges his oath on Trevrizent's reliquary, and that night, after the day's oppressive heat, half freezes in the forest during the unseasonal snowfall. The whole of Book VI takes place on the following day, September 19, and at the end of that day, after being cursed by Cundrie, Parzival sets out to find the Grail anew. Gawan simultaneously sets out to answer, within forty days, the untrue accusation of having murdered the King of Ascalun. Book VII recounts an adventure of Gawan's on the way to Ascalun, while Book VIII recounts his adventure at Ascalun itself, where he has arrived toward the end of the stipulated forty days. The action of Book VIII must, therefore, be dated in the last three days of October. The story is now into its second year.

More particularly, Books III and IV presented a spring sequence, while Books V through VIII have presented an autumn sequence. Book IX begins with a snowy Good Friday five years later, and all the rest of the poem will present a continuous spring sequence again. Clearly the spring-autumn-spring pattern reflects the joy-sorrow-joy pattern of the poem as a whole.

Lost in sorrow, unaware of the day or even of how long he has wandered, Parzival comes through the snowy woods to Trevrizent's hermitage. It is a Good Friday, for which the date of March 20 has been arbitrarily selected. Trevrizent informs him from his Psalter calendar that it is four years, six months, and three days since Parzival last visited this spot on the occasion when he swore on the reliquary to Jeschute's innocence (460). The count backward establishes that day as September 18. In Book XIII (646) Queen Ginover makes a parallel computation from the arrival of Gawan's messenger at that point, and says it is four years, six months, and six weeks since Gawan set out from Joflanze for Ascalun. Her count establishes that departure as September 19.

At the close of Book IX we are told that Parzival leaves Trevrizent after a stay of fifteen days. The date would be April 3. The remaining seven books of the poem occupy the months of April and May. On April 27 Gawan meets Orgeluse, defeats Lischois, and spends the night at the ferryman's (Book X). On the 28th he undergoes the trials of the Castle of Wonders (Book XI). On the 29th he encounters Gramoflanz (Book XII) and sends his page as messenger to Arthur and Ginover (Book XIII). The page delivers his message apparently on the next day, April 30, and Ginover makes her computation of time. By May 5 Arthur has arrived just outside the Castle of Wonders; shortly after midday of May 6 he is encamped at Joflanze. On the 7th Gawan and Parzival meet in battle, unaware of each other's identity (Book XIV); on the 8th Parzival defeats King Gramoflanz; on the 9th he fights his hardest battle, that with his half brother Feirefiz, which ends with the joyous discovery of their blood kinship and their arrival together at Arthur's camp on Joflanze meadow by the banks of the Plimizoel (Book XV). The next day, May 10, is Pentecost Sunday. The great Round Table is held on the flowery field, and there before all the assembled company Cundrie appears with her momentous news that Parzival has been declared King of the Grail. With her as their guide, Parzival and Feirefiz leave for Munsalvaesche. On May 11 the wondrous cure of Anfortas is effected, and on that same day Parzival consults once again with Trevrizent (Book XVI). In the grey dawn of May 12 Parzival is reunited with Condwiramurs on the banks of the Plimizoel, at the very spot where once the blood-drops on the snow formed her image. Darkness falls upon the returning party before they can reach Munsalvaesche, yet there is still time for the Grail banquet at which Feirefiz falls in love with Repanse de Schoye. On May 13 he is baptized so that he may marry her. For eleven days he remains at the Grail castle, and on the twelfth, May 24, he and his bride begin their long journey to India.

All these dates depend upon our first arbitrary assumption of March 20 for Good Friday, but it must be understood that their interrelation within the text remains constant and that they will all move forward together with any other Good Friday date up to April 23, the latest permitted by the church calendar. The spring-autumn-spring pattern is constant in any case. It is worth mentioning that Wolfram and his audiences may well have been familiar with snowy Good Fridays. On twelve occasions between 1155 and 1212 the holy day fell on March dates, ranging from the 22nd to the 27th, but only once in the twelfth century, in the year 1136, had it actually fallen on March 20.

13. THE TRANSLATION

Parzival offers many problems for the translator, probably more than any other medieval German work. The usual explanation for this is the so-called "obscurity" of Wolfram's style. His style is usually, however, not so much obscure as it is complicated and often elliptical. The translators have tried to convey something of the complexity in the translation, hence a number of long English sentences which may seem unduly awkward to the reader but which do indicate an important characteristic of Wolfram's style. The ellipses we have not reproduced, for fear of merely confusing the reader; indeed, we have very occasionally added a word or phrase not in the original in order to make the meaning clear. Puns are always a problem in translation, and Wolfram has his share of them. Here we have done the best we could, but we are quite aware of the impossibility of doing full justice to a pun in a foreign language. We were also faced with another perennial problem, especially in translating older literature, passages where the meaning is really in doubt and where various interpretations are possible. Sometimes the footnotes call attention to a troublesome passage, but usually, since such spots are quite numerous in *Parzival,* we have simply chosen the interpretation we thought best without distracting the reader by all too many notes.

In any translation one has the problem of trying to find the right word to give the proper meaning and tone, but in translating medieval German one is faced with a problem which does not exist in other languages. Medieval German has two words for "love," "minne" and "liebe." The conventional distinction in the lyric of the period, that "minne" is courtly love and of a higher nature, and that "liebe" is love which includes erotic love, does not hold for *Parzival.* Even if it did hold, there would be only one available word in English, but at least footnotes could make clear to the reader which word was used. The use of these terms by Wolfram, however, is so complicated, and the nuances in meaning are so many and so varied, that not only is an adequate translation impossible, but no helpful hints can be given to the reader. The topic is far too broad to deal with here, but an example or two will show the seriousness of the difficulty. In reference to the relationship between Parzival and Condwiramurs, which is truly affectionate and at the same time delicately erotic, Wolfram uses both words. He also uses both words in regard to Gawan and Antikonie, whose relationship is frankly erotic. Both words are also used in reference to God.

More important of course for the understanding of the work is the recognition of Wolfram's ability to portray love relationships on many different levels, the childlike innocence of Obilot's love for Gawan, the sensual love between Gawan and Antikonie, Sigune's martyrdom for love, the intensely erotic but genuine love between Gawan and Orgeluse, Bene's selfless devotion to Gawan, the fairy-tale love sight unseen of Gramoflanz and Itonje, and at the highest level the delicate and tender love of Parzival and Condwiramurs, which is fully consummated, almost sanctified, at the close when their reunion is associated with Parzival's reunion with the Grail.

The present translation endeavors to stay as close as possible to the original within the limitations of English style.

The division into books, which may be Wolfram's own, has been retained, and the subdivisions of thirty lines each, each of which represents one page of the manuscript, are indicated by the numbers in the margin of the page. Each number stands opposite the line where a new unit of thirty lines begins. Names of persons are given in one of the variant spellings of the original manuscripts except for a very few so close to the English that we have used the English form. Geographical names, except where obviously recognizable as present-day places, are given in the original spelling. The one exception is the use of "Britain" and related words for "Bertane" and its related words. These words were for Wolfram undoubtedly associated with Brittany, though originally in the history of the Arthurian legends they referred to the island of Britain. We have retained Wolfram's use of French words, a general characteristic of the German romances which were derived from the French. The line is not always easy to draw here, for many French words were already, at Wolfram's time, an integral part of the medieval German language. At two points in the text the English word "beloved" has intentionally been substituted for the French word "ami." This word has in modern French unfortunate connotations which we felt would distort the meaning of these two serious passages in the text; indeed, even in Chrétien's text the word "ami" has a different meaning from Wolfram's use of it. Chrétien always uses the word to refer to an extramarital relationship. Wolfram often uses it, or the feminine form, to refer to husband and wife.

In general we have followed the Lachmann text (*Wolfram von Eschenbach,* edited by Karl Lachmann, revised by Eduard Hartl, Berlin, 1952), but we have felt free to use the Leitzmann text whenever it seemed to give a preferable reading (*Wolfram von Eschenbach,* edited by Albert Leitzmann, vol. I, 5th edition, Halle, 1948; vol. II, 3rd edition, Halle, 1947; vol. III, 2nd edition, Halle, 1933). We also wish to acknowledge our debt to the helpful notes in the Bartsch and Marti edition of *Parzival und Titurel* (edited by Karl Bartsch and revised by Marta Marti, 4th edition, 3 vols., Leipzig, 1929-1935) and to other translations, both German and English. The only other complete translation in English is the verse translation by Jessie L. Weston, 2 vols., London, 1894. There are also two partial English translations to which we have referred, one by Margaret F. Richey in prose (Oxford, 1935), the other in verse by Edwin H. Zeydel and Bayard Quincy Morgan (Chapel Hill, 1951). There are many German translations, among them the meticulous prose translation by Wilhelm Stapel (Hamburg, 1938, revised in 1943, reprinted in Munich, 1950). The verse translations by Karl Pannier (Reclam, 1897) and Wilhelm Hertz (1898) are still widely read, but were not useful for our purposes.

The bibliography on Wolfram's *Parzival* and on the history of Arthurian legend is tremendous. For the reader who wishes to pursue his study of *Parzival* further, an excellent selection from the bibliography is given in an article by Otto Springer, "Wolfram's *Parzival*," in *Arthurian Literature in the Middle Ages,* edited by Roger Sherman Loomis, Oxford, 1959; and Hugh Sacker's *An Introduction to Wolfram's Parzival,* Cambridge, 1963, presents a very good interpretative analysis intended particularly for beginning students but so well and vividly written as to hold the interest of the general reader as well.

PARZIVAL

BOOK·I

If inconstancy is the heart's neighbor, the soul will   1
not fail to find it bitter. Blame and praise alike befall when
a dauntless man's spirit is black-and-white-mixed like the
magpie's plumage. Yet he may see blessedness after all, for
both colors have a share in him, the color of heaven and the
color of hell. Inconstancy's companion is all black and takes
on the hue of darkness, while he of steadfast thoughts clings
to white.

This flying metaphor will be much too swift for dullards.
They will not be able to think it through because it will
run from them like a startled rabbit. Mirrors coated on the
back with tin, and blind men's dreams, these catch only the
surface of the face, and that dim light cannot steadfastly
endure even though it may make fleeting joy real. Anyone
who grabs the hair in the palm of my hand, where there
isn't any, has indeed learned how to grab close. And if I
cry Ouch!, it will only show what kind of a mind *I* have.
Shall I look for loyalty precisely where it vanishes,   2
as fire in running water, dew in the sun?[1]

[1] This obscure paragraph, like the following one, may consist of
cryptic remarks in reply to hostile critics of previously "published"
sections of the poem. There is reason to believe that the Introduction
was added after several books (most probably iii-vi) of the total work
were already familiar to the public.

Never have I met a man so wise but that he would have liked to find out what authority this story claims and what good lessons it provides. On that score it never wants for courage, now to flee, now to charge, dodge and return, condemn and praise. Whoever can make sense out of all these turns of chance has been well treated by Wisdom, or whoever does not *sit* too tight, or *walk* astray, but in general under*stands*. The thoughts of a false man lead to hell-fire, but they beat upon high dignity like hail; his loyalty has a tail so short that it couldn't slap back at the third bite if it were flicking flies in a forest.[2]

These various definitions are by no means directed at men solely: for women I will set up these same goals. Any woman willing to mark my advice shall know where to bestow her praise and honors, and, accordingly, on whom to bestow her love and respect, so that she will not rue   3 the giving of her purity and devotion. I pray to God that good women may follow the proper mean. Modesty is a capstone over all virtues; I need not wish them anything better than that. She who is false shall win false praise. How durable is thin ice that gets the hot August sun? Just so quickly will her renown decay. Many a woman's beauty is praised afar, but if the heart within is counterfeit, I would praise her as I would praise a jewel of blue paste set in gold. I count it no trifling thing if someone mounts a noble ruby, with all its magic virtue, in paltry brass. To such a jewel I liken a faithful woman's way. Any one true to her womanhood I will not examine as to her complexion or the heart's external roof, for if she is well protected *within* her heart, her praise will not be paid amiss.

If I were to tell of men and women aright, as I understand them, it would be a long tale. But now listen to the manner of this story. It will bring you word of both joy and sorrow, and delight and distress accompany it as well. Assuming there were three men instead of me   4

[2] A twelfth-century English satirist (Nigel Wireker, in his *Brunellus*) tells of a cow whose tail froze and broke off in the ice in winter, and hence could not flick flies in the summer.

alone, each possessed of ability equal to mine, it would still be fantastic skill if they set forth to you what I, single-handed, mean to set forth. They would find it a task indeed. I mean to tell you once again a story[3] that speaks of great faithfulness, of the ways of womenly women and of a man's manhood so forthright that never against hardness was it broken. Never did his heart betray him, he all steel, when he came to combat, for there his victorious hand took many a prize of praise. *A brave man slowly wise*—thus I hail my hero—sweetness to women's eyes and yet to women's hearts a sorrow, from wrongdoing a man in flight! The one whom I have thus chosen is, story-wise, as yet unborn, he of whom this adventure tells and to whom many marvels there befall.

❦⒬❧

It is still the custom as it used to be the custom wherever Latin law prevails and formerly prevailed, and, as you have heard without me, it is the custom still in a corner of our German land as well, that whoever was the ruler of a country over there would command, without any feeling   5 of wrongdoing—this is the truth and no mistake! —that the eldest brother should have his father's entire inheritance. This was the misfortune of the younger ones, since death deprived them of the rights which were theirs while their fathers were still alive. Before, it was held in common, whereas this way the eldest alone possessed it. A wise man ordained that age should have property, for youth has many a thing of value, while age has sighs and sorrows. Never was anything so wretched as old age and poverty. That kings, counts, dukes—and I am telling you no lie—should be dispossessed of their lands to an eldest child, that is a strange custom.

In this fashion Gahmuret, the warrior gallant and brave, lost the castles and land where his father had borne scepter and crown in splendor and with great royal power until he

[3] The verb *niuwen* may mean "tell once again" or "introduce you to a story hitherto unknown to you."

lay dead in knightly combat. Thereupon he was deeply
mourned. He had maintained all loyalty and honor until
his very death.   6

His eldest son then summoned before him the princes of
the land, and in knightly fashion they came, for by rights
they should receive great fiefdoms from him. When they
had come to court and their claims had been heard and
they had all received their fiefdoms, now hear what they
said. They made, as their loyalty bade them do, rich and
poor alike, the whole crowd of them, earnest but futile request that the king should increase his brotherly fidelity to
Gahmuret and do honor to himself by not driving him
away but by assigning him an estate within the country, so
that it might be clear on what the lord based his claim to
free status and a name.

The king was not at all displeased, and he said, "You
know how to make fitting requests. I will grant this and
more besides. Why not call my brother Gahmuret the Angevin? Anjou is my country: let us both take our names
therefrom." And the noble king went on to say: "My
brother may look to me for further steadfast help   7
than I can quickly mention here. He shall be one of my
household, and I shall clearly show you all that one mother
bore us both. He has little and I have plenty, and this my
hand shall so share with him that my salvation shall not be
forfeit before Him Who giveth and Who taketh away, as
both those things beseem Him."

When the mighty princes all heard their lord profess such
good faith, it was a glad day for them. Each one bowed before him. Nor did Gahmuret remain silent at their assent,
but spoke as his heart prompted. Graciously he said to the
king: "My Lord and brother, if I were to be of your or any
man's household, I would have everything arranged for my
comfort. But now, as you are honorable and wise, test my
worth, counsel me as to what is proper, and then assist me
therein. I have nothing but my armor. If I had accomplished
more in it, it would bring me far more renown and I should
somewhere be remembered." And Gahmuret went on to
say: "I have sixteen squires, six of them equipped   8

with armor. Give me in addition four pages of good breeding and high lineage. For them nothing shall be stinted that
my hand may ever win. I want to see the world. I have already traveled a bit. If luck sticks by me, I shall gain a
good woman's greeting. If I then serve her, and if I am
worthy to do so, my best thought will direct me to act with
true loyalty. May God show me the ways of blessedness.
We have ridden together, you and I, while our father Gandin still had your kingdom, and many a grievous pain have
we both suffered for Love's sake. You were both knight
and thief; you could serve a lady and yet dissemble. If only
I too could steal love! O, if I only had your skill and the
true favor of women!"

The king sighed and said, "Alas that I ever saw you,
since with jesting unconcern you have hacked to pieces my
heart that was whole before by proposing that we
part. My father left us both riches aplenty, and in   9
respect to these I shall stake out equal limits with you, for
you are dear to my heart. Bright jewels, red gold, attendants, weapons, horses, garments, accept as many of these
from my hand as you wish, to travel as you will and to
maintain your knightly generosity. Your manhood is of a
rare sort, and if you were born in Gylstram[4] or if you came
from Ranculat,[5] I would still like to keep you here with me
because I am so fond of you. You are my brother."

"Sir, you praise me perforce because your knightly breeding so commands. Let your help be shown accordingly. If
you and my mother share your riches with me I shall rise
and not go down. My heart, however, yearns upward to the
heights. I do not know why it is so full of life that the left
side of my breast swells to bursting. O where is my desire
driving me? That I shall find out if I can! But now my
day of parting has come."

The king granted him everything, more than he had
asked: five choice and tested horses, the best in all   10
his land, brave, strong, and not slow, and many a precious

---

[4] Gylstram, unidentified; the extreme west is meant.
[5] Ranculat, believed to be Hromgla on the Euphrates, hence the
extreme east. See XI, 563.

golden vessel and many a bar of gold. Nor did the king begrudge in the least filling four traveling chests for him, into which went many a jewel until they were full to the brim. And the pages in charge of all these things were handsomely dressed and mounted.

Then there was no lack of grieving when he went to see his mother, and she clasped him tightly to her. *"Fils du roi* Gandin, will you not stay any longer with me?" said that womanly woman. "Alas, I gave you birth, and you are also Gandin's child. Is God in His help blind, or is He deaf, that He does not heed me? Must I now have fresh grief? I have buried my heart's strength, the sweetness of my eyes. If He robs me still further, when He is supposed to be a judge, then the story lies that speaks about His help, for He has abandoned me."

Then the young Angevin said, "God comfort   11 you, Lady, for my father. We shall both mourn for him. But no one can bring you mournful tidings about me. For my valor's sake I go to seek knightly deeds in foreign lands. That, Lady, is how matters stand."

Then the queen said, "Since you are turning your mind and your service to lofty love, dear son, do not disdain to take of my wealth upon your journey. Bid your attendants receive from me four heavy traveling chests which contain bolts of pfellel-silk, whole ones that have not been cut, and many a bolt of precious samite. Sweet boy, let me know the time when you will come back again, for you are the source of my joy."

"Lady, I have no notion in what country I shall be. Only, wherever I go, you have bestowed your nobleness upon me as was befitting for a knight. Moreover, the king has released me in such a fashion that my service shall show my gratitude. I assure you that you will hold him in greater respect because of it, however things may go with   12 me."

As the story tells us, this dauntless hero had, through love and a woman's friendship, received gifts worth a thousand marks. Even today they could be pawned to a Jew for that amount and he would not disdain them. These were sent by one who was his beloved. By his service he had gained women's love and greetings, but seldom had he been granted consolation for the pangs of love.

The warrior took his leave. Never again did his eye behold mother, brother, or country. That was a great loss to many. To anyone who had shown him a favor of any kind, before his departure he paid great thanks. He deemed their favor more than enough, and in his courtesy it never occurred to him that they had done only what duty required. His nature was plainer than plain. Anyone who tells his own value will meet disbelief; his fellow men should tell it, and those who beheld his actions away from home: 13
then the story would be credited.

Gahmuret's ways were those that moderation dictated, and no other. Boast he rarely did, great honor he meekly bore, haughtiness had no part in him. Yet this noble man felt there was no one who wore a crown, neither king nor emperor nor empress, of whose household he wished to be, except one who had supreme power on earth over all lands. Such was his heart's will. He was told that in Baghdad there was a man so powerful that two-thirds of the earth, or more, was subject to him. To heathens his name was so great that he was called "The Baruch," [6] and such was his power that many kings were vassals to him and subject were their crowns. The office of Baruch exists today, and just as Christian law looks to Rome, as our faith enjoins, there the heathen order is seen and from Baghdad they take their papal rule—deeming this entirely proper—and the Baruch gives them absolution for their sins.   14

From two brothers of Babylon,[7] Pompey and Ipomidon, the Baruch had taken Niniveh, which had belonged to all

[6] "Baruch" = Hebrew: "the blessed one." From stanza 40 of *Titurel* we learn that his name is Ahkarin. The Caliph of Baghdad (Wolfram's "Baldac") is presumably meant. The Caliph had his seat in Baghdad until 1245.

[7] I.e., Cairo.—The Egyptian Babylon was founded in 525 B.C. by colonists from Babylon in Mesopotamia, according to Strabo, just after the Persian conquest of the Nile Valley. The Romans made the town a legionary headquarters, and through them Babylon in Egypt was well known. Modern Cairo lies a few miles north of the ruins of Babylon.

their ancestors, and they had waged a stout defense. Now
came the young Angevin, to whom the Baruch showed great
favor, and for his services Gahmuret the worthy knight accepted pay.

Allow him now to have a coat of arms other than the one
Gandin his father had previously given him. As one with
high aspirations, the knight chose an anchor, ermine-white,
to be sewn on his horse's caparison, and others, necessarily
identical, on his shield and on his garment. Greener than
emerald was his saddle gear, while of the hue of achmardi[8]
—that is a silk material and superior to samite—he had his
surcoat and gambeson made, with anchors of ermine sewn
thereon and golden ropes looped through them. His anchors
had not tasted cape nor continent nor been cast anywhere. This knight was to bear that weight of her-   15
aldry to many a foreign land, noble stranger that he was,
and despite the sign of the anchor he was never to find any
place to dwell or tarry.

Through how many lands did he ride? Around how
many did he sail in ships? If I were to swear to that, my
word as a knight, given in lieu of an oath, would tell you
just what the story says—I have no other evidence—and it
says that his manly strength won fame throughout heathendom from Morocco to Persia. Elsewhere too his hand
prevailed, before Damascus, and before Aleppo, and wherever knightly deeds were done; before Arabi, and throughout all Araby, till he was free from challenge from any man
whatsoever: such was the reputation he acquired. His
heart's desire thirsted for fame. All their deeds melted
away before him and became almost as nothing. That is
what every man was taught who jousted with him, and in
Baghdad people said of him that his courage never faltered.   16

From there he traveled to the kingdom of Zazamanc,
where they were all mourning for Isenhart, who had lost
his life in the service of a lady. Thereto he had been driven
by Belacane, that sweet lady without guile, and because she

---

[8] Actually a color: Arabic *azzamradi* (from Greek *smáragdos*) =
"emerald-green."

never granted him her love, he lay dead of love for her. His kinsmen were now avenging him openly and secretly by besieging the lady with an army. She was in the midst of a brave defense when Gahmuret came to her country, which Fridebrant the Scotsman with ship-borne army had laid waste before he departed.

Now hear how things went with our knight. The sea with such a storm cast him there that he barely escaped with his life, but into the harbor he came sailing toward the queen's great hall, down from which he was observed by many. He looked around across the field where many a tent was pitched on all sides of the city except toward the sea, and there two powerful armies were encamped. He bade his men inquire whose castle this was, for neither he nor any of his shipmen knew. His messengers   17 were informed that it was Patelamunt, and graciously was the answer made to him. They implored him by their gods to help them: their need was urgent, they were fighting with death itself.

When the young Angevin heard of their grievous distress he offered his services for hire, as many a knight still does, and asked them to tell him what would be the prize for incurring the enemy's hatred. With one voice the sick and the well declared all their gold and all their jewels should be his; he should be master of it all and have a fine life among them. But he required little pay, for of the gold of Araby he had brought along many an ingot. Black as night were all the people of Zazamanc, and he felt ill at ease; yet he gave orders for lodgings to be taken. It pleased them to give him the best.

The ladies were still leaning out of the windows to see him, and they had a good look at his pages and his   18 armor with its adornments. On his ermine shield the generous hero displayed I don't know how many sable pelts, which the queen's marshal discerned as an anchor, and the sight did not displease him. Then his eyes told him that he had seen either this knight or his double before, and that must have been at Alexandria when the Baruch was besieging that city. No one equaled his achievement then.

Thus he who was rich in courage rode cheerfully into
the city. Ten pack horses he ordered loaded, and through
the streets they went, twenty squires riding behind them.
His household staff were seen up ahead, for pages, cooks,
and the latter's helper-lads had gone on up front. Stately
was his retinue: twelve highborn youths rode next after the
squires, all well bred and with sweet manners, several of
them Saracens. Next came eight horses, caparisoned in
sendal-silk one and all. The ninth bore his saddle,   19
while a shield I have mentioned before was carried by a
squire of cheerful mien walking alongside. After these rode
trumpeters, who are still required today, and a drummer
kept hitting his drum and swinging it high in the air. The
master would not have thought much of the lot if flute
players had not been riding along with the rest, and three
good fiddlers. None of these was in any great hurry. He
himself rode last, and with him his ship captain, a man
famed and wise.

All the people in the city, men and women alike, were
Moors. Now the master beheld many a shattered shield
riddled with spears, many of them being hung out on display on walls and doors. Sorrow enough they had. At the
windows, so placed as to get the air, was the bed of many
a man so badly wounded that even if he could get a doctor
he still would never recover. These had really faced the
foe. So it goes with a man who is unwilling to flee.   20
Numbers of horses were led past him, pierced and hacked
with weapons. To right and left he saw many a dusky lady
with complexions of the raven's hue. His host received him
graciously—a thing that brought him joy later on—and he
was a man rich in courage who had dealt many a thrust
and many a blow with his hand when he was guarding a
gate. With him he found many a knight whose arms hung
in slings and whose heads were in bandages. Their wounds
were such that they still performed knightly service in spite
of them, and had not abated their powers.

The governor of the city then graciously bade his guest
not to refrain from making any claim whatsoever upon his
goods and person. Next, he conducted him to his wife, who

kissed Gahmuret, little as he relished it. Then they went to breakfast, and when that was over the marshal left him directly to go to the queen and ask her for a very considerable messenger's reward.[9] "Lady," he said,   21 "our distress has ended in joy. This man we have welcomed here is a knight of such a kind that we shall ever have to thank our gods, who brought him here, for bethinking themselves to do so."

"Now tell me by your loyalty who this knight may be."

"Lady, he is a doughty warrior, a soldier in the pay of the Baruch, and an Angevin of high lineage. O how little does he hold back when they set him on the enemy! How skillfully he dodges and returns this way and that way! He teaches the enemy trouble! I saw him fight once when the Babylonians were supposed to be liberating Alexandria and when they were trying to drive the Baruch away by force.[10] What a lot of them were killed off in their defeat! Then that wonderful man did such feats that they had no choice but to run for it. Besides, I heard people say of him that he should be recognized as having won the highest honors over many a country by his own right hand."   22

"Now find out when and how, and arrange for him to see me here! There is a truce all day long, so the hero can ride up here to see me—or should I go down there? He is of a different color from us. O, I do hope he won't be offended by that! I should have liked to find out first whether my people advise me to offer him honors. And if he deigns to come to me, how am I supposed to receive him? Is he of high enough birth for me so that my kiss will not be misbestowed?"

"Lady, he is known to be the kin of kings, I pledge my life on that. I will tell your princes, Lady, to put on rich apparel and wait here with you until he and I ride over to see you. You may so advise your ladies. For when I ride

[9] Bringers of news, particularly of good news, were regularly compensated for their trouble with *botenbrot,* "messengers' bread."

[10] It is to be understood that Babylonians were marching from Cairo to relieve fellow Babylonians besieged inside of Alexandria by the Baruch.

down now I will bring you up this worthy guest, who never lacked for sweet virtue."

Very little of this was left unperformed, and the marshal worked deftly to carry out his lady's behest. Rich apparel was quickly furnished Gahmuret, which he put 23 on. I heard reported that it was elegant. Anchors heavy with Arabian gold were sewn thereon as he desired. Then that Reward of Love mounted a horse that a Babylonian had ridden in a joust against him—he had knocked him off it and the fellow didn't like that at all. And did his host ride with him? Yes, he and his knights as well, and indeed they were happy to do so. Together, then, they rode and drew rein in front of the palace, and up there were many knights all dressed, of course, in their finest. His pages entered ahead of him, two by two, hand in hand, and their master discovered a host of ladies within, resplendently attired. The great queen's eyes caused her grievous pain when they beheld the Angevin, who, being of Love's color, unlocked her heart whether she wished it or not. Her womanliness had kept it locked until then. She advanced a little way toward him and invited her guest to kiss her. She took him by the hand, and along the wall that faced the 24 enemy they sat down on a broad window seat on an upholstered cushion of samite beneath which a soft mattress was spread.

If there is anything brighter than daylight—the queen in no way resembled it. A woman's manner she did have, and was on other counts worthy of a knight, but she was unlike a dewy rose: her complexion was black of hue. Her crown was a lucent ruby[11] through which her head could be seen. The hostess told her guest that his coming gave her pleasure. "Sir, I have heard much report of your knightly achievement. In your courtesy do not take offense if I make lament to you of the sorrow which I carry close to my heart."

"My help, Lady, will not fail you. Let my hand be

[11] The crown consists of a single huge ruby, just as Gahmuret's helmet (II, 53) consists of a single huge diamond, and just as the drinking cups (II, 85) are individual gems hollowed out.

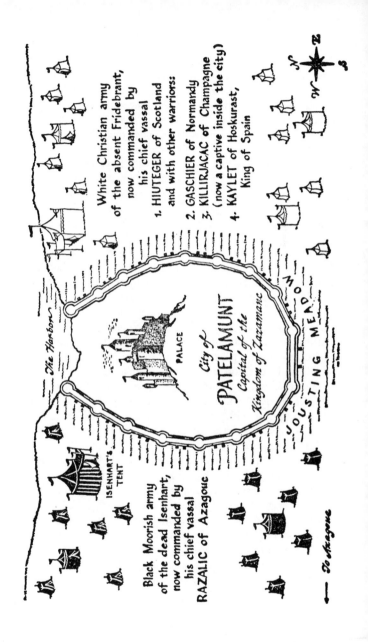

The Harbor

White Christian army
of the absent Fridebrant,
now commanded by
his chief vassal
1. HIUTEGER of Scotland
and with other warriors:

2. GASCHIER of Normandy
3. KILLIRJACAC of Champagne
(now a captive inside the city)
4. KAYLET of Hoskurast,
King of Spain

ISENHART'S
TENT

City of
PATELAMUNT
Capital of the
Kingdom of Zazamanc

PALACE

JOUSTING MEADOW

Black Moorish army
of the dead Isenhart,
now commanded by
his chief vassal
RAZALIC of Azagouc

To Azagouc

N
W — E
S

marked for your service wherever it can avert what it is or was that troubles you. I am only one man, but, though it may impress the enemy but little, I offer you my shield against anyone who is doing or has done you harm."

Courteously one prince spoke up: "If we had a leader we wouldn't spare the enemy much, now that Fride-   25 brant is gone—he is defending his own country out there. A king named Hernant, whom he slew for Herlinde's sake, *his* kinsmen are doing him damage aplenty and show no signs of letting up. He left heroes behind here—like Duke Hiuteger, whose knighthood has caused us many a grief, and his associates—and their fighting has skill and force. Then too, Gaschier of Normandy, that wise and great warrior, has many a soldier here. Kaylet of Hoskurast has even more knights here, and angry guests they are, too! All these were brought into this country by the Scotsman, King Fridebrant, and his comrades four,[12] together with many a fighting man. To the west there along the sea lies Isenhart's army, tears flowing from their eyes. Never has any man beheld them in public or in private but that he has marveled at their immense grief. Their hearts' showers have brought on floods since their lord perished in the joust."

With knightly courtesy the guest said to his hostess, "Tell me, if you will be so kind, why you are   26 being attacked with anger and violence. You have many a bold knight. It grieves me that they are so weighed down with the enemy's hatred to their harm."

"That I shall tell you, Sir, since you ask. —I was served by a knight, and a worthy man he was, a blossoming branch of virtues, a hero bold and wise, a root-taking fruit[13] of loyalty. His courtesy outweighed the courtesy of all others, he was more modest than a woman, and daring and bravery were contained in his person. A knight more generous never grew before in any land—of what may grow in times hereafter I know nothing: let other people tell of that. To all false conduct he was deaf, and in blackness of hue he was,

---

[12] The four are apparently Hiuteger, Gaschier, Killirjacac, and Kaylet.

[13] Wolfram's own mixed metaphor.

like me, a Moor. His father was Tankanis, a king, and he too had high renown. My beloved's name was Isenhart. My womanhood was ill advised when I accepted his service in love, because it did not turn out to his joy, and for that I must bear sorrow forever. They imagine that I had him murdered, but I am little capable of treachery, 27 though his men accuse me of it. He was dearer to me than to them. I am not without witnesses for what I have to prove, and my gods and his gods both know the real truth. He caused me many a grief, but my over-modest womanhood delayed his reward and lengthened my own sorrow. My virgin reticence spurred the hero on to much knightly fame—I was testing him to see whether he could be my friend. That was soon demonstrated. For my sake he gave all his knightly equipment away. (What stands yonder like a palace, that is a lofty tent which the Scotsmen brought to this field.)[14] Once the hero was without his armor, his body was little spared. Life seemed pointless to him, and he sought out many an adventure, unarmed. When things stood thus, a prince named Prothizilas, one of my household and free of all cowardice, rode out to adventure, where great harm did not miss him: in the forest of Azagouc he found no mock death in a charge against a brave man, who likewise met his end there. That was 28 my beloved Isenhart. They both felt a spear through their shields and through their bodies. And I, poor woman, still grieve for this; both deaths distress me still. Grief flowers in the soil of my loyalty. I have never become the wife of any man."

Gahmuret reflected how she was a heathen, and yet never did more womanly loyalty glide into a woman's heart. Her innocence was a pure baptism, as was also the rain that wet her, that flood which flowed from her eyes down upon the furs about her bosom. The practice of sorrow was her delight and the true instruction received from grief.

She went on to say: "Then from across the sea came the

[14] The knightly equipment included his tent, which Belacane's eye catches as she is sitting there by the window, speaking. Isenhart gave the tent and other equipment to his vassal Fridebrant.

King of Scots against me with his army, for my friend was
his maternal uncle's son, but they could do me no more
hurt than had been done me by Isenhart, I must confess."

The lady fetched frequent sighs and through her tears
cast many a shy glance, as strangers will, at Gahmuret. Her
eyes told her heart that he was handsome, and she   29
could also judge of fair complexions, for she had seen many
a fair-skinned heathen before. Between the two there sprang
up a genuine desire. She looked at him, he looked at her.
Then she ordered them to pour the parting wine cup. That
she would have left undone if she had dared, and it vexed
her that it could not be left undone, because it always drove
the knights away who liked talking to a woman. Yet she
was now his, and he had given her the feeling that his life
was now the lady's life.

Hereupon he stood up and said, "Lady, I am inconven-
iencing you, I have sat longer than I should, and that was
thoughtless of me. I most humbly regret that your sorrow
is so great. Make disposition of me, Lady, wherever you
will, and there my vengeance will be. I shall serve you in
any way I may."

"Sir," she replied, "I am fully confident you will."

His host the governor now left little undone to pass the
time for him. He inquired whether he would like to take a
ride out "and you can see where we are fighting   30
and how our gates are defended." Gahmuret, that worthy
warrior, said he would like to see where deeds of knighthood had taken place. Several knights of doughty mien
rode down with the hero, some of them seasoned, some of
them fresh. They led him around by sixteen gates, explain-
ing to him that not one of these had been shut "since Isenhart has been being avenged in anger upon us. By night
and by day our fighting has been the same: we have not
closed one of them since. Before eight gates Isenhart's
loyal men do battle with us. They have done us much injury and they fight in anger, these princes high born, these
king's vassals of Azagouc." Over brave companies before
each gate flew a bright flag with a transfixed knight thereon.
After Isenhart lost his life, such was the coat of arms his

men had chosen. "But against that device we have another
with which we assuage their grief. Our banner may be
recognized by the two fingers it shows outstretched   31
from a hand to represent the oath: that never did anything
so grievous befall her as when Isenhart lay dead. That
brought my lady heart's sorrow. So there stands the queen,
the Lady Belacane, sharply outlined in black upon white
samite, and ever since we saw *their* emblem—their loyalty
brings them grief—*these* banners fly over the gateways
high. —Before the other eight gates proud Fridebrant's
army still attacks us, baptized men from across the sea.[15]
Each gate is commanded by a prince who leads the sallies
out with his banner. We have captured a count of Gaschier's, who is offering us a good deal of money. He is
Kaylet's sister's son,[16] and whatever Kaylet does to us, *he*
has to make good. Such luck seldom comes our way. Of
green meadow there is mighty little, but it is perhaps thirty
horse-charge lengths of sandy land from the moat out to
their tents, and there many a joust takes place."

His host had this report to give him: "One   32
knight never fails to come out for jousting. If he were to
do his service in vain for her who sent him out, what then
would be the use of his bold challenge? This is the proud
Hiuteger. About him I would like to tell you more. Ever
since we have been under siege here that reckless fellow has
appeared every morning before the gate opposite the great
hall. What is more, many a lady's favor has been taken
from that brave man by virtue of his ramming them
through our shields, and these have been declared of great
value when the heralds have picked them off. He has
brought down many a knight of ours, he loves to be seen,
and *our* womenfolk praise him too. And when women

---

[15] Eight of Patelamunt's sixteen gates face west toward the black
Moorish army of the late Isenhart, King of Azagouc, and of his avenger,
the Moorish Razalic; the other eight gates face east toward the army
of white Christian fighters: the currently absent Fridebrant of Scotland,
Gaschier of Normandy, Kaylet of Spain, and Hiuteger the Scottish
Duke.

[16] This is the youthful Count Killirjacac of Champagne; see I, 46,
below.

praise a man, he is known; he has the prize at hand and his heart's desire."

Now the weary sun had gathered its bright rays in, and the ride had to come to an end. The guest rode back with his host and there he found supper ready.

I must tell you about their meal. It was set out with propriety and he was served in knightly fashion.   33
Resplendent, the great queen appeared at his table. Here was heron, there was fish. She had ridden down to see to it herself that he was being properly attended, and her maidens had come with her. She knelt down—to his displeasure—and with her own hand cut up a portion of the knight's food.[17] The lady was delighted with her guest. Then she served him his wine and took good care of him. He also observed her gestures and her words. At the foot of his table sat his minstrels, and opposite sat his chaplain.

Shyly he looked at the lady and with some embarrassment said, "I am not accustomed, Lady, to being served with such honor as you offer me here. If I may say so to you, I would have requested such treatment this evening as I am worthy of, and you would not have ridden down here. If I may venture to request it of you now, Lady, allow me to live in proper moderation. You have shown me too much honor."

Still she would not desist, and going over to   34
where his pages were sitting, she urged them to eat heartily. This she did by way of honor to her guest. These young gentlemen were one and all charmed with the queen. Nor did the lady then forget to go over to where the governor was sitting with his wife. The queen raised the drinking cup and said, "Let me commend our guest to you: the honor is yours. This I urge upon you both." She made her farewells, and yet she walked over once again to her guest. His heart felt the burden of love for her, and the same was true of her for him. Her heart and her eyes declared it, for they shared the burden with her. Courteously the lady said,

[17] The table, which consists of a "board" placed on a folding trestle, is low; hence Belacane is obliged to kneel in order to cut the meat on Gahmuret's plate.

"Command, Sir, and whatever you desire I shall perform, for you are worthy of it. Now grant me permission to withdraw. If good repose is granted you, we shall be most happy." —Of gold were her torch holders, and four torches were borne before her. In this way she rode up to where there were torches aplenty.

Now they went on eating no longer. The lord was both joyous and sad. He was pleased to be shown great   35
honor, but on the other hand distress tormented him, and that was mighty Love, who bows lofty spirits down. The hostess retired for the night immediately. Then a bed was prepared with care for the hero, to whom the host said, "Sleep soundly and rest well tonight: you will need it." With that he bade his followers leave. The guest's pages had their beds arranged in a circle around his, with their heads all toward his, as was his custom. Tall candles stood there, brightly burning. The hero found it irksome that the night was so long, for again and again he felt his helplessness before the black Moorish queen of the land. He kept twisting like a willow withe so that his joints cracked.

War and love were what he wanted:
Now pray that these to him be granted.

Loud was the throbbing of his heart as it swelled with yearning for knightly deeds till his warrior's breast strained as the bow strains the bowstring: his desire was all   36
too intense.

Sleepless the hero lay till he saw the grey of dawn, though it was not yet bright daylight. Then one who was his chaplain was ready for Mass, which he sang for God and for him.[18] They brought him his armor and he rode out to where the jousting was. Directly he mounted a horse that was capable of both headlong charges and swift leaps, responding agilely when it was checked. He was seen wearing his anchor on his tall helmet as he rode toward the gate, and there men and women declared they had never seen a

[18] A humorous formula: "for the honor of God and the spiritual welfare of the knight."

knight so handsome; their gods were supposed to look like
him. Stout spears were brought up. And how was he
equipped? His horse wore iron covering for its protection
against blows, and over this was laid a second covering that
was light of weight and made of green samite. His surcoat
and gambeson were also a green achmardi made in the city
of Arabi. I tell you no lie when I say his shield   37
straps and the fastenings that went with them were un-
bleached thongs studded with precious stones; refined in
fire was the red gold of his shield-boss. His service was for
Love's reward, and a sharp fight weighed lightly with him.
The queen was sitting in the window with her ladies about
her.

Look now: there was Hiuteger at the very spot where he
had often won the prize before, and when he saw this
knight coming toward him at a gallop he thought, "When
and how did that Frenchman get into this country? Who
sent that proud man here? If I ever took him for a Moor,
my best wits would have been a fool." They did not delay
the onslaught. Both spurred their horses from a gallop to
full career. A fine show of knightly valor they made of it,
too, and did not fail to provide each other a joust. The
splinters of bold Hiuteger's lance flew into the air, and his
opponent's fighting knocked him backward off his horse
onto the grass—something he was not accustomed to. Over
to him rode Gahmuret and trampled him down,   38
but he picked himself up again with energy and showed a
will to put up a defense. Gahmuret's lance, however, had
pierced his arm, and he asked for guarantee of safety in
surrender. He had met his master. "Who is it that has conquered me?" asked the bold man; to which the victor replied, "I am Gahmuret the Angevin." The other said, "I
give you my guarantee." This was accepted and he sent
him into the city. And much praised he was by the ladies
who had witnessed it.

Now Gaschier of Normandy hurried up, that proud warrior, rich in valor and a stout jouster, and the undaunted
Gahmuret waited in readiness for the second onrush. The
iron head of his spear was broad and its shaft firm. The

two strangers met, but with unequal prowess, for Gaschier was thrown, horse and all, in a joust fall and was compelled to guarantees of surrender whether he liked it or not. Gahmuret the warrior said, "Your hand has given   39 me guarantee, after having put up a manly defense. Now ride to the Scottish army and bid them spare us their attacks, if they will be so kind, and follow me into the city." Whatever he ordered or bade was carried out exactly. The Scots were forced to cease their warfare.

Up now rode Kaylet, but from him Gahmuret turned away, for he was his mother's sister's son—how, then, could he do him an injury?—though the Spaniard called after him enough. An ostrich he wore on his helmet, and the man was dressed, as I must tell you, in pfellel-silk wide and long. The field rang in the hero's wake, for the little bells he wore set up a ringing.[19] A flower of manly beauty was he! In the battle of beauty his features carried the day until the coming of two who lived hereafter: Beacurs,[20] son of Lot, and Parzival, who were not present here; they were as yet unborn, but later they were esteemed for their beauty.

Gaschier seized him by the bridle. "Your wildness will turn very tame, I tell you on my honor, if you at-   40 tack the Angevin, who has my oath of guarantee. Heed my advice, Sir, and my request as well. I have promised Gahmuret that I would dissuade all of you from warfare and I vowed it in his hands. For my sake give up your effort, or he will show you his strength in battle."

Then King Kaylet said, "If it is my cousin Gahmuret, *fils du roi* Gandin, I will give up my warfare with him. Let go of my bridle!"

"I will not let go of it until first my eye has seen your uncovered head: *mine* is still dazed."

Therewith he untied his helmet and took it off.

It was now around mid-morning. Gahmuret did find still more fighting, by which the people of the city were made

---

[19] Knights sometimes had their garment seams, particularly on the sleeves, sewn with small spherical bells.

[20] I.e., Beau-corps. He probably is the character whom Malory calls Gareth.

glad as they witnessed that joust. They all went out on the
bastions, and in their view he was a snaring-net where
everything that came under it was caught. As I heard it
told, the worthy man mounted a second horse that flew and
hugged the ground with equal adroitness, bold   41
when a charge was on, easily checked or wheeled. And
what did he do on this horse? I must say, it was bravery.
He rode out where the Moors could see him from where
their army lay westward along the sea.[21]

There was a prince there named Razalic, the most powerful man in Azagouc—his race was a guarantee of that, for
he was of royal birth—and never did this man let a day go
by without coming out toward the city for a joust. There
the hero from Anjou put checkmate to his power. A black
lady who had sent him out was to lament that someone
overthrew him. A squire, without so much as being asked
to do so, brought his master Gahmuret a spear with a
bamboo shaft, and with that he rammed the Moor back
off his horse onto the gravel; nor did he let him lie there
very long, but his hand forced him to guarantees of surrender. Therewith the conflict subsided and a great prize
was his. Gahmuret now saw eight banners streaking on
toward the city, and these he ordered the brave but   42
victoryless man to send back;[22] he further ordered him to
follow him inside the walls. This he did: there was no help
for it.

Gaschier, too, had not failed to arrive, and from him the
governor had meanwhile learned that his guest had sallied
forth.[23] If he did not eat iron like an ostrich and if he did

[21] Having defeated the leaders of the white Christian army east of
Patelamunt, Gahmuret now turns his attention "around mid-morning"
to the black Moorish army west of the city.

[22] Eight vassals of Razalic are riding to attack, apparently unaware
that their lord has been defeated. They take their orders from Razalic,
who from this moment on must take orders, in turn, from Gahmuret.

[23] It is a little odd that the governor in charge of the city's defenses
("burcgrave," "comte du château") should still be unaware of the
fighting which the whole population has been watching. Gahmuret,
after defeating the white army must have ridden around the city wall
to his encounter with the black army leader, rather than through the
city itself.

not chew rocks, it was because he didn't have any at hand. His anger growled and roared like a lion; he tore his hair and said, "I have put my old age to a great greenhorn's uses! The gods sent me a brave and worthy guest, and if he now has more fighting than he can manage, I will never know honor again. What good are shield and sword to me? Anybody that reminds me of this will revile me!" With that he turned away from his people and galloped off in the direction of the gate.

A squire brought him a shield which was painted inside and outside with the figure of a transfixed man, made in Isenhart's country; he also brought a helmet in his hand, and a sword which Razalic had taken bravely to   43 the fight but from which he was there parted, that brave and black-complexioned pagan. —Far and wide went his fame, and if he later died unbaptized, may He who has all miracles within His power have mercy on that warrior brave. —When the governor saw that, he was never so delighted with anything. Recognizing the coat of arms, he went out the gate at a gallop to where he saw his guest, his young guest not at all old, eagerly awaiting further knightly combat. There his host, Lahfilirost, overtook him and quickly led him back in: never did he strike down another opponent there.

"Sir," said Lahfilirost, *le comte du château,* "tell me, did hand of yours conquer Razalic? If so, our country is safe from war for good and all, for he was over all the army of the Moors, those vassals of loyal Isenhart who have done us injury. Our sufferings are at an end. An angry god gave them the command to attack us here with their army: now their champion is brought low."

He brought Gahmuret in, loath as the latter was to come. The queen rode down to meet him and with   44 her hand she grasped his bridle and untied the fastenings of his mouth guard. The governor was obliged to surrender the bridle to her. Nor did his pages forget to come running to their master. Through the city the wise queen was seen leading her guest, who had won the victory. At the moment she deemed proper she dismounted: "Oh! but your pages are devoted! —You seem to think you are going to lose this man. He will be well attended without you. Take his horse and lead it away. Here *I* am his friend."

Up there he found numerous ladies, but his armor was removed by the black hands of the queen. In a bed beautifully adorned and with a coverlet of sable there was granted to him an intimate honor. No one was present—the maidens had gone out and shut the door after them—and the queen bestowed a sweet and noble love, as did Gahmuret, her heart's beloved. Yet their skins were not alike in color.

Offerings aplenty the inhabitants of the city brought to their gods. And what commands did brave Razalic   45 receive when he came off the battlefield? Whatever they were, he performed them faithfully, and yet his grief was renewed for his master Isenhart. The governor was informed that he had arrived, and then there was a jubilation! To Gahmuret princes came from all parts of the queen's land of Zazamanc to express their gratitude for the victory he had achieved. In formal joust he had overthrown four-and-twenty knights and brought back the horses of most of them; captured were princes three; in their retinues rode many a knight into the courtyard up at the palace.

Well rested now and breakfasted, and in fine-made garments splendidly arrayed was the country's supreme lord. She who was formerly termed a maiden was now a wife, and as she led him forth by the hand she said: "My person and my country are now subject to this knight, provided enemies will allow it so to be." [24]

Then compliance was accorded to a courteous request of Gahmuret's: "Come nearer, my lord Razalic, you   46 shall kiss my wife. The like shall you do also, lord Gaschier." And Hiuteger the Scotsman proud he bade kiss her on the lips; he still bore his wounds from the joust. Now he bade them all be seated, and, remaining standing himself, he said good-naturedly, "I would be happy to see here also my cousin, if that might be with the permission of

[24] Gahmuret is proclaimed King of Zazamanc; by virtue of his defeat of Razalic, Isenhart's successor, he is already King of Azagouc.

the man who took him captive. As his kinsman I have no course but to set him free." With a happy smile the queen bade them fetch him quickly. In through the crowd the lovable *beau comte* made his way. Knightly deeds had left him with wounds but he had done many a brave action in the course of them. Gaschier the Norman had brought him there; courteous he was; his father was a Frenchman, and he was the child of Kaylet's sister; his journey had been made in a woman's service; his name was Killirjacac; and he surpassed the beauty of all men.

When Gahmuret saw him—their faces attested their kinship, for they very much resembled one another—he bade the great queen kiss him and embrace him, and 47 then he said, "And now come over here to me also," and the lord kissed him too. They were delighted to see each other. But then Gahmuret said, "Alas, sweet young man, whatever brought your tender self to this country? Tell me, did a woman give you such a command?"

"They give few commands, Sir, to me. It was my uncle Gaschier who brought me here, and he well knows the reason why. I have a thousand knights here for him, and I am in his service. To Rouen in Normandy I went to answer his call to arms, and took those young heroes to him, and for his sake I made the journey from Champagne. Now Harm will turn her skill and cunning against him unless you act to your own honor. If you will so permit, allow him to profit from his kinship to me and allow me to relieve his distress."

"I will leave the matter up to you. Now go with my lord Gaschier and bring Kaylet to me here."

Directly they set about fulfilling the hero's request and brought him in as he had bidden. Then he too was graciously received and embraced by the great queen. 48 She kissed the warrior graciously, as well she might in honor do, for he was her husband's aunt's son and by lineage a noble king.

Laughingly the host[25] went on to say, "God knows, Lord

25 I.e., Gahmuret.

Kaylet, that if I were to take Toledo from you, and your country Spain, for the advantage of the King of Gascony who in his anger is doing you much injury, that would be disloyal of me, for you are my aunt's son. The best men, the very core of knighthood, are here with you: who forced you into this expedition?"

To which the proud young warrior replied, "My uncle, Schiltung, whose daughter Fridebrant married, ordered me to serve Fridebrant, and thus the latter, for his wife's sake, has from me alone six thousand well-known knights here, and they have hands that are brave. I brought him still more knights besides, but a good share of them have gone away. In support of the Scots there were here these brave contingents: from Greenland battle-seasoned heroes came to him, and two kings with strong forces; a flood of   49 knighthood they brought, and many a ship. That contingent pleased me mightily. Here too for his sake was Morholt, whose prowess has both strength and skill. These have now gone home, and with my men I shall do as my lady here instructs. My service shall be manifest to her, but for my service you have no cause to thank me: our kinship requires as much. These dauntless heroes are now yours. If they were baptized men as mine are, and of the same color of skin, there would never be a man crowned but that he would get his fill of fighting from them. —But I am amazed to see you here. Tell me about that, and how it happened."

"I arrived yesterday, and today I became master of this country. The queen took me captive with her own hand, and with love I defended myself, for my wits so counseled me."

"I gather that that sweet weapon of defense has overcome both armies."

"You mean because I avoided battle with *you?* You shouted loudly to me: what did you want to get from me by force? Let me bargain with you some other way!"

"I did not recognize your anchor. My aunt's hus-   50 band Gandın never wore it."

"But I recognized your ostrich perfectly well, and the serpent-head on your shield, too;[26] your ostrich stood tall without a nest. I saw by the look of you that you didn't much like the oaths of surrender that two men had given me; they had put up a stiff fight."

"It could easily have gone the same with me. I would have to admit even to a devil whose ways I can never get to like, that if he had put up such a battle against stout heroes as *you* did, the women would eat him like sugar."

"Your mouth grants me too much praise."

"No, I cannot flatter. But look for other support from me."

They called for Razalic to come over and join them.

Courteously Kaylet said, "My cousin Gahmuret has taken you prisoner with his hand."

"That he has, Sir. I have recognized the hero as the man from whom the land of Azagouc will never withhold homage, now that our Lord Isenhart may not wear the crown there. He was slain in the service of her who is now your cousin's wife; for her love he gave his life. But my   51
kiss to her has abolished that account. I have lost my lord and kinsman and am now ready to do homage as a knight to your aunt's son, and, if he will compensate me for that loss, I will pledge my hand to him. Thus he will have riches and honor and everything that Tankanis bequeathed to Isenhart. Embalmed amid the army there Isenhart lies, and on his wounds I have gazed every day since this spearhead broke his heart." And he drew it forth from his bosom on a silken ribbon. Then the warrior put it back again against his bosom next to the bare skin.

"It is still broad daylight, and if my lord Killirjacac will carry the message to the army as I request, my princes shall ride along as his escort." He sent a ring along as token.

Then those who were of hell's color came, all the princes that were on hand, up through the city to the castle hall. With conferral of flags his hand bestowed fiefs of land upon

[26] The word *sarapandratest* is probably French *serpent à tête,* 'serpent-head," though *tête de serpent* would be expected.

the princes of Azagouc. Each was delighted with his portion, yet the best portion remained for Gahmuret their lord.   52

These came first, and now those of Zazamanc pressed forward with grand display, not shabby at all, to receive from him, as their lady bade, lands and usufructs, to each one as was fitting. Poverty fled from their lord.

Now Prothizilas, who was a prince of high lineage, had left a dukedom, which Gahmuret now bestowed upon a man who had gained much honor with his hand and who from battle had never shrunk back: Lahfilirost, *le comte du château*, received it that day amid conferral of flags.

Then the lordly princes of Azagouc took the Scotsman Hiuteger and Gaschier the Norman and led them before their lord, who pronounced them free upon their request. For this they thanked Gahmuret. Turning to Hiuteger the Scotsman, they urged him earnestly: "Leave the tent here for our master as a reward for his adventure. Isenhart's life was taken from us when he gave away his armor and equipment to Fridebrant; the pledge of his joy was lost, he himself lies upon his funeral bier, and unrequited service brought him excessive grief. To Fridebrant the equipment was given, that treasure of our country, and never on earth was anything so fine: the helmet was thick and strong and made of diamond, a good companion in battle."   53

Thereat Hiuteger's hand vowed that, when he got to his master's country, he would gather all the equipment and send it back here in prime condition. This he did from no constraint.

All the princes present now begged the king for permission to withdraw, and forthwith they left the palace.

Devastated though his land might be, Gahmuret could nevertheless lavish such gifts by way of rewards as if gold grew on his trees. He distributed rich presents and his vassals and kinsmen accepted his wealth. This was the queen's wish. Many a battle had preceded the wedding festivities, but they were all set right in this way. I did not think this up by myself: I was *told* that Isenhart was buried

like a king by the men who had known him. The taxes
from his lands, to the amount of a year's income,   54
they expended on the costs, and did so of their own free
will. Gahmuret bade Isenhart's people keep his great wealth
for each of them to enjoy for himself.

Next morning the foreigners before the fortress vacated
the country. All who were there departed, and many a
stretcher they carried as they went. The field stood bare of
shelters save for one tent, and that was a large one. The
king ordered it carried on board ship, saying to the people
that he was going to transport it to Azagouc—but with
those words he deceived them.

Here the proud man remained until he began to grieve
because he found no knightly activity, and then his joy was
pawned to sorrow. Yet his black wife was dearer to him
than his own life. Never was there a woman more endowed
with charms, and that lady's heart never failed to include
in its retinue a worthy company of womanly virtues and
true modesty.

In the city of Seville was born the man whom, some time
later, he asked to take him away. He had already guided
him many a mile; he had brought him here; he   55
was not like a Moor in color. And this ship captain replied,
"You must quietly conceal this from those whose skins
are black; my boats are so swift that they can never overtake us, and we shall get away."

He ordered his gold put on board ship. And now I must
tell you of departure. By night the worthy man went away,
and it was done secretly. And when he deserted his wife
she had within her body a child twelve weeks alive. The
wind bore him swiftly away. In her girdle purse that lady
discovered a letter written by her husband's hand. In
French, a language which she knew, the writing informed
her:

"To one Love another Love sends love:
    By this journey I am a thief: I steal it from you to
spare you grief. I cannot conceal from you, Lady, the

fact that, were your faith of the same law as mine, I would yearn for you eternally, for I do suffer for your sake always, even so.

If the child of us two should in his features resemble a man, then he will indeed be rich in valor. He is born out of Anjou; Love will be his lady; in battle he   56 will be a storm of hail, to foes a hard neighbor. My son should know that his grandfather was named Gandin and that he died from knightly deeds.

His father before him suffered the same fate, and his name was Addanz. Rarely did his shield remain whole. He was by race a Briton, he and Utepandragun being offspring of two brothers who are named herewith: one was called Lazaliez and the other Brickus.

The father of these was named Mazadan; into Famorgan he was taken by a fairy, and her name was Terdelaschoye, and he was a fettering chain upon her heart. From these two is my line descended, which will shine in brilliance forever; each one since has worn a crown, and each has had no lack of honor.

Lady, if you will receive baptism, you may yet win me back."

Nor did she wish it otherwise. "Alas! how swiftly this has come about! If only he will come back, I shall do just that. In whose charge has his manly courtesy left   57 the fruit of his love here behind? Alas for loving companionship! Now sorrow with its power must control my life forever. To do honor to his God," the lady said, "I would gladly agree to be baptized and live as he desired." Grief brought warfare to her heart. Her joy sought the withered bough, as the turtledove still does, for that bird was ever of the same mind:

> *When she a loved one loses, she*
> *Will perch upon a withered tree.*

In due time this lady was delivered of a son who was of two colors and in whom God had wrought a marvel, for he was both black and white. Immediately the queen kissed him over and over again on his white spots, and on her little child the mother bestowed the name of Feirefiz Angevin. He was to become a waster of forests, for the jousts of his hand were to shatter many a spear and riddle many a shield with holes. Like a magpie was the color of his hair and of his skin.

It was more than a year now since Gahmuret had been so much praised there in Zazamanc and his hand   58 had wrested triumph. Now he was still sailing the sea and the swift winds were bringing him woe. He saw a silken sail glowing red, and the boat that bore it was also bearing the messengers sent by the Scotsman Fridebrant to the Lady Belacane. He was begging her to forgive him, although he had lost his kinsman on her account, for ever having attacked her. They had with them the diamond helmet, a sword, a coat of mail, and a pair of leg guards. You may see a great marvel in the fact that their boat encountered him, as the story vowed to me it did. They gave him the knightly equipment, and he swore that his lips would be the guarantee of their message when he came to her. Whereupon they parted.

I was told that the sea brought him to a harbor, and from there he made his way to Seville. With gold the brave man rewarded the ship captain for his labors. Whereupon they parted, to the latter's regret.

BOOK·II

In the land of Spain he knew the king: it was his cousin Kaylet, and he traveled on to Toledo to see him.[1] But he had left there on a knightly expedition where shields   59 were not to be spared. So Gahmuret also gave orders, as the story assures me, for spears to be made ready, with painted shafts and green sendal-silk pennons, each spear with a pennon attached to it and three ermine anchors thereon, so proud that people talked about their richness. Long and broad they were and hung right down to the hand when tied a span below the spear point. A hundred of them were prepared for the brave man and they were carried behind him by his cousin's men. Well might they honor him and treat him with distinction: their doing so did not displease their master.

He pressed onward, I don't know for how long, until in the land of Waleis the tents of strangers came into view. There before Kanvoleis many a pavilion had been pitched on the plain. Now I tell you this without any doubt, and if you will have it so, then it is true: he ordered his men to halt and sent his dapper chief squire on in ahead of him. The latter asked, as his lord had instructed him,   60 to take lodgings in the city. He was in a great hurry, and

---

[1] Kaylet is therefore King of Castile. Toledo was recovered from the Moors in 1085.

pack horses were being led behind him. Not a house did he see but that shields formed a second roof for it, and the walls were all hung with spears round about.

The Queen of Waleis had proclaimed a tournament at Kanvoleis, so planned that many a coward is still scared when he sees anything like it being arranged: his hand has no part in it. She was a maiden, not a wife, and she was offering two countries and her own person to whoever won the prize. This offer knocked many a man back off his horse onto the ground, and those who got these throws were called thrown and lost. Dauntless heroes made display of their knightly bravery, to full career of onslaught many a horse was spurred, and many were the swords that rang.

On the plain the current of a stream was traversed by a bridge guarded by a gate. This a squire readily opened as he was minded to do. Over the gate was built the   61 great hall, and inside by the windows sat the queen with many noble ladies. They looked to see what these squires were about, for the latter had decided on a plan of action and were putting up a tent—a tent which a king had lost for the sake of unrequited love when Belacane had driven him to it. With labor now that tent, which required thirty pack horses to transport, was erected, and richly did it show. The meadow was broad enough so that the tent ropes stretched way out.

At the same time Gahmuret, the worthy man, was having breakfast on the other side of the city, after which he made careful preparations for riding forth in courtly fashion. With no loss of time his squires tied up his spears, five to a bundle, while the sixth, adorned with a pennon, they carried in their hands. Thus the proud man came riding.[2]

In the queen's presence the news was heard that a guest whom no one knew had arrived from a distant country.   62

"His attendants are of fine manners, both heathen and French, and several of them, to judge by their speech,

---

[2] Gahmuret now covers the same route already traversed by his chief squire: through the city, over the bridge, and out onto the Leo Meadow where his tent is now ready for him.

may well be Angevins.[3] Their bearing is proud, their attire splendid and well tailored. I spent some time among his squires, and they are free of misconduct. They say that anyone desiring riches has but to seek out their master and he will deliver them from want. I inquired about him, and without hesitation they told me he is the King of Zazamanc." —This report a page made to her. —"*Ah voilà!* What a pavilion! Your crown and your country could be pawned for only half of its value!"

"You need not praise it so to me. My mouth will tell you this: it must belong to a distinguished man who knows nothing about poverty." So said the queen. "But when will he himself arrive there?" She bade the page inquire about that.

In courtly fashion the hero now came riding through the city, waking sleepers as he came. Many a shield he saw shining. Ahead of him along his way shrill trum-   63
pets loudly raised a din, and there was a sound of two drums alternately swung aloft and thumped with stout blows so that the noise re-echoed through the town. Along the route their melody was spelled with flutes sounding a march tune. Now we must not neglect how their master approached. Fiddlers rode alongside him, and the warrior worthy had one leg stretched out in front of him on top of his horse; he displayed two boots pulled up on his bare legs. His mouth shone in its redness like a ruby or as if it were on fire, and a full mouth it was, not thin at all. His whole body was noble; fair and curling was his hair as far as it could be seen outside his hat, and that was a rich headgear. Of green samite was his cloak, with sable trim showing black on the front of it, and set off against a shirt that was white. There was a great press around him to get a look, and many a time the question was asked: who was this beardless knight that made display of wealth like this? In no time the news was abroad, for his people answered them directly.   64

Now they were coming to the bridge, both his men and other people as well, and at sight of the bright glow that

[3] Distinction is apparently made among dialects of French.

emanated from the queen he quickly brought his leg down to his side and he braced himself, that warrior worthy, like a falcon set to fall on its prey. The quarters met with his approval—such was the hero's taste—and they did not displease his hostess, Waleis's queen.

Then the King of Spain learned that out on the Leo Meadow[4] there stood a tent which at brave Razalic's bidding had been given to Gahmuret before Patelamunt. A knight so informed him. Whereat he was a soldier of Joy and leaped up like a deer. And the knight added further: "I saw your aunt's son coming in pomp as he used to. There are a hundred pennons set up beside a shield on the green meadow in front of his high tent, and they are all green. The hero bold also has three ermine anchors brightly blazoned on every banner of green silk."

"Is he in battle array? O then people will see how 65 he turns their onrushes to confusion! The way he parries their onslaughts! Haughty King Hardiz has now this long time been directing his angry zeal against me: now Gahmuret's hand shall bring him down with his jousting. My fate is not with the lost."

With that he sent his messengers over to where Gaschier the Norman was camped with a large company, and the handsome Killirjacac, both of whom were present there at his request. To the pavilion they came with Kaylet and with their retinues, and warmly they welcomed the worthy King of Zazamanc. They said it was much too long a time not to have seen him before this, and they spoke in all sincerity.

He asked them what knights were here.

His aunt's son replied: "From distant lands there are knights here whom Love has sent, many heroes bold and dauntless. King Utepandragun has many a Briton here, for it pains him like a thorn that he has lost his wife, 66 she who was Arthur's mother. She went off with a cleric who spoke magic spells, and Arthur has ridden in pursuit of him. It is now the third year since he has been without

[4] *Leoplan* ("Leo Meadow") may be the poet's misunderstanding of the Old French common noun *lee plaine*—"broad meadow."

son and wife. Here too is his daughter's husband, expert in knightly doings, Lot of Norway; slow in treachery and swift to fame is that warrior bold and wise. Here too is Gawan, his son, but too young to be capable of any knightly action. He was with me, the little fellow, and he says that, if he could break a lance and if his strength would allow it, he would gladly do a knightly act. How early his eagerness for it has begun! And here the King of Patrigalt has a whole forest of spears. But his airs count for nothing because the men of Portugal are here—we call them the dashing ones because they thrust right through shields. The Provençals have bright-colored shields here too. And the men of Waleis are here. By dint of the numbers of their   67
fellow countrymen they manage to keep on riding as they will, right through their opponents' onrush. Many a knight whom I cannot identify is here for a woman's sake, but all those of us whom I have named are quartered here with our large retinues in the city—no mistake about that—as the queen requested us to do. I will now tell you who are quartered out in the field[5]—and they have slight regard for our fighting. There is the worthy King of Ascalun,[6] and the proud King of Aragon, Cidegast of Logrois, and the King of Punturtois, whose name is Brandelidelin; and there is the bold Lehelin; and there is Morholt of Ireland, who wrests precious hostages from us. Out on the plain are encamped the proud Alemans:[7] the Duke of Brabant has come to this country on account of King Hardiz, because that King of Gascony had given him his sister Alize, and thus his service has received its reward in advance. They both have it in for me here. Now I shall rely on you. Remember our kinship and in your affection look   68
out for me."

Then the King of Zazamanc said, "You owe me no

[5] These will constitute the "outer army"; the foregoing belong to the "inner army."

[6] This is Kingrisin, of whose death Gawan will be accused in Book VIII.

[7] *Alemans* (= *les Allemands*) is the French word for Germans in general. In this German poem, "the proud Alemans" are on the "enemy" side.

thanks for what my service may accomplish here to your honor. We shall be of one will. Does your ostrich still stand without a nest? You shall bear your serpent-head against his half griffon. My anchor shall be firmly cast and will land squarely in the clash of his onset so that he will have to look for a ford on the gravel behind his horse. If they let us at one another, either I will bring him down or else he will bring me down. That much I guarantee you for sure."

Overjoyed, his worries gone, Kaylet rode to the tents. Up went a war cry over two heroes proud, Schiolarz of Poitou and Gurnemanz de Graharz, who were jousting on the meadow, and then and there began the vesper games.[8] From one side rode out six, from the other side three, and quickly a detachment came out in support of them. Then they started in on knightly deeds for fair and nothing could stop them.

It was still only the middle of the day and the King of Zazamanc was resting in his tent when he dis-   69 covered that the charges on horseback were taking place from one end of the field to the other, all in accordance with knightly rules. He set out in that direction with many a banner of bright color. He was in no hurry to get into swift action; rather, he wanted to watch leisurely how things were being done by both sides, and so his carpet was laid out on the meadow where the charges were crisscrossing and horses were whinnying at the jabs of the spurs. A ring of squires formed around him, and on past them there was a clang and a clatter of swords. How they fought for victory, those men whose swords thus rang! And a mighty cracking of spears there was. He had no need to inquire of anyone: Where? Onsets of horsemen formed his tent walls and hands of knights wove the designs. So near was the knightly action that the ladies could easily gaze down on the heroes' labors, but the queen was sorry that the King of Zazamanc did not mingle with the others. She said, "Alas, why has he come, this man of whom I have heard such marvels reported?"

[8] Unofficial warm-up games on the eve ("vesper") of the official tournament

Now the King of France was dead, whose wife had often enough brought Gahmuret into great peril by her love. The worthy queen had sent to inquire for   70 him and to find out whether he had yet returned from heathendom to his own country at last. The power of great love forced her to that step.[9]

A mighty good showing was made there by many a brave fellow, who, however, did not aim so high as the winning of the queen's person and lands: their objective was lesser winnings.[10]

Now Gahmuret too was in armor—armor by which his wife was informed of a reconciliation: Fridebrant of Scotland had sent it to her as a gift of restitution for her losses, for he had overburdened her with warfare.[11] Nothing on earth was so fine. He looked at the diamond headgear, and what a helmet it was! Upon it was attached an anchor in which precious stones were set, large ones, by no means small. But it was a heavy weight of a thing. Arrayed was this visitor now. How was his shield adorned? A precious boss of gold of Arabi was fixed thereon, massive as he carried it, and such was the brilliance of the red gold that one could see himself in it as in a   71 mirror. Underneath that there was an anchor of sable.—*I* would like to be able to afford what he wore on his person, for it was worth many a mark.

His surcoat was very full. I fancy no one since has worn so fine a one in battle. Its length reached to the carpet. Let me see if I can describe it. It shone like living fire in the night. A faded color was what it did not have. No glance could miss its radiance, it slashed weak eyes with pain. Picture-embroidered it was with gold which at Montagne à Caucasus was torn from the crags by griffons' claws, for griffons guarded it then and still guard it there today.

[9] We leave these oddly intrusive lines, with their anticipation of later developments, in their manuscript position. Removing them to 71 (Lachmann) or to 64 (Stapel) offers little advantage.

[10] The author commends knights who (like himself) are brave but poor.

[11] A curious statement, since, as far as we know, Belacane never received it See 58, at the conclusion of Book I.

From Arabi people go there and get it by cunning—there is nothing so precious anywhere—and bring it back to Arabi, the place where they also weave the green achmardi and the precious pfellel-silk. It was, in short, like no other garment.

Now he raised his shield to his neck. A horse in splendid array stood close at hand, stoutly armored to its very hooves. Here, you pages! Call out now, call out!   72
Up he leaped onto its back as it stood there. Many were the stout spears that the hero's hand scattered in the fray, and he scattered the horsemen too that rushed him: right through their midst every time and out the other side. And after the anchor followed the ostrich.

Gahmuret unhorsed Poytwin de Prienlascors and many another worthy man besides, exacting from all of them oaths of surrender, and any cross-bearing knights that rode that day got the benefit of the hero's efforts. The horses he won he gave to them, so that in him they found their great gain.[12]

Out against him came four identical flags—brave troops rode beneath them and their master knew how to fight— and each one bore the device of a griffon's tail. That hinder part proved a hailstorm of knightly valor. The fore part of the griffon was carried by the King of Gascony on his shield.[13] This fine-bred knight was arrayed as well as women could do. When he caught sight of the ostrich he advanced to fight in front of the others, but the anchor got to him first, and back off his horse he was thrown by the   73
worthy King of Zazamanc, who took him prisoner. Then

[12] Scholars are divided as to whether there "cross-bearing knights" (gekriuzte ritter) are Crusaders (Kreuzritter) or, in a rather elaborate pun, knights bearing the "cross" of poverty. Thus Gahmuret may be piously giving to religion, or he may be spontaneously helping out the poor fellows referred to in 70 above.

[13] The front half of the heraldic griffon is displayed by King Hardiz of Gascony; the rear half of the same heraldic beast is displayed apparently by his vassal and brother-in-law, Duke Lambekin of Brabant. Their personal foe is Kaylet, whose device is the ostrich, but when they attack him, Gahmuret, wearing the anchor, intervenes. Gahmuret defeats King Hardiz, and in 74 below Kaylet defeats Duke Lambekin.

there was a grand free-for-all, deep furrows were stamped smooth, and the hair of many was combed down with swords. There forest timber was squandered and many a knight unhorsed. These made their way rearward—so I heard it told—to where the cowards tarried. The fighting was so near that the ladies one and all saw clearly who deserved the prize.

From the spear of love-seeking Riwalin[14] there snowed a fresh path of splinters; he was the King of Lohneis, and his horse-charges hit with a resounding crash.

From Gahmuret Morholt stole a horseman by lifting him out of his saddle and setting him in front of him on his own horse—a grossly improper action—and this was Killirjacac.[15] From him King Lac[16] had previously been dealt such payment as he might pick up off the ground where he fell: he had done some good fighting there. The powerful Morholt was eager to conquer him with a sword, and thus he captured that worthy warrior.

Kaylet's hand unhorsed the Duke of Brabant, a prince named Lambekin. And what did his men do then?   74 They shielded him with swords: those heroes were craving for battle.

Then the King of Aragon unhorsed the aged Utepandragun, bringing that King of Britain down on the meadow. Many were the flowers that stood there in bloom around him. —O how accommodating I am in allotting that worthy Briton so handsome a bed there before Kanvoleis: there, where peasant's foot never trod nor—if I am to tell you the truth—is ever likely to tread, he was not allowed to retain

---

14 Riwalin, King of Lohneis (Lyonesse) is the father of Tristan. Knights at the Kanvoleis tournament belong to the generation preceding the famous heroes: Utepandragun is the father of Arthur, Riwalin father of Tristan, Lot father of Gawan, and Gahmuret father of Parzival.

15 Morholt (who will one day be slain by Tristan) is of giant size, Killirjacac is a youth.

16 Lac, King of Karnant, is the father of Hartmann von Aue's hero Erec and also of the Lady Jeschute, who will enter the story in Book III. This cross referencing to characters in well-known romances by other authors no doubt delighted Wolfram's audiences.

his seat on the horse whereon he had sat till now. His men did not forget him for very long but protected him as they fought above him, and then there was no lack of mighty clashes of arms.

Now along came the King of Punturtois, who here before Kanvoleis was thrown down onto his horse's tracks so that he lay there behind the animal. This the proud Gahmuret did. Trample him down, my lord! Trample him down!—Trampled down in the fighting they found his aunt's son, Kaylet: men of Punturtois had taken him captive. Then the faring became very rough. Since King Brandelidelin had been snatched away from *his*   75 men, *they* took a different king prisoner. Then many a worthy man in iron clothing went running hither and thither, and their hands were tanned by horses' hooves and by cudgels till they were black and blue. Those gracious heroes got bruises there.

Not for embellishment do I say this—repose was there disdained—it was love that drove those worthy men on, many a painted shield, and many a helmet bedecked, for which the dust was now a cover. Part of the field had flowers growing, and short green grass grew everywhere: thereon fell those worthy men, to whom honor was accorded.—*My* mind can go along with such desires as theirs, provided *I* am left astride my foal.

Now the King of Zazamanc rode to a place where no one pursued, and sought a horse that was fresh and rested. They removed his diamond helmet, but only for the sake of the cool breeze, not because of any dare-devil bravery. They removed his coif of mail. His mouth shone red and proud.

A lady whom I have mentioned before, along   76 came one who was her chaplain, and three young pages; stout squires rode with them, leading by hand two pack horses. These messengers had been sent by the Queen Ampflise. Shrewd was her chaplain and he immediately recognized this man. In French he greeted him: "*Soyez le bien venu, beau sire,* to my lady and to me. *La reine de France* is she who is struck by the lance of your love."

Into his hand he delivered a letter wherein the lord found a greeting and a little ring as an accompanying token, for its lady had received it once from the man of Anjou. As he perceived the handwriting he made a bow.

Would you care to hear what she said?

"Love and greeting I send you—I who have never been free of grieving since first I knew your love. Your love is the lock and the bolt of my heart and of my heart's rejoicing. Love of you will be the death of me. If your love must be far away, then love cannot fail to do me harm. Come back, and from my hand   77 accept a crown, a scepter, and a country: these have descended to me by inheritance, these have been won by your love. Receive also as a reward the costly presents contained in the four packing cases. Moreover, you shall be my knight in the land of Waleis and before the capital city of Kanvoleis. I do not care whether the queen sees it; it can do me no serious harm. I am richer and more beautiful and I can more lovingly give love and receive love. If you are willing to live in accordance with worthy love, take my crown as reward in accordance with my love."

He found nothing further in the letter.—A squire's hand pulled his coif of mail back over his head, and grief fled from Gahmuret. They fastened his diamond helmet on: thick and hard it was. He craved exertion. The messengers he bade be conducted beneath his pavilion to rest.

Wherever there was a press of fighting, there he opened up a space. One man lost, another won, and there a man could find a second chance if he had missed his knightly action. In one place there was opportunity aplenty   78 for jousting one against one, in another place for thrusting away in formations.[17] They gave up those little taps that people call friendly pokes, and intimate brotherhoods were now torn to pieces in real anger. The crooked was rarely

[17] See Additional Notes, number 6, pp. 435-436, for the five types of knightly combat.

made straight and there was little mention of chivalric rights: whoever won anything kept it and did not care if he earned the hatred of the other. Of many lands they were, these men whose hands plied the knightly trade and feared no injury at all. There Gahmuret performed Ampflise's bidding to be her knight: her letter had conveyed her word to him. O how he now set on! Did love and valor impel him? Great love and strong loyalty made his strength like new. Now he saw King Lot lifting his shield against oncomers; he was almost being forced to flight. But Gahmuret's hand prevented that. He broke the onset with a clash and with his spear shaft thrust the King of Aragon backward off his horse. Schafillor was the king's name. The spear with which he downed that warrior proud had no pennon attached to it; he had brought it with him out of heathendom. The worthy king's followers defended him valiantly, but he took him prisoner all the same. Now the inner army made the outer army do some fast galloping across the meadow. These vesper games had brought both sides a goodly income of fighting. They could well be considered a tournament, for many a broken spear was left behind.

Then Lehelin in fury said, "Are we to be dishonored this way? This comes from that fellow wearing the anchor. Before the day is over, one of us is going to bring the other down where he will lie pretty uncomfortably. They have all but gained the victory over us." [18]

Their clash opened up plenty of space around them, and then the matter went beyond a childish game. Under the whittling of their hands the wood began to disappear, yet neither had any wish other than: "Spears, Sir! Spears! More spears!" All the same, Lehelin had to endure disgrace and pain, for the King of Zazamanc thrust him off his horse to the length of a spear point plus the length of the shaft in which it was fixed. Then Gahmuret picked up his oath of surrender.—*I* would be more comfortable picking ing up sweet pears, no matter how easily those knights fell

[18] Lehelin, who was mentioned casually in 67 above, is a sinister character who will repeatedly appear on the periphery of the narrative.

before him.—And many a man of those that stood his onset set up the cry: "Here comes the anchor! Worse luck!
Worse luck!"

Right toward him came charging a prince of Anjou—
Grief was his lady-mistress—with inverted shield.[19] That
brought Sorrow's news to Gahmuret, for he recognized the
coat of arms.—Why did he turn away from him? I'll tell
you about that, if you wish.—That coat of arms had been
assigned in times past by Galoes, *fils du roi* Gandin, his ever-
faithful brother, before love had brought about his death in
a joust. Then he unfastened his helmet. No more did his
fighting take its path across the grass or the dust: Sorrow so
commanded. He cursed himself for not so much as asking
Kaylet, his aunt's son, what his brother was doing that he
was not taking part in this tournament. Sad to say, he was
unaware that he had died in combat before Munthori. One
sorrow was already his companion, for noble love of a great
queen[20] tormented him. *She* was later to sicken   81
from yearning for him and die from the faithfulness of her
grieving.

Weighed down with grief though Gahmuret was, he had
nevertheless in that one half day broken in two so many
spears that, if the tournament had taken place, the forest
would have been wiped out. A hundred painted ones had
been allotted to him, and these that proud man had used
up. His bright pennons were given to the heralds, as was
their due.[21] Then he rode to his tent.

The page of the Queen of Waleis followed him, and to
him was given that precious surcoat, now tattered and torn,
which he carried to his lady. It was still valuable for the gold
in it, and it gleamed like a glowing coal. Its richness was
easily seen, and then the queen said, "Some noble woman
sent you with this knight to my country.—But my dignity
prompts me that the other knights must not be offended,

---

[19] The carrying of the shield upside down, i.e., with the pointed
end up and the rounded or straight end down, indicated the death of
the knight's lord.

[20] Belacane presumably.

[21] Compare 32 in Book I above.

whom adventure has brought here. Let all of them perceive my good will, for by Adam's rib they are all my kinsmen. I feel, however, that Gahmuret's fighting has   82
won the highest prize."

The others continued the chivalric contests with such
furious persistence that they went on battling away almost
till nightfall. The inner army had forced the outer army
back to their tents. Had it not been for the King of Ascalun
and Morholt of Ireland, they would have ridden down
their tent ropes. Winnings and losses there were, and plenty
of them had sustained injuries; the rest had praise and
honor.

Now it is time to send them their separate ways. No one
can see a thing here. Without a stakes-holding innkeeper
to furnish light, who would want to shoot craps in the
dark? It is more than these tired men can manage.

Darkness was quite forgotten, however, where Gahmuret
was sitting. There it was like daylight—not real daylight—
but there was a tremendous number of lights there and
many a cluster of small candles. Upon olive branches many
a sumptuous cushion was placed, and carefully spread in
front of these was many a broad carpet.[22] Up as far as the
tent ropes rode the queen, with numerous noble ladies; she
desired to see the noble King of Zazamanc. Many   83
tired knights pressed after her. The tablecloths had been
removed before they arrived in the pavilion. The host sprang
to his feet with alacrity, and four captive kings with him,
each of them accompanied by several princes. After the manner of courtesy he received her, and she was well pleased
with him as soon as she set eyes on him.

With joy the woman from Waleis said, "Here where I
find you, you are the host; yet I am the mistress-ruler of
this country. If you desire that *I* should bestow the kiss of
welcome upon *you*, I am quite willing to do so."

To which he replied, "Your kiss shall be mine, provided
these lords are also to be kissed; but if king or princes

[22] With Leitzmann's punctuation of the *MHG* text, it would be the
candles which were placed on olive branches. In any case, however, the
scene is inside the great tent, not in an illuminated olive orchard.

are to be deprived of it, I shall not venture to ask you for it either."

"So shall it be, indeed. I had not noticed any of them before." And she kissed those present who merited it, as Gahmuret desired her to do.

He bade the queen be seated. My lord Brandelidelin courteously sat down by the lady. Green rushes wet with dew were lightly strewn upon the carpets whereon sat he who was the delight of the noble woman from Waleis; 84 love for him constrained her. He sat down so close in front of her that she took hold of him and drew him back so he was right next to her on the other side. She was a maiden and not a wife, she who allowed him to sit so near her.— Would you like now to hear what her name was? She was Queen Herzeloyde; and her cousin Rischoyde was the wife of Kaylet, whose aunt's son was Gahmuret. From the lady Herzeloyde was shed such radiance that, if all the candles had been extinguished, there would from her alone have been sufficient light. Had it not been that great sorrow toppled the peak of his joy afar, he would readily have offered her his love.

They had exchanged greetings as propriety required, and some time later cup bearers came forth with precious objects from Azagouc, the great richness of which escaped no one. Noble youths carried them. Costly goblets they were, broad, not small in the least, and made of precious stones entirely without gold. They were the tribute from that country which Isenhart had more than once offered to the lady Belacane as the price of relief from love's pain. Drink was proffered now in many a jewel of bright color, 85 emerald and carnelian, and some consisted of a single ruby.

To the pavilion came riding now two knights who were at liberty on their pledged word. They had been taken captive by the outer army and were coming in to the inner army. One of them was Kaylet, and when he saw King Gahmuret sitting there with the mien of sadness, he said, "Why do you look this way? The prize is acknowledged yours, you have won the lady Herzeloyde and her country.

All tongues here agree on that, Briton and Irishman alike, and whoever speaks a Romance tongue, and men of France and Brabant—they all agree and grant that no one can match you in such skillful sport. I read the true attestation of the fact right here, for your brave strength was not asleep when these lords met their downfall; never did their hands offer oath of surrender before: my lords Brandelidelin and bold Lehelin, Hardiz and Schafillor. Ah! and then there was also Razalic the Moor, to whom you taught surrender before Patelamunt! On his account your 86 fame in battle finds both height and breadth!"

Gahmuret said, "My lady here will think you are out of your mind, overpraising me this way. You can't sell me, you know, because *somebody* is sure to see the flaws in me. Your lips have been heard in too much praise.—Tell me, how did you get back here?"

"The good people of Punturtois have allowed me, and this fellow from Champagne here, to go completely free. My nephew shall have his liberty from Morholt, who stole him, provided my lord Brandelidelin is set at liberty by you. Otherwise we are still both hostages, I and my sister's son. Have mercy upon us. Vesper games have been held here of such a kind that the tournament before Kanvoleis will now be called off. I know the fact of the matter, because here sits the outer army's best strength. Tell me, with whom or how could they make a stand before us? You are master of much fame."

From her heart the queen spoke a sweet request to Gahmuret: "Whatever claim I may have upon 87 you, allow me to assert it; I crave it as a favor. If it impairs your fame to grant me both claim and favor, permit me to withdraw."

Up leaped the chaplain of Ampflise, the queen gracious and wise, and cried, "No! He should by rights belong to my lady, who sent me to this country in the interests of her love! She lives amid consuming love of him, her love has a claim vested in him, and she shall retain possession of him, for she is fonder of him than all other women are. Here are her messengers, princes three, noble youths of all misconduct free. One is named Lanzidant, of noble lineage from Greenland; he has come to Kärlingen[23] and has made the language here his own. The second is named Liadarz, *fils du comte* Schiolarz."

Now listen and you shall hear the story of who the third one was: his mother's name was Beaflurs, his father's Pansamurs, and they were of fairy race; their son was called Liahturteltart.

All three ran up to Gahmuret and said, "Lord,   88 *la reine de France* will deal you winning dice-throws of worthy love if you are wise, and you can play without stakes; joy will be yours at once, without any worries."

When that message was heard, Kaylet, who had come up meanwhile, went over and sat down beside the queen and beneath a corner of her robe.[24]

To him she said, "Tell me, has any further injury befallen you? I noticed wounds upon you." Then that lovely lady touched his bruises with her gentle hands so white— God's artistry was manifest in them—and found his cheeks crushed and bruised, and his chin, and part of his nose. The queen who did him the honor of drawing him close to her, was his wife's niece. Courteously she turned to Gahmuret and said, "The noble Frenchwoman is making you a firm offer of her love. Honor now all womankind in me and let me have recourse to law. Stay here until I have obtained a decision. Otherwise you will abandon me to shame."

The worthy man vowed to her that such would be done.   89

Then she took her farewell and rode away. Kaylet, the warrior worthy, lifted her, without use of footstool, onto her horse, and then walked back inside, where he saw his friends.

To Hardiz he said, "Your sister Alize once offered me her love, which I accepted. But she is married to another, and

---

[23] I.e., France. Only here (and once in *Willehalm*) does Wolfram use this old word which designates the land of the Carolingians.

[24] I.e., in the position of a suppliant, as in paintings of the Madonna. Kaylet's liberation is jeopardized if Gahmuret goes to Ampflise and leaves the winner of the tournament yet to be determined.

more advantageously than to me. I beg you by your courtesy not to be angry. Prince Lambekin has her to wife. Although she does not wear a crown, she has nevertheless acquired high dignity: Hainaut and Brabant are subject to her, and many a goodly knight. Turn your good will toward me, allow me to be in your favor, and take me back into your service."

To which the King of Gascony replied, as his manly courage prompted, "Your words were always sweet; but anyone treating you kindly after you have done him much harm would be overlooking the injury out of fear. —However, your aunt's son did take me prisoner."

"He will not harm anyone. You will be set free by Gahmuret. That will be my first request. Once you are free of constraint, I will again know a time when you will   90 accept me as your friend. You will have had time to get over your disgrace. But whatever *you* may do to me, your sister wouldn't murder me."

Their talk raised general laughter. But then sorrow invaded their merriment, and their host's fidelity prodded him to feel grief anew, for grief is a sharp goad. Everyone noticed that he was wrestling with sorrow and that his joy furnished weak support.

Whereat his aunt's son said with irritation, "You are being very impolite!"

"No, I cannot help but feel remorse. I yearn for the queen. I left in Patelamunt a sweet woman of purest kind, and my heart is sore because of it. Her noble dignity compels me to sorrow for her love. She gave me her people and her country. Lady Belacane robs me of manly gladness; yet it is perfectly manly to be ashamed of love that wavers. The lady's protectiveness held a tight bit on me, so that I could not get to knightly action, and then I fancied that knightly action would rid me of the bonds of discontent.   91 Here I have done my share of knightly deeds. Now many a misinformed man imagines that her black complexion drove me from her, and yet I looked upon her as the sun. Her womanly excellence now causes me grief, for she is the boss upon the shield of excellence. For that reason I cannot help but grieve—and for this reason besides: I have seen my brother's shield borne with point inverted."

Ah! those words! The report was so sad that the worthy Spaniard's eyes were filled with tears: "Alas, foolish queen, for love of you Galoes lost his life, over whom all women should weep sincerely from their hearts if they wished their lives to win praise whenever people thought of them. Queen of Navarre, however little it distresses you, it was because of you that I have lost my kinsman, who met his knightly death from a joust, a fatal joust wherein he wore your favor. Princes who were his comrades give evidence of their heartfelt grief and have turned the broad edges of their shields toward the ground in keeping with Sorrow's   92 custom; deep mourning so instructs them, and in this fashion they go about their knightly deeds. They are overwhelmed by the force of grief since Galoes, my aunt's son, shall no longer perform feats in the service of love."

When Gahmuret learned of his brother's death, that was his second sorrow, and in his grief he cried out, "How my anchor's tooth has with remorse fixed itself in harbor!" Forthwith he divested himself of that coat of arms. Grief taught him heart's anguish. From the depths of his feeling the hero exclaimed, "Galoes of Anjou! Henceforth let no one ask for more manly chivalry, for such was never born! Out of your heart sprang the fruit of true generosity. I mourn your excellence."

To Kaylet he said, "How fares Schoette, my mother poor in joys?"

"So that God might well be moved to pity. When Gandin died, and Galoes your brother as well, and when she did not have you with her either, death broke her heart also."

Then said King Hardiz, "Bring now your man-   93 hood to bear. If you have manhood in you, you will mourn with due restraint."

Unfortunately his grief was too great, and a flood of tears poured from his eyes. He dismissed the knights to their rest and himself went to his chamber, in a small tent of samite. That night he passed a time of grieving.

When the new day came they all agreed, both the inner and the outer armies, that no one there present in warrior's gear, be he young or old, timid or bold, was to engage in jousting. It was bright mid-morning, but they were so worn out from combat and the horses had been so excessively put to the spurs, that the brave knightly company was still bowed down with weariness. Then the queen herself rode out to the worthy men in the field and brought them back with her into the city. The best knights in her city she bade ride out to the Leo Meadow, nor was her behest disregarded. They arrived just as Mass was being sung for the sorrowful King of Zazamanc, and as Benediction was being pronounced the Lady Herzeloyde herself arrived.   94 She stated her claim upon Gahmuret, demanding what had been agreed upon as her right.

To which he replied, "Lady, I have a wife, dearer to me than I am to myself, and even if I did not have her, I would still know a story that would cause you to give me up, if anyone were to concede me my right."

She answered, "You should renounce the Moorish woman for my love's sake. The sacrament of baptism has superior power.[25] Therefore give up your heathenry and love me by our religion's law, because I yearn for your love. Or am I to be done injustice because of the French queen? Her messengers spoke sweet words and they played out their story to the last move on the board."

"Yes, she is my real lady. I took to Anjou the training in chivalry fostered by her counsel. Her assistance is with me still by virtue of the fact that my education in chivalry came from my lady, from whom Womanly Wrongdoing fled afar. We were children then together, yet always delighted to see each other. The Queen Ampflise dwells close by Womanly Excellence. Gracious lady that she was, she gave me the best revenues in her country—I was poorer   95 then than now—and I accepted them willingly. Count me among the poor even now: my noble brother is dead. Have

[25] Wolfram's audience would readily accede to the notion that marriage between a Christian and a heathen had no validity.

mercy on me, Lady. In your courtesy do not press me. Turn
your love where there is joy, for with me there is nothing
but sorrow."

"Do not leave me to waste away any longer. Tell me,
what defense do you have left?"

"I shall tell you as your question desires. A tournament
was proclaimed here, but it did not take place. There is no
lack of witnesses to grant me that."

"Vesper games drained its strength. The brave men here
are so worn out that the tournament has been ruined as a
result."

"I fought in defense of your city, with men who put up a
brave fight. Therefore you should spare me any arguments
in self-defense. Many a knight performed there better than
I. Therefore your claim on me has no force. Only the greeting you give to everyone, *that* I would welcome, if I might
have it from you."

The way the adventure tells it, the knight and the
maiden then had recourse to a judge in the matter of the
lady's complaint. It was getting on toward noon when a
verdict was handed down: 96

"Any knight having once fastened on his helmet here
and come here for the purpose of chivalric combat, if he
won the prize therein, then the queen shall have him."

This verdict was then ratified.

Whereupon she said, "Sir, you now belong to me. I shall
serve you so as to win your favor, and I shall provide you
such a share of delights that after all your sorrow you shall
come to joy."

Despite all this he still knew the pain of sorrow.

April had now passed, and thereafter had come the short,
small, green grass—the field was green from end to end—
that makes faint hearts bold and gives them high spirits.
Many a tree stood in blossom from the sweet air of the
May-time. Now the fairy strain in him made him love and
yearn for love, and this his beloved most willingly granted

him. He looked at the Lady Herzeloyde and courteously his sweet mouth said, "Lady, if I am to be happy with you, you must leave me free of your watchful care. If misery's power ever releases me, I would like to practice the knightly art. If you do not allow me to go jousting, I still know the old trick that I used when I left my wife 97 —whom I also won through feats of knighthood. When she applied the checkrein to keep me from battle, I forsook a people and a country."

She said, "Sir, you shall set the terms. I bow to your will."

"I want to break many a spear yet. One tournament a month, Lady, you must be resigned to allow me to attend."

To this she agreed, I was told. And thus he came into possession of both the country and the maiden too.

Among those present when the verdict was given and ratified stood those three pages of the Queen Ampflise and her chaplain, so that he heard and saw it all. Privately he said to Gahmuret, "It was reported to my lady how you won the highest prize before Patelamunt and how you ruled over two kingdoms there. She too has a country and is willing to give you her person and her property."

"Since she bestowed knighthood upon me, I am obligated to obey the force of its laws unfalteringly, as the trade of the knight requires. Had I not acquired my shield through her, all the rest of this would not have happened. Whether it makes me glad or sad, I am in this case bound 98 by chivalric verdict. Go back and tell her that I serve her, that I am still her knight, and that, even if all the crowns in the world were mine, my supreme desire would still be for her."

He offered them his immense wealth, but they refused to accept his gifts. The messengers journeyed home, having brought no dishonor upon their lady. As often happens even today in anger, they did not ask permission to leave. And as for the lady's princely pages, those lads wept themselves well nigh blind.

As for those who had carried their shields with point inverted, their friend in the field[26] informed them: "Lady Herzeloyde has won the Angevin."

"Who was here from Anjou? Our master is elsewhere, unfortunately, off to the Saracens in search of knightly fame, and that is our most grievous sorrow."

"The man who won the prize here, the one that brought down so many knights, the one that thrust and struck so well, the one that was wearing the precious anchor on his helmet with the bright jewels, that is the man you mean. King Kaylet tells me that the Angevin is Gahmuret. And he has certainly met with success here!"   99

Then they ran to their horses, and with their garments wet with tears came to where their master was sitting. They welcomed him and he welcomed them, and joy and sorrow were there commingled. He kissed those loyal men and said, "You must not grieve to excess for my brother. I well may take his place. Turn your shields upwards after their proper fashion and bear yourselves after the manner of joy. I shall wear my father's coat of arms, because my anchor has found its anchorage. The anchor suits a wanderer knight: let anyone who wants it take it and wear it. But I must now live an ordered life. I am the lord of a land, and if I am to be the ruler over a people, my grief would be harmful to them. Lady Herzeloyde, help me to beg, you and I together, these kings and princes present here to remain here as vassals of mine until you grant me the enjoyment that love desires from love." This request was made by both of them, and immediately the noble knights voiced agreement. All retired to their quarters.

To her beloved the queen said, "Yield now to my tending!" and she guided him by private ways. His   100 guests were well looked after, let their host be where he might. The two corps of servants were now merged into one, and yet he proceeded alone, except for two pages. Certain maidens and the queen guided him to a place where he found delight and where all his grieving disappeared. Vanquished was his sorrow, and his high spirits became as

[26] This informant is not identified.

new: this could only have been because of love. Lady Herzeloyde the Queen there surrendered her maidenhood. Lips were not spared as now they began to consume them with kisses and to fend off sorrow from delights.[27]

Thereafter he did an admirable thing: those whom he had taken captive he set free. Hardiz and Kaylet, they were made friends by Gahmuret. And then followed such a festival that anyone who has equaled it since has had great means at his disposal. Gahmuret was determined his wealth was not to be stinted. To poor knights one and all Arabian gold was distributed; upon kings Gahmuret's hands bestowed jewels, as also upon all princes who were   101 there. Traveling minstrels were made happy, for they received a share of rich gifts. Let them ride away who had been his guests: the Angevin permitted them to leave.

Upon his shield was now attached in sable the panther[28] which his father had worn. And over his shirt of chain mail he wore a fine, white, silken garment of the queen's, which had lain next to the naked body of her who had now become his wife. Eighteen were pierced through and riddled by sword thrusts before he departed from that lady, and these she in turn laid against her naked skin each time her beloved returned from those knightly expeditions where he hacked many a shield to slivers. And both their loves held true.

Achievements enough he had had already when his manly courage took him over seas to face battle. I mourn his voyage. True report reached him that his lord the Baruch was overridden by the forces of the Babylonians, one named Ipomidon, the other named Pompeius. The story calls the latter by this name, and a proud and worthy man he was. (He was not the one who fled Rome before   102

---

[27] In medieval times consummation of marriage preceded the wedding ceremony.

[28] The emblem of historical Anjou was the leopard. Bartholomew Glanville (Bartholomans Anglicus) in the thirteenth century wrote that the leopard and the panther are one and the same animal. The fourth century "Physiologus" claimed that, among all beasts, the panther considered only the dragon as its enemy.

Julius.[29]) His mother's brother was Nebuchadnezzar, who
in deceitful books read that he was supposed to be a god.
Nowadays people would laugh at such a thing. These two
brothers, who spared neither themselves nor their wealth,
were of high lineage, descended from Ninus, who ruled
before Baghdad was founded. He was also the founder of
Niniveh. Shame and disgrace now afflicted them, for the
Baruch had declared them his vassals. On this account
much was won and much was lost on both sides, and heroes
were seen in combat. And so Gahmuret sailed over seas and
found the Baruch under arms. With joy he was received,
though I mourn his voyage.

What was happening in one place, how things were going
in another place, which way matters stood as to winnings
and losses, of all this the Lady Herzeloyde knew nothing.
She was like the sunlight and made for love. Wealth and
virtue that woman had, and of joys more than too much,
for she had surpassed the limits of desire. Her heart was
turned to the knowledge of the good, and hence   103
she won the favor of the world. The life of Lady Herzeloyde the Queen won praise, and her virtue was declared
most admirable. Queen over three countries was she: over
Waleis and Anjou, and she wore the crown of Norgals in
her capital of Kingrivals. Her husband was so dear to her
that if ever lady won so noble a beloved, it was nothing to
her: she could countenance it without envy. When he
had been away for half a year she did indeed expect his return, for on that her life depended. Then the sword blade
of her joy snapped in two at the hilt. Alas and well-a-day
that goodness should bear such misery and loyalty forever
rouse such grief! Such is the way of the world: joy today,
tomorrow sorrow.

One noonday the lady was sleeping a troubled sleep,
when a fearful shock befell her. She thought a falling star
was sweeping her into the air where fiery thunder-
bolts struck upon her with violence. These flew at   104
her all at one time, and then her braids crackled and sang

---

[29] I.e., Julius Caesar, when he crossed the Rubicon.

with sparks. With a crash the thunder made its rush and burst in a gust of burning tears. As she came to consciousness, there a griffon wrenched her right hand away. Then all was changed. She imagined fantastic things—how she was nurse to a dragon that tore her womb, and how this dragon took suck at her breasts, and how he swiftly fled away and left her so that she never saw him again. Her heart was bursting out of her body, and yet her eyes could not help but see that thing of terror. Seldom has anguish the like of that befallen a woman in her slumber. Previous to this she had been radiantly fair, but alas! how all that is changed: now she became of sorrow's color. Long and broad her grief became, and future affliction drew near her. Then that lady began to do what she had been incapable of doing before: she writhed and wailed and cried aloud in her sleep. Many maidens were sitting close by, and they rushed to her and woke her up.

Then came riding Tampanis, her husband's wise   105
chief squire, and many young noblemen besides. Then the borders of joy were crossed and left to rearwards. With lamentation they reported her lord's death. At that news Lady Herzeloyde felt pain and collapsed unconscious.

The knights wondered: "How could my lord have been conquered in his armor and as well armed as he was?"

His squire, pursued though he was by grief, nevertheless explained to the heroes: "Long life deserted my master. He had removed his coif of mail, forced to do so by the great heat. Accursed guile stole away that hero good. A certain knight filled a tall glass with a he-goat's blood and poured it on the diamond helmet, whereat the helmet became softer than a sponge.[30] May He Whom painters show us as the Lamb holding the Cross between His hooves, have mercy on what followed. When they rode out in troops against one another, ah! what a battle was there!

---

[30] In the twelfth-century *Bestiary* translated by T. H. White, we read under "Hyrcus the He-Goat": "The nature of goats is so extremely hot that a stone of adamant [the word here translated as 'diamond'], which neither fire nor iron implement can alter, is dissolved merely by the blood of one of these creatures."

The knights of the Baruch fought with all the force of
bravery, and on the plain before Baghdad many a shield was
run through as they rushed each other. Charges   106
of horsemen crisscrossed and interwove, banners were jum-
bled in confusion, and many a good knight perished.

Then came Ipomidon riding, and repaid my master with
death for having unhorsed him once before Alexandria
where thousands of knights could see it. My master void of
guile turned to face this king, but he whose joust was to
teach him to die, split his helmet, and his spear point bored
through his head; a splinter of it was found lodged there.
Still in his saddle, but dying, the warrior rode out of the
conflict to a wide meadow, and there his chaplain came
and stood over him. Then in a few words he spoke his confession and sent us here to bring this garment and the very
spear point which parted him from us. He died without sin.
His squires and pages he commended to the queen.

He was taken to Baghdad. The Baruch gave no con-
sideration to the costs. With gold his coffin was   107
adorned, and great treasure of precious stones was expended on it. Within lies the blameless one. His youthful
body was embalmed, and many were those that mourned
for him. Over his grave was set a precious ruby through
which he clearly shines. We were permitted to place a Cross
on his grave for his comfort and for the defense of his
soul, after the manner of the Passion by which Christ's
death redeemed us. Its cost was borne by the Baruch, and it
consists of a single precious emerald. This we did without
the help of the heathens, for their ways cannot cherish the
Cross by which Christ's death gave us redemption. In all
seriousness the heathens now pray to Gahmuret as their
noble god, but not for the honor of the Cross nor for Baptism's law which at final Judgment shall loose our bonds.
His manly fidelity and his contrite confession give him a
bright radiance in heaven, for falseness in him was shallow
indeed.

An epitaph was engraved upon his diamond helmet,
which was made fast to the cross above his grave.   108
This is what the letters say:

Through this helmet a joust slew a man who was brave.

GAHMURET

*was his name, a mighty king over three countries. Each
one avowed him a crown and rich princes followed after.
He was born in Anjou and before Baghdad he gave his
life for the Baruch. His fame towered so high that no
one shall achieve its equal, however knights may be
esteemed. The man is not born of mother to whom his
courage vowed surrender—I mean any who works at
the knightly trade. Help and manly counsel he unfail-
ingly gave his friends; for women's sake he endured
sharp pain; he was baptized and supported the Christian
law, yet his death was a grief to Saracens. This is true
and no lie. All his years of reason his bravery so strove
for fame that he died with knightly glory. Over treachery he triumphed.*

Wish him bliss who lies here!

And it was as the squire reported. Many a man of Waleis
wept. Well might they weep.   109
The lady was pregnant with a child that was stirring
within her body, and they left her there helpless. Eighteen
weeks the child had been alive within the mother[31] who
was now wrestling with death, Lady Herzeloyde the Queen.
The others were weak of wit for not helping the woman,
for within her body she bore him who will be the flower of
all chivalry, if death misses him now. Then came a wise old
man and stood over the lady to lament with her as she was
struggling with death. He forced her clenched teeth apart
and they poured water into her mouth. With that she regained consciousness.

"Alas!" she cried. "What has become of my beloved?"
With a scream she vented her grief. "My heart's full joy
was Gahmuret's high worth, but his audacious aspiration
has robbed me of him. I was much younger than he, and

[31] The law recognized the life of an unborn infant as beginning with
the first stirring inside the womb after the eighteenth week of preg-
nancy. Hence the "eighteen weeks" of the text indicate "thirty-six
weeks," or nine months, to the modern reader.

yet I am both his mother and his wife. I bear him here
within me and also the seed of his life which our two loves
gave and received, but if God is true, let Him grant me
that it shall ripen into fruit! I have suffered too   110
much because of my proud and noble husband. What a
blow death has dealt me! He never received a woman's love
without being happy in her happiness, without suffering at a
woman's grief. His manly faithfulness so instructed him,
for he was void of guile."

Listen now to a further story of what the lady did then.
—Clasping child and womb within her arms and hands,
she said, "God send me the noble fruit of Gahmuret: that
is my heart's prayer. God avert such senseless anguish from
me, for it would be Gahmuret's second death if I were to
kill myself while I am bearing that which I received from
his love, from him who showed me a husband's fidelity."

Unconcerned as to who might see it, she tore the garments away from her bosom, clasped her soft, white breasts,
and pressed them to her red mouth with the wisdom of
mother-wit. "You are the holders of an infant's nourishment," that wise woman said; "the infant has been filling
you in advance ever since I felt him alive within   111
my body." The lady found satisfaction in seeing that
nourishment lying above her heart, that milk in her breasts,
and pressing some of it out, the queen said, "You come
from faithful love. If I had never received baptism, I would
want you to be my baptismal water. I shall anoint myself
with you and with my tears, both in public and in private—
for I shall mourn for Gahmuret."

The lady bade them bring closer that shirt of the color
of blood in which, amid the Baruch's host, Gahmuret had
lost his life and met his warrior's death with true manly
will. The lady inquired also for the spear point that dealt
Gahmuret his death. Ipomidon of Niniveh, that proud
and noble Babylonian, had paid such a warrior's debt that
the shirt was a tattered rag from his blows. The lady
wished to put it on as she had done on previous occasions
when her husband returned from knightly expeditions, but
they took it out of her hand. The noblest in all the land

buried both the spear point and the cloth of blood   112
in the minster, as a dead man is buried. Then in Gahmuret's land there was lamentation.

On the fourteenth day thereafter the lady gave birth to a
child, a son, and of such a size that she hardly survived.

Herewith this adventure's dice are cast and its beginning determined, for only now has he been born to whom
this tale is devoted. His father's joy and sorrow, his life
and death, you have heard a deal about these. Know, then,
whence he comes to you and how he was cared for, the hero
of this tale.

They hid him away from all chivalry until he should
come to the age of reason. When the queen recovered
consciousness and took her baby into her arms, then she
and the other ladies intently observed the tiny pizzle between his legs. He could not be other than fondled and
cherished, for he was possessed of the organ of a man.
Later on, he was to be a very smith for the swords with
which he struck fire from helmets, and his heart had manly
courage. It was the queen's delight to kiss him   113
over and over again, and always she kept calling him *"Bon
fils, cher fils, beau fils."*

Directly the queen took those little brownish-pink buds
of hers—I mean the tips of her little breasts—and pressed
them into his tiny mouth, for she who had borne him in
her womb was also his nurse. She who fled from all
womanly misconduct clasped him to her bosom, fancying to
herself that she had prayed Gahmuret back to her arms.
Toward haughtiness she did not lean: humility was her
way.

Wisely the Lady Herzeloyde said, "The supreme Queen
gave her breasts to Jesus, Who afterwards for our sake met
a bitter death in human form upon the Cross and Who kept
faith with us. Whoever underestimates His anger, his soul
will fare ill at Judgment, however good he has been. This
I know to be a true report."

The country's mistress bathed in the dew of her heart's
affliction, and upon the boy rained down the tears of her
eyes. A woman's true fidelity was hers. Her lips could form

in both sighs and laughter: in the birth of her son   114
she did find delight, but her mirth drowned in fording the
flood of her sorrow.

❦

If there is anyone who praises women better than I, I will
surely not be the one to hold it against him. I would be glad
to hear their joys extended far and wide. For only one of
them am I unwilling to do loyal service, and against her my
anger is still fresh—ever since I found her in disloyalty. I
am Wolfram von Eschenbach, and I know a thing or two
about poetry, and I am a tongs at holding my anger against
a woman. This one has offered me such an offense that I
cannot do other than hate her. On account of this the others
hate *me*. Why, alas! do they do so? Though their hatred
troubles me, it is their womanhood that is to blame, since I
did go too far and I have done myself harm. This will
probably never happen again, but they should not be over-
hasty to storm my bastion, or else they are likely to run
into defensive combat. I have not forgotten how to judge
both their manners and their lives. To any woman   115
following propriety I shall be a defending champion of her
reputation: her distress troubles me to the depths of my
heart.

A man's praise limps like a spavined horse when he de-
clares all women are off the board just to show his own lady
to advantage.[32] Any lady that wants to inspect my rights,
both see them and hear them, I will not deceive her. My
birth was to the knightly trade, and if my bravery is under-
rated by one who loves me for my poetry, I consider that
she is weak in her wits. If I seek a good woman's love, and
if I am not to win her love's reward by my shield and my
spear, then let her bestow her favor accordingly. A man

---

[32] Perhaps a rebuke to Reinmar von Hagenau, who so praised his
lady to the detriment of all other ladies in a poem which had the refrain: *"daz ist in mat."* ("That checkmates them," i.e., takes them off
the board and out of the game.)

aiming at love through knightly deeds is, after all, playing for very high stakes.

If the women would not take it for flattery, I would add further unknown words to this story for you, I would continue the adventure for you. But if anyone requests me to do so, let him not consider it a book. I don't know a single letter of the alphabet.[83] Plenty of people get their material that way, but this adventure steers without books. Rather than have anybody think it is a book, I would sit   116 naked without a towel, the way I would sit in the bath— if I didn't forget the bouquet of twigs.[84]

[83] This is the line: *"ine kan decheinen buochstap,"* endlessly disputed as to whether it is to be understood literally or in broad irony.

[84] The bouquet of twigs used in steam baths to stimulate circulation. "Fig leaf" would be the equivalent for Western readers.

BOOK·III

It grieves me that so many share the name of woman. They all have the same clear voices, but plenty of them are quick to falsity, while others are free from falsity, and thus things vary. But that they should bear the same name, shames my heart. Womanhood, with your true nature goes fidelity, and always has gone. A good many people say that poverty serves no good, but anyone enduring it for fidelity's sake, his soul will escape hellfire. There was a woman who endured it for fidelity's sake, and thereby her gift was compensated in heaven with eternal giving. I fancy there are few such now alive who would renounce the world's riches while still young for the glory of heaven. *I* know of none such. Man or woman, they are all the same, all alike shirk it.

Lady Herzeloyde, the mighty, became a stranger to her three kingdoms, bearing with her the burden of joy-lessness. Falsity had so utterly vanished from her heart that neither eye nor ear could detect it. For her the sun was a mist. She fled the world's delight. To her night and day were the same; her heart dwelt on sorrow alone.

This lady full of sorrow withdrew from her kingdom to a forest, to the clearing in Soltane, and not for the sake of flowers on the meadow. Her heart's grief was so complete that she cared for no garland, neither red nor faded. And there, for refuge, she brought noble Gahmuret's child. The people who are with her have to clear and till. *She* well knew how to care for her son. Before he came of years she summoned her people before her and charged them on their lives, men and women alike, never to utter a word about knights. "For if my heart's darling should find out what knights' life is, it would pain me deeply. Now use your wits and keep all knighthood from him."

The custom traveled an anxious road. The boy thus hidden away was brought up in the forest clearing of Soltane, cheated of his royal heritage except on one   118 count: with his own hands he whittled himself a bow and little arrows and shot many birds that he came upon. But whenever he shot the bird whose song was so loud before, he would weep and tear his hair—and his hair came in for grief. His body was fair and proud. Every morning he washed in the stream by the meadow. Of sorrow he knew nothing, unless it was the birdsong above him, for the sweetness of it pierced his heart and made his little bosom swell. Weeping he ran to the queen, and she said, "Who has hurt you? You were out on the meadow." He could tell her nothing, as is still the way with children.

For a long time she kept pursuing the matter. One day she saw him gaping up at the trees toward the song of the birds, and then she realized it was their voices that made her child's bosom swell. His heritage and his desire thus compelled him. Without quite knowing why, Lady Herzeloyde turned her anger against the birds and wanted to destroy their song. She bade her plowmen and her   119 field hands make haste to snare the birds and twist their necks. The birds were better mounted. Quite a number of deaths were avoided and a share of them remained alive, which afterwards were merry with singing.

The boy said to the queen, "What do they have against the birds?" and asked peace for them at once.

His mother kissed him on the mouth and said, "Why should I alter His commandment Who is, after all, Supreme God? Should birds lose their delight because of me?"

Then the boy said to his mother, "O, what is God, Mother?"

"Son, I will tell you in all earnest. He is brighter than the daylight, yet He took upon Himself the features of man. Son, mark this wisdom and pray to Him when in trouble, for His fidelity has ever offered help to the world. But there is one called the Master of Hell, and he is black and faithlessness is his mark. From him turn your thought away, and also away from inconstant wavering!" His mother fully explained for him the dark and the light. And then his alacrity was off and away.   120

He learned the swing of the javelot and with it brought down many a stag, which his mother and her people put to good use. Thaw or snow, his shooting brought the wild animals grief. Now hear a strange thing: when he shot a weight that would have been load enough for a mule, he would carry it home carcass-whole.

One day he went out hunting along a mountain slope. He broke off a branch from a tree for the whistle the leaf would make. Right near him ran a path, and there he heard the sound of horses' hooves. He began to brandish his javelot and said, "What is this I hear? O, if only the Devil would just come along now in his furious rage! I would stand up to him for sure. My mother says he is a terror, but I think her bravery is a little daunted." And thus he stood eager for battle, when look! there came three knights galloping along, as fair as anyone could wish and armed from the feet upward. The lad thought for sure that each one was a god, and so he stood there no longer but fell to his knees on the path. Loud cried the lad then,   121
"Help, God! You surely have help to give!"

The rider in front flew into a rage to see the lad lying there in the path: "This stupid Waleis is holding up our swift journey."—A thing we Bavarians get praise for I have to say about Waleis people too: they are stupider than Bavarian folks, and yet, like them, of manly stout-heartedness. Anyone born in these two countries grows up a marvel of cleverness.

Just then there came along at a gallop a splendidly

adorned knight who was in a great hurry. He was riding in
pursuit of those who had got a head start on him, two
knights, namely, who had abducted a lady in his land. He
considered this a disgrace and grieved at the plight of the
maiden, who had ridden on before him in a deplorable state.
These three knights here were his own vassals. He was
riding a fine Castilian horse; there was very little of his
shield that was whole; and his name was Karnahkarnanz,
le comte Ulterlec. "Who is blocking our way?" said he,
and rode over to the lad, to whom he seemed to have
the form of a god, for never had he seen anything so
bright. His surcoat swept the dew, his stirrups,   122
adjusted to either foot to just the right length, rang with
little golden bells, and his right arm chimed with bells
whenever he raised it in greeting or to strike. It was meant
to ring loud at his sword strokes, for this hero was eager
for renown. Thus rode the rich prince, wondrously adorned.

Then of him who was a garland of all the flowers of
manly beauty Karnahkarnanz asked, "Young Sir, have you
seen two knights ride past who could not keep the knightly
code? They are perpetrating rape and are lacking in honor.
They are abducting a maiden."

But say what he might, the lad still thought he was God,
just as Lady Herzeloyde the Queen had told him when she
explained His bright shining.[1] And so he cried out in all
seriousness, "Help me now, God of help!" And *le fils du roi*
Gahmuret fell down in an attitude of prayer.

The prince said, "I am not God, though I gladly do
His commandment. What you see here are four
knights, if you would only look aright."   123

The lad asked further, "You speak of *knights*: what is
that? If you do not have God's kind of power, then tell me:
who bestows knighthood?"

"That King Arthur does. Young Sir, if you come to his
house, he will give you the name of knight so that you will
never need to be ashamed of it. You may well be of knightly
race."—And by the warriors he was scrutinized, and God's

[1] The author makes a gallant compliment to the knightly class to
which both he and his audience belonged.

handiwork was manifest in him.—I have this from the adventure, which with truth was told me so. Never had man's beauty been more nobly realized since Adam's time, and hence his praise was wide among women.

But then the lad spoke again, and laughter arose at it, "Ay, Knight God, what may you be? You have so many rings tied around your body, up there, and down here." And therewith the lad's hand laid hold of iron wherever he could find it on the prince, and he began to inspect the armor. "My mother's ladies wear their rings on strands and they don't fit so close together as these." The lad spoke further to the prince, just as the thoughts came   124 to him, "What is this good for, that fits you so well? I can't pick it off."

Then the prince showed him his sword. "You see, anyone seeking battle with me I ward off with blows, and to protect myself against his, I have to put this on, and both for shot and for stab I have to wear armor like this."

But the lad quickly replied, "If stags wore pelts like that, my javelot would not wound a single one. And a good many fall dead before me."

The knights were chafing at his delay with the lad who was so simple. "God shield you," said the prince. "Would that your beauty were mine! God would have conferred upon you the uttermost that could be wished for, if only you had intelligence. May God's power keep you from harm."

He and his men rode on at rapid gait and soon came to a field in the forest where the courteous man found Lady Herzeloyde's plows at work. Never did greater distress befall her people. Those whom he saw plowing now, began to sow and then to harrow, wielding their goads upon stout oxen. The prince bade them good morning and   125 asked whether they had seen a maiden in distress.

There was no way out of it: what he asked, that they answered: "Two knights and a maiden rode past this morning, the lady lamenting and those that had the maiden using their spurs liberally." It was Meljacanz,[2] whom

2 Meljacanz will appear briefly in Book VII.

Karnahkarnanz now outrode, taking the lady from him by force. Joyless enough had she been until then. Her name was Imane of the Beafontane.

The farm hands were dismayed as the heroes spurred past them. "How did this happen?" they said. "If our young master has glimpsed the dinted helmets on those knights, we have not kept a good lookout. We will hear the queen's hatred for this, and rightly so, for he came along here with us this morning while she was still asleep."

As a matter of fact the lad no longer cared who shot the stags small and large. He went straight to his mother and told her the story. At which she collapsed. So greatly was she terrified by his words that she lay unconscious   126 before him.

When the queen came to her senses again—whereas before she had not been equal to it—she spoke: "Son, who told you about the order of knighthood? How did you come to know of it?"

"Mother, I saw four men more shining than God, and they told me about knighthood. The royal power of Arthur shall in knightly honor turn me to chivalric service."

Here was a fresh sorrow. The lady did not rightly know what stratagem to invent to keep him from his purpose.

The simple yet noble lad kept begging his mother for a horse, so that she grieved in her heart. "I will not deny him," she thought, "but it must be a thoroughly bad one." And the queen thought further, "People are much given to mockery. Fool's clothing shall my child wear on his fair body. If he is pommeled and beaten, perhaps he will come back to me again."—Alas for her grievous sorrow!—The lady took sack cloth and cut for him shirt and   127 breeches which, all of a piece, came halfway down his white leg. Such was the regular garb of fools. On top was a hood, while from a hide of untanned calfskin boots were cut for his feet. But all this did not keep sorrow away. The queen, having pondered the matter, begged him to stay yet that night. "You shall not leave here until I teach you cunning:

On untrodden ways you must beware of dark fords;
where they are shallow and clear, there ride boldly in.

You must be polite and give people your greeting.

If a man grey with age is willing to teach you behavior, as he well knows how to do, you must follow
him willingly and not show him temper.

Son, bear this in mind: wherever you can win a
good woman's ring and greeting, take them; it will set
you free from care. You must make haste to kiss her
and clasp her tight in your embrace. That brings happiness and a stout spirit, if she is chaste and   128
good.

"You must know further, my son, that the proud, bold
Lehelin wrested two countries away from your nobles,
which were to have served your hand, Waleis and Norgals.
One of your vassal princes, Turkentals, met death at his
hand. Your people he slew or took captive."

"This I will avenge, Mother. God willing, my javelot
will wound him yet."

Next morning when daylight came the lad quickly made
up his mind that he would go straight to Arthur. Lady
Herzeloyde kissed him and ran after him. Then the sorrow
of the world befell. When she no longer saw her son—he
rode away: who could be glad of that?—then that lady without falsity fell upon the ground, where grief stabbed her until she died.—Her death from sheer loyalty saved her from
the pains of hell. Well for her that she became a mother!
Thus she traveled the journey that brings reward, a root of
goodness she, and a branch of humility. Alas that we do
not now have her like even to the eleventh generation!
Lacking such, many are turned to falseness. Yet   129
all loyal women should wish this lad well, who has ridden
away and left her.

Then this handsome lad turned toward the forest in
Brizljan,[3] where he came upon a brook as he rode. A
rooster could probably have crossed it, but there were

---

[3] Brizljan = Fr. Broceliande, a forest usually said to be located in
Brittany.

flowers and grass there which made its stream so dark that the lad avoided fording it. All day he rode alongside, as befitted his wits. He spent the night as best he could until the bright day shone upon him.

Then the lad went on all by himself to a fine clear ford. On the other side was a meadow adorned with a tent upon which great luxury had been expended. It was of samite in three colors, high and wide, and with fine ribbons attached to the seams. Above it hung a leathern screen that could always be pulled over it when the rain came on.

Inside he found the wife of Duke Orilus de Lalander, the noble duchess, Jeschute by name, winsomely reclining like a knight's beloved. The lady had fallen asleep.   130 She bore Love's weapon, a mouth gleaming red, the heart's sorrow of a yearning knight, and as she slept her lips parted, warm with the fire of Love's ardor. So lay this marvel of uttermost desire. Of snow-white ivory, and small and close-set, were her teeth.—I guess no one will ever get me accustomed to kissing such high-praised lips. I have seldom known anything of the sort.—Her sable coverlet reached only to her hips, for because of the heat she had pushed it down when her lord had left her by herself. She was beautifully shaped and molded; no art had been spared on her, for God Himself had fashioned her sweet body. This lovely lady had also a slender[4] arm and a white hand, and there the lad discovered a ring which drew him toward the bed for a struggle with the duchess. He was thinking of his mother who had counseled him about women's rings. And so the handsome lad leaped from the carpet onto   131 the bed.

The sweet, chaste lady was rudely startled to find the lad lying in her arms. Naturally she could not help waking. With shame in which there was no laughter the gently bred lady said, "Who has dishonored me? Young Sir, you presume too far. You might choose a different goal!"

Loudly the lady protested, but he paid no heed to what she said and he forced her mouth to his. Then it was not

---

[4] We accept Stapel's deduction, based on comparison with 157,27, that *langen* must here mean "slender."

long before he hugged the duchess to him and took her ring besides. On her smock he caught sight of a brooch, and he roughly snatched that. The lady had only a woman's weapons; *his* strength was to her a whole army. All the same, there was a great struggle there.

Then the lad complained of hunger. The lady's body was radiantly lovely.

"You shan't eat *me!*" she said. "If you were sensible, you would take some other food. There stand bread and wine, and two partridges too, though when the young lady brought them she by no means had you in mind."

He paid no heed to where his hostess sat,[5] but   132 ate a good bellyful and then drank lusty drafts.

To the lady his stay in the pavilion seemed all too long. She thought he was a boy who had lost his wits. Her shame began to sweat; yet the duchess said, "Young Sir, you must leave my brooch and my ring here. And now begone. If my husband comes, you will endure some anger that you had better avoid."

To which the well-born lad replied, "What do I care for your husband's anger? But if it does any harm to your honor, I will be off." And with that he went up to the bed and there, to the dismay of the duchess, another kiss was taken. Without saying farewell the lad rode off, and yet he did say, "God shield you. That's what my mother told me to say."

The lad was delighted with his spoils. When he had ridden on for a time, perhaps a mile, there arrived he of whom I am about to tell. By the dew he perceived that his lady had had a visitor. Some of the tent ropes had been ridden down, and around them some lad had trodden   133 down the grass. Inside, this noble and renowned prince found his wife all woebegone.

"Aha! my lady!" said the haughty Orilus. "For what have I devoted my service to you? A shameful end to many a knightly prize: you have another *ami.*"

[5] Medieval etiquette would have required an invitation from the hostess to sit at her side.

With tear-filled eyes the lady protested that she was innocent, but he did not believe her story. Timidly, however, she went on to say, "A fool came riding along here. Of all the people I have ever known, I never saw anybody so comely. And against my will he took my brooch and my ring."

"Oh, so he pleases you, and you gave him your company!"

"God forbid!" she said. "But his boots and javelot were all too close to me just the same. You should be ashamed to talk that way. It does not beseem a noblewoman to accept love from the likes of that."

But the prince said, "Lady, I have done you no harm, unless you are ashamed of one thing, that you   134 gave up the title of Queen to receive the title of Duchess by marrying me. I have the worst of the bargain. But my manhood is so mettlesome that your brother Erec, my brother-in-law, *le fils du roi* Lac,[6] may well hate you on account of it. All the same, that clever man knows that I am of such renown as can nowhere be gainsaid, except that he unhorsed me in the lists at Prurin. But afterwards, at Karnant, I paid him back richly. In the single combat with lance my hand knocked him backwards off his horse to get his oath of surrender. My lance carried your token right through his shield.[7] Little then did I intend your love would go to some other lover, my Lady Jeschute. Lady, I want you to realize that the proud Galoes, *fils du roi* Gandin, fell in death before my jousting. And you were right there when Plihopliheri rode against me in a tourney and did not spare me his battleskill. But my thrust toppled him from his horse so his saddle didn't pinch him any more. I   135 have often won renown and I have brought down many a knight. But now I can no longer profit from that: a great disgrace tells me so. They hate me, every one of them at the Round Table, eight of whom I unhorsed where many

---

[6] Wolfram makes a peripheral character of the titular hero of Hartmann von Aue's romance, which was a translation-adaptation of the *Erec* of Chrétien de Troyes.

[7] Compare 32 in Book I and 81 in Book II.

a noble maiden could see it at the joust for the sparrow hawk at Kanedic. For you I won the prize, and victory for myself. You saw that, and so did Arthur, in whose house lives my sister, the sweet Cunneware. Her mouth cannot produce laughter until she beholds him to whom the highest praise is given. If only that man would come! Then there would be a battle like the one this morning when I fought and did some harm to a prince who had challenged me with his jousting. *He* fell dead from *my* joust. I will forbear to mention that many a man has beaten his wife in anger for a lesser fault. If I owed you service or homage, you would have to do with the lack of it. No longer will I bask in those white arms of yours where, for   136 love's sake, I used to lie many a blissful day. I'll turn your red mouth pale and put redness in your eyes. I'll undo your joy and teach your heart to sigh."

The princess looked at the prince and her lips said piteously, "Honor in me your knightly fame. You are faithful and wise, but you also have such power over me that you can inflict great pain on me. You should first hear my defense. In the name of all women, deign to do so—you can still make me wretched enough after that. If I lay dead at another's hands, so long as it did not impair *your* honor, that hour would be sweet to me, even if I died at once, since your hatred is turned against me."

But the prince went right on: "Lady, you're getting just too proud for me, and I'm going to curb that in you. Our companionship is over, so is our common eating and drinking, and our common bed shall be forgotten. You'll receive no clothing from me except what I find you sitting in now. Your bridle shall be a cord of bast, your horse   137 shall go hungry, your saddle with all its adornment shall be despoiled!" And all of a sudden he ripped and tore the samite covering from it, and when that was done he smashed the saddle in which she rode—her chasteness and her womanhood had to endure his hatred—and with bast cords he tied it together again. His hatred had come all too soon upon her. And then he said, "Lady, now we shall ride. I would be happy to come upon him who shared your love here. I would face him in battle even if his breath blew fire like a wild dragon."

Unsmiling, full of tears, this lady rich in sorrow departed wretchedly. What had happened to *her* did not distress her: what distressed her was her husband's chagrin. His sorrow grieved her greatly; she would rather have been dead. Now you shall lament for her faithfulness' sake, for now she begins to endure high affliction. —Even if all women hated me, the Lady Jeschute's sorrow would still grieve *me*.—And so they rode following the trail. The lad ahead of   138 them was also very swift. Nor did that dauntless youth know that he was being pursued. Whenever his eyes caught sight of someone, he would approach him and the good lad would greet him and say: "That's what my mother told me to do."

Thus our simple boy came riding down a slope. He heard a woman's voice. There, beside a cliff, a lady was wailing in real anguish. Her true joy had been torn in twain. The lad quickly rode over to her. Now hear what the lady was doing. There was Sigune tearing her long brown braids out of her head for grief. The lad looked, and there was Schianatulander the Prince, dead in the maiden's lap. She was aweary of all mirth.

"Sad or of joy's color, my mother bade me greet everybody. God help you!" said the lad. "I find a piteous object here in your lap. Who gave you the wounded knight?" And eagerly the lad went on, "Who shot him? Was it   139 done with a javelot? I think he is dead, Lady. Won't you tell me something about who killed the man? If I can overtake him I will gladly fight him."

The good lad reached into his quiver and found sharp javelots aplenty there. He was also still carrying both the tokens which he had wrested from Jeschute when he committed his stupidity there. If he had learned his father's habitual ways, he would have hit the target better, since the duchess was alone. But she was yet to suffer much grief because of him: more than one whole year she missed the welcome of her husband's body. Injustice was done that woman.

But now let me tell you about Sigune, who might well bemoan her sorrow. She said to the lad, "You have virtue in you. Honor be to your sweet youth and to your lovely face. In truth you will be rich in blessings. This knight did not die by the javelot, he perished in a joust. Fidelity was born in you, that you can feel pity this way for 140 him." Before she allowed the lad to ride on she asked him his name, remarking that he showed the evidence of God's handiwork.

"'Bon fils, cher fils, beau fils,' that is what I was called by those who knew me at home."

As soon as he said this she recognized him by those names. Now hear him more correctly named so that you will know who is the lord of this adventure.

As he stood there with the maiden her red mouth made haste to speak: "In truth, your name is Parzival, which signifies 'right through the middle.'[8] Such a furrow did great love plow in your mother's heart with the plow of her faithfulness. Your father bequeathed her sorrow.[9] I tell you, and not to boast: your mother is my aunt. And without any base deception I tell you the sure truth of who you are: your father was an Angevin, and you were born a man of Waleis on your mother's side, at Kanvoleis. I know this for a certainty. You are also the King of Norgals, and in your capital city of Kingrivals your head shall some day bear the crown. This prince was slain for your 141 sake because he defended your lands steadfastly. Never did his fidelity slacken. O fair, sweet young man, those two brothers have done you much harm: Lehelin seized two kingdoms of yours, and this knight, as well as your father's brother, was slain by Orilus. And he it was who left me

[8] On the basis of the Old French form of the name *Perceval* Wolfram etymologizes: *perce à val!* = "pierce through!" A subsequent poet, Heinrich von der Türlin, will explain in his poem *Diu Krone* that *val* means both "valley" and "furrow," an interpretation which clarifies Wolfram's next sentence here. Chrétien offers no etymology at all in *Li Contes del Graal.*

[9] The text seems to imply an etymology for "Herzeloyde" as "heart's sorrow" (*herz* + *leide*), but linguistic analysis will not support this poetically appropriate interpretation.

in the grief you here behold. This prince of your kingdom served me in unstained honor. I was then your mother's ward. Dear, good cousin, hear how this came about. It was a hound's leash that brought him mortal pain.[10] In the service of us two he gained death for himself and for me the grievous yearning for his love. What a fool I was not to grant him my love! Utter sorrow has cut my joy to pieces. Now that he is dead, I love him."

Then he said, "Cousin, I grieve for your sorrow and for my own disgrace.[11] If I can avenge these things I will surely do so."

He was eager for battle then and there, but she showed him the wrong direction, fearing that he would lose his life and that she would thereby only sustain   142
greater harm than before. Then he took a road, smooth-trodden and wide, that led to the Britons. And to whomever he met, afoot or on horseback, knight or merchant, he gave his greeting and said that that was what his mother had told him to do. And she had given him that advice with no thought of ill.

Evening was coming on and suddenly great weariness came over him. Then Simplicity's companion caught sight of a house of fair size. There dwelt a greedy owner of the sort that still spring from base birth, a fisherman who lacked all kindliness. Hunger instructed the lad to turn in there and tell the owner of hunger's pangs.

But he said, "I wouldn't give you half a loaf of bread, not in thirty years. Anybody that looks for my generosity for nothing is wasting his time. I don't care about anybody but myself, and after that, about my children. You won't get in here today. If you had money or valuables, I would keep you, sure enough."

Whereat the lad offered him Lady Jeschute's   143
brooch.

[10] This statement is not clear in context, but the second fragment of Wolfram's stanzaic romance, *Titurel,* recounts the story of Schianatulander and the hound's leash.

[11] Parzival's disgrace lies in the fact that Schianatulander has died fighting in his service, and with no vengeance for his death.

As soon as the churl saw that, his mouth became a smile and said, "If you would like to stay, dear child, all who live here will show you honor."

"If you will feed me tonight and in the morning show me the way to Arthur—I am in his service—the gold can stay with you."

"That I will," said the churl. "I never did see such a handsome fellow. And just for a change I'll take you up to the King's Table Round."

And so the lad passed the night there, but the morrow saw him elsewhere.

He could hardly wait for daylight. His host also made ready and ran on in front while the lad rode after, and both were in a hurry.

Sir Hartmann von Ouwe! [12] To the house of your Lady Ginover and your lord, King Arthur, a guest of mine is coming. Please to protect him from mockery there! He is neither a fiddle nor a rote: let them get some other plaything and out of courtesy amuse themselves with that. Or else your Lady Enite and her mother Karsnafite will be put through the mill and have their fame bent down.   144
If I am forced to misuse my mouth for mockery, then with mockery I will defend my friend.

Then the fisherman and the brave lad came to where they could see a capital city close by, and that was Nantes.

Then the fisherman said, "Child, God shield you! Look now, there is where you ride in."

The lad, scant of wit, said, "You must lead me further than this."

"I should say not! Those courtiers are all so high bred that if ever a peasant came near them it would be a serious offense."

So the lad rode on by himself across a meadow not too broad that was bright with the color of flowers. No Cur-

---

[12] Hartmann von Aue (Ouwe), Wolfram's older contemporary, had been the first poet to adapt French chivalric romances to his own language. *Erec,* the earliest of these, was composed in the 1190's, and its heroine was Enite.

venal had brought him up.[18] He knew nothing of *courtoisie,* as is the way with those who have not traveled. His bridle was made of bast, and his pony was mighty weak so that it stumbled to many a fall, and his saddle was nowhere covered with new leather. Of samite or downy ermine there was very little to be seen on him, he had no use for tie cords to a cloak, and instead of fur-lined jacket and surcoat he carried his javelot. His father, who was adjudged   145 a model knight, was better attired on that carpet before Kanvoleis.

He who never knew the sweat of fear now saw a knight riding toward him. He greeted him in his usual fashion: "God keep you! That's how my mother taught me."

"Young Sir, may God reward you and her," said the son of Arthur's aunt.

This warrior had been brought up by Utepandragun and claimed hereditary rights to the land of Britain. Ither von Gaheviez was his name, though people callled him the Red Knight. His armor was so red that it made your eyes red to look at it. His swift horse was red, all red was his horse's hood piece, red samite were its trappings, his shield was redder than a flame, all red was his gambeson and tailored full, red was his spear shaft, red was his spear point, and at the hero's own desire his sword had been dyed red, though tempered for sharpness all the same. This King of Kukumerlant [14] had in his hand a goblet of red gold and finely engraved, snatched away from the Round Table.   146 White was his skin, red was his hair.

Straightforwardly he said to the lad, "Blessed be your sweet body: a pure woman brought you into the world. Well for the mother that bore you! I have never seen anyone so fair. You are the very luster of love, her defeat and her victory. Much joy in woman will triumph in you, but afterwards grief will weigh you down. Dear friend, if you

---

[18] Curvenal was Tristan's tutor. Wolfram points up the elaborate knightly training of Tristan in contrast to Parzival who had learned nothing.

[14] I.e., Cumberland.

intend to ride in here, then tell the King for me, and all his men, that I have not taken flight and that I will gladly wait here for anyone who may be preparing to joust. Let none of them think it strange. I rode up to the Round Table to claim possession of my kingdom. In token of my claim my hand picked up this goblet, but the wine spilled in Lady Ginover's lap. If I had overturned the torches I would have got my skin all sooty, so I chose not to do that." [15] The bold warrior went on: "Not that I did this as a theft. Being a king, I have no need for that. Now tell the Queen, friend, that I spilled the wine on her unintention- 147 ally. And those worthy gentlemen sat there and offered no defense. Kings or princes they may be, but why do they let their host die of thirst? Why don't they come out here and get his golden goblet for him? Otherwise their reputations will be lost."

"I will do as you have told me," the lad said, and rode away from him into Nantes. There the children followed him to the courtyard in front of the palace where all sorts of things were going on. A crowd gathered dense around him. Up ran Iwanet, a lad free of falseness, and offered to bear him company.

The lad said, "God keep you! as my mother told me to say before I left her house. I see many Arthurs here: which one will make me a knight?"

Iwanet burst out laughing and said, "The right one you do not see, but it won't be long before you do." He led him inside the great hall where the worthy company was.

In spite of the din he was able to say, "God keep you gentlemen all, and especially the King and his wife. My mother charged me on my life to greet 148 *them* in particular. And those that have a place at the Round Table because of their deserved renown, she bade me greet them too. But one piece of knowledge I lack: I don't know which one of you is the host. To *him* a knight has sent a message—I saw him and he was red all over—

[15] Seizure of the goblet and inverting a torch as though to set fire to a field were both symbolic gestures representing seizure of the territory which the King of Kukumerlant claims from Arthur.

and he says he will wait for him outside there. I think he wants to fight. Also, he is sorry that he spilled wine on the Queen. O, if only I had received those clothes of his from the King's hand! I would be very pleased: they look so knightly!"

The free-spoken lad was much elbowed about, hustled this way and that. They noticed his beauty. Their own eyes saw that never was more lovely form lorded or ladied, for God was in a good humor when He created Parzival. And thus he who feared terror but little was brought before Arthur. No one could be hostile to him in whom   149 God invented perfection. The Queen too gazed at him before she left the great hall where she had had the wine spilled on her.

Then Arthur looked at the lad, and to the simple youth he said, "Young Sir, may God repay your greeting. I will gladly serve you with my life and my possessions. I am indeed of a mind to do so."

"God grant that that is really so! The time seems to me a year since I was supposed to become a knight, and that is more bad than good. Now do not make me wait any longer, grant me the honor of knighthood!"

"That I will, and gladly," said his host, "if my dignity suffices. You are so pleasing that my gift to you shall be of precious worth. Indeed I will not fail to do it, but you must wait until tomorrow morning and I will fit you out properly."

The high-born lad halted there awkward as a crane, and said, "I will not beg for anything here. A knight came riding toward me. If I can't get his armor I don't care who talks about kingly gifts. Those my mother can give me, for after all she is a queen."   150

Then Arthur said to the lad, "That armor is worn by such a man that I would not dare give it to you. I have had to live with worry as it is, and through no fault of mine, ever since I lost his homage. He is Ither of Gaheviez, who rammed sorrow through my joy."

"A generous king *you* would be, if a gift like that were too great for you!" said Keie then. "Let him have it, and let him go out there and face him on the meadow! As long as someone has to bring us the goblet, here is the string and there is the top: let the boy do the spinning. He will be praised for it among the women. He will often have to risk quarrels and take such chances, and I don't care about either of their lives. You have to lose a dog or two to get a boar's head."

"I hate to deny him," said Arthur in good faith, "only I fear he may be killed just when I am about to help him to knighthood."

But the lad obtained the gift, from which subsequently was to come grief. Now he was in a hurry to leave the King. Young and old crowded after him. Iwanet took him by the hand and led him past a roofed balcony not   151 too high up but that he could see the length and breadth of it. In fact, the balcony was so low that he saw and heard something there that grieved him greatly. The Queen herself chose to be at the window with knights and ladies around her, and they were all looking at him. There too sat Lady Cunneware, the proud and fair, she who was never to laugh until she beheld him who had won, or was to win, supreme honor, otherwise she would die never having laughed. She *had* never laughed—until the lad came riding past, and then her lovely mouth burst forth laughing. Her back paid for that later in soreness, for Keie the seneschal took Lady Cunneware de Lalant by her wavy hair and wound her long fair braids around his hand and fastened them without a bolt. Her back had taken no oath on a judge's staff,[16] and yet on her back a staff was used until, by the time the whirr had gone out of it, it had cut right through her clothes and through her skin.

Then the unwise fellow said, "Your noble repu-   152 tation is brought to a disgraceful end, but I am the net that catches it, and I'm going to pound it back into you till you feel it in every limb. To King Arthur's court and household has come riding so many a worthy man for

---

[16] The allusion is to the legal procedure whereby a person swearing an oath laid his hand on the judge's staff of office.

whom you failed to laugh, and now you laugh for a man
who has no knightly breeding at all."

Many odd things happen in anger. No ɪoyal decree would
have awarded him the right to flog that maiden, who was
much pitied by her friends. Even if she had been a knight, it
was a disgraceful way to beat her, and she was a princess by
birth. If her brothers, Orilus and Lehelin, had seen it, there
would have been fewer blows.

Her laughter and the speech of silent Antanor, who because of his silence was considered a fool, were dependent
on the same event: he was never to speak a word unless she
laughed, she who was flogged. But when she did laugh, his
mouth said to Keie, "God knows, Sir Seneschal,   153
that Cunneware de Lalant is being thrashed because of that
lad, but by his hand your own joy will yet be destroyed,
however far away he may go."

"Since your first words are a threat to me, I think they
will bring you little joy yourself!" Then *his* hide got tanned,
and fists whispered a lot of things into that clever fool's
ears: that is what Keie did with no delay.

Young Parzival could not help seeing this misery of Antanor's and of the lady's, and his heart was sick beholding
their distress. More than once he seized his javelot, but
there was such a press around the Queen that he refrained
from the throw.

Then Iwanet took leave of *le fils du roi* Gahmuret, whose
trip was made alone out to Ither on the meadow. To him he
reported that there was no one inside who wanted to joust.
"The King bestowed a gift on me. I told him, just as you
had told me, how it happened unintentionally that you
spilled the wine, and how you were sorry for your   154
clumsiness. None of them wants to fight. Now give me
what you're riding on there, and all your armor too, because that is what I was given at the great hall, and I have
to be made a knight in it. I'll deny you my greeting if you
refuse it to me. So give it to me, if you're in your right
mind."

The King of Kukumerlant said, "If Arthur's hand has

made you a gift of my armor, he would do as much with
my life—if you could win it from me. That's the way he
loves his kinsmen. Tell me though, was he ever so well
disposed toward you before? Your service has won its reward so fast."

"I dare to earn whatever I deserve, and he did give it to
me. Hand it over, and stop this foolish talk. I'm not going to
be a squire any longer. I'm going to carry the shield of a
knight." He reached over and grabbed his bridle. "Maybe
you are Lehelin about whom my mother complains."

The knight reversed his spear shaft and struck the lad
with such force that both he and his pony were tumbled
onto the flowers. That hero was quick to anger   155
and he struck him with his shaft so the blood spurted from
his scalp. The good lad Parzival stood there furious on
the meadow. Then he seized his javelot. Just where the
helmet and the vizor had holes over the cap beneath, there
the javelot went through his eye and right on through his
head, so that he fell dead, that foe of falsity. Women's sighs
and the rending of hearts were the result of the death of
Ither of Gaheviez, and all women who loved him found
their eyes wet with tears. Their joy was ridden down, their
delight was defeated and led onto rough roads.

The simple Parzival rolled him over and over but did not
know how to get the armor off him. Here was something
odd: neither helmet laces nor kneepieces could his strong
white hands untie or pull off, though he tried again and
again in his simplicity. Now both steed and pony set up
such a whinnying that Iwanet heard it, Lady Gin-   156
over's page and kinsman, where he was standing at the end
of the moat by the city wall. When he heard the outcry from
the horse, and when he saw no one on it, the nimble-witted
lad hurried out—he did so from the loyalty he bore Parzival
—and found Ither dead and Parzival in childish distress. He
ran over to both of them. Then he praised Parzival for the
fame his hand had won over the King of Kukumerlant.

"God reward you for that! Now tell me what to do. I
don't know how to go about this. How do I get it off from
him and onto me?"

"I can soon show you that," said the proud Iwanet to *le fils du roi* Gahmuret.

And the armor was stripped from the dead man right there on the meadow before Nantes and put onto the living one, whom great simplicity still ruled.

"Those boots won't go with iron hose," said Iwanet. "You have to wear knightly attire now."

These words vexed the good lad Parzival, and he said, "Anything my mother gave me is not going to be cast off, whether for the better or for the worse." 157

To Iwanet that seemed odd enough—*he* was courtly-bred—but he had to comply all the same. He was not angry with him at all. So he shod him with two shiny iron hose over the boots. With them went two golden spurs, and these he fastened on, not with leather straps, but with two bands of ribbon. Before offering him the gorget he tied on the kneepieces, and in short order there was the impatient Parzival in armor from the foot upward.

Then the lad asked for his quiver too.

"I won't let you have a javelot," said Iwanet, the worthy lad. "Knighthood has forbidden you that."

And he girded a sharp sword around him, and taught him how to draw it, and told him he must never flee. Then he brought over the dead man's Castilian, with its long slim legs. The youth leaped in full armor into the saddle without asking for stirrups. People still talk about his swiftness. Iwanet did not think it too much trouble to teach 158 him how to use his shield properly and how to aim for an opponent's harm. Then he put a spear into his hand, but he would have none of that.

"What's the good of that?" he asked.

"If someone comes riding against you in a joust, you're supposed to break it on him boldly and run it through his shield. The more you do of that, the more you will be praised before the women."

As the adventure tells us, he sat better upon his horse than any painter from Maestricht or Cologne could have painted him.

Then to Iwanet he said, "Dear friend and comrade, I

have won here what I asked for. Commend my service to
King Arthur in the city. Take his golden goblet back to
him and tell him also about the great insult to me. A knight
forgot himself with me and beat a maiden because she was
moved to laughter at me. Her cries of pain trouble me yet.
The lady's undeserved suffering does not touch just the
edge of my heart but lies at its very center. Now do this, by
our friendship, and feel for me in my grief. God   159
keep you. I leave you now. May He preserve us both."

Ither of Gaheviez he left lying pitiably on the meadow,
who was so fair in death and who had, in life, known the
fullness of joy. If knightly action had been the cause of his
death in a joust, with a spear through his shield, who then
would mourn the great calamity? But he died by a javelot.
Then Iwanet brought him bright flowers for a covering.
The javelot shaft he set in the ground at his side, and in the
manner of Christ's Passion this lad pure and proud pressed
a piece of wood through the javelot blade to make a cross.
Nor did he fail to go back to the city and tell the news, at
which many a woman was dismayed and many a knight
wept as they gave vent to their faithful grief. Great was the
lamentation. The dead man was brought in in state. The
Queen rode forth from the city and bade them lift up the
Monstrance over the King of Kukumerlant whom Parzival's
hand had slain.

Lady Ginover the Queen spoke words of sor-   160
row: "Alas and alas, the renown of Arthur may break in
twain at this strange event, that he who had been destined
to win the highest fame of those about the Round Table
lies here slain before Nantes. He claimed his heritage and
they gave him death. He was of our company here, and no
ear ever heard of any misdeed on his part. In wildness of
treachery he was tame, for that had been stripped from him.
Now I must bury all too soon this treasure-lock of fame.
His heart wise in courtesy, a seal upon that lock, taught
him the noblest conduct wherever a man should with
bravery show a man's fidelity for a woman's love. A seed
bearing ever new fruit of sorrow is sown among women.
Grief wafts from your wounds. So red was your hair that

your blood could not make these bright flowers any redder.
You have banished laughter from women." [17]

Ither the rich in renown was buried as a king,   161
and his death taught sighing to women. His armor had cost
him his life; the simple Parzival's desire for it was the
cause of his death. Later, when he learned better, he would
not have done it.

There were certain qualities in his horse: it took great
exertion as nothing; cold weather or hot, over rocks or tree
trunks, it never sweated from travel; there was no need to
tighten its girth by a single notch even if he rode for two
days. In his armor that simple man[18] rode further that day
than a sensible man without armor would have ridden in
two. He rode at a gallop, rarely at a trot, because he did not
know how to check the speed.

Toward evening the pinnacle and roof of a tower came
into view. The simple man actually thought that more and
more towers were growing up out of the ground, for there
were a great many of them on a house. He imagined that
Arthur had planted them, and therefore thought of him as
a saint whose blessings reached far and wide.

"Well," said the simple man, "my mother's peo-   162
ple don't know how to farm. Their crops don't grow this
tall, any that she has them sow there in the forest. She always gets too much rain."

Gurnemanz de Graharz was the name of the lord of this
castle toward which he was riding. In front of it there stood
a broad linden tree on a green meadow that was neither
broader nor longer than the proper size. The horse, and the
road too, led him to where he found sitting him to whom
the castle and the land belonged. A great weariness made
him carry his shield improperly, swinging it too far back or
too far forward but not at all in the manner that was
deemed praiseworthy there. Gurnemanz the Prince was sit-

[17] It is puzzling why the Queen should publicly and so eloquently
lament for her husband's challenger, but the role of Ither is puzzling
in other respects as well. It is possible that the author was seeking to
reconcile conflicting traditions of this episode.

[18] The author here first terms his hero a man and not a lad.

ting alone. The linden's mass cast its shade—as it should—
upon that captain of true courtesy. Then he, whose ways
were a refuge from falsity, received the guest, as was his
duty. He had neither knights nor squires with him.

Then from his simple wits and without delay Parzival
answered him thus: "My mother told me to accept advice
from any man having grey hair. I will serve you for
it, since that is what my mother said."   163

"If you have come here for advice, you will have to
guarantee me your friendliness before I assent to give you
such advice."

Then the famed prince cast from his hand a yearling
sparrow hawk that swooped off into the castle. It wore a little golden bell that tinkled. That was a messenger, and immediately there appeared a number of handsomely attired
pages whom he bade escort the stranger in and attend his
needs.

"My mother was right," said he. "There is no danger
from an old man's talk."

They took him in at once to where he found many noble
knights. At one spot in the courtyard they all begged him to
dismount.

But he in whom simplicity was evident said, "A king
bade me be a knight, and I don't care what happens, I'm
not going to get off this horse. My mother told me to greet
all of you."

They thanked both him and her, and then when the
greetings were over, though the horse was tired and so was
the man, they thought up many a plea before they got him
off the horse and into a warm room. Then they   164
all began to urge him: "Let them take your armor off and
lighten your limbs."

Directly his armor was removed, but when the attendants
saw the rough boots and the fool's garment they were
startled. With much embarrassment this was reported at
court, and the host was all but overcome with shame.

But one knight, of fine manners, said, "Truly, my eye has
never beheld one so noble. In him there is surpassing beauty,
as well as a lofty nature pure and sweet. How is it that the

glory of love should be dressed like this? I am grieved to find the World's Joy in such attire. And yet, well for the mother that bore him, for in him there is all that can be desired. His knightly gear is rich and his armor was gallantly worn before it was removed from the handsome fellow. But I noticed the bloodstains of a great bruise on his body."

"This," said the host to the knight, "has been done for some woman's sake." [19]

"No, Sir, his manners are such that he would not know how to ask a woman to accept his service, al-   165 though his looks are of Love's color."

"Well," said the host, "let us go and have a look at this fellow whose clothes are so very strange."

They went to Parzival and found him wounded with a spear—an unbroken spear. Then Gurnemanz took him under his special care, care such that no father who strove for loyalty to his children could treat them any better. With his own hand the host washed and bandaged the wound. Then supper was laid, of which the youthful guest was in need, for great hunger had not passed him by. He had ridden away from the fisherman that morning without breakfast. His wound and the heavy armor that he won before Nantes had brought him weariness and hunger, as well as the long day's travels from Arthur of Britain. Everywhere they had let him fast. The host bade him eat with him, and the guest fell to with a will. He tackled the manger with such eagerness that he put away a quantity of food. That amused the host, and Gurnemanz, the rich in loyalty, earnestly bade him go right on eating and forget his fatigue.   166

When the time came and the table was removed, the host said, "I guess you are tired. Were you up early?"

"God knows my mother was still asleep. She can't stay awake so much."

The host could not help laughing. Then he took him to the sleeping quarters and told him to slip out of his clothes. He did so unwillingly, but it had to be. An ermine coverlet was laid over his naked body: never did woman bear fairer

[19] I.e., the fool's garb is a disguise or a penance relative to some love adventure.

fruit. Great weariness and sleep kept him from turning on one side and the other. Thus he waited for day to come.

Then the famed prince ordered a bath to be prepared for mid-morning at the foot of the couch where he lay—this was regularly done in the morning—and roses were strewn in the water. As little noise as they made around him, the sleeping guest still awoke and went, that sweet and worthy young man, directly to the bath.

I don't know who told them to, but maidens in   167 rich apparel and lovely to see came in with all propriety, and with their soft white hands washed and rubbed away his bruises. He had no cause to be surprised, that orphan of wisdom, and he just enjoyed the pleasure and *aise,* nor did they mind his simplicity. Thus maidens modest yet bold tended him, but chatter as they might, he merely remained silent. He could not imagine it was too early, for a second daylight shone from them. Thus radiance clashed with radiance, until *his* brightness outshone them both—he did not lack in that. They offered him a bath sheet but he would have none of it: he was so ashamed before ladies that he would not put it around him. The maidens had to leave, they dared not stay any longer. —I think they would have liked to see if anything had happened to him down below.

> *Womanhood is loyal ever;*
> *Friend's woe is their endeavor.*

The guest walked over to the bed, where a gar-   168 ment all of white was ready for him. Through it they passed a gold and silken belt, and hose of scarlet wool they drew up smooth on the legs of him whom bravery never failed. Ah! How fine his legs looked in them, and how his fine form was revealed! Of gleaming scarlet wool and well cut, both lined with ermine white, were his long coat and mantle, and trimmed in front with wide sable fur both black and grey. These the fine young man put on. Girt with a costly belt, the coat was fastened and beautifully adorned with a precious brooch. His lips burned red as well.

Then came the loyal host followed by proud knights, and greeted his guest. When this was over, the knights all said

they had never seen anyone so handsome, and in all sincerity they praised the woman who had given the world such
progeny. From their courtly breeding and in honesty too
they said, "He will be well rewarded wherever he seeks for
favor. Love and greeting await him. May he profit   169
by his worth." All said the same, and so did all who saw
him thereafter.

The host took him by the hand and they walked off together. The famed prince inquired how his rest had been
that night under his roof.

"Well, I would not be alive now if my mother had not
advised me to come here that day when I left her. May God
reward you and her, Sir! You do me great kindness."

Then our simple-witted hero went where Mass was being
sung for God and for his host. During Mass the host taught
him the things that increased blessedness: how to make his
offering, how to make the sign of the Cross, and how to foil
the Devil thereby. Then they went to the palace hall where
the table was laid, and there the guest sat down with his
host and ate with gusto.

Courteously the host said, "Sir, you must not mind my
asking where you come from."

He explained to him how he had ridden away and left his
mother, and about the ring and the brooch, and   170
how he had won the armor. The host had known the Red
Knight and now sighed in pity at his fate. His name he
now transferred to his guest and called *him* "the Red
Knight."

When the table was removed, then a wild will received
its taming. The host said to his guest, "You talk like a little
child. Why not stop talking about your mother and think of
other things? Follow *my* advice: it will keep you from
wrongdoing. I will begin thus:

> See that you never lose your sense of shame. A man
> without a sense of shame, what good is he? He
> lives in a molting state,[20] shedding his honor, and
> with steps directed toward hell.

[20] The metaphor refers, of course, to falcons.

You have beauty and bearing, you may well be the lord
of some people. If you are of high origin and rising still higher, bear in mind that you must have
compassion on the host of the needy. Shield them
from distress with generosity and with kindness,
and strive for humility. The poor man of good
birth may well wrestle with shame—it is a sour
business—and you should be ready with   171
help. When you lighten his load God's blessing is
near you. He has it worse than those who come to
the window for bread.

Be both poor and rich appropriately: if a lord squanders,
that is not lord-like; if he hoards treasure too
much, that is dishonor also. Make your rule the
true mean.

I have observed that you are in need of advice.

Leave bad manners to their own quarrel.

Do not ask too many questions.

Do not disdain thoughtful answers that go straight to
the question of one who is sounding you out with
words. You can hear and see, taste and smell: these
should bring you wisdom.

Let mercy go along with daring. *There* will be the test
of my counsels. Once a man gives you his oath of
surrender in battle, take his word of honor and let
him live, unless he has done you such wrong as
would burden your heart with grief.

You will frequently have to wear armor. As   172
soon as it is removed, see that you wash your hands
and around your eyes to get the iron rust off. That
way you will be of love's color, and women's eyes
will note that.

Be manly and cheerful of spirit: that is good for winning honor and praise.

Let women be dear to you, for that enhances a young
man's worth. Do not waver a single day toward
them: that is true manly conduct. If you choose to
tell them lies you may deceive many of them, but
in true love base deception does not enjoy honor

long. It is the prowler's complaint that the dry
branches in the park snap and crack and rouse the
watch. Pathless places and felled-tree barriers, there
is where many a battle thrives. Measure this
against love. Noble love has judgment with which
to outwit sly deceptive trickery. If you incur her
disfavor you will be dishonored and suffer painful
shame forever. Take this lesson to heart.

I will tell you more about womankind. Husband and
wife are one, as are the sun that shone to-   173
day and the thing called day itself; neither can be
separated from the other; they blossom from a
single seed. Strive to understand this."

The guest bowed thanks to his host for his counsel. He
gave up talking about his mother—in his speech, but not in
his heart, as is still a true man's way.

The host spoke what redounded to his honor. "Also, you
must learn more skill in knightly arts. The way you came
riding here to me! I have seen many a wall where I found
the shield more properly hung than yours was around your
neck. It is not too late: let us go out on the field and learn
some skills. Bring him his horse and me mine, and every
knight his. Have squires come too, and have each one take
a stout spear and bring it along, and see that they are new
ones."

Then the prince came out on the meadow, and there some
practice was had at riding. He showed his guest how to
bring the horse out of a gallop with a sharp dig of the
spurs, how to urge it to the charge by a pressure   174
of the thighs, how to lower the spear properly, and how to
bring up the shield in front against a spear thrust. Then he
said, "Be so good as to do the same."

Thus he saved him from mishap better than the lithe
switch that tears the skin of wayward children. Then he
called for hardy knights to come out against him in joust
and himself led him to the lists against one of them. There
the youth made his first spear thrust through a shield, so
that all were astonished, and there he knocked a stout

rider, who was no slight fellow, back off his horse. A second jouster had come up, and Parzival had taken a fresh strong spear. His youth and strength and spirit, this sweet young man without a beard, and his heritage from Gahmuret, together with innate manhood, drove him on. He rode at full career head on and aimed at the four rivets.[21] His host's knight did not keep his seat but measured the field in a fall. Little bits of splintered lance were   175 all around. In this manner he struck down five of them. Then the host took him and led him home. He had won the prize in the games: later he was to prove adept at real combat. All who saw him ride and who understood these matters said that he had skill and courage.

"Now my lord[22] will see the end of his cares and he can become young again. Let him bestow his daughter, our lady, on him for a wife. If he is sensible his sorrows will be at an end. Here is someone that has ridden into his house to make up for the deaths of his three sons. Fortune has not passed him by."

And so the prince came in at evening, the table was set, and he bade his daughter come to table with them—that is how I heard the story.

Now hear what the host said to the lovely Liaze when he saw the maiden coming: "Allow this knight to kiss you, and do him honor. He travels with Fortune's instruction. —And you, Sir, are supposed to leave my daughter her ring —assuming she has one. But she hasn't. Nor any   176 brooch either. Who would give her such expensive things as were given to the lady in the forest? *She* had someone from whom she received those things that you managed to take, but from Liaze there is nothing to be taken."

The guest felt shy, but all the same he kissed her on the lips, and they were the color of fire. Liaze was lovely to look at and rich in true purity besides. The table was long and

---

[21] The four rivets that held the shield boss formed an opponent's target.

[22] The speaker is one of the knights referred to in the foregoing sentence.

low, and the host was crowded by no one but sat alone at one end. His guest he bade sit between him and his daughter, and at his command her soft white hands had to cut up whatever was to be eaten by this man whom they called "the Red Knight." No one was to disturb them if they exchanged little intimacies. The maiden with all propriety was doing her father's will. She and the guest made a comely pair. Directly thereafter the maiden withdrew.

In this way our hero was entertained until the fourteenth day. His heart was troubled by just one thing: he   177 wanted to have fought better before enjoying the warmth of what they term "a lady's arms." He felt that noble striving was a lofty goal both in this life and yonder. And that is still no lie.

One morning he asked permission to depart, and thus he left Graharz the town. His host rode out with him, but then a new heart's sorrow came to pass.

"You are the fourth son that I have lost," said the prince, truest of the true. "I thought that I had recompense for those three sorrows. There were, after all, only three of them. But now if someone were to take his hand and strike my heart into four pieces and carry each piece away, I would be glad of it, one for you—you are riding away— and the other three for my noble sons who died bravely. But such is knighthood's reward; it has a knotted whip of sorrows for a tail.

"One death lamed all my joy, that of my fair son whose name was Schentaflurs. Since Condwiramurs was not willing to bestow herself and her kingdom, helping   178 her, he lost his life at the hands of Clamidê and Kingrun.[23] From that, my heart is slashed by sorrow so that it has holes like a fence. You have ridden away from me all too soon, disconsolate as I am. O, to think I cannot die, since Liaze the lovely maid and my country do not satisfy you!

"My second son was Count Lascoyt, who was killed by

[23] Clamidê, the King of Iserterre, and his seneschal Kingrun are still besieging Condwiramurs, the Queen of Brobarz, and Parzival will soon be involved in that struggle.

Ider, *fils de* Noyt, in a contest for a sparrow hawk.[24] Because of that I am empty of joy.

"My third son's name was Gurzgri. With him rode Mahaute in her beauty, whom her haughty brother Ehkunat had given him for a wife. To the capital city of Brandigan he rode to Schoydelakurt,[25] where death did not fail to find him. Mabonagrin slew him. Wherefrom Mahaute lost her beauty, and my wife, his mother, died. Great grief drew her after him."

The guest perceived his host's sorrow, for he had recounted it so clearly, and he said, "Sir, I am not wise, but if I ever win knightly fame so that I am fit to ask for love, you shall give me Liaze your daughter, the   179 lovely maid. You have told me too much sorrow. If I can relieve it then, I will not let you bear so great a burden of it."

Then the young man took his leave of that loyal prince and of all his retinue. With that, the prince's trey of sorrows was sadly raised to a four.[26] He had just suffered his fourth bereavement.

[24] The allusion is to the sparrow-hawk contest at Kanedic in Chrétien's and in Hartmann's *Erec*.

[25] Schoydelakurt (= *Joie de la cour*) was the adventure in a garden of evil enchantment, guarded by the red knight Mabonagrin, in Chrétien's and in Hartmann's *Erec*. Gurzgri's head must then have been one of those numerous heads which Erec saw impaled on stakes there before he overcame Mabonagrin and undid the evil spell on the place.

[26] The metaphor, as so often in Wolfram, is from dice playing.

BOOK·IV

So departed Parzival, bearing knightly ways now and the looks of a knight, except, alas, as he was troubled by many a twinge of unsweet discomfort. To him width seemed too narrow and breadth too close, all greenness looked withered to him, and his red armor seemed white. So did his heart constrain his eyes. For now that he had lost simplicity, the spirit of Gahmuret would not allow him to stop thinking of the lovely Liaze, that gracious maid who in friendship had offered him every honor except love. His horse might choose any road, he was too deep in sorrow to check it   180 whether it ran or trotted. Wayside cross and wattle fence and ruts of wagon wheels, none of these marked his forest way. Many a trackless path he traveled where the plantain weed did not grow, and hill and valley were alike unknown to him. Lots of people are in the habit of saying that whoever rides astray will find the sledge-hammer, and signs of a sledge-hammer were here aplenty, if huge tree trunks are what sledge-hammers are used on.[1]

But he did not ride too far astray, for keeping straight ahead he arrived from Graharz that day in the kingdom of Brobarz, through wild, high mountains. Day was drawing toward evening when he came to a swift stream that was loud with the rushing of its waters. Cliffs, from one to the

[1] The allusion is apparently to a proverb unknown to us.

next, hurled it down. He rode downstream until he came
to the city of Pelrapeire, which King Tampenteire had bequeathed to his daughter and where many people now share
her distress. The ·water rushed like arrows that are well
feathered and trimmed and shot with twanged string from
the flexed bow. Spanning it was a drawbridge   181
made of wickerwork, and at that point it emptied into the
sea. Pelrapeire was well defended! As children sway in
swings and we do not want to stop them from swinging, so
swayed the bridge, but without a rope—*it* was not that
young any more.

On the further side stood sixty knights or more with
their helmets on. "Go back! Go back!" they shouted, and
waving their swords those weak men sought battle. They
thought it was Clamidê, whom they had often seen there,
because the stranger rode so royally up to the bridge from
across the field so wide. And now they shouted to this young
man with such loud cries that, spur his horse as he would,
it was frightened and refused the bridge. Then he from
whom cowardice ever fled dismounted and led his horse
onto the swaying bridge. A coward's spirit would have
sickened at approaching such odds of battle, and besides,
there was another thing he had to watch out for, the fear
that his horse might fall. The noise on the other   182
side died down. The knights carried their helmets and
shields and shining swords back in and shut their gates.
They were afraid a larger force was behind him.

So crossed Parzival, and as he rode, he came to a battlefield where many a man had tasted death for the sake of
knightly renown before the high and splendid gate of the
great hall. On the gate he found a knocker which he lost no
time in seizing. No one heard his call except one maiden
of comely looks, and from a window this maiden saw the
hero halted there unafraid.

The pretty girl said courteously, "Do you come as an
enemy, Sir? There is no need for that. There are enough of
those already without you, both by land and by sea, to attack us, an angry and brave host of them."

But he said, "Lady, you see here a man who will serve

you, and if I can, your greeting shall be my reward. I am
eager to do your service."

Then the girl prudently went to the queen and helped
him to get in—a thing which averted great dis-   183
aster from them later on. And thus he was admitted.

On both sides of the street stood a great crowd of people. Slingers and foot soldiers, a long line of them, came
bearing arms, and a large number of dart throwers. At the
same time he saw many brave foot soldiers, the best in the
country, with long stout lances, sharp and whole. Also, as I
heard the story, many merchants stood there too with axes
and javelots, as their guild masters had ordered. They all
had skins slack from hunger. The queen's marshal led
him with difficulty through their midst as far as the courtyard. There defenses had been prepared. There were towers
over the living quarters, mural towers, tower keeps, and
half turrets, certainly more of them than he had ever seen
before. From all sides knights came forth to greet him,
some on horseback, some on foot, and this sorry crowd was
also all the color of ashes or sickly clay. —My   184
master, the Count of Wertheim, would not have liked to be
a soldier there: he couldn't have survived on their allow-
ance. —Want had reduced them to starvation. They had
neither cheese, nor meat, nor bread; they had no use for
toothpicks, and no grease from their lips soiled the wine
they drank. Their bellies had caved in, their hips were pro-
truding and lean, and their skin was shriveled right to their
ribs like Hungarian leather. Hunger had driven their flesh
away, and from privation they could do nothing but endure
it. There was mighty little to drip into their fires. It was a
worthy man, the proud King of Brandigan, who had driven
them to this pass: they were reaping the harvest of
Clamidê's wooing. Rarely did mead brim over in can or
tankard, rarely did a Trüdingen pan of fritters sizzle. *That*
tune was no more. —But if I were to twit them about it, I
would show very poor sense, for where I have often dismounted and where I am addressed as Sir, at home in my
own house, it is uncommon for a mouse to find   185
delight. Mice have to steal their food, but I, from whom no-

body has to hide it, can't even find it openly. And it happens all too often to me, Wolfram of Eschenbach, that I put up with such comfort!

But enough of my complaint. Back now to the story of how Pelrapeire was full of troubles.

There a tax was levied on the people's joy. Those heroes rich in loyalty lived in wretchedness; their true manhood so commanded. Have pity on their distress! Their very lives are now at stake unless the Hand Supreme redeem that pledge. Now hear more about those poor people, and may they rouse your pity! Shamefaced, they received their brave guest, who seemed to them so distinguished that he would not have needed to ask *them* for lodgings in their condition. He knew nothing of their great distress.

A carpet was laid on the grass where a linden tree was enclosed by a wall and trellised for shade, and there attendants removed his armor. He was not of their complexion when once he had washed off the iron   186
rust with well water, for then he all but outshone the sun in its bright glory. Then they deemed him a worthy guest indeed. He was given a mantle to match the coat he was wearing, and the sable fur had a fresh, wild smell. They said, "Do you wish to see the queen, our lady?" and the steadfast hero said he would gladly do so. They walked toward a great hall approached by steep steps. The light of a lovely face, a sweet sight to his eyes, a bright radiance shone from the queen before she received him.

Kyot of Catalonia[2] and noble Manpfilyot, dukes both, led forth their brother's child, the queen of that land. They, for the love of God, had renounced their swords. And now these noble princes, grey-haired and comely, with great courtesy escorted the lady midway down the steps, and there she kissed the worthy warrior. Red   187

---

[2] Katelangen = Catalonia, the district of northeastern Spain, linguistically distinct from the rest of Spain by virtue of its own variety of Romance speech. Politically, it had formed part of the Spanish March which Charlemagne regained from the Moors; from 874 to 1037 it was known as the County of Barcelona or Catalonia; from 1037 to Wolfram's time it constituted a unit within the Kingdom of Aragon.

were the lips of both. Then the queen gave him her
hand and led Parzival back inside, where they both sat
down. All the ladies and knights that stood or sat there
were weak of strength. Both mistress and retinue had abandoned joy. And yet, wherever the beauty of ladies was
judged and one was praised as the best, there Condwiramurs in her radiance was singled out above these: Jeschute,
Enite,[3] and Cunneware de Lalant. Her glory outshone theirs,
and the beauty of both Isaldes too.[4] Yes, Condwiramurs
won the prize. She had the true *beau corps*[5]—in German:
"beautiful body." They were indeed excellent women that
had given birth to those two sitting there together now.
Neither men nor women could do anything but gaze at the
two of them there together. Good friends he found there
among them.

The guest was thinking—I will tell you what: 188
"That was Liaze there, this is Liaze here. God means to
lighten my sorrow, for now I behold Liaze, noble Gurnemanz' child."

But Liaze's beauty was a mere breath compared with this
maiden sitting here: in *her* God had not omitted any wish,
she was the mistress of the land, and like the rose washed
with the sweet dew that from its bud sends forth its new
and noble glow, red and white together. This caused her
guest great perplexity. For his manly courtesy was so perfect since the worthy Gurnemanz had cured him of his simplicity and counseled him against questions, unless they
were discreet ones, that he sat there with that noble queen
without opening his mouth to speak a word, right close by
too, not at some distance away. Still, many a man more
experienced with ladies will fail to talk.

The queen thought to herself, "I guess this man scorns

[3] Enite is the heroine of Hartmann's (and Chrétien's) *Erec.*

[4] Isalde, the beloved of Tristan, and Isalde of the White Hands. The
spelling with "a" is that used by Heinrich von Veldeke. Wolfram seems
to ignore his contemporary Gottfried from Strassburg, who spelled
the name with an "o."

[5] I.e., Old French: *bea curs.* (In Book I, 39,25, this word occurred
as a given name for a brother of Gawan and son of King Lot of Norway.)

me because I am wasted away. No, he is doing it deliberately. He is the guest, I am the hostess, and the first speech
should be up to me. For he has been looking so
kindly at me since we have been sitting here, and   189
has shown me courtesy. I have held back too long from
speaking. Let there be no more of this silence."

To her guest the queen said, "Sir, a hostess must speak.
My kiss earned me your greeting, and besides, you did offer your service when you arrived—so one of my maidens
told me. Guests have not accustomed us to that, but my
heart has longed for it. Sir, I inquire whence your journey
has brought you?"

"Lady, I rode away today from a man whom I left in
sorrow, a man of flawless loyalty. That prince's name is
Gurnemanz and he is called 'of Graharz.' From there I
rode today into this kingdom."

Then the noble maiden said, "If anyone else had told me
this I would not believe it, that it could be done in one day.
Whenever one of my messengers has ridden there, the swift-
est has never taken less than two days. His sister was my
mother, your host's sister, that is. Moreover, his daughter's
beauty has reason to fade from sorrow. Many a bitter day
we have spent, I and the maid Liaze, lamenting with tear-
ful eyes together. If you are fond of your host, ac-   190
cept such entertainment here tonight as we here, men and
women, have long known. In a way, you will be serving
him too thereby. I will tell you of our plight, for we have to
endure severe privation."

Then her uncle Kyot said, "Lady, I will send you twelve
loaves of bread and three smoked shoulders and hams;
add to that eight cheeses and two butts of wine. And my
brother shall also contribute tonight, for the need is great."

Then Manpfilyot said, "Lady, I will send an equal
amount."

Thereat the maiden was full of joy, nor did she stint her
great thanks to them.

They took their leave and rode to their hunting lodge
near by. The two old men lived in a wild mountain glen

without defenses, yet they were left in peace by the army.
Their messenger came posting back bringing relief for the
famished people. The citizenry had done beautifully without this food: many a one was dead from starvation before
these provisions arrived. The queen ordered them portioned out, the cheese, the meat, and the wine,   191
among the starving people. Parzival, her guest, so advised.
Thus for the two of them hardly a morsel remained, but
they shared it without an argument.

The supplies were consumed, and many a man's death
averted, whom hunger left alive. The guest was shown to
his bed, a soft one I am prepared to believe. If the citizens
had been hunting-birds, their crops would not have been
overstuffed, as the courses served to them will testify. They
all showed the mark of hunger, except young Parzival,
who now said good night and went to bed.

Were his candles tallow butts? No, they were a good deal
better than that. Now the handsome youth got into a magnificent bed regally adorned, not of poverty's sort, and with
a carpet spread before it. The knights he dismissed and
would not allow them to stand there waiting any longer.
Pages removed his shoes, and then he slept—until true sorrow summoned him and the rain of heart's tears from
bright eyes: these awakened the noble knight. This came
about as I shall now tell you.   192

The proper limits of womanhood were not broken. Restraint and modesty marked that maiden of whom a bit will
now be told. Distress of war and the deaths of dear supporters had forced her heart to break and her eyes to wake,
and she came now, not for such love as gains the name of
changing maids to women, but for help and a friend's advice. She wore raiment of combat, a nightgown of white
silk—what could be more battle-like than a woman coming
thus to a man?—and around her she had thrown a long
mantle of samite. She came because grief compelled her to.
Ladies-in-waiting, chamberlains, and whoever else served
her, she left them all asleep, and slipped softly without a
sound into the chamber where it had been arranged that

Parzival was sleeping alone. Around his bed the candle light was as bright as day. Her way took her up to his bed, and there before him, on the carpet, she knelt down. Neither he nor the queen had any notion   193 of passionate love, and the wooing here was of this fashion: the maiden was bereft of joy and the shame of it distressed her. Will he take her into his bed? Unfortunately he has no such skill. And yet it *was* done, skill or no skill, and with such conditions of truce that they did not join their bodies together. Little did they think of such a thing.

So great was the maiden's grief that many tears flowed from her eyes upon young Parzival, and he heard the sound of her weeping so that he awoke and gazed upon her. Both pain and pleasure befell him as he did so.

The young man raised himself up and said to the queen, "Lady, are you mocking me? You should kneel this way only to God. Be so kind as to sit down here beside me" —such was his request and his desire—"or lie here where I was lying. Let *me* lie wherever I can."

She said, "If you will do yourself honor and show such moderation toward me as not to wrestle with me,   194 I shall lie here right beside you."

Truce was at once declared by him and she crept into bed. It was still so dark that not a rooster was crowing, but, in fact, the chicken roosts were empty. Famine had shot the fowl off from them.

Courteously the lady rich in sorrow asked him if he would be willing to hear her lament. "I fear," she said, "that if I tell it to you it will prevent your sleep, and that would be to your harm. King Clamidê and Kingrun his seneschal have devastated our castles and land up as far as Pelrapeire. My father Tampenteire left me as a poor orphan in frightful straits. Kinsmen, lords, and vassals, rich and poor, were subject to me, a great and brave force of them, but half of them or more have perished in my defense. Wretched as I am, how should I be happy? Now it has reached the point where I am ready to kill myself before I surrender maidenhood and body to become Clamidê's wife. His hand slew Schentaflurs, whose heart bore   195

great knightly praise. He was a blossoming bough of manly
beauty, that brother of Liaze, and he knew how to hold
falseness in check."

At the mention of Liaze Parzival was full of sorrow, re-
calling his pledge of service, and his high spirits sank. Such
was the effect of his love for Liaze. To the queen he said,
"Lady, can anyone's consolation be of help to you?"

"Yes, Sir, if I could be free of Kingrun the seneschal. In
formal combat his hand has struck down many a knight of
mine, and he will be coming here again tomorrow. He
thinks his lord will lie at last in my arms. You have seen
my palace hall: it is not so high but that I will throw myself down into the moat before Clamidê shall have my
maidenhood by force. That way I will thwart his boast."

Then he said, "Lady, let Kingrun be a Frenchman or a
Briton or let him come from whatever land he may, you
shall be defended by my hand as far as in my power
lies."
                                                        196
The night came to an end and day arrived. The lady rose
and bowed and did not omit her great thanks. Then she
slipped away, and no one was so wise that he perceived her
going, except Parzival the fair. Nor did he sleep any longer.
The sun was swiftly climbing aloft and its brilliance pierced
the clouds. Then he heard the ringing of many bells, and
churches and minster were filling with the people whom
Clamidê had severed from joy.

The young man rose. The queen's chaplain sang Mass
for God and for his lady, and her guest could gaze at her
until the benediction was pronounced. Then he called for his
armor and soon he was cased in it. A brave knight he
proved, too, with true manly fighting skill. On came Clamidê's army with many a banner, and ahead of the rest rode
Kingrun swiftly on a horse of Iserterre. As I heard the
story, from the gates had issued also *le fils du roi* Gahmuret, who had the prayers of the citizenry, for   197
this was his first sword fight. He began his charge from
such a distance that from the shock of the onset the saddle
girths of both horses were broken and both horses recoiled
on their haunches. Those who had been mounted did not

forget their swords now: they found them right in their sheaths. Kingrun had wounds on his arms and chest. This joust taught him the loss of such renown as he had had up to this day of pride's vanishing. Such valor had been attributed to him that he was said to have brought down six knights opposing him on a single field of encounter. But Parzival with his brave hand paid him back so well that Kingrun Seneschal had the odd feeling that a catapult was raining rocks on him. But a different kind of assault laid him low: a sword rang right through his helmet. Parzival brought him down and planted one knee on his chest. Then Kingrun offered what he had never offered any man before: his guarantee of surrender.   198

He who fought with him would not accept his oath there on the battlefield but bade him go and take it to Gurnemanz.

"No, Sir, you would do better to kill me, for I slew his son; I took the life of Schentaflurs. God has bestowed much honor on you, and if people say that your strength has prevailed over me and that you have conquered me, you have had your success."

Then said young Parzival, "I will give you another choice. Make your surrender to the queen, to whom your master in his wrath has caused great sufferings."

"There I would also be lost. My body would be hacked with swords to bits as tiny as float in a sunbeam, for I have inflicted grievous harm on many a brave man inside there."

"Then go from this field to the land of Britain and take your oath of surrender to a maiden who because of me suffered pain that she should not have suffered if a certain person had known what was just. And tell her that, whatever may befall me, she will never see me happy until I avenge her and pierce a shield for her sake. Tell   199 Arthur and his wife, both of them, that my service is theirs, and all their retinue as well, and say that I will never come to them until I have purged myself of a shame which I bear in common with her who offered me her laughter—from which she suffered grievous pain. And tell *her* that I am her knight to serve her, bound to her in humble service."

To this command obedience was given, and the heroes were seen to part.

Back now came the citizens' comfort in battle to where his horse had been caught and held. Later those citizens were to be delivered by him. Uncertainty beset the outer army now that Kingrun had been defeated in battle. Parzival was now conducted to the queen, who embraced him and clasped him close and said, "I shall never be the wife of any man on earth unless it be the one I have just embraced." She helped in the removal of his armor and did not stint her service. After his great exertions 200 there was lean fare made ready. The citizens came in and swore homage to him, all of them, declaring that he should be their lord, and the queen declared further that he should be her *ami,* since he had won so fine a victory over Kingrun.

From the ramparts now two brown sails were espied, with a strong wind driving them into the harbor. Their cargoes were such as to rejoice the citizens, for these consisted of nothing but food. God in His wisdom had so ordained it. Down from the battlements they rushed and ran to the boats, a hungry crowd bent on plunder. They could well have flown like dry leaves, these famished and withered people whose flesh had no weight and whose skins were empty of padding. The queen's marshal proclaimed amnesty for the ships and announced he would hang any person that touched either of them. Then he escorted the merchants into the city and to the presence of his lord. Parzival ordered them to be paid double the price of their wares. The merchants were overwhelmed; never- 201 theless at that rate their wares were paid for. Now grease dripped into the citizens' fires; gladly would I be a soldier there now, for now no one there drinks beer, and they have wine and food aplenty. Then Parzival the pure did as I shall tell you. First, he portioned out the food himself in small lots and fed the good people whom he found there. Not wishing to have their empty stomachs overtaxed, he dealt out a proper share to each. They were pleased with his dispensation, and that night he gave them more, that gentle man without pride.

Asked if they wished to share one bed, both he and the queen said yes. He lay with such propriety as would surely not satisfy many a woman who was so treated nowadays. —To think that they will enhance their manners in order to torment a man, and adorn themselves especially for the purpose! Before strangers they are all modesty, but their hearts' desires belie whatever may be in their outward behavior. They exasperate their lovers in private with their tenderness. The faithful and constant man who   202 ever preserves moderation knows how to treat his beloved considerately. He thinks—as is indeed the truth—"I have served this woman all my years in hope of reward; she has accorded me consolation, for now here I lie. It would once have been enough for me if with my bare hand I might have touched her garment. If I took her now greedily, I myself should be false. Should I trouble her and broaden the shame of both of us?" —Sweet talk before sleeping suits ladies' ways far better. So lay the Waleis, and slight was his harshness. He whom they call "the Red Knight" left the queen a maiden. And yet she thought she was his wife, and as a sign of his love she next morning tied on the headdress of a matron. Then this virgin bride gave him castles and country, for he was the beloved of her heart.

Two days and the third night they were happy   203 with one another in their affection. To him there often came the thought of embracing her, as his mother had counseled him—and Gurnemanz too had explained to him that man and wife are one. And so they entwined arms and legs, if I may be allowed to tell you so, and he found the closeness sweet. The custom, old and ever new, dwelt with the two of them there, and they were glad and nowise sad.

Now hear also how Clamidê, approaching with might, was distressed by bad news. A squire whose horse's flanks were gashed from the spur thus began: "On the plain before Pelrapeire there has been a noble show of knighthood, and sharp too, at a knight's hand. The seneschal has been defeated, and Kingrun, commander of the army, is on his way to Arthur of Britain. The soldiers are still camped before the city as he ordered them when he went away. You and both your armies will find Pelrapeire well guarded. Inside there is a noble knight who wants nothing but battle. Your soldiers are all saying that the queen has sent for Ither of Kukumerlant from the Round   204 Table, for his weapons appeared in the joust and were borne gloriously."

Then the king said to the squire, "Condwiramurs is willing to have me, and I want her and her country. My seneschal Kingrun gave me a true report that they would surrender the city from starvation and that the queen would offer me her noble love."

The squire got nothing but hatred. The king rode ahead with his army. But they were met by a knight who was not sparing *his* horse either, and he reported the same thing. Then Clamidê's joy and knightly spirits sank with heaviness and he realized his great loss.

One of his vassals, a prince, then said, "Kingrun did not fight as a representative of all our bravery, he fought there for himself alone. Suppose he *has* been killed, are two armies supposed to give up on that account, this one and the one before the city?" He bade his master stop grieving. "We should make another try, and if they are willing to offer defense, we will give them plenty of battle yet   205 and put an end to their joy. Urge every man and kinsman on and attack the city with two flags. We can ride on horseback along the slope to meet them; the gates we can attack on foot. Then we'll make them pay for their merriment!"

This advice was given by Galogandres, Duke of Gippones, and he brought the citizens to great distress before he found death beside their outworks. So too did Count Narant, a prince from Uckerlant, and many another poor fellow whom they carried away from there dead.

Now hear further report about how the citizens looked to their fortifications. They took long tree trunks and drove stout pegs into them—these hurt the attackers—and suspended them by ropes. These logs were manipulated on wheels.[6] All this had been tested out before Clamidê at-

[6] I.e., on pulleys.

tacked them after Kingrun's defeat. Moreover, the wild
heathen fire[7] had been imported into the country along with
the food supplies. The engines outside were burned by it;
the movable towers and the catapults, and what-   206
ever advanced on wheels, battering rams and portable sheds
in the moats, the fire wiped them out.[8]

Kingrun the seneschal had arrived in the land of Britain
and found King Arthur at a hunting lodge called Karminal
in the forest of Brizljan. There he did as Parzival had bidden him when he was captured: he presented his oath of
surrender to Cunneware de Lalant. The maiden was delighted that her distress was faithfully lamented by him
whom people called "the Red Knight." The news was heard
everywhere. Then this conquered nobleman appeared before
the King, and to the latter and to all the company he stated
what had been enjoined upon him.

Keie was startled and grew red; then he said, "Is it you,
Kingrun? Alas! how many a Briton your hand has conquered, you, Clamidê's steward! Your captor may never
favor me, but you shall enjoy your office all the same, for
the stew kettle is subject to us, to me here and to you in
Brandigan. Help me by your valor to win Cunne-   207
ware's favor with good large doughnuts!" He offered her
no other compensation.

Let us leave this talk and hear what is happening back
where we left the story before.

To Pelrapeire came Clamidê, and great battles were not
avoided then. Those inside fought with those outside. They
had spirit and strength, those heroes were found gallant,
and thereby they won the field, Far out in front of them
fought their country's lord Parzival, and the gates stood
open. His arms swung to the dealing of blows and his sword
clanged through hard helmets. The knights he struck down

---

[7] The famous "Greek fire."

[8] The technical terms here are: 1. *ebenhoehe* ("equal height"), a
movable platform or tower of the same height as the wall being at
tacked (*turris ambulatoria*); 2. *mangen,* "catapults"; 3. *igel* ("hedge-
hog"), a battering ram with iron-studded head; 4. *katzen* ("cats"), a
portable shed or roof under which men operated the battering ram.

came to a bitter end, for this is what was done: at the gussets of their armor the citizenry took their revenge and stabbed them through the slits. This Parzival forbade them to do, and when they heard of his displeasure, they took twenty of them alive before they left the battle.

Parzival observed that Clamidê and his forces were avoiding knightly combat near the gates, choosing battle on the other side of the city. The youth of hardy heart   208 turned to that trackless area and made haste to circle around the city and get close to the king's banners. Now see! There Clamidê's soldiers earned their pay to their harm! The citizens fought till their hard shields were hacked right out of their hands. Parzival's own shield was riddled with shots and blows. But however little they profited from it, the attackers that saw this all gave him praise. Galogandres was carrying the king's banner—he knew how to spur an army on—but now he lay dead at the king's side. Clamidê himself was in danger, and woe befell him and his men. Then Clamidê forbade the attack, for the manhood of the citizens had had its effect and won the day.

Parzival the worthy knight ordered the captives to be well taken care of until the third morning. The outer army was in difficulties. The proud young master in his joy accepted the oath of surrender from the captives, saying, "Come back when I send you word, good people." He bade them keep their armor. Then they made their   209 way back to the army outside the city. Although they were flushed with wine, their comrades in the outer force said, "You must have suffered from hunger, you poor fellows." —"Don't waste your pity on us," answered the captive knights. "There is plenty of food inside there, and if you camped here for a year they could feed both you and themselves. The queen has the handsomest man for a husband that ever knightly service has known. He may well be of high lineage, he combines the honor of all knights."

When Clamidê heard this he rued his exertions for the first time. He sent messengers back into the city to ask who it was that shared his bed with the queen: "If he is of rank to do combat so that she has recognized him as fit to defend her and her country in battle with me, then let there be a truce in both armies."

Parzival was overjoyed that the message called for single combat, and the undaunted youth said, "Let my word of honor be my pledge that not a hand shall be raised within the inner army in my defense."   210

Between the moat and the outer army this truce was established. And then those smiths of battle put their armor on. The King of Brandigan mounted an armored Castilian horse, Guverjorz by name, which, together with precious gifts, had been presented to Clamidê by his nephew Grigorz, the King of Ipotente, from north across the Uker Sea. Le comte Narant had brought it, and two thousand fighting men besides, all in armor but without shields. Their pay was paid in advance for two whole years, if the adventure tells the truth, and Grigorz had sent him excellent knights, five hundred of them—each one wore a helmet bound upon his head—who knew a thing or two about fighting. Then Clamidê's army had laid siege to Pelrapeire by land and by sea, so that the citizenry had their troubles.

Out rode Parzival to the field of ordeal, where God was to indicate whether He meant to leave him King Tampenteire's daughter. Proudly he came riding. His   211
horse broke immediately into a gallop and from that into full career. The horse was well armored for trials, but over its iron covering lay a covering of red samite, while he himself displayed a red shield and a red gambeson. Clamidê began the attack. A short spear of unwrought wood he carried to fell his opponent in the joust, and with it he began his onrush from afar. Guverjorz leaped to the onset. Good was the jousting by those two beardless youths and faultless. Never did man or beast fight a harder fight. Both horses were steaming from weariness. They fought until their horses could endure no more and collapsed under them at the same moment. Then each tried for the fire in the other's helmet. They had no wish to be idle, there was work for them to do. Their shields flew in splinters as if someone were tossing feathers into the wind for fun. And yet Gahmuret's son was not weary in   212

any limb. Clamidê, however, thought the truce was being broken by those from the city and told his opponent to keep honor and stop this bombardment by catapults, for great blows *were* raining on him and they did seem like stones from catapults. But the country's master answered, "I think you are safe from catapults: my word of honor guarantees you from that. But if you had peace from my hands, no catapult would be beating your chest and head and thigh."

Over Clamidê came a weariness—all too soon, it seemed to him. Victory won and victory lost, so the struggle went back and forth. Yet King Clamidê was beheld in defeat as he was jerked to the ground. Parzival's grip was such that the blood gushed from his eyes and nose and made the greensward red. He uncovered his head, removing both helmet and coif of mail, and there was the defeated man awaiting the death blow.

The victor said, "Now my wife shall be free of you. Now learn what death is!"   213

"Oh no! noble knight and brave! By me your honor will be increased thirtyfold. Now that you have defeated me, what greater glory could come to you? Condwiramurs can well claim that I am the luckless man and that your fortune has the gain. Your country is delivered. As though someone were bailing out a boat till it is much lighter, so my power is fainter; manly joy has run thin for me. What, then, is the good of killing me? I must bequeath shame to all my descendants, while you have the glory and the gain. If you do any more to me it is pointless. I bear a living death since I am separated from her who by her power held fast my heart and my mind, although I gained nothing from her. Now, unhappy mortal that I am, I must yield her and her country to you."

Then he who had the victory thought of Gurnemanz' advice, that brave manhood must be quick to pity.   214
So he heeded that advice and said to Clamidê, "I will not let you go unless you take your oath of surrender to Liaze's father."

"No, no, Sir! I have done him grievous harm. I slew his

son. You mustn't do that to me. For Condwiramurs' sake Schentaflurs fought with me, and I would have died at his hand if my seneschal had not helped me. Gurnemanz de Graharz had sent him to the land of Brobarz with a doughty army's strength, and there fine knighthood was displayed by nine hundred knights that fought well—they all rode mail-clad horses—and twelve hundred fighting men that I found armored in battle, except for shields. I thought his force too great for me, but at the harvest he hardly got seed grain back. I have lost more warriors since. But now I lack both honor and joy. What more do you want of me?"

"I will soften your terrors. Go to the land of the Britons —there Kingrun has preceded you—to Arthur the   215 Briton. Assure him of my service, and ask him to lament with me an insult I sustained there. A maiden laughed on seeing me, and never have I so grieved over anything as that they beat her on my account. To that same maiden say that I am sorry, and take your oath of surrender to her so that you perform her commands, or else choose death here and now."

"If that is the choice, I will not argue about it," said the King of Brandigan, "I will start on the journey right now."

With that vow he departed, whose pride had betrayed him. Parzival the warrior went to where he found his exhausted horse and leaped onto its back—his foot had never reached for a stirrup yet—and the horse, turning in circles, scattered the shivered bits of shield around him. This outcome delighted the citizens, but the outer army was downcast. Their flesh and bones ached. King Clamidê was led to where his attendants were, and he had the dead conveyed on stretchers to their rest. The strangers left the   216 country. Clamidê the noble rode off toward the land of Löver.[9]

All the members of the Round Table happened to be together at Dianazdrun with Arthur the Briton, and if I haven't told you a lie, the plain of Dianazdrun had to get

[9] Löver represents a separate development, along with Logrois, of "Lloegr," the Welsh word for "England."

used to supporting more tentpoles than there are trees in the Spessart.[10] With such a retinue and with many ladies Arthur was encamped for Pentecost holiday. Many a banner and many a shield was to be seen there too, with individual coats of arms upon them,[11] and many a tent circle splendidly adorned. Nowadays this would be considered a marvel: who could provide the traveling apparel for so many ladies? And besides, any lady there would have considered her reputation lost if she did not have her *ami* along. —*I* wouldn't have done it for anything, with all those young fellows there. Even now I wouldn't like to bring my wife into such a large crowd: I would be afraid of the press of strangers. This one or that one might tell her he   217
was stung with love for her and that his passion was dimming his joy, that if only she averted his distress, he would be at her service forever. I would be in a hurry to get her away from there.

But I have been speaking about personal matters.—Now hear how the circle of Arthur's tents was distinguishable by itself. There the company, surpassing the others in sumptuous *joie,* ate in his presence, many a noble man devoid of falseness and many a maiden proud, for whom jouster friends were nothing but arrows to be sped against the foe; and if battle brought the man grief, their hearts were ready to recompense him with kindness.

Into that tent circle rode Clamidê the youth. His mail-clad horse and mail-clad self Arthur's wife saw, his helmet too, and his splintered shield, and all the ladies saw him, for that was the way he had come to court. You heard previously how he was forced to come. He dismounted, and great was the press around him until he was able to find Lady Cunneware de Lalant.

But then he said, "Lady, it is you whom I am   218
to have the honor to serve. True, I am largely forced to it. The Red Knight assures you of his service. He wants to assume the entire responsibility for the harm done to you.

---

[10] The Spessart (Wolfram's Sphehteshart) is a famous forest region in west-central Germany.

[11] I.e., of independent "guest" knights.

He also asks you to make complaint of it to Arthur. I
gather that you were beaten on account of him. Lady, I
bring you an oath of surrender. That was the command of
him who fought with me. I will be glad to take the oath
right now, if you will. My life was forfeit to death."

Lady Cunneware de Lalant grasped his iron-clad hand.
The Lady Ginover was sitting right there, dining with her
but without the King. And Keie was standing by the table
too, so that he heard this statement. It gave him a start, but
the Lady Cunneware was delighted.

Then he said, "Lady, whatever this man has done here
in your presence, he was downright forced to it. But I think
he has been misled. What I did, I did for the sake of
courtly usage, and hoped to improve you thereby. I earned
your hatred from it.—But I would suggest you have this
captive's armor removed. He may find this standing here a
bit tedious."

The maiden proud bade him take off his hel-   219
met and his coif of mail, and when they untied the one and
pulled back the other, then he was recognized as Clamidê.

Kingrun darted a glance of recognition at him, then began to wring his hands so they cracked like dry twigs.
Clamidê's seneschal pushed away the table and asked his
master what had happened. He found him empty of joy.

He said, "I was born for misfortune. I have lost a gallant
army. Never did a mother give her breast to one who has
experienced greater loss than I. The loss of my army I do
not regret so much, but the grief of losing love weighs me
down with such a weight that joy is a stranger to me and
high spirits an absent guest. Condwiramurs is turning me
grey. Whatever vengeance their Creator took on Pontius
Pilate[12] and on that sorry Judas who was ready with a kiss
when Jesus was betrayed, I would not refuse their torments if the Lady of Brobarz loved me and were   220
my wife. If I could once embrace her, I wouldn't care what
happened to me afterwards. But unfortunately her love is
far away from the King of Iserterre, and my country and

---

[12] Wolfram's text has "Pilatus von Poncia."

my people in Brandigan must forever be in sorrow.[18]
My uncle's son Mabonagrin also endured long suffering on
her account.[14] And now, King Arthur, I have ridden here
to your house, compelled by the hand of a knight. You are
well aware that many an offense has been committed against
you in my country. Forget that now, noble man. While I
am a captive here, free me from such hatred! May the Lady
Cunneware also shield me from danger, who accepted my
oath of surrender when I appeared before her in arms."

Arthur's faithful lips forgave him his guilt at once.

Now men and women learned that the King of Brandigan
had ridden into the tent circle. Press closer now, press
closer! The news was quickly spread about.

Courteously Clamidê the joyless asked for com-   221
pany: "Commend me to Gawan, Lady, if I am worthy of it,
for I know that he too would desire it. If he performs
your command, he will honor both you and the Red
Knight."

Arthur bade his sister's son[15] bear the king company—
but that would have come about in any case. Then the
conquered man free of falseness was graciously received
by the noble company.

To Clamidê Kingrun said, "Alas! that ever a Briton
should see you in defeat in his house! You were richer
than Arthur in vassals and possessions, and you have the
advantage of youth. Is Arthur to win credit because Keie in
anger beat a noble princess whose heart's wisdom chose by
her laughter the man truly destined for supreme glory?
These Britons think they can now hoist the bough of their
renown aloft. Without any effort on their part it has come
about that the King of Kukumerlant was sent back here
dead and that my master has conceded victory to the
man who fought against him. That same man de-   222

---

[13] Clamidê refers to himself. His capital city is Brandigan, but his
country is Iserterre, which is mentioned only here and, obliquely, in
196 above.

[14] Mabonagrin guarded the grisly garden in Hartmann's *Erec*. See
Footnote 26, p. 98.

[15] I.e., Gawan.

feated me too, and without any tricks. The people saw how
the sparks flew off our helmets and how the swords whirled
in our hands."

But now everyone, rich and poor alike, agreed that Keie
had behaved improperly.

Here we shall leave this story and return to our course.

⤜§§⤛

Out where Parzival was wearing the crown, the devastated
country was being rebuilt and joy and jubilation were to be
heard. His father-in-law Tampenteire had left him bright
jewels and red gold in Pelrapeire, and these he now divided
up, and was beloved for his generosity. With many
banners and fresh shields his country was adorned, and
many a tourney was fought by him and by his men. Along
the marches of his territory the youthful knight undaunted
more than once displayed his bravery, and his deeds toward
those outsiders were praised as the best possible.

Now hear also about the queen. How could she be any
happier? That sweet and noble young woman had   223
the utmost that could be wished for on earth. Their love
stood in such strength that no wavering could affect it. This
she had recognized in her husband, and each found it in
the other. He was as dear to her as she to him.

But if I take up the story now and come to where they
have to separate,[16] *there* will be grief for them both. And

[16] The interval of time indicated in the two preceding paragraphs
must, by the nature of the facts reported, be a matter of, at least,
months. Professor Weigand's shrewdly reasoned time analysis of the
total poem, however, demonstrates that Parzival passes some fifteen
months here in Brobarz, from the Pentecost and Maytime of one year
until the September of the following year. By the arbitrary selection
of the earliest possible date (March 20) for the Good Friday of Book
IX, we establish September 16 as the day of Parzival's departure from
Condwiramurs. But with any of the possible dates for Good Friday
the departure must, in any event, fall on some day between September
16 and latter October.

Chrétien's version presents all action as continuous—which is hu-
manly impossible—up to the Good Friday scene. Thus all of the hero's
experiences up to this point are, in the French tale, assigned only five

how sorry I feel for that noble woman. His hand had saved her people, her country, and herself from great tribulation, and in return she had offered him her love.

One morning he said courteously—many a knight heard and saw it—"If you will allow me, Lady, I will with your permission see how things are faring with my mother, for I know nothing at all as to whether she is well or ill. So for a brief time I will travel to her, and also for the sake of adventure, for, if I serve you well in that, your love will reward me for it." Thus he asked her for permission to depart.

He was dear to her, so the story says, and she had no desire to deny him. From all his vassals he then took his leave and rode away alone.

---

days, with the departure almost immediately following, perhaps on the morning of the sixth day.

BOOK·V

Whoever cares to hear what is the present destiny   224
of him whom Lady Adventure sent forth shall observe most
wondrous things. Let the son of Gahmuret ride on! Wherever there are people of good will, may they wish him well,
for great suffering lies in store for him, albeit joy and
honor also. One thing troubled him sorely, that he was
separated from her who was more beautiful and virtuous
than any other woman of whom lips had ever read or told.[1]
Thoughts of the queen began to trouble his mind, and he
might have lost it completely had he not been such a courageous man. The horse pulled the dragging reins over
fallen trees and through marshy land, for no one's hand
guided it. The story tells us that on that day he rode so
far that a bird could only with difficulty have flown all
that way. If the story has not deceived me, he did not travel
nearly so far on the day when he shot Ither nor, later,
when he came from Graharz to the land of Brobarz.

Would you like to hear how things go with   225
him now? At evening he came to a lake. There fishermen,
whose domain these waters were, had cast their anchor.
When they saw him ride up, they were close enough inshore to hear quite well what he said. One man he saw in

---

[1] Wolfram is thinking here of a narrator who either reads his story
from a book or simply tells it.

the boat whose apparel could not have been richer if all
lands had been subject to him. His hat was trimmed with
peacock feathers. Of this fisherman he made inquiry, asking
him to advise him in God's name and by the dictates of
his knighthood where he might find lodging for the night.

The sorrowful man replied and said, "Sir, I know of
neither land nor water for thirty miles around with human
habitation. There is only one house nearby, and in all good
faith I advise you to go there, for where else could you go
so late in the day? At the end of the cliff turn right and
ascend the hill. When you have reached the moat—there, I
guess you will *have* to stop—ask them to let down the
drawbridge for you and open the approaches."

He did as the fisherman advised and took his   226
leave. "If you do get there," the fisherman said, "I myself
will be your host tonight. You may thank me then, according to how you are treated. Be careful, though! Those
roads lead no one knows where. You can easily ride astray
on the slopes, and *that* I would be sorry to see."

Parzival set off and began to trot jauntily up the right
road till he reached the moat. There the drawbridge was
up and the castle well defended. It stood as though turned
on a lathe, and nothing, unless it flew or were blown by
the wind, could have harmed it by an attack. Its many turrets and halls had marvelous fortifications. If besieged by
all the armies on earth, these people would not in thirty
years have given so much as a loaf of bread for the trouble
it caused them.

A squire noticed Parzival and asked him what he wished
and where he had come from. "The fisherman sent me
here," he said. "I thanked him just for the hope of a
lodging. He said you should lower the drawbridge, and he
told me to ride straight in."   227

"Sir, you are very welcome. Since the fisherman gave you
his promise, and it was he who sent you here, we shall give
you all honor and comfort for his sake," the squire replied
and lowered the bridge.

In through the castle gates rode the bold lad, and into a
courtyard large and wide where short green grass grew

everywhere untrampled by knightly sports, for tourneys were not practiced there, and banners were as rarely seen flying above it as over the field of Abenberc.[2] Little gaiety had there been here for many a day; the knights were too sad of heart.

Yet they did not let Parzival feel this, and welcomed him, young and old alike. Many pages ran out to seize the bridle of his horse, each one trying to be the first, and held his stirrup for him to dismount. Some knights bade him enter the castle and led him to his chamber, where they quickly and skillfully removed his armor. When they then looked upon the youth, with his boy's face, still beardless, and saw how beautiful he was, they confessed that he was indeed richly blessed.

The young man asked for water and washed   228 the rust from his hands and from under his eyes. It seemed then to both old and young as though from him a new day shone, so handsome was this friend as he sat there. They brought him a cloak of flawless Arabian silk, and the fair youth put it on, leaving it open with the tie cords hanging loose; they praised him for so doing.

Then the courteous chamberlain said, "It was worn by Repanse de Schoye, my lady the Queen, but she is lending it to you since clothing has not yet been made for you.[3] I could ask this of her with good conscience, for if I have judged you rightly, you are a worthy man."

"May God reward you, Sir, that you say so. If you are right in your judgment, then I have been fortunate indeed. Such fortune is the gift of God."

They poured him drink and tended him. These sad knights were joyful with him and showed him all respect and honor. They had more provisions there than he had found in Pelrapeire, the land he saved from great distress.

His armor was removed and taken away. This   229 he regretted a moment later when he was made the butt of

[2] The fortress of Amberg near Schwabach, east of Wolfram's home town of Eschenbach.

[3] It was the custom to provide a guest with clothing especially made for him.

a jest which he did not understand. A man of the court, known for his ready wit, now invited the valiant guest to join his host, but in an all too arrogant tone, as though he were angry. For that he came near to losing his life at the hands of the young Parzival, who, finding his bright sword nowhere at hand, clenched his fist so tightly that the blood gushed out from beneath his nails and wet the sleeve of his cloak.

"O Sir, not so," said the knights, "he is a man who likes to jest, however sad we are like to be. Show yourself courteous toward him. He merely wanted to tell you that the fisherman has arrived. Go in—you are his honored guest —and cast off the burden of your wrath."

They went up to a great hall. A hundred chandeliers all aglow with candles gave light from above to the household assembled there, and little candles were burning all around on the walls. A hundred couches he saw there—servants whose duty it was had prepared them—and a hundred quilted coverlets lay on them. The couches, set   230 some distance apart, could seat four knights apiece, and in front of each lay a round carpet. Such luxury the *fils du roi* Frimutel could well afford. And another thing was not omitted, since they had not to count the cost—three square fireplaces made of marble, and in them fires were burning, of the wood called *lign aloe*.[4] Such great fires no one has ever seen here in Wildenberg[5] before or since. All those things were costly indeed. The lord of the castle was brought into the hall and placed, as he bade, on a cot facing the central fireplace. He had paid his debt to joy; his life was but a dying.

Into the great hall came the radiant Parzival, and he who had sent him there gave him a gracious welcome, bidding him stand no longer but come nearer and sit "here beside me. If I should let you sit farther away, I would be treat-

---

[4] Latin *lignum* (wood) + Greek *aloe,* the name of an aromatic East Indian tree. In the Middle Ages this wood was believed to have curative powers.

[5] Wildenberg is an actual castle in the Rhineland, presumably the seat of one of Wolfram's patrons.

ing you too much like a stranger." Thus spoke the sorrowful host.

He, because of his illness, kept blazing fires and   231
wore warm clothing. The jacket of fur and the cloak over
it were lined outside and in with sable skins wide and long.
The poorest skin was yet worth praise, for even *it* was
black and gray. On his head he wore a covering overlaid
inside and out with the same costly sable fur. An Arabian
border encircled its crown and in its center was a small
button, a glittering ruby.

There where sat many a valorous knight, Sorrow itself
was borne into their presence. In through the door dashed
a squire, bearing a lance in his hand. This rite sharpened
their sorrow. Blood gushed from the point and ran down
the shaft to the hand that bore it and on into the sleeve.
And now there was weeping and wailing throughout the
whole wide hall. The people of thirty lands could not have
wept so many tears. The squire bore the lance in his hands
all around the four walls until he reached the door again
and ran out. Stilled then was the people's mourn-   232
ing, called forth by the sorrow of which they had been reminded by this lance borne in the hand of the squire.

If it will not weary you, I shall tell you now with what
courtesy service was offered here. At the end of the great
hall a door of steel was opened and in came two maidens
of noble birth—now note how they are attired—so fair that
they could have given love's reward if any knight there
had earned it with his service. Each wore a wreath of
flowers on her loose-flowing hair[6] and bore in her hand a
golden candlestick in which was a burning candle. Their
hair was wavy, long, and fair—but we must not forget to
tell how they were dressed. The Countess of Tenabroc and
her companion wore gowns of brown wool, each drawn
tight with a girdle about the waist. Following   233
them came a duchess and her companion, their lips aglow
like the red of the fire, carrying two little ivory stools.
They bowed, all four, and the two set the stools in front

---

[6] Only married women wore head coverings, not young girls.

of the host. This service was performed to perfection. Then they stood in a group together, all four dressed alike and fair to see.

But look how quickly they have been joined by more ladies, four times two, who had a duty to perform. Four carried tall candles, the other four were not displeased to be the bearers of a precious stone so clear that in the day the sun shone through. It was a garnet hyacinth, long and wide, and he who measured it for a table top had cut it thin that it might be light to carry. At this sumptuous table the host ate. All eight maidens went straight to the host and bowed their heads before him. Four laid the table top on the snow-white ivory of the stools placed there before, and stepped back decorously to stand with   234 the first four.

The dresses these eight ladies wore were greener than grass, of samite from Azagouc, cut long and full, gathered in at the waist by long, narrow girdles, richly wrought, and each of the eight fair ladies wore a little wreath of flowers in her hair.

The daughters of Counts Iwan of Nonel and Jernis of Ril had come a distance of many miles to take service here. These two princesses were seen approaching now, most beautifully dressed. They carried two knives as sharp as fishbones, displaying them, since they were so rare, on two cloths, each one separately. They were of silver hard and white and wrought with cunning skill, so keenly sharpened they could very likely have cut even steel. Preceding the silver knives came other ladies needed for service here, four maids of a purity free from reproach, carrying candles that cast a gleam upon the silver. So they came forward, all six. Now hear what each one did.

They bowed, and the two who carried the sil-   235 ver knives approached and laid them down on the beautiful table. Then courteously they all withdrew and joined the first twelve. If I have counted right, there must be eighteen ladies standing there. *Ah vois!* Six more are now seen coming arrayed in costly garb, one-half of a silk that was interwoven with gold, the rest of pfellel-silk from Niniveh. They and the six who went before wore gowns alike, of priceless worth, each made of two fabrics combined.

After them came the queen. So radiant was her countenance that everyone thought the dawn was breaking. She was clothed in a dress of Arabian silk. Upon a deep green achmardi she bore the perfection of Paradise,[7] both root and branch. That was a thing called the Grail, which surpasses all earthly perfection. Repanse de Schoye was the name of her whom the Grail permitted to be its bearer. Such was the nature of the Grail that she who watched over it had to preserve her purity and renounce all falsity.

Before the Grail came lights of no small worth, 236 six vessels of clear glass, tall and beautifully formed, in which balsam was burning sweetly. When they had advanced a proper distance from the door, the queen and all the maidens bearing the balsam bowed courteously. Then the queen free of falsity placed the Grail before the host. The story relates that Parzival looked often at her who bore the Grail, yet thought only that it was her cloak he was wearing. The seven now withdrew, as was fitting, to join the first eighteen. Their noblest member they placed in the center, with twelve on either side, I was told, and the maiden with the crown stood there in all her beauty.

For the knights assembled in the great hall stewards were assigned, one for each group of four, all bearing heavy gold basins and followed by comely pages carrying white towels. Splendor enough was there to be seen. A hundred 237 tables—there must have been that many—were now brought into the hall, each was placed before four of the noble knights, and white cloths were spread carefully upon them. The host then took water for washing his hands—he had long since lost his joyful spirits—and Parzival too washed in the same water and, like his host, dried his hands on a bright-colored silk towel which a count's son on bended knee was quick to offer them. In the spaces between, where

[7] Wolfram frequently uses this phrase to describe the Grail. There is no one English word which reproduces adequately the meaning of the word *wunsch* in the original. It connotes an absolute ideal, the supreme good.

no tables were, four squires were stationed to serve those who sat at each table. Two of them knelt and carved; the other two brought food and drink and attended them zealously.

Listen now as I tell you more of this splendor. Four carts brought costly vessels of gold to every knight who was there. Around the four walls they were drawn, and four knights with their own hands placed the vessels on the tables, each one followed by a clerk whose duty it was to collect and count them later after the meal was   238 over.

Now listen and you shall hear more. A hundred squires, so ordered, reverently took bread in white napkins from before the Grail, stepped back in a group and, separating, passed the bread to all the tables. I was told, and I tell you too, but on *your* oath, not mine—hence if I deceive you, we are liars all of us—that whatsoever one reached out his hand for, he found it ready, in front of the Grail, food warm or food cold, dishes new or old, meat tame or game. "There never was anything like that," many will say. But they will be wrong in their angry protest, for the Grail was the fruit of blessedness, such abundance of the sweetness of the world that its delights were very like what we are told of the kingdom of heaven.

In small vessels of gold there were dressings for every dish: gravy, pepper sauce, and fruit broth. The temperate eater and the glutton too both had their fill. All were served with great courtesy, and whatever drink one held   239 out his goblet for, whatever drink he might name, mulberry juice, wine, or red sinopel, he found the drink in his glass, all by the power of the Grail, whose guests the noble company were.

Parzival did not fail to notice the richness and the great wonder, but for courtesy's sake he refrained from questions. "Gurnemanz counseled me in all sincerity not to ask many questions," he thought. "What if my stay here proves to be like my stay with him? Then without any questions I shall hear how this knightly company fares."

As Parzival was reflecting thus, a squire approached bearing a sword. Its sheath was worth a thousand marks, a ruby formed the hilt, and its blade seemed to be the source of great wonders. The host presented it to his guest and said, "Sir, I carried it often in the heat of battle before God wounded me. May it be your recompense if perhaps there is some fault in our hospitality. You are fit to wear it anywhere, and once you have tried it, you will find   240 it a sure defense in battle."

Alas that he did not ask the question then! I still sorrow for him on that account. For when the sword was put into his hand, it was a sign to him that he should ask. And I pity too his sweet host whom God's displeasure does not spare and who could have been freed from it by a question.

But now the feast was ended, and the attendants set to work to remove the tables and also the dishes, which they had loaded again on the four carts. Each maiden performed her task, those who had been the last now being the first. Once more they led the queen to the Grail, and she and all the maidens bowed courteously to the host and Parzival. Then they carried out again by the same door what they had brought in before.

Parzival gazed after them and saw, before they closed the door behind them, on a couch in an outer room, the most beautiful old man he had ever beheld. I say it and do not exaggerate—he was greyer even than mist.

Who he was you shall learn later. And you   241 shall hear from me, when the proper time has come, clearly and without any protest or delay, the name of the host, his castle, and his land. I tell my story like the bowstring and not like the bow. The string is here a figure of speech. Now *you* think the bow is fast, but faster is the arrow sped by the string. If what I have just said is right, the string is like the simple, straightforward tales that people like. Whoever tells you a story like the curve of the bow wants to lead you a roundabout way. If you see the bow and it is strung, you must admit the string is straight—unless it be bent to an arc to speed the shot. Of course if I shoot my tale at a listener who is sure to be bored, it finds no resting place, but travels a roomy path, namely, in one ear and out

the other. It would be labor lost if I annoyed such a one
with my tale. A goat would understand it better, or a rotten tree trunk.[8]

But I want to tell you more about this sorrow-   242
ful company to whom Parzival had come. Seldom did one
hear there sounds of joy, whether of bohourt[9] or dance.
They grieved so constantly that they had no thought for
pleasure. A smaller company than this often enjoys some
amusement now and then, and here every nook was filled
as well as the great hall. The host spoke to his guest and
said, "I think your bed is ready. If you are tired, I advise
you to go to bed now and sleep." Now I should cry Alas!
that they parted so. It portends ill for both.

The courteous Parzival rose up from the couch, and his
host bade him good night. The knights all sprang up from
their seats, and a group of them came to lead the young
man to his room. It was richly decorated, with a bed so
sumptuous that I am irked at my own poverty in a world
which contains such riches. There was no poverty   243
about that bed. A bright pfellel-silk covered it, the colors
glowing as if on fire. Parzival, seeing that there were no
beds save the one, bade the knights go to their rest. They
took their leave, and pages came in to assume their duties.
The many candles and his fair coloring glowed in rivalry
with each other. How could daylight be brighter? Beside
his bed stood a couch covered with a quilt. Here he sat
down while the nimble pages, all handsome youths of gentle birth, made haste to serve him. They drew off his shoes
and hose from his white legs and removed the rest of his
clothing too.

Then in came four fair maidens to see if the guest had
been properly tended and lay comfortable in bed. Each

---

[8] In comparing his story to the bowstring, Wolfram seems to be
claiming that he tells a straightforward tale with no digressions. But as
he develops the metaphor, he shows that the string has to be arched.
Thus it takes on even more of a curve than the bow itself. This is a
playful defense of Wolfram's own style, which was criticized by contemporaries for its digressiveness.

[9] The *buhurt* was jousting in groups.

was preceded by a squire, so the adventure told me, carrying a brightly burning candle. Parzival, the agile knight, leaped under the bed cover. "Please stay awake a 244 little longer for our sake," the maidens said. As in a children's game, Parzival had raced against time and won, but his bright face, as he peeped from under the covers, gladdened their eyes before he gave them greeting, and their hearts were moved at the sight of his mouth so red and the smoothness of his skin which showed not even half a hair, so young was he.

Hear now what each of these fair maidens bore. In their white hands three of them carried mulberry juice, wine, and claret, and the fourth brought, on a white cloth, fruits of the kind which grow in Paradise. She, the last, knelt down before him. He bade her be seated, but she replied, "It is better not, my lord. If I were to sit, you would not receive the service which I have been ordered to render you." He took of the drinks and ate a little, not neglecting to give them all a friendly word as he did so, and when they had left he lay down to sleep. Pages placed his candles on the carpet, and when they saw that he was asleep, they withdrew.

Parzival did not lie alone. Until the dawn of day 245 deep distress was his companion. Future suffering sent him its heralds in his sleep, so that his dream was no less terrible than his mother's dream in the night when she yearned after Gahmuret with such forebodings. His dream was stitched with sword thrusts round the hem, and in the center with mighty jousts. From the hurtling onrush of horses he suffered in his sleep great pain. Had he been awake, he would rather have died thirty times. Such was the wage which misery meted out to him.

These agonies awakened him. His very veins and bones were in a sweat. Daylight shone through the windows. "Oh, where are the pages," he said, "that they aren't here with me? Who will bring me my clothes?" So the warrior waited for them until once again he fell asleep. No one spoke and no one called. There was no one to be seen.

The morning was half spent before he again woke up,

and now the brave youth rose immediately. On   246
the carpet the noble warrior saw his armor lying and two
swords. The one his host had given him, the other was the
one from Gaheviez. Then he said to himself, "Alas, why
have they done this? True, I must put on my armor. While
asleep I suffered such pain that surely some ordeal must be
awaiting me today upon my waking. If my host is hard
pressed by foes, I'll gladly obey his command, and hers also
who of her goodness lent me this new cloak. Would that
it were her pleasure to accept my service! That would
please me well for her sake, though not for the sake of her
love, for my wife the queen is as fair as she, or fairer, that
is true."

He did as he had to do. He armed himself from his feet
up in readiness for battle and girded on the two swords.
Out through the door went the noble warrior, and there
was his horse tethered at the foot of the stair, shield and
spear leaned alongside. This was just as he wished.

Yet before Parzival the warrior mounted his   247
horse, he ran through many of the rooms, calling out for
the people, but not a one did he hear or see. At this he
burst into a passion of grief and anger. He ran out to
where he had dismounted the evening before upon arrival.
Here earth and grass were trampled down and the dew
drops scattered.

Screaming, the young man ran back to his horse and
mounted, scolding angrily the while. He found the gate
wide open and through it the tracks of many horses leading
out. No longer did he hesitate but rode briskly out onto
the bridge. A squire, hidden from view, pulled the rope so
sharply that the end of the drawbridge almost struck down
the horse as it sprang clear. Parzival looked back, intending
to ask what this meant.

"Ride on," said the squire, "and bear the hatred of the
sun. You are a goose. If you had only moved your jaws
and asked your host the question! But you weren't interested in winning great honor."

The guest shouted back, demanding an expla-   248
nation, but no answer came. He called again and again, but

the squire behaved quite as if he were sleeping as he walked, and slammed the portal shut. Too sudden a parting it is for him who has lost so much and who must now pay interest on his joy when the joy is a thing of the past. The dice had been thrown when he found the Grail, with sorrow as the stake, but it was a throw with *his* eyes,[10] without dice and without a hand to throw them. Grief may arouse him now, but it is a thing he has not been accustomed to, nor did he much long for it.

Parzival set off, following hard on the tracks which he saw, and thought to himself, "Those who rode before me must, I think, be fighting manfully today in my host's cause. If they but wished it, their ranks would not be weakened by my presence. I would not falter, but would help them in their need and so would earn my bread and this wondrous sword as well which their noble lord gave to me. I wear it now unearned. Perhaps they think I am a coward."

So he, the enemy of falsehood, followed the   249 horses' tracks. I grieve that he left this place. His adventures begin now in earnest. Presently the tracks began to grow fainter, for they who were riding ahead had gone different ways. The track, which had been broad before, now became narrow, and at last, to his great dismay, he lost it entirely.

Suddenly the valiant warrior heard the voice of a woman lamenting. From her the young man now heard tidings which filled his heart with grief. The ground was still wet with dew. Before him, in a linden tree,[11] sat a maiden whose faithfulness in love had brought her great distress. A knight, dead and embalmed, was leaning against her, clasped in her arms. Whoever should see her sitting thus and feel no pity, I would call heartless. Parzival turned his horse toward her, but did not recognize her, though she was his mother's sister's child. All earthly loyalty was like a fleet-

---

[10] This is a pun on the eyes of a person and the eyes of the dice.

[11] In fairy tales women are frequently found thus, and the Vienna manuscript of Wolfram's *Parzival* shows Sigune sitting in the linden tree.

ing breeze when weighed against the constancy one saw
in her.

Parzival greeted her and said, "Lady, I am grieved for
your longing and distress. If in anything you need my
service, I am at your command."

She thanked him, but sadly, in sorrow's fash-   250
ion, and asked him whence he came. "It is not wise," she
said, "for anyone to venture a journey into this wild region.
Grave harm can befall a stranger here. I have heard and
also seen how many have lost their lives here and found
their deaths in combat. Turn back if life is dear to you.
But tell me first where you spent the night."

"It is a mile from here or more. I never saw a castle so
magnificent, with all manner of riches. I left there just a
short while ago."

"You should not, with such a lie, make sport of one who
has trusted you," she said. "You bear the shield of a stranger. This forest may have been too much for you if you
rode here from cultivated land. For thirty miles around no
wood was ever cut nor stone ever hewn for any building,
save for one castle which stands here all alone. Rich it is in
all earthly perfection. He who diligently *seeks* it will not
find it, alas. Yet many do search for it. He who shall see
the castle must chance upon it unawares. I think,   251
Sir, it is not known to you. Munsalvaesche is its name, and
the kingdom of the lord of the castle is called Terre de
Salvaesche. The aged Titurel bequeathed it to his son. *Le
roi* Frimutel was the name of that brave warrior. Great
fame did his hand win, but at last he lay dead from a
joust done at the bidding of love. He left four noble children. Three of them, though rich, live in sorrow. The
fourth has chosen poverty, for the love of God making
atonement for sin. His name is Trevrizent. His brother
Anfortas can only lean, he cannot ride nor walk nor lie nor
stand. He is the lord of Munsalvaesche, and God's displeasure has not spared him. Sir," she continued, "if you
had indeed come there to that sad company, their lord
would have been freed from the suffering he has borne so
long."

The Waleis said to the maiden, "I saw great marvels there and many a fair lady."

By the voice she recognized the man and said, "You are Parzival. Tell me, did you see the Grail and its   252 lord, forsaken by joy? Let me hear good tidings. If he has been released from his evil, may you be blessed for that fortunate journey. You shall reign over all things, whatsoever the air touches, all creatures, tame and wild, shall serve you, and the utmost of power and riches shall be yours."

Parzival the warrior said, "How did you recognize me?"

She answered, "I am that maiden who once bewailed her sorrow to you and who told you your name. You need not be ashamed that we are kin, for it is your mother, my aunt, who makes us so. She is a flower of womanly virtue, pure without being washed by dew. May God reward you that you so grieved about my friend who for my sake died in combat. I have him here. Now perceive what sorrow God has given me through him, in that he should no longer live. He was an excellent man and kind. His death fell heavy on me then, and always since, day after day, I have mourned him anew unceasingly."

"Alas, what has become of your red mouth? Are you Sigune, who told me who I was, without dissembling? And your head—it is bare—what has become of   253 your wavy long brown hair? In the forest of Brizljan I saw you in all your loveliness though you were heavy with grief. You have lost your strength and color. This burdensome company you keep would weary me if it were mine. Let us bury this dead man."

For answer, the tears streamed down her cheeks and wet her gown. No such thought had come to her as the counsel Lunete[12] gave her mistress when she said, "Permit this man to live who slew your husband. He can give you recompense enough." Sigune desired no such recompense as do women who are fickle—but I shall speak no more of

[12] A reference to *Iwein* by Hartmann von Aue. Iwein had killed the husband of the heroine, Laudine. Her maid and confidant, Lunete, advises her to overlook that and take Iwein as her husband.

them. Listen, rather, to more about Sigune's faithfulness.

"If anything can give me joy," she said, "then only one thing, that he shall be released from his death agony, that sorrowful man. If you left deliverance behind you, you are indeed worthy of high renown. You are wearing his sword girded about you, and if you know its magic charm, you may engage in combat without fear. Its edges run exactly parallel to each other. It was wrought by Trebuchet,[18] of noble race. Near Karnant there flows a spring, and from it King Lac derives his name. The   254 sword will withstand the first blow unscathed; at the second it will shatter. If you then take it back to the spring, it will become whole again from the flow of the water. You must have the water at the source, beneath the rock, before the light of day has shone upon it—the name of this spring is Lac. If the pieces are not lost and you fit them together properly, as soon as the spring water wets them, the sword will become whole again, the joinings and edges stronger than before, and the signs engraved on the blade will not lose their shine. The sword requires a magic spell. I fear you forgot to learn it there. But if your mouth did learn the words, the power of fortune will sprout and grow with you forever. Dear cousin, believe me, all the wonders which you found there will render you allegiance, and exalted over the noblest men you can rightly wear the crown of bliss. You shall have all your uttermost wish on earth. There is no one so rich that he can compare with you in splendor if you did ask the question as was right."

He said, "I did not ask."   255

"Oh, alas, that my eyes behold you,"[14] the sorrowful maiden cried, "since you were too faint of heart to ask a question. Yet you saw such great marvels there—to think that you could fail to ask when you were in the presence of the Grail! You saw the many ladies free of falsity, the noble Garschiloye and Repanse de Schoye, the cutting silver and the bloody spear. Alas, why do you come to me? Dis-

---

[18] The famous smith of French romance.

[14] Sigune here changes, in addressing Parzival, from the intimate *du* ("thou") to the formal *ir* ("you"), indicating her displeasure.

honored and accursed man! You had the fangs of a ven-
omous wolf, so early did the gall[15] take root in you and
poison your loyalty. You should have felt pity for your
host, on whom God has wrought such terrible wonders,
and have asked the cause of his suffering. You live, and
yet are dead to happiness."

"Dear cousin mine," he said, "show me a friendlier
spirit. I shall make atonement if I have done anything
amiss."

"You may spare yourself the atonement," answered the
maiden. "I know well that you lost your honor and your
knightly fame at Munsalvaesche. You will get no other
answer from me." Thus Parzival parted from her.

He felt a deep remorse, the valiant hero, that   256
he had been so slow to question as he sat by the side of
his sorrowful host. His self-reproaches and the heat of the
day brought the sweat pouring from him. To get the cool
of the air he removed his helmet and carried it in his hand.
He also loosened his visor, and through the grime of the
rust his face shone fair. He came upon a fresh track where
before him went a well-shod charger and a horse not shod
at all.

The last, with the lady riding on it, he could see, and
he rode along on the path behind her. Her horse had long
since been pawned to misery; you could have counted all its
ribs through the skin. It was white as ermine, with a bridle
of hemp, and its mane hung down to its hooves. Its eyes
were sunk deep in their sockets and the poor beast looked
neglected and worn. It must often have awakened from
hunger at night, for it was as dry as tinder. It was a wonder it could walk at all. The gentle lady who rode it had
seldom taken care of a horse.

On its back was a very narrow saddle from   257
which saddlebow and bells were missing. The only addition
to the horse's harness was the increase in things that were

---

[15] The derivation of this word (Latin *galla*) is the same for English,
Middle High German, and Old French. It means a swelling in the
tissues of plants, caused by the attack of certain parasites and certain
aphids. Hence the association here with poison.

lacking. The sad, far from merry, lady had for her saddle-girth a hempen cord. She was of too gentle birth for that. Branches and thorns had torn her clothing, and Parzival saw how she had knotted the tattered strips of cloth together to conceal the holes, yet beneath, her skin shone through, whiter than a swan. Her clothing was nothing but knots, and where they had covered the skin he saw how white it was, but where the rags did not cover, her skin had been scorched by the sun. Whatever may have been the cause of her suffering, her mouth was still red, so glowing a color it could have kindled a fire. From whichever side one might approach her, that was her exposed side, but if one called her *vilan,* one would have done her great injustice, for actually she had very little on.[16]

Believe me, by your courtesy, the hatred she endured was undeserved. She had never forgotten her womanly virtue. I have told you much of her poverty, but why? With her, poverty is wealth. I would rather have her, bare and in rags, than many a well-dressed woman.

When Parzival greeted her she looked at him   258 and in that instant recognized him. He was the fairest in all lands, and by that she knew him. "I have seen you before," she said, "and that day was the source of all my suffering. May God give you more joy and honor than you, by your treatment of me, have deserved! Because of you my clothing is shabbier than when you last saw it. If you had not come near me then, no one would have doubted my honor."

"Lady," Parzival answered, "pay better heed against whom you direct your hatred. Never have you nor any other woman suffered shame at my hands—that would have been dishonor for me—since I first won my shield and learned the ways of chivalry. Yet I am grieved for your sorrow."

The lady rode on, weeping; the tears rolled down on her breasts which stood out white and round as if they had been turned on a lathe. Never was there a turner so skillful that

16 A pun on the Old French *vilan* ("low born," "peasant") and the Middle High German *vil an* ("much on").

he could have shaped them better. Lovely though she was as she sat there on her horse, yet Parzival the   259 warrior pitied her with all his heart as she tried with hands and arms to cover herself from his view.

Then he said, "Lady, in God's name let me serve you and take my gambeson as covering."

"Sir, though all my joy depended on it, I would not dare to touch it. If you want to save us from death, ride away and put distance between us. Not that I care what may befall me, but I fear lest you may meet your death."

"Lady, who would take our lives? God's power gave us life, and though a whole army should wish to take it away, you would see how I would defend us."

She said, "It is a noble warrior who wants to take your life. He is so keyed to battle that six of you would be hard pressed. Your riding with me disturbs me. Once I was his wife, but now, in my wretched state, I could not even be this hero's servant, so great is his anger against me."

"How many men does your husband have with him?" Parzival asked the lady. "If I took your counsel and fled, you might well condemn me. I would rather die   260 than learn to flee."

The naked duchess answered, "He has no one here except me, but that is small warrant of victory in a combat."

No part of her gown remained untorn but the knots and the hem of the collar, yet she wore, in all her poverty, the wreath of womanly purity. She was possessed of true goodness, so that there was no falsity in her.

Parzival put on his helmet again, ready to ride into battle, and tightened it, adjusting the visor so that he could see comfortably. At that moment his horse bent its head to the lady's mare and began to neigh. He who was riding on before Parzival and the naked lady heard the sound and angrily wheeled his horse around, almost forcing it off the path, to see who was riding beside his wife.

Poised for battle, Duke Orilus halted, ready to ride to the joust with a warrior's zeal. The spear he bore came from Gaheviez, with gaily colored shaft, the same colors as his armor. Trebuchet had wrought his helmet,   261 and his shield had been made in Toledo, Kaylet's land, with sturdy rim and boss. From Alexandria in the land of the heathen had come the fine pfellel-silk of the gambeson and surcoat which the proud hero wore. The covering for his horse was made in Tenabroc of close-welded metal rings, and, a sign of his pride, over the iron cover lay a splendid pfellel-silk which anyone could see was costly. Rich, yet light in weight were his greaves, gorget, and coif of mail. Iron kneeguards too the brave fighter wore, made in Bealzenan, chief city of Anjou. The naked lady who rode so sadly behind him wore garments very unlike his, but she had indeed no choice of anything better. His breastplate had been forged in Soissons, and his horse came from Lake Brumbane in Munsalvaesche.[17] His brother, King Lehelin, had won it there in a joust.

Parzival, no less prepared, rode his horse at a   262 gallop toward Orilus de Lalander, upon whose shield a dragon faced him as if it were alive. A second dragon, fastened to the helmet, reared its head, and many tiny dragons of gold, with insets of rare stones and rubies for their eyes, decorated his gambeson and the trappings of the horse. And now the two brave heroes, riding back, measured a long distance for the charge. Great splinters, freshly broken, sprang into the air at their clash. I would boast of it if I had seen such a joust as this tale has told me of. Then the two horses were set at full career, and even Lady Jeschute thought in her heart that she had never seen a more beautiful joust. She stood there watching and wringing her hands, for, bereft of joy, she wished neither man any harm.

Both strove for victory, and the horses were   263 bathed in sweat. The flashing of the swords, the blaze that sprang from the helmets, and the sparks from many a mighty blow lighted up the air about, for the best of heroes, renowned and bold, were met here in combat, whether the end be for good or for ill. Alertly responsive as the horses

17 Wolfram says here, *Salvasche ah muntane*. This is simply a rearrangement of the word *Munsalvaesche*.

were that both were riding, they used their spurs to urge them on, nor were their bright swords idle.

Parzival deserved great honor that he could thus defend himself against one man and a hundred dragons too. One dragon was sorely wounded, the one in Orilus' helmet. Many rare stones, so clear that the day shone through them, were hammered out of it. And this was a fight on horseback, not on foot! [18] The hands of a fearless hero, with the play of his sword, won for Lady Jeschute once more the friendly greeting of her husband. With such impact of blows the two dashed against each other so often that the rings, though of iron, burst from their kneeguards. If you will permit me to say it, they fought a valiant fight.

I shall tell you why the one was so angry. Because his well-born wife had once been assaulted. Yet he was her proper lord to whom she should look for protection. He fancied her woman's heart had turned away from him and that she had betrayed her purity and honor with another lover. This disgrace he felt to be his own and passed so harsh a judgment on her that, barring death, never did a woman suffer greater misery—and through no fault of hers at all. He could deny her his favor if he wished. No one could hinder that, if husbands have authority over their wives.

But Parzival, the bold warrior, meant to regain Orilus' favor for Lady Jeschute by means of the sword. In this sort of thing I have usually heard friendly requests, but these two were far from having such charming manners. I think they are both in the right. If He who created both, the crooked and the straight, can decide the issue, may He so turn the struggle that it end without death to either. They are already doing enough harm to each other.

The battle was sharp and hard, each staunchly 265 defending his knightly renown against the other. *Le duc* Orilus de Lalander fought as one who had learned the art well. I suppose there was never a man who had fought so

18 This was a *tour de force;* the swordfight was customarily fought on foot.

much. He fought with the strength and skill which had often given him the victory in many a battle such as this. Confident of that, he seized the strong young Parzival in his arms, but the latter, quick as a flash, closed with him, jerked him out of his saddle, caught him under his arm like a sheaf of oats, and springing from his horse, flung him down over a fallen tree and held him there. Then one who had never been accustomed to defeat had to learn what it meant.

"You are reaping the reward for all that this lady has endured because of your anger. Now you are lost unless you receive her again into your favor."

"That won't happen quite so fast," said Duke Orilus. "I am still unconquered."

Parzival the noble warrior gripped him so hard that a rain of blood spouted through his visor. Thus this hero was forced to grant what was demanded of him, and, 266 as he had no wish to die, he said to Parzival, "Alas, strong youth, what have I done to deserve that I should lie dead before you?"

"I will gladly let you live," said Parzival, "if you will grant this lady your favor."

"That I will not do. Her guilt toward me is far too great. She was held in high esteem, yet she forfeited this and plunged me into despair. Anything else you ask I will gladly do if you grant me my life. That I once received from God; now your hand has become His messenger, and I shall owe it to your honor as a knight." Thus Orilus spoke and added shrewdly, "I will pay a good price for my life. My brother, who is rich and powerful, wears the crown of two lands. Of these take whichever you choose if only you do not slay me. He loves me and will ransom me for whatever payment I agree upon with you. I will also take my duchy from you as my fief and acknowledge you my liege lord. Your knightly renown has won great honor 267 through me. Now release me, brave warrior and bold, from a reconciliation with this woman and demand of me something else which will do you honor. With the dishonored duchess I shall not make peace no matter what may happen to me."

Parzival the noble-spirited said, "Neither people nor lands nor the possessions of this world can help you if you do not give me your surety that you will ride to the land of Britain, and in no wise delay your journey, to a maiden who because of me was beaten by a man on whom, unless she plead for him, I shall yet have revenge. You shall pledge allegiance to that high-born maiden and assure her of my service, or you shall die here and now. And to both Arthur and his wife give the same assurance, and ask that they reward my service by making recompense to the maiden for the blows she suffered. Moreover, I wish to see this lady restored to your favor in true reconciliation. If you refuse, you shall ride away from here, dead, on a bier. Mark my words and give me your oath that you   268 will suit your action to them."

Then Duke Orilus replied to King Parzival thus, "If ransom paid cannot release me, then I must needs do what you ask, for I do wish to live."

For fear of her husband the lovely Lady Jeschute shrank from separating the contestants. Yet she grieved for her foe's plight. Parzival allowed him to rise when he promised reconciliation with Lady Jeschute.

Then the conquered hero said, "Lady, since this my defeat in battle came about because of you—well, come here, you shall be kissed. I have lost great honor for your sake. What matter? That is a thing of the past."

The lady, naked as she was, leaped swiftly from her horse to the grass, and not caring that blood from his nose had reddened his mouth, she kissed him as he had commanded.

The three tarried there no longer, but rode to a hermit's cave in the wall of a cliff. There Parzival found a casket with holy relics and, leaning beside it, a spear painted in bright colors. The hermit's name was Trevrizent.

Then Parzival did as a man who is true must   269 do. He took the holy casket and swore an oath upon it of his own free will. And he framed the oath thus, "Upon my honor as a knight—whether I have honor myself or not, whoever sees me bear my shield will know me a member of knighthood's order—the power of this name, so the code of chivalry teaches us, has often won great fame and its name is still exalted today. May I stand disgraced forever before the world and all my honor be lost, and as pledge for these words let my happiness, with my deeds, be offered here before the Hand Supreme—that, I believe, God bears. May I suffer shame and scorn forever by His power, in body and in soul,[19] if this lady did do anything amiss when I snatched her brooch from her and took her golden ring as well. I was a fool then, not a man, and not yet grown to wisdom. Many tears did she shed, and she sweat in anguish at what she suffered there. She is truly an innocent woman. Of this let all my happiness and all my honor serve as pledge. I pray you, believe in her innocence. See, 270 here is her ring. Give it back to her. Her brooch was given away and lost—I have my own folly to thank for that."

The valiant warrior accepted the gift and, wiping the blood from his mouth, he kissed his heart's beloved. Then Orilus, the famous prince, put the ring on her finger again and gave her his cloak to cover her nakedness. It was of fine pfellel-silk, wide and full, and if torn, it was by the hand of a hero.

I have seldom seen ladies wearing warriors' cloaks which were so rent from battle. Never did Jeschute's battle cry summon knights to a tourney, or cause a spear to be broken when one took place. The good squire and Laembekin would be better at organizing a joust.[20] Thus the lady was freed from her sorrow.

Prince Orilus then said to Parzival, "Hero, your unforced oath gives me great joy and little pain. I have suffered a defeat which has brought me happiness. Now I can with all honor make amends to this noble woman for cast- 271

[19] What Wolfram says here is "in both lives," meaning this life and the life hereafter. The Middle High German word for life, *lip*, means both body and soul.

[20] This puzzling sentence may refer to a lost story in which these characters played a part.

ing her out from my favor. Since I left her alone, the sweet, how could she help what befell her? But when she talked of your beauty, I thought you were her lover. May God reward you that she is free of falsehood. I have done her a great wrong. I had ridden out that day into the *jeune bois* on this side of the forest of Brizljan."

Parzival took away with him the spear he had found. It had come from Troyes; the wild Taurian, brother of Dodines,[21] had left it standing there. Now tell me, where and how will our heroes spend the night? Their helmets and shields had suffered damage; one could see they were hacked to pieces. Parzival took farewell of the lady and her beloved. The wise prince invited him to share his hearth, but ask as he might, it did him no good. And so the heroes parted.

Lady Adventure told me a further tale, how when Orilus of great renown came to where his tent and a part of his retinue were, the people rejoiced with one accord that their lord was reunited with the kind and gracious duchess.

Without further delay Orilus' armor was re-   272
moved, and he washed off the blood and grime. Then taking the lovely duchess by the hand, he led her to the place of reconciliation, where he ordered two baths prepared for them. And then Lady Jeschute lay weeping beside her beloved, not from grief but for love, as is the way of good women.

Everyone knows: Eyes that weep, mouth that is sweet. Of that I would say more. Great love is born of joy *and* sorrow both. If you lay the story of a love upon the scales to weigh it, you will find that this cannot be otherwise. A true reconciliation took place there—that I do believe.

Then they went to their separate baths. Twelve fair maidens one could see with her. They had tended her ever since she, though guiltless, bore the wrath of her beloved husband. At night she had lain well covered, however threadbare she had ridden by day. They bathed her now, rejoicing.

---

[21] Taurian and Dodines are knights of the Round Table mentioned in other romances.

Now would you like to hear how Orilus heard the news of Arthur's journey? A knight informed him   273 thus, "I saw a thousand tents or more pitched on a field. Arthur, the rich and noble King, lord of the Britons, is encamped not far from us here with a host of lovely ladies—perhaps a mile cross-country. A loud throng of knights is there too. Down by the Plimizoel they are camped, on both banks of the river."

Duke Orilus hastily left his bath, and fair Jeschute too, the sweet and gentle, left her bath and went straightway to his bed. There they found release from sorrow, and her limbs earned a better covering than they had worn for many a day. In close embrace they found unchanged the joyous rapture of their love.

Then the maidens came to dress their lady, and Orilus' armor was brought to him. Jeschute's dress was something to admire. And with good appetite they ate birds which had been caught in snares. As they sat there together on their couch, Lady Jeschute was kissed more than once, and it was Orilus who kissed her.

Then they brought for the lovely lady a beau-   274 tiful, strong horse, well-paced, richly bridled and saddled, and lifted her up that she might ride away with her brave lord. His horse was quickly clad in armor just as when he had ridden to combat. The sword with which he had fought that day was hung on the saddlebow.[22] Armed from head to foot Orilus stepped to his horse, and there, where his duchess was waiting, he sprang to the saddle, and he and Jeschute rode away. He bade all his retinue return forthwith to Lalant, but first to wait for the one knight who was to show him the way to Arthur. They came so near to Arthur that they could see his tents stretching out downstream for nearly a mile. Then the lord sent the knight who had shown him the way there back to the company.

Fair Lady Jeschute was his retinue, and no one else besides. The kindly, modest King Arthur had gone to an open meadow where he ate his evening meal, and around him

---

[22] Orilus as a defeated knight may not wear the sword at his side.

sat his court of noble knights and ladies. Orilus, true to his
word, came riding up to the circle. His helmet   275
and shield were so cut to pieces that no one could recognize
the markings on them. Parzival had dealt these blows.

The brave man dismounted, while Lady Jeschute held
his reins. A crowd of pages came running up and thronged
close around them both. "We will see to the horses," they
said.

Orilus the noble warrior laid his battered shield on the
grass and asked after her for whose sake he had come.
They showed him where she was sitting, Lady Cunneware
of Lalant, and praised her courteous ways. In full armor he
approached, and the King and Queen greeted him. He
thanked them and made his pledge of fealty to his fair
sister.

By the dragons on his cloak she had recognized him perfectly well, but was in doubt about one thing, for she said,
"You are a brother of mine, either Orilus or Lehelin. I
shall take no pledge from either of you. You were always
ready to serve me, both of you, when I asked you. It would
mean 'checkmate' to my loyalty if I dealt with you as a
foe and thus betrayed my own courtesy."

The hero knelt before the maiden and said,   276
"What you have said is true. I am your brother Orilus. The
Red Knight forced me to give my word that I would pledge
fealty to you, and with that word I bought my life. Accept
my pledge so that what I promised him may be fulfilled."
Then she took, in her white hand, the oath of loyalty from
him who wore the dragon. Having done so, she set him free.

After that had taken place, he rose and said, "In loyalty
to you I shall and must protest. Who has beaten you, alas?
Blows given you will always grieve me. When the time
comes for me to avenge them, I shall show anyone who
wishes to see that they are also an affront to me. And the
bravest man that ever a woman brought into the world
shares my indignation. He calls himself the Red Knight.
My lord the King and my lady the Queen, he sent to you
both the assurance of his service, but most especially to my
sister. He asks that you reward his service by making

recompense to this maiden for the blows she has received. I would have fared better at the hand of this dauntless hero had he known how close my ties with her and how her suffering touches me."

Now Keie earned fresh hatred from the   277 knights and ladies sitting there on the bank of the Plimizoel. Gawan and Jofreit, *le fils d'*Idoel, and he whose misfortunes you have already heard, the vanquished King Clamidê, and many another noble man—I could name them, but I do not wish to make this too long—all began to throng around. Their service was accepted courteously. Lady Jeschute was fetched from her horse, on which she was still sitting. King Arthur and also the Queen, his wife, bade her welcome, and many of the ladies kissed her in greeting.

Arthur said to Jeschute, "Your father, Lac, King of Karnant, I knew for a gallant man, and I have grieved for your trouble from the time I was told of it. And you yourself are so lovely your friend should have spared you that. The prize was yours at Kanedic for the brightness of your beauty. You won the hawk because you were so fair, and it rode away on your hand. However great the wrong done me by Orilus, I did not wish you any suffering,   278 and I shall always be grieved if anything happens to you. I am pleased to see you restored to favor and, after your great ordeal, wearing garments befitting a lady."

"Sir," she said, "may God reward you! With these words you enhance your honor."

Then Lady Cunneware de Lalant led Jeschute and her *ami* away. On the field off to one side of the royal circle of tents, and right above the source of a spring, stood her tent. At its peak was a dragon that looked as though he had the top in his claws, grasping the half of the apple-shaped knob of the tent. From the dragon four ropes were strung down, just as if he were alive and flying and were pulling the tent up into the air. By this Orilus recognized it, for the arms he bore were the same. In the tent he removed his armor, and his sweet sister could offer him honor and comfort.

But all the knights were saying that the might of the Red

Knight had gained a companion, renown. This they said and not in whispers.

Keie asked Kingrun to serve Orilus in his stead. Kingrun could easily do it, for he had often done 279 such service for Clamidê in Brandigan. Keie gave up his office because his evil star had caused him to thrash the duke's sister too roundly with his staff. So for courtesy's sake he withdrew. Besides, the high-born maiden had not forgiven him this offense. But he prepared food in abundance, and Kingrun served it to Orilus. Cunneware, who knew what was viewed with approval, cut the food for her brother with her soft, white hands, and Lady Jeschute of Karnant ate with ladylike delicacy.

Arthur the King did not neglect to come to where the two were sitting and eating together like lovers, and he said, "If you do not eat well tonight, it will not have been my fault. You have never sat at the table of a host who offered you bread with a better will and a heart so free from faithlessness. My Lady Cunneware, care for your brother well. May God give you a good night!"

Then Arthur went to his rest, and Orilus was so bedded that his wife Jeschute could bear him company until the next day dawned.

BOOK·VI

Would you like to hear now why Arthur left his 280
country and his castle at Karidoel? He had followed the
counsel of his retinue and, with noble knights of his own
and of other lands, so the story says, he was now riding for
the eighth day in search of him who called himself the Red
Knight, that same knight who had done him the honor of
delivering him from great distress by slaying King Ither
and by sending Clamidê and Kingrun, each one singly, to
the Britons and to his court. He wished to invite him to
become one of the company of the Round Table, and for
this reason rode in search of him.

He had made the following decree: All those who belonged to the profession of knighthood, both the lowly and
the powerful, had to pledge in Arthur's hand that whatever
knightly deeds they might see, they would, by virtue of this
oath, refrain from any joust unless they asked him for his
permission to fight.

"We must ride into many a land," he said, "where
knightly deeds may well challenge us. Upraised 281
spears we shall certainly see. If you then vie with each other
and rush out like wild mastiffs whose master slips their
leash, that I do not wish. I shall prevent such turbulence.
But I will help you when there is no other way. You may
rely on my valor."

This was the oath, as you have heard it. Now will you hear where his journey has taken Parzival the Waleis? That night fresh snow had fallen thick upon him. Yet it was not the time for snow, if it was the way I heard it. Arthur is the man of May, and whatever has been told about him took place at Pentecost or in the flowering time of May. What fragrance, they say, is in the air around him! But *here* this tale is cut of double fabric and turns to the color of snow.

Arthur's falconers from Karidoel had ridden out in the evening for hawking along the Plimizoel and had suffered the misfortune of losing their best falcon. It had suddenly taken flight and remained in the woods all night. This came of overfeeding, for it spurned the food put out to lure it. All night it stayed near Parzival, for the forest   282 was strange to both, and they very nearly froze.

When Parzival saw the daylight, he found his pathway covered over with snow and rode then at random over fallen tree trunks and stones. The day steadily shone brighter, and the forest began to thin out into a meadow, level except for one fallen tree toward which he slowly rode, Arthur's falcon following along. Resting there were perhaps a thousand geese, and a great cackling went up. Like a flash the falcon darted among them and struck at one so fiercely that it barely managed to escape under the branches of the fallen tree. Pain no longer let it fly.

From its wounds there fell upon the snow three red drops of blood. These brought Parzival great distress, from the trueness of his love. When he saw the blood-drops on the snow which was so white, he thought, "Who created this color so pure? Condwiramurs, this color does in truth resemble you. God must wish to give me fullness of bliss, since I have found here something which resem-   283 bles you. Honor be to the hand of God and to all His creatures! Condwiramurs, here lies your image, for the snow offered the blood its whiteness, and the blood reddens the snow. Conwiramurs, your *beau corps* is like these colors. That you must confess."

From the way the drops lay on the snow, the hero's eyes

fancied two as her cheeks and the third as her chin. His love for her was true and knew no wavering. And thus he mused, lost in thought, until his senses deserted him. Mighty Love held him in thrall. Such distress did his own wife bring him, for she had the very same colors, the Queen of Pelrapeire. She it was who robbed him of his senses.

So he remained still as if he were sleeping. And who came running up to him there? A squire of Cunneware's had been sent out on an errand to Lalant. Just then he saw a helmet with many wounds and a much-battered shield. And there was a warrior in armor—in the service   284 of the squire's lady[1]—with spear erect, as if he were waiting to do combat. The squire quickly retraced his steps. If he had recognized him as his lady's knight, he would not have raised such a hue and cry. He urged the people out to attack him as if he were an outlaw. He wanted to do him harm, but he lost thereby his name for courtesy. Never mind, his lady was also thoughtless.[2]

"Fie upon you, fie, you cowards," cried the squire. "Do Gawan and the rest of this company of knights deserve knightly honor, and Arthur the Briton?" So cried the lad. "The Round Table is disgraced. Someone has ridden your tent ropes down."

Then there was a great clamor among the knights. They all began to ask whether a battle were going on. When they heard that a single man was there ready for combat, many a one regretted the oath he had given to Arthur. Quick as a flash, not walking, up leaped Segramors, always eager for a fight, and broke into a run. Whenever he sus-   285 pected a fight, they had to tie him hand and foot or he would be in the midst of it. Nowhere is the Rhine so wide but if he saw combat on the opposite shore there was no feeling if the bath were warm or cold—in he plunged, the reckless warrior.

Speedily the youth arrived at court in Arthur's circle of tents. The worthy King was fast asleep. Segramors ran in

[1] Parzival is serving Cunneware, who is the squire's lady.
[2] What Wolfram means by this is not explained in the poem. Cunneware always behaves very properly.

among the tent ropes, burst through the doorway of the tent, and snatched off the sable cover from the King and Queen as they lay there sleeping sweetly. They were awakened, yet they could not help laughing at his impudence.

"Ginover, my lady the Queen," he said to his mother's sister, "everyone knows we are kin, and far and wide it is known that I can count on your favor. Now help me, Lady, speak to Arthur your husband and say he must grant me this—there is an adventure nearby—that I be the first to the joust."

Arthur replied to Segramors, "You promised   286 me on your oath that you would abide by my will and hold your folly in check. If you engage in a joust here, then many another man will ask me to let him ride out to combat and seek for fame in battle, and my own defense will be weakened. We are nearing the host of Anfortas which rides out from Munsalvaesche to defend the forest in combat. Since we do not know where the castle lies,[8] things might well go hard with us."

But Ginover pleaded with Arthur so well that Segramors' wish was granted. When she won him this adventure, he would have done anything in return—except perhaps die for joy. Not for the world would he have given anyone a share in the adventure and his coming glory, that proud youth, still beardless.

Both he and his horse were armed, and away rode Segramors *le roi.* Galloping *par le jeune bois,* his horse leaped over tall underbrush, and many a golden bell rang on the horse's trappings and on the man. One could have thrown him into the briars like a falcon to start   287 the pheasant. If you wanted to look for him in a hurry, you would find him by the loud jingling of the bells.

So the reckless hero rode toward him who was so completely in thrall to love, but refrained from blow or thrust until he had given him his challenge. Parzival remained rooted to the spot, lost to all around. Such was the power of the three blood drops and of that relentless love—which often robs me also of my senses and disquiets my heart. O,

[8] No one knows where the castle of the Grail is.

the grief one woman is causing me! If she wants to vanquish me thus and seldom give me succor, then she may
take the blame and I shall flee from any solace she may
offer.

Now hear about those two knights, how they met and
how they parted. This was what Segramors said, "You behave, Sir, as though you were pleased that a king with his
following is encamped so near. For all that you take it so
lightly, you will have to pay him dearly for that, or I shall
lose my life. In your search for combat you have ridden too
close to us. Yet for courtesy's sake will I beg you to give
yourself into my power, else you will make me such swift
restitution that your fall will make the snow fly.   288
You would do better to make an honorable peace before."

Parzival made no response in spite of the threat. Lady
Love was speaking to him of other cares. The bold Segramors wheeled his horse around to gain the proper distance
for the charge. At that Parzival's Castilian also turned, and
the eyes of the fair Parzival, who had been sitting there in
a trance, staring at the blood, were turned away from the
drops. Whereby his honor was restored. When he saw the
drops no longer, Lady Reason gave him his senses back
again.

Here came Segramors *le roi*. Parzival lowered his spear,
the spear from Troyes, firm and tough and gaily colored,
which he had found outside the chapel. He received one
thrust through his shield, but his return thrust was so
aimed that Segramors, the noble warrior, was forced to quit
the saddle. But the spear which taught him what falling
was remained whole. Without a word Parzival rode back to
where the blood drops lay, and when his eyes found them,
Lady Love drew her chains tightly about him and   289
he spoke no word at all, for he had parted again from his
senses.

Segramors' Castilian set off for its stall, while he himself
had to stand up to rest, that is, if he wanted to go and
rest at all. Most people lie down to rest, you have heard
that often enough. But what rest could he get in the snow?
—I, for one, would find it very uncomfortable. It has al-

ways been thus—the reward for the loser is scorn, for the victor the help of God.

The army was encamped so near that they saw Parzival halt and stay motionless as before. He had to acknowledge the triumph of Love, which vanquished even Solomon. It was not long before Segramors returned to camp, as amicable to those who hated him as to those who wished him well—he rewarded them all with abuse.

"You know very well," he said, "that fighting is a game of chance and that a man can fall in a joust. A ship can sink, too, in the sea. I tell you there is no doubt he would never have dared to face me if he had recognized my shield. But then he was too much for me, he who is still   290 waiting there for combat. Well, even he is worthy of praise."

The brave Keie straightway brought this news to the King, how Segramors had been unhorsed and how a sturdy youth was waiting out there, still intent on combat. "Sir," he said, "I shall always regret it if he gets away without being punished. If you think me worthy, let me attempt what he wants, since there he waits with spear erect, and that in the presence of your wife. I can remain no longer in your service, and the Round Table will be dishonored, if he is not checked in time. His challenge is a threat to our fame. Give me leave to fight. If we were all blind or deaf, you would have to defy him yourself—and that very soon."

Arthur gave Keie permission to fight, and the seneschal was armed. He meant to use up the forest for spears against the unbidden guest. Yet the stranger already bore the heavy burden of love; snow and blood had laid it upon him. It is sinful to harass him further now. And Love gains but little fame thereby, for she had long since set her mighty seal upon him.

Lady Love, why do you so? Why do you   291
make the unhappy man glad with a joy so briefly enduring and then leave him all but dead?

Is it fitting for you, Lady Love, to cause manly spirits and courage bold and high to be so humiliated?

Whatever on earth opposes you in any way, be it contemptible or noble, you have always quickly vanquished.

In all truth, without deception, we must grant that your power is great.

Lady Love, you can claim but one honor, and little else beside: Lady Affection is your companion, else your power would be riddled for fair.

Lady Love, you are disloyal in ways that are old, yet ever new. You rob many a woman of her good name, you urge upon them lovers blood kindred to them. And it is by your power that many a lord has wronged his vassal, friend has wronged friend, and the vassal has wronged his lord. Your ways can lead to Hell. Lady Love, you should be troubled that you pervert the body to lust, wherefore the soul must suffer. Lady Love, since you have the power to   292 make the young old, whose years are yet so few, your works are insidious treachery.

Such words would be seemly only for one who never received consolation from you. Had you been of more help to *me,* I would not be so slow to praise you. To me you have allotted privation, and have thrown me such luckless dice that I have no trust in you. Yet you are far too highly born that my puny wrath should bring a charge against you. Your thrust has so sharp a point, and on the heart you lay a heavy burden.

Heinrich von Veldeke, with true artistry, fitted his tree to your nature.[4] If he had only taught us more of how to keep you! He has given us only a splinter from the tree—how one can win you. From ignorance many a fool must lose his precious find. If that was my lot in the past and is still to be my lot in the future, I blame you, Lady Love, for you keep Reason under lock and key.

Neither shield nor sword avails against you, nor

[4] In his *Eneit,* based on Virgil's poem, Veldeke substitutes a tree for Virgil's cave, where the two lovers, Dido and Aenas, have their rendezvous.

swift horse, nor high fortress with stately towers—
your power transcends any defense. What can   293
escape your attack, by land or by sea, swimming or flying? Lady Love, you proved your power when Parzival, the warrior bold, took leave of his wits because
of you, as his fidelity directed him. His noble, sweet,
and lovely wife, the Queen of Pelrapeire, sent you as
messenger to him. And Kardeiz, *le fils de* Tampenteire,
her brother, you killed. If one must pay you such a
price, it is well for me that I have nothing from you—
unless you gave me something more pleasant. I have
spoken for all of us.

Now hear what was happening there. The mighty Keie
came riding out in knightly armor, as if he would do battle.
And battle, I think, the son of King Gahmuret gave him.
All ladies who know how to vanquish men should wish
him safekeeping now, for a woman brought him to such a
pass that love chopped away his wits.

Keie withheld his charge, first saying to the Waleis, "Sir,
since it has so happened that you have insulted   294
the King, if you will take my advice, I think your best
course is to put a hound's leash about your neck and let
yourself be led like that before him. You cannot escape me,
I shall take you there by force in any case, and then they
will deal with you in a rather unpleasant fashion."

The power of love held the Waleis silent. Keie raised his
spear shaft and gave him such a blow on the head that his
helmet rang. "Wake up!" he said. "You shall sleep, but not
between sheets. I am aiming at something quite different—
on the snow you shall find your bed. Even the beast that
carries the sack from the mill would rue his indolence if he
got such a beating as I have given you now."

Lady Love, look here, this is an insult to you. Only a
peasant would speak so about what has been done to my
lord. And Parzival would also protest if he could speak.
Lady Love, let him seek revenge, the noble Waleis. If you
set him free from your harshness and the bitter burden of

your torment, this stranger would defend himself well, I
think.

Keie charged hard against him and in so doing   295
forced his horse to turn around so that the Waleis lost sight
of his bitter-sweet distress, the image of his wife the Queen
of Pelrapeire—I mean the red against the snow. Then Lady
Reason came to him as before and gave him his senses back.
Keie set his horse at a gallop, and the other came on for
the joust. Both knights lowered their spears as they charged.
Keie aimed his thrust as his eyes directed and drove a wide
breach in the Waleis' shield. This blow was repaid. At the
countercharge Arthur's seneschal Keie was thrown right
over the fallen tree where the goose had taken refuge, so
that horse and man both suffered harm. The man was
wounded, his horse lay dead. Caught between the saddlebow and a stone, Keie's right arm and left leg were broken
in this fall. Saddlegirth, bells, and saddle were shattered by
the crash. Thus did the stranger avenge two beatings; the
one a maiden had suffered for his sake, the other he had
endured himself.

Once more Parzival, the uprooter of falseness,   296
was shown by his fidelity where to find the three snowy
drops of blood that set him free of his wits. His thoughts
about the Grail and the Queen's likeness here—each was a
painful burden, but heavier lay on him the leaden weight of
love. Sorrow and love can break the strongest spirit. Can
these be called adventure? They both should better be
called pain.

Courageous men should lament Keie's misfortune. His
manly spirit sent him bravely into many a fight. Far and
wide it is said that Arthur's seneschal Keie was a rogue. *My*
tale acquits him of this charge and calls him honor's companion. Though few may agree with me—Keie was a brave
and loyal man—this I do maintain.

I will tell you more about him. Many strangers came to
Arthur's court, seeking it as their goal, worthy and worthless alike. By those of dapper manners who practiced trickery Keie was not impressed. But the man of cour-   297
tesy who was an honest friend, him Keie could respect and

was always ready to serve. I grant you, he was a carper.
Yet the harshness which he displayed was for the protection
of his lord. Tricksters and hypocrites he separated from the
noble folk, and on them he descended like harsh hail,
sharper than the sting of a bee's tail. You see, these are the
ones who defamed Keie's name. He always practiced manly
loyalty, yet from them he got only hate.

Herman, Prince of Thuringia,[5] some of those I have seen
residing *in* your house should better be residing *out*. You
too could use a Keie, for your true generosity has brought
you a motley following, in part a mean and worthless band,
in part a noble throng. This is why Sir Walther sings, "I
greet you one and all, the base and the good." [6] Where such
a song is sung, there false men are too highly honored.
Keie would not have allowed this, nor Sir Heinrich of
Rispach either.[7]

Now listen to more of the strange things that happened
on the field of the Plimizoel. Keie was carried   298
away and brought into Arthur's pavilion. His friends began
to bewail him—many ladies and many men as well.

Then came Sir Gawan too and bent over Keie where he
lay. "Unhappy day," he said. "Alas that this joust was ever
fought, in which I have lost a friend." And grievously he
mourned for him.

But the angry Keie spoke out, "Sir, are you pitying me?
Let old wives make such laments. You are the son of my
lord's sister. Would that I could still serve you as you
wished! When by God's grace my limbs were whole, my
hand never shirked from fighting often for you. I would do
so still if I could. Now lament no longer and leave the pain

[5] Landgrave of Thuringia from 1190 to 1217 and patron of the arts.
He was one of Wolfram's patrons. His residence was the Wartburg,
the famous castle where the contest of the minstrels is said to have taken
place early in the thirteenth century. Wolfram supposedly took part in
this contest.

[6] Walther von der Vogelweide (ca. 1170-ca. 1228), a lyric poet who
also resided for a time at Herman's court. No such poem as this has
been preserved.

[7] Nothing is known concerning this person. Rispach is Reisbach,
not far from Landshut and not far from Wolfram's home.

to me. Your uncle, the noble King, will never find such a
Keie again. You are too highly born to take revenge for me.
But if *you* had lost even a finger there I would risk my
head to avenge it. Believe me or not, as you please. Far be
it from me to urge you. He can hit hard, the one   299
who waits out there, and he is not fleeing, either at a gallop or a trot. As for you, a single hair of a woman, be it
ever so thin and fine, would be a chain strong enough to
stay your hand from a fight. A man of such gentle de-
meanor is an honor to his mother indeed; bravery comes
from the father's side. Follow your mother, Sir Gawan,
then you will turn pale at the flash of a sword and your
manly strength will become soft."

Thus was this well-respected man attacked where he had
no defense, with words. He could not respond in kind.
Shame seals the mouth of a man of breeding, while the
shameless know no restraint.

In answer to Keie, Gawan said, "Where blows of sword
and thrusts of lance were aimed at me in battle, no one, I
think, has ever seen my color pale from either thrust or
blow. You have no cause to be angry with me. I have always been ready to serve you."

With that Sir Gawan left the tent and bade his horse be
brought. Without a spur and without a sword the noble
warrior mounted and rode out to where he found   300
the Waleis, whose wits were still in pawn to Love. His
shield showed three punctures, made by the hands of heroes,
for Orilus too had pierced it. Gawan came riding up to
him, but not galloping his horse nor poising his lance for a
thrust. He wanted to come in peace and discover who it
was who had done this fighting.

He gave greeting to Parzival, but Parzival scarcely heard.
So it had to be—Lady Love showed her power over him
whom Herzeloyde bore. The heritage of suffering from
father and from mother and from uncounted ancestors
bereft him of his senses. So the Waleis heard little of the
words Sir Gawan's mouth was uttering.

"Sir," the son of King Lot said, "you must want to do
combat, since you refuse to greet me. But I am not so timid

that I dare not question you further. You have brought dishonor to the King's men and his kin, even to the King himself, and have heaped disgrace upon us. Yet if   301 you will follow my counsel and come with me to the King, I can move him to show you mercy and pardon you your offense."

For the son of King Gahmuret threats and pleas alike were as a mere breath. But Gawan, the pride of the Round Table, was well versed in such pangs from his own painful experience when he had driven the knife right through his hand.[8] To this the power of love had forced him and the favor of a noble woman. A queen had saved him from death when the bold Lehelin in a splendid joust had vanquished him so completely. The sweet and gentle lady offered her head as ransom for him. *La reine* Inguse de Bahtarliez was the name of that loyal woman.

And Sir Gawan reflected, "What if love holds this man enslaved as it enslaved me then, and what if his faithful memories force him to yield the victory to love?" He observed how the Waleis was staring, and followed the direction of his gaze. Then taking a scarf of faille from Syria, lined with yellow sendal-silk, he flung it over the drops of blood.

Once the faille had covered the drops so that   302 Parzival could no longer see them, the Queen of Pelrapeire gave him his wits again. But not his heart, that she kept with her.

Hear now the words which he spoke, "Alas, my lady and my wife," he said, "who has taken you from me? Did this hand of mine really win with knightly service your noble love, a crown and country? Am I the one who delivered you from Clamidê? I found distress and misery among those who were serving you, and many a brave heart heavy with sighs. And here in bright sunlight a mist before my eyes has taken you from me, I know not how. Alas," he said, "what has become of my spear, which I brought here with me?"

---

[8] The allusion is to a Gawan romance unknown to us.

Then Sir Gawan said, "It was broken in jousting, my lord."

"With whom?" asked the noble warrior. "You have neither shield nor sword. What honor could I gain in fighting you? Yet though I must bear your mockery now, you will perhaps speak better of me in time. I too have often jousted and I kept my seat. If I cannot fight with you, the lands around are large enough for me to find honor and travail there and suffer both joy and affliction."

Sir Gawan then replied, "The words I spoke to   303 you just now are clear and kindly meant; they are not dark with hidden meanings. What I ask of you I shall earn by my service. A king is encamped nearby with many knights and many a lady fair. I will bear you company there if you will allow me to ride with you, and I will protect you from any attack."

"I thank you, Sir. Your friendly words I would gladly repay with my service. Since you offer me your escort, tell me, who is your lord, and who are you?"

"I call a man my lord from whom I have received much wealth. A part of it I will tell you here. He was always kindly disposed toward me and showed me true knightly courtesy. His sister was given King Lot as wife, and it was she who brought me into the world. Such as God made me, I am pledged in service to him. King Arthur is his name. My name is also not unknown, and nowhere is it concealed. Those who know me call me Gawan. I and this name are at your service if you do not shame me by refusing."

"Are you Gawan?" said Parzival. "Small honor   304 can I take to myself that you show me such kindness now, for I have always heard it said of you that you treat everyone with kindness. Still I accept your service, but only if I can repay it in kind. Now tell me, to whom do all the tents belong which are set up over there? If that is Arthur's camp, I do regret that I cannot with honor see him or the Queen. I must first avenge a beating I saw, which has grieved me since the day I left them. The reason is this: A noble maiden laughed when she saw me, and because of me the seneschal beat her so that splinters flew as at the felling of a forest."

"That has been avenged already," said Gawan, "in a most ungentle manner. His right arm and left leg are broken. Ride over here and look at the horse and the stone too. And here on the snow lie splinters of your spear which you asked about before."

When Parzival saw this proof, he questioned further and then said, "I trust to you, Gawan, that this was the same man who insulted me then. If that is so, I shall ride with you wherever you like."

"I am not lying to you," Gawan said. "Here   305 Segramors also fell in the joust, a hero in combat, ever famous for his knightly prowess. You vanquished him before Keie was felled, and from both you have gained renown."

They rode on together then, the Waleis and Gawan. In the camp a crowd of people, on horseback and on foot, gave them friendly greeting, Gawan and the Red Knight, as their courtesy bade them. Gawan turned toward his pavilion. Lady Cunneware de Lalant had her tent-ropes just next to his. She was happy indeed and welcomed with joy her knight who had avenged the wrong Keie did her. She took her brother by the hand and Lady Jeschute of Karnant, and it was thus Parzival saw them approaching. His armor had been removed, and through the marks of iron rust his face shone fair as though dewy roses had flown there. He sprang to his feet when he saw the ladies.

Now hear what Cunneware said. "In God's name first, and then in mine, be welcomed, since you have remained a manly and courteous knight. I had refrained from any laughter until my heart came to know you, and   306 Keie then beat me so and robbed me of my joy. That you have richly avenged. I would kiss you, if I were worthy to be kissed."

"I would have asked that myself today, at once, if I had dared," said Parzival, "for your welcome makes me very happy."

She kissed him and bade him be seated again. One of the

maidens with her she sent to her tent to fetch costly garments. They were already cut and sewn, of pfellel-silk from
Niniveh, and King Clamidê, her prisoner, was to have worn
them. The maiden brought them, but spoke her regret that
the cloak was lacking a tie cord. Cunneware drew a lacing
from her dress against her own white skin and pulled it
through his cloak.

Young Parzival then asked leave to wash the rust from
his face; this done, his skin shone fair against the red of
his lips. Quickly the warrior was dressed, and how proud
and handsome he then appeared! All who saw him declared
him the flower of all men. His beauty richly deserved this
praise, for his garb became him well. With a green emerald
they fastened his cloak at the neck, and Cunne-   307
ware gave him even more, a beautiful, costly girdle with
a border of animals formed of precious stones and a ruby
for the clasp. How did the beardless youth appear when
adorned with this belt? Well enough, the story says. All the
people felt their hearts drawn to him. Whoever saw him,
man or woman, held him worthy of respect.

Arthur the King had heard Mass, and they saw him approaching now with the knights of the Table Round, not
one of whom was false. They had all heard by now that
the Red Knight had come to Gawan's pavilion. Arthur,
the Briton, was on his way there, but Antanor, once so
roundly thrashed,[9] ran ahead of the King the whole time
until he caught sight of the Waleis.

"Are you the one," he asked, "who avenged me and
Cunneware de Lalant? To your hand everyone gives great
praise, for Keie has had to pay his debt. His threats are
now at an end. I need not fear his blows; his right arm is
far too weak."

Young Parzival looked, save that he had no   308
wings, like an angel come into flower upon this earth. Arthur and his brave knights welcomed him affectionately,
and all who saw him there were full of good will toward
him. To praise of him their hearts said "Yes," and no one
said to it "No," so winsome did he appear.

9 By Keie.

Arthur then said to the Waleis, "You have caused me both sorrow and joy, yet you have brought and sent me more honor than I have ever received from a man before. Measured against yours, my service to you till now has been slight, even had you attained no more than this, that the duchess, Lady Jeschute, has been restored to favor. And Keie's offense would have been atoned *without* revenge, had I only spoken to you before."

Arthur told him further the request he wished to make and why he had traveled to this place and through other lands as well. Then all the knights added their voice to the King's and begged him to pledge, to each member of the Table Round, his knightly fellowship. Their request made him very happy, as he had good right to be.   309 Parzival gave them his assent.

Now listen and judge for yourselves whether the Table Round can observe its rules this day. For Arthur was its lord, and on one custom he was firm—no knight ate at his table on the day when Adventure failed to visit his court. But Adventure is now obliging him—this honor the Round Table now had.

Though the Table had been left behind at Nantes, they transferred its rights and privileges to a flowery field with no tents or shrubs in the way. King Arthur ordered it so, to honor the Red Knight, and thus his valor there received its reward. A cloth of pfellel-silk from Acraton in far-off heathendom was chosen for this purpose, cut not square, but circular, according to the custom of the Round Table, for that custom prescribed that the seats were all of equal rank and no one might claim the place of honor facing the host. King Arthur ordered further that noble knights and ladies should be seated around the circle. All those esteemed for worth and honor, maid, woman, and man, ate there together at court.

Then came Lady Ginover with many a lady   310 fair and many a noble princess, all lovely to look upon. The ring had been made so large that without any crossing or strife many a lady could sit beside her *ami*. Arthur, the loyal and true, led the Waleis by the hand. Cunneware de

Lalant walked on the other side of him. She was now freed
of her sorrow.

Arthur looked at the Waleis, and now you shall hear what
he said. "I intend to let my old wife kiss you in greeting,
you handsome lad. You would of course hardly need to
ask anyone here for a kiss, since you come from Pelrapeire
where the sweetest of kisses is yours. One thing I will ask
of you. If I ever come as a guest to your house, see that
you repay this kiss in kind."

"I shall do whatever you ask of me," said the Waleis,
"there or anywhere else."

The Queen took a few steps toward him and welcomed
him with a kiss. "I now forgive you truly," she said, "that
you left me in grief, grief that you caused me when you
took the life of King Ither." As the Queen made   311
her peace with him, her eyes grew wet at the recollection,
for Ither's death brought all women sorrow.

King Clamidê was given a seat on the bank of the Plimizoel, and beside him sat Jofreit, *le fils d*'Idoel. Between
Clamidê and Gawan, the Waleis had his place, so the adventure told me. In this circle sat no one who ever sucked
a mother's breast whose nobility stood the test so well, for
the Waleis brought with him here strength with youth and
beauty joined. If you would judge him rightly you will say,
many a woman has gazed at herself in a mirror less bright
than were his lips. And I can tell you that the coloring of
cheek and chin was so fair it could serve as a tongs; this
would hold constancy fast, which then can pare fickleness
away.[10] I am thinking of women who waver and forget the
old love for the new. His radiance held women's constancy
enchained, and their fickleness vanished before him. When
they saw him they were drawn to him in loyalty; through
their eyes he entered into their hearts. Men and women
alike were fond of him, and thus he enjoyed esteem until the end came filled with sighs.   312

Here came she of whom I have to speak, a maiden much
praised for her loyalty but whose courtesy was consumed
in rage. Her tidings brought grief to many. Let me tell you

[10] Constancy is here pictured as a sharp instrument.

what the maiden was riding—a mule as tall as a Castilian horse, fallow in color, its nostrils slit and sides branded like Hungarian war horses.[11] Harness and bridle were rich and costly and wrought with great skill, and the mule came along at a good firm pace. No lady was she in appearance. Alas, what did her coming mean? Nonetheless, she came— so it had to be. To Arthur's host she brought distress.

The maiden was so learned that she spoke all languages well, Latin, French, and heathen.[12] She was versed in dialectic and geometry and even in the science of astronomy. Cundrie was her name, with surname *la sorcière*. Her tongue was far from lame, for it had quite enough to say, and she struck down great rejoicing.

The learned maiden looked quite unlike those 313 whom we call *belles gens*. A cape of fine cloth from Ghent, even bluer than lapis lazuli and well tailored in the French fashion, she wore about her, this hailstorm that beat down joy, and beneath it a dress of rich pfellel-silk. A hat from London, trimmed with peacock plumes and lined with cloth of gold, was hanging on her back—the hat was new and the tie ribbon was not old. The news she bore was a bridge which carried sorrow across, arching over joy. She robbed them of pleasure enough. Over her hat swung a braid of her hair, so long that it touched the mule. It was black and hard, not pretty, and soft as the bristles of a pig. She had a nose like a dog's, and two boar's teeth stuck out from her mouth, each a span in length. Both eyebrows were braided and the braids drawn up to the ribbon that held her hair. —Only for truth's sake has my courtesy so offended as to speak thus of a lady. No other can reproach me for saying the like of *her*. —Cundrie had ears like a bear's, and no lover could desire a face like hers, hairy and 314 rough. In her hand she carried a whip with thongs of silk

[11] In the Middle Ages a horse's nostrils were slit if it had difficulty in breathing, in the belief that this would enable it to breathe more easily. If a horse or mule had a wound or a sore, the spot was branded, and if the animal was sickly, it was often covered with burns. Cundrie's mule is thus in reality a miserable nag.

[12] I.e., Arabic.

and a ruby handle, and the hands of this charming dear looked like a monkey's skin. Her fingernails were none too fine, and, as the adventure tells me, they stuck out like a lion's claws. Rarely was a joust fought for *her* love.

So she came riding into the circle, the source of sorrow, the oppressor of joy. She went to where she found the host. Arthur was dining there in state, at his side Lady Cunneware de Lalant, and the Queen of Janfuse had the seat on the other side of Lady Ginover. Cundrie halted before the Briton and spoke to him in French. Though I must put her message into German for you, I am not happy at her tidings.

"Fils du roi Utepandragun, what you have done here has brought shame to yourself and to many a Briton. The best knights of all lands would be sitting here in honor, were their honor not now mixed with gall. The Round Table is ruined; falsity has joined its ranks. King Arthur,   315 you were praised above your peers. But your rising fame is sinking, your swift renown now limps, your high praise is dwindling, your honor has proven false. The fame and power of the Round Table are lamed now that Sir Parzival has joined its company, though he also bears, as he sits over there, the outward signs of a knight. You call him the Red Knight, after him who died before Nantes. The lives of the two were quite unlike, for no knight's lips have ever read of one so completely noble as he." [13]

From the King she rode over to the Waleis and said, "You are the one to blame that I deny my proper greeting to Arthur and his retinue. A curse on the beauty of your face and on your manly limbs. If I had peace and accord to give, you would find it hard to get them. You think me an unnatural monster, yet I am more natural and pleasing than you. Sir Parzival, why don't you speak and tell me why, as the sorrowful fisherman sat there, joyless and comfortless, you did not release him from his sighs? He showed you his burden of grief. Oh, faithless   316 guest! You should have taken pity on his distress.

"May your mouth become empty, I mean of the tongue

[13] I.e., read aloud.

within it, as your heart is empty of real feeling! You are destined for hell, in heaven before the hand of the Highest, and also upon this earth if noble men come to their senses. You bar to all salvation, you curse of bliss, you scorn of perfect merit! You are so shy of manly honor and so sick in knightly virtue that no physician can cure you. I will swear by your head, if someone will administer the oath to me, that never was greater falsity found in any man so fair. You baited lure! You adder's fang! Your host gave you a sword, of which you were never worthy. Your silence earned you there the sin supreme. You are the sport of the shepherds of hell. Dishonored are you, Sir Parzival. Yet you saw the Grail borne before you and the silver knives and the bloody spear. You death of joy and bestowal of grief!

"Had you but asked at Munsalvaesche—the city of Ta-bronit in heathendom has riches enough to sat-   317
isfy all earthly desire, yet they cannot compare with the reward your question would have brought you here. The queen of that land was won in hard knightly combat by Feirefiz the Angevin. In *him* that manhood which the father of both of you also possessed has never failed. Your brother is a strange and wondrous man. He is both black and white, the son of the Queen of Zazamanc.

"But now my thoughts turn to Gahmuret in whose heart all falseness was weeded out. Your father had his name from the land of Anjou, and he left you a heritage other than the one you have won for yourself. Your good name is destroyed. If your mother had ever strayed from virtue, I might believe you were not their son. But no, her faithfulness taught her grief. Believe only good of her, and that your father was of manly loyalty and far-reaching fame. He liked to join in merriment, a generous heart did his breast enclose, and little of gall. He was fishpound and weir alike, and his manly valor knew how to catch fame like a fish. Your fame has turned into falseness.   318
Alas that I ever learned that Herzeloyde's child had failed of finding honor."

Cundrie herself succumbed to grief. Weeping, she wrung

her hands, and many a tear overtook another as great sorrow pressed them from her eyes. It was loyal devotion taught the maiden to pour out her heart's distress. She returned to where the host was sitting and gave him further tidings.

"Is there here no noble knight," she said, "who craves to win fame by his strength and fair ladies'[14] love as well? I know of four queens and four hundred maidens whom any knight would gladly look upon. They are in the Castle of Wonders, and all other adventures are but a breath compared with what may there be won, a worthy reward for noble love.[15] Burdensome as the journey is, I shall be there yet tonight."

The maiden, grieving and joyless, rode away from the ring without a farewell, but more than once looked back at them, weeping. Now hear her parting words. "Oh, Munsalvaesche, place of sorrow! Alas that there is no one to comfort you!"

Cundrie *la sorcière,* unlovely but yet proud, left   319 the Waleis troubled. What help to him now was his brave heart, his manliness and true breeding? Still another virtue was his, a sense of shame. Real falsity he had shunned, for shame brings honor as reward and is the crown of the soul. The sense of shame is a virtue above all others.

Cunneware was the first to begin to weep that Parzival, the bold warrior, had been so abused by Cundrie *la sorcière,* a creature so strange. Heartfelt sorrow brought tears to the eyes of many another noble lady, and their weeping was plain to see. Cundrie, the cause of their grief, rode away.

And now there came riding toward them a proud bold knight, clad from head to foot in armor so fine that one could tell it was costly indeed. His gear was rich; both man and horse were accoutered in knightly fashion. He found the whole circle sad, maid and man and woman, as he

[14] Wolfram uses here an untranslatable phrase, *hohe minne.* A knight who serves a noble lady for her favor, but not necessarily with a view to marriage, is seeking such "high love." Parzival's relationship to Cunneware is *hohe minne.*

[15] This is another attempt to translate *hohe minne.*

came riding up. Now hear how proud was his   320
spirit, and yet how full of grief. I shall tell you the cause
of these two feelings. His manhood moved him to pride,
but grief taught him sorrow of heart.

He rode up to the outside of the circle. Did they meet
him and crowd around him? Yes, many pages ran quickly
toward him and received the worthy man. His shield and
he were strange to them. He did not remove his helmet,
the joyless knight, and held his sword, still sheathed, in
his hand. "Where are Arthur and Gawan?" he asked.
Pages pointed them out to him.

So he passed through the wide circle. Costly was his
gambeson of beautiful, gleaming pfellel-silk. Before the host
of the company in the circle he halted and said, "God save
King Arthur, his ladies and his men! To all whom I see
here I offer my service and greeting. Only one is free of
my service, and never will he have it. From him I want
nothing but hate. Let him give me what hate he can. I
shall give him back blows of hatred. I must tell   321
you who he is. Oh wretched man that I am! Alas that he
wounded my heart so sorely! The grief is too great that I
have from him. It is Sir Gawan here, who has often done
deeds of prowess and won high honor from them. Dishonor
ruled him then when base desire misled him to kill my
lord as he gave him greeting. It was the kiss of Judas
that prompted him to such purpose. There is grief in many
thousand hearts that my lord died such a bitter, murderous
death. If Sir Gawan denies this, let him answer for it in
battle, forty days from today, before the King of Ascalun,
in the high city of Schanpfanzun. I summon him to meet
me there, ready to oppose me in combat. If he does not
shrink from pursuing his knightly calling, I admonish him
further by the honor of the helmet and by the rule of the
life of chivalry: to this life are given two rich possessions,
good faith and a true sense of shame, which bring honor,
today as of old. Sir Gawan must not lose his   322
shame if he wishes to take his place in the company of the
Round Table, which stands there. Its rule would then be
broken if a faithless man retained his seat. I did not come

here to reprove. Believe me, for you have heard it yourselves, I am asking for battle, not wrangling, and its end
shall be either death or life with honor, as Fortune decrees."

The King remained silent, sorely troubled. Then he made
answer thus: "Sir, he is my sister's son. Were Gawan dead,
I would undertake the combat rather than let his bones lie
disgraced by the charge of faithlessness. If Fortune so wills
it, Gawan's hand shall prove to you in combat that he has
always kept his faith and has held himself free from falsity.
Perhaps some other man has done you injury. If so, you
had best not proclaim so openly his guilt which has yet to
be proved. For if he proves his innocence and wins your
favor, what you have said about him in this brief space will
damage your own good name, if people show good judgment."

The proud Beacurs, brother of Sir Gawan,   323
sprang to his feet and said, "Sir, I will be Gawan's surety
wherever the battle shall be. The slander of him makes me
angry. If you will not exonerate him, then address yourself
to me. I shall be his surety and shall take his place in the
combat. Words alone cannot degrade the high renown
which no one can deny to Gawan."

Then he turned to where his brother was sitting, and
falling to his knees he implored—now hear how: "Think,
brother, how you have always helped me to win honor. Let
me, in return for your trouble, be your proxy in battle. If I
win safely through, the honor will still be yours." And he
continued to plead for this knightly prize, urging his claim
as a brother.

Gawan answered, "I am wise enough, my brother, not to
grant you your brotherly desire. Indeed, I do not know why
I am to fight, and fighting for its own sake gives me no
pleasure. I would be loath to deny you this, save that I
should have to bear the shame."

Beacurs pressed his cause still more urgently.   324
The stranger stood where he was and said, "I am offered
battle by a man wholly unknown to me, and I have no
claim on him. Strong, brave, handsome, true-hearted and
richly-attired—if he possesses all of these, he may all the

better act as a substitute, but I bear no hatred against him. He was my lord and kinsman for whom I raise this strife. Our fathers were brothers who were true to each other through thick and thin. No man was ever crowned whom I, equal in birth, could not challenge to battle to seek revenge on him. I am a prince of Ascalun, Landgrave of Schanpfanzun, and my name is Kingrimursel. If Sir Gawan values fame, he cannot refuse to meet me in combat there. And I give him safe-conduct through all the land, save from attack by my hand alone. By my faith I promise him peace outside the field of combat. God keep all whom I part from here—except one: He Himself knows why."

So he took his leave, that man of high renown,   325
from the field by the Plimizoel. The moment the name Kingrimursel was heard—oh, then he was recognized, for the wise prince was famous and respected far and wide. They all agreed that Sir Gawan would have cause to be afraid of battle with a man of such unquestionable courage as the prince now riding away. And only the stress of their sorrow had hindered many a one there from showing him due honor. The news they had received this day, as you have already heard, was such as could easily cause a host to neglect the proper greeting to a guest.

From Cundrie they had also learned Parzival's name and lineage, that a queen had borne him and how the Angevin had won her. "I remember well," said many a one, "it was in a tournament at Kanvoleis that with many a hurtling charge and well-aimed thrust of the spear his dauntless courage won the gracious maid. The noble Ampflise had taught the hero Gahmuret the ways of courtesy. Now every Briton should be glad that this hero has come to   326
us. His fame, like Gahmuret's, is justly deserved and known to all. True valor was his companion."

To Arthur's company had come on this day both joy and sorrow; such a chequered life was the lot of these heroes then. They all rose from their seats, upon them a sadness beyond measure, and approaching the Waleis and Gawan, as the two stood there side by side, they said what they could to comfort them.

The well-born Clamidê thought his loss greater than that of any of the others there and his suffering too great to bear, and he said to Parzival, "Even if you were now in the presence of the Grail, I must still say in all seriousness that whatever one has heard tell of riches, in the heathen land of Tribalibot, or the mountains in Caucasus, or even of the splendor of the Grail—all these could never compensate me for the suffering that was mine at Pelrapeire. Alas, unhappy man that I am! It was your hand robbed me of joy. Here is Lady Cunneware de Lalant—yet even   327 this noble princess is so devoted to you that she will permit no knight to serve her, though richly she could reward such service. And she might well be weary of having me her prisoner here for so long. If I am ever to recover the joy I once knew, help me to prevail on her to do herself honor so that her love may repay me a part of what I lost through you when the highest joy passed me by. I would have kept it, had it not been for you. Now help me to win this maiden."

"That I will do," said the Waleis, "if she in her *courtoisie* will grant my request. I would gladly offer you recompense, for she is mine, for whose sake you say you are grieved, I mean Condwiramurs, she of the *beau corps.*"

The heathen lady from Janfuse and Arthur and his wife and Cunneware de Lalant and Lady Jeschute of Karnant also went over to comfort him. Was there anything more they could do? Cunneware they gave to Clamidê, who yearned for her love so grievously. To her, as reward, he gave himself and for her head a crown.

When the heathen lady from Janfuse saw this,   328 she said to the Waleis, "Cundrie named a man who, I grant, might well be your brother. His power extends far and wide. Two wealthy lands obey in fear his rule, on water and on land. Azagouc and Zazamanc are powerful, by no means unimportant. Nothing can compare with his wealth, wherever it is spoken of, save that of the Baruch and the riches of Tribalibot. He is worshipped like a god. His skin has a wonderful sheen, but in color it is different from that of other men, for it is both white and black. I passed through his realm on my way here, and he would have liked to prevent me from journeying further, but he did not succeed, much as he begged me. I am the daughter of his mother's sister. He is a noble king, and I shall tell you more wonderful things about him. In a joust with him no man has ever kept his seat. He is known for lavishness, and a more generous man never sucked at a mother's breast. His conduct is without falsity. Feirefiz the Angevin —he has endured suffering in women's service.

"I came here, strange though everything here   329 might be to me, to see new things and to seek adventure. Now surely if good bearing means anything, and your fair looks and manly ways, which everyone says you have and with truth, and added to these your strength and youth, then the highest gift is yours, whose fame has brought honor to all baptized folk." The rich, wise heathen lady had acquired such learning that she spoke French well.

Then the Waleis answered her in this fashion, "May God reward you, Lady, that you give me such kind words of comfort. But I cannot cast off my sorrow, and I shall tell you why. I can find no words for my suffering as I feel it within me when many a one, not understanding my grief, torments me, and I must then endure his scorn as well.[16] I will allow myself no joy until I have seen the Grail, be the time short or long. My thoughts drive me toward that goal, and never will I swerve from it as long as I shall live. If I am to hear the scorn of the world because I   330 obeyed the law of courtesy, then his counsel may not have been wholly wise. It was the noble Gurnemanz who advised me to refrain from impertinent questions and resist all unseemly behavior.

"Here I see many a noble knight. Counsel me now by your courtesy how I can win your favor. A sharp, stern judgment has been passed against me here. If for that I have lost any man's favor, I shall not reproach him. But if in the days to come I win fame, treat me then accordingly. I must hasten to leave you now. You all gave me fellowship when I enjoyed the fullness of fame. Of this I absolve you

[16] This is perhaps a reference to Clamidê, Cundrie, and Sigune.

now until I have set right that thing for which my verdant joy is withered. Great sorrow shall tend me so that my heart will give rain to my eyes, for I left at Munsalvaesche what thrust me out from all true joy and, alas, from many a fair maid as well! No one has ever told of wonders so great but the wonders of the Grail surpass them. The host lives a life heavy with sighs. Oh, Anfortas, forlorn of help, what did it help you that I was there?"

They could remain there no longer; the time   331 for parting had come. Then the Waleis asked Arthur the Briton and all the knights and ladies to give him leave to depart. None was pleased to see him go. That he rode away in sorrow—*that*, I think, grieved them all.

Taking his hand, Arthur pledged him that if ever his kingdom should suffer such distress as it had known from Clamidê, he would treat the offense as if it were done to him. And he said it grieved him that Lehelin had robbed him of two rich crowns. Many knights assured him then of their loyalty, but the stress of sorrow urged him on and away from them.

Lady Cunneware, that maiden fair, took the brave hero by the hand and led him aside. The manly Sir Gawan kissed him and said to the valorous hero, "Friend, I know very well that your path will not be free of strife. God give you good fortune in battle! And may He also help me to serve you some day as I would! May His power grant me that!"

The Waleis said, "Alas, what is God? If He   332 were mighty, if God could rule with power, He would never have imposed such disgrace on us both. I was in His service, since I hoped to receive His grace. But now I shall renounce His service, and if He hates me, that hate I will bear. Friend, when it comes your time to fight, may a woman be your shield in battle and may she guide your hand—a woman in whom you have found both virtue and womanly kindness. May her love keep guard over you! I do not know when I shall see you again. May my wish for you be fulfilled!" Their parting gave both a cruel partner —sorrow.

Lady Cunneware de Lalant led Parzival to her pavilion, where she bade his armor be brought, and with her own soft, lovely hands she armed Gahmuret's son. "This is my proper duty," she said, "since I owe it to you that the King of Brandigan wishes to wed me. My concern for your honor fills my heart with sighs and grief. So long as you are without defense against sadness, your sorrow will consume my joy."

His horse was saddled and armed, and now his   333 own misery was quickened afresh. The handsome warrior was clad in silvery gleaming armor of iron.[17] Gambeson and surcoat were adorned with precious gems without flaw. Only his helmet he had not yet laced on. Then he kissed Cunneware, the lovely maiden, so I was told. That was a sad parting for those two so fond of each other.

Away rode the son of Gahmuret. Let no one judge these adventures by others which have been told until he has heard what Parzival now undertakes, in what direction he turns his course, and where he travels. Anyone *shirking* knightly deeds should not think of him during this time, though pride may prompt him to do so.

Condwiramurs, often and often will your lovely *beau corps* be remembered. How many adventures shall be undertaken in your service! The art of knighthood will be practiced unceasingly by him whom Herzeloyde bore, co-heir to the Grail for which he strives.

Then many of Arthur's retinue set out for the   334 place where they should see an arduous adventure, the Castle of Wonders, where four hundred maidens and four queens were held captive within. —I do not begrudge them what they won there. I have had but scanty rewards from women.

Then the Greek, Clias, spoke. "There I was once delayed." To everyone there he said this. "To my shame the Turkoite[18] thrust me from my horse. But he told me the

---

[17] The armor, as Wolfram describes it here, does not seem to be the red armor traditional with Parzival as the "Red Knight."

[18] What this name means is not known. It may be a title of some sort. Its bearer, Florant of Itolac, enters the story in Book XII, 624.

names of four ladies there who have the right to wear
crowns. Two are old, two are still young. Itonje is the
name of the one, the second is called Cundrie, the third
Arnive, and the fourth Sangive." [19]

All the knights there were eager to see these things for
themselves. Their journey did not give them this reward.
Instead they suffered great injury there—which I also lament, but not too much, for he who endures great stress
for the sake of a woman is rewarded with joy, though sorrow sometimes prevails in the end. Thus, very often, does
love make recompense.

Then Sir Gawan made ready too and armed   335
himself for the meeting with the King of Ascalun. At this
many a Briton grieved, and many a woman and maiden,
and heartfelt were their laments at his departure for the
combat. The Table Round was an orphan, bereft of its
glory.

Gawan considered with care how he could gain the victory. Old shields, sturdy and solid—he did not care how
they looked—had been brought up on pack animals by
merchants, but not for sale. He acquired three of these.
And seven horses too he got, this truly valorous hero,
selected especially for battle. From his friends he received
twelve sharp spearheads made in Angram, stuck into strong
reed shafts from a moor in the heathen land of Oraste
Gentesin. Gawan took his leave and with dauntless courage
rode away. Arthur was generous with him. He gave him
costly gifts, bright gems and red gold and many a sterling-
weight of silver. Gawan's fortunes were rolling now toward
danger.

The young Eckuba left to sail for her home, I   336
mean the rich heathen lady, and the company assembled
at the Plimizoel scattered in all directions. Arthur went to
Karidoel. Cunneware and Clamidê had taken leave of him
before. Orilus too, the famous prince, and Lady Jeschute of
Karnant had bidden Arthur farewell, but they remained

[19] Itonje and Cundrie are sisters of Gawan and nieces of Arthur;
Arnive is Arthur's mother, and Sangive is Arthur's sister. The Cundrie
mentioned here is not the same person as Cundrie *la sorcière*.

there three days longer to celebrate Clamidê's marriage.
Not the royal wedding festival—that was held later with
great pomp in his homeland. His generosity was so great
that he took back to his kingdom with him many a needy
knight and wandering minstrel. And as a token of his
esteem for them he gave them rich gifts of his wealth, nor
did he turn anyone away deceitfully. Lady Jeschute and
Orilus, her beloved, also went with Clamidê to Brandigan,
and that in honor of Lady Cunneware, Orilus' sister, who
was there crowned queen.

Now I know that any reasonable woman who   337
sees this story written, if she is also true of heart, will own
to me in truth that I can *speak* better of women than I
did in the songs I *sang* to one. Queen Belacane was without reproach and devoid of falsity when a dead king besieged her castle. Later, a dream gave Lady Herzeloyde a
heart filled with sighs. How grievously did Lady Ginover
lament on the day of Ither's death! And how deeply was I
moved that the daughter of the King of Karnant, Lady
Jeschute, known for her purity, had to ride in such disgrace! And how Lady Cunneware was held fast by her hair
and beaten! But now these two are well avenged, their
shame has gained them honor.

Would that some other man would take up this story,
one who knows how to relate adventures and how to speak
his rhymes, who can link his lines with rhymes and can
separate them with other rhymes as well. I would gladly
tell you more myself if only certain lips would but give the
command, lips which are borne by quite other feet from
those which move in *my* stirrups.

BOOK·VII

Now for a while he whose conduct was never   338
dishonorable shall claim this adventure for his own, a man
known to all as noble—Gawan. In this story many a man
appears beside or even above the one who is its hero—
Parzival. He who continually exalts his favorite to the heavens will fail to get the listeners' praise. But he who praises
only when praise is due could profit from the people's approval, else whatever he speaks or has spoken, his words
will never find a friendly shelter. Who will accept words of
wisdom if wise men do not do so? A false and lying tale
—that I think had better lie homeless out in the snow so
that the lips ache that spread it as the truth. Thus God
would have dealt with him according to the wish of all
good people whose honesty earns them only ingratitude.
Anyone who is eager to compose such tales, which deserve
only reproach—if a noble man favors him with praise then
folly must be his teacher. He would refrain from that if
he had a sense of shame. Shame is the virtue he should
take as his guide.

Gawan, the brave knight, was saving of his   339
strength, yet so that true cowardice never impaired his
glory. On the battlefield his heart was a fortress, towering
so against sharp attacks that he could always be seen in the
thick of the fray. Friend and foe acknowledged that his

battle cry rang loud in pursuit of fame, though gladly would Kingrimursel have wrested that fame from him in combat.

Now the valiant Gawan had journeyed away from Arthur for I do not know how many days,[1] and with his company the bold warrior was riding a straight course out of a forest and through a narrow valley. There on the hill he saw a thing which could have caused fear, but which only heightened his courage. He clearly saw many banners and a mighty host that followed after. "The way is too long," he thought, "to flee back again to the woods." Then he bade them saddle quickly a horse which Orilus had given him, without his so much as asking for it. Its name was Gringuljete[2] with the red ears, and it had come   340 from Munsalvaesche. Lehelin had won it in a joust by the lake of Brumbane from a knight whom he had struck dead from his horse with the thrust of a spear, as Trevrizent subsequently related.[8]

Gawan thought to himself, "Anyone who is such a coward that he flees before he is pursued is too hasty for his own honor. I'll ride a little closer to them, whatever may come of it. Most of them have seen me already, but I'll manage somehow."

Then he sprang from his horse just as if he were about to lead it to its stall. Countless was the host riding together toward him. He saw many finely fashioned garments and many a brightly painted shield, but he did not recognize the colors nor any of the banners among them. "I'm a stranger to this army," said the noble Gawan, "since I don't know any of them. If they want to be hostile because of this, I'll certainly give them a joust with my own hand before I turn away from them." Then Gringuljete, who in

---

[1] According to Book VI, 321, it must be well under forty days.

[2] Chrétien has "le gringalet" or "le guingalet," the first of which already was, or later became, the common noun meaning "homme chétif" or "cheval maigre et alerte," but Professor Loomis shows that it is Welsh "guin-calet" (white-hardy) or "keincalet" (handsome-hardy), Gawan's traditional horse. In Celtic lore heroic horses are white with red ears, and of divine origin.

[8] In Book IX, 473.

many a perilous pass had been urged to the joust,   341
was girthed. And this was to be his destiny today.

Gawan saw many costly helmets, adorned with precious
ornaments. And myriads of new white spears they carried
to battle, each painted in its own colors and floating the
pennon of the lord whose page bore it in his hand.

Gawan, *le fils du roi* Lot, saw the great press of the
throng. Mules which had to carry the armor and many a
heavy-laden wagon were eagerly pushing on toward quarters. Behind them came the tradesmen with their strange
and wondrous wares, as was to be expected. Of ladies there
was also aplenty, and some of them were wearing their
twelfth girdle as guaranty for their love. No queens were
they; these wenches were called soldier-girls. And with
them went a rabble, some young, some old, their limbs
weary from the march. For many, a rope around the neck
would have been more fitting than swelling this army and
bringing disgrace to honorable people.

The army, which Gawan had awaited, had   342
passed by, on horse or on foot. Those who saw the hero
tarrying there thought that he was one of them. Never this
side of the sea nor beyond did there march a host more
splendid; they had spirit.

Now there came riding after them, close upon their track
and in a great hurry, a squire of courteous bearing, dressed
finely in clothes well-cut. He had another horse on the lead
and carried a new shield. With both spurs he goaded his
horse unsparingly, so eager was he to get to combat. Gawan
rode up to the squire and, after greeting him, asked him to
whom this company belonged.

"Sir," said the squire, "you are mocking me. If I have
earned this humiliation through any discourtesy of mine,
any other distress I might have suffered would serve my
honor better. For God's sake, abate your anger. You know
one another better than I. Why do you ask me? You must
know the answer as well, a thousand and one times better
than I."

Gawan swore many an oath that the host   343
which had ridden past him was completely unknown to

him. "It is shameful for me who have traveled so much," he said, "that I cannot honestly say that I have ever seen one of them before this day in any place where I was called upon for service."

"Sir," the squire said to Gawan, "then I was in the wrong. I should have answered your question before, but my better judgment failed me. Now judge my guilt with leniency. I will gladly tell you what you asked, but first let me lament my discourteous behavior."

"Then tell me, young man, by your distress which shows your courtesy, who they are."

"Sir, he who rides *before* you and whose journey no one can prevent is *le roi* Poydiconjunz and with him Duke Astor of Lanverunz. In their company rides an ill-bred man to whom no woman ever gave her love. He wears the crown of discourtesy and his name is Meljacanz.[4] Any love he ever won, from woman or maid, he took by force. For that he ought to be killed. He is the son of Poy-   344 diconjunz and wants to engage in knightly combat here. Full of courage, he often fights dauntlessly, but what good is his manliness? Even a mother sow would fight to defend her piglets running along at her side. I never heard any man praised if his courage was without true courtesy, and many agree with me in this.

"Sir, listen to another extraordinary thing which I especially want to tell you. Following *behind* you is a great army led by a man whose incivility drives him to battle, King Meljanz of Liz. He has displayed haughty anger unnecessarily—improper love prompted him to it. Sir, I shall tell you what I saw myself," the squire went on courteously. "The father of King Meljanz, when he lay on his death-bed, summoned before him the princes of his land. His life as a gallant knight was forfeit now and could not be redeemed; it had to yield to death. In his grief at the approaching end he commended the handsome Meljanz to the

---

[4] Meljacanz (Chrétien's Meleagant) is always an abductor of ladies in the Arthurian romances. He is seen briefly in his stock role in Book III, 125, where the first knights Parzival ever saw were riding in pursuit of this same abductor.

loyalty of all who were there. He chose one 345
among them, the foremost of all his vassals, whose loyalty
was so tried and true that there was no falseness in him,
and asked this prince to rear his son. 'To him you can now
give proof of your loyalty,' he said. 'Bid him have respect
for both strangers and friends, and when the needy ask for
help, bid him give them of his wealth.' Thus the youth was
given over to his care.

"And Prince Lippaut did all that his lord, King Schaut,
had asked of him in his dying hour, neglecting nothing,
but obeying every request exactly. The prince took the lad
back home with him where he had children of his own who
were dear to him then as they still are now, of course. One
daughter, who in nothing was lacking save that people said
at her age she should be some knight's *amie,* was called
Obie, and her sister's name is Obilot. It is Obie who is
causing us all this trouble. One day things reached the
point where the young king asked her to reward his service
with love. She denounced these ideas of his and 346
asked him how he could be so presumptuous and why he
had taken leave of his senses. 'If you were so old,' she said,
'that for five years of your life, with shield in hand and
your helmet on your head, you had won fame and honor
in glorious battles fraught with danger, and if you had
come back to me ready to be at my bidding—if I then said
yes to what you desire, I would still be granting your wish
all too soon. You are as dear to me (who will deny it?) as
Galoes was to Annore—who died for his sake only after
she had lost him in a joust.' [5]

" 'I am sorry, my lady,' he answered, 'to see you so
enamored that your ill humor turns against me. Service
is rewarded with good will when loyalty is rightly valued.
Lady, you go too far when you mock this way at my reason. You were much too hasty there. I would like to re-
mind you that your father is my vassal and that he holds
many a castle and all his land in fee from me.'

" 'Then let him to whom you give a fief serve 347

[5] This is of course ironic. The implication is that Annore continued
to live until she died a natural death.

you for it,' she said. 'I have a higher goal in mind. I do not want to have a fief from anyone. My sovereign freedom is great enough for any crown which earthly head has ever borne.'

" 'You were taught these ideas,' he answered, 'so your arrogance has increased. It was your father who gave you such counsel. He shall pay for this insult. I shall arm myself and there will be thrusts of spear and blows of sword, be it in battle or in tournament. And many a spear will be broken.'

"In anger he left the maiden, and his wrath was much lamented by all the company, and Obie too lamented it. In the face of this misfortune Lippaut offered to appear before a court of princes and to make other compensation as well, innocent though he was. Whatever the verdict, just or unjust, he demanded the right of judgment by his peers, the princes assembled at court, and swore he had been brought to this strait through no fault of his own. Most earnestly he besought the gracious favor of his lord, but the latter's anger checkmated any friendly impulse.

"Lyppaut could not bring himself to seize his   348 lord and take him prisoner, for he was his host, and a loyal vassal does not do such things. The king left without a word, obeying the counsel of his own folly. His squires, the sons of princes, who had been there with the king, burst into tears from grief. Lippaut had nothing to fear from them, for he had reared them loyally and taught them proper behavior. Except perhaps for *my* lord alone, though he too had known the prince's loyalty. My lord is a Frenchman, *le châtelain de* Beauvais, and his name is Lisavander. All the squires had to renounce allegiance to the prince when they undertook their knightly calling. Just today many princes and other young men were dubbed knights by the king.

"The vanguard is in the charge of a man who is skilled in rough fighting, King Poydiconjunz of Gors, and he has many a well-armed horse. Meljanz is his brother's son, and both are alike in their arrogance, the young one and the old one. A plague upon them both! Anger has   349

so run away with them that both kings want to go to
Bearosche where the favor of ladies must be earned in the
heat of battle. There many a spear will be broken, in onset
and in thrust. But Bearosche is so strongly defended that if
we had twenty armies, each one larger than the one we
have, we would have to leave it undestroyed.

"The rear army is unaware that I have ridden ahead. I
stole away from the other squires, bringing this shield along,
for perhaps my lord, with the very first shield that he
bears,[6] may find here a joust with a hurtling charge and a
well-aimed thrust of spear."

The squire looked around and saw that his lord was
swiftly overtaking him, three horses and twelve white spears
racing along at his side. I think no one was deceived—his
eagerness showed how much he wanted, by rushing ahead,
to get the first joust for himself. So the adventure told me.

Then the squire said to Gawan, "Sir, allow me to take my
leave," and turned back to his lord.

What would you have Gawan do now except look into
these matters? Yet he was sorely troubled by doubt. "If
I look on at the fighting and don't take part in   350
it," he thought, "my fame will be extinguished. But if I
join the battle and let it delay me, then in truth all my
earthly fame will be destroyed. I simply won't do it, I must
wage *my* battle first." His distress grew more intense—it
was all too dangerous to remain here when he should be
riding to his own battle, but how could he just ride on?
He said, "May God preserve my strength and manly
courage!" And Gawan rode toward Bearosche.

Fortress and city lay before him—a more beautiful dwelling no one could have. Well adorned with turrets, it shone
toward him in splendor, a crown among all other fortresses.
On the plain before it the army was encamped, and my
lord Gawan saw there many a sumptuous tent circle.
Wealth upon wealth was there, and he saw many wonderful
banners and all sorts of people strange to him. Doubt cut
his heart like a plane with sharp anxiety.   351

Gawan rode straight through their midst, though one

[6] He has just been made a knight.

tent rope crowded the next. The camp was broad and long,
and he could see how it was arranged and what this or that
person was doing. Whenever anyone said to him, *"Bien
venu,"* he responded with a *"Grand merci."* At one end a
large company of foot soldiers from Semblidac was encamped, and near them, but separate, the Turkish archers
from Kaheti. Strangers are often unwelcome, and so as
the son of King Lot rode along, no one invited him to stop.
Gawan turned toward the town. "If I am to be a by-
stander," [7] he thought, "I shall be safer there in the town
than here with them. I am looking for no profit—I just
want to keep what is mine—and may Fortune be kind to
me."

Gawan rode up to a gate, and there he was vexed at
what the townspeople had done. They had not spared the
cost, but had walled up all their gates and all their mural
towers, and on every rampart stood an archer with his
crossbow ready to shoot. They were busy readying   352
their defenses for battle.

Gawan rode up the hillside, unfamiliar though he was
with the way, until he came to the castle. There he saw
many noble ladies. The mistress of the castle[8] had herself
come up to the great hall to look out, together with her
two lovely daughters, radiant in their beauty. Presently he
heard what they were saying.

"Who was that who just came here?" said the old duchess. "What kind of procession can that be?"

Then her elder daughter spoke. "It's just a merchant,
Mother."

"But they are carrying his shields."

"Merchants often do that."

Then her younger daughter said, "You're accusing him of
something that never happened, sister. You ought to be
ashamed of yourself. No one ever called *him* a merchant.
He is so handsome, I want to have him for my knight. He

---

[7] Such bystanders at the tourneys were not knights, but other men
who sought to make a profit, sometimes in questionable ways, on the
booty there available.

[8] The wife of Duke Lippaut, often referred to as "the old duchess."

is probably seeking reward for his service, and I want to give it to him because he pleases me."

Then his squires noticed a linden and some olive trees down by the wall, and a welcome discovery it seemed to them. What do you suppose they will do now? Noth-   353
ing more than that the son of King Lot dismounted where he found the best shade. His steward brought a mattress and cover on which the proud and noble man sat down. Above him an army of women surged like a flood. The squires who had come up with him unloaded his clothing and his armor from the pack horses and then took shelter beneath the other trees.

The old duchess spoke and said, "Daughter, what merchant would behave in such a courteous fashion? You should not speak so badly of him."

And the young Obilot said, "This is not the worst of her discourtesy. On King Meljanz of Liz she turned the sting of her arrogance when he asked her for her love. Such manners are a disgrace!"

Then Obie spoke, not without anger. "He seems to me quite vulgar. That's nothing but a peddler sitting there. He will probably do a good business here. The pack boxes are being well watched—the boxes of your knight, my silly sister. He is doing the watching himself."

Every word they said reached Gawan's ears.   354
But let them go on talking as they like and hear now how the town is faring. A navigable river flowed past it under a large stone bridge, not on the side where the enemy lay, but on the other side which was free of troops. At this moment a marshal came riding up to the bridge, and on the plain before it he marked out a broad space for a camp. His lord and the others who arrived now with him came at the right time. I will tell you, if you do not yet know it, who it was who rode to the aid of the prince[9] and fought for him loyally. From Brevigariez came his brother, *le duc* Marangliez, and brought with him two brave knights, the noble King Schirniel, who wore the crown of Lirivoyn, and his brother, the King of Avendroyn.

[9] I.e., Lippaut.

When the townspeople saw that help was near they regretted having done what had previously seemed to all a
good course. Prince Lippaut then spoke. "Alas, that it ever
came to pass that Bearosche had to wall up its gates! For if
I turn my knightly skill against my own lord, my   355
honor as a knight is doomed. His grace would profit me
more and be more fitting than his raging hate. What if he
should aim a thrust at my shield with his own hands and
pierce it, or what if my sword should hack his shield to bits,
the shield of my noble lord? If ever a wise woman calls
this good, she is all too frivolous. And say that I held my
lord prisoner in my tower keep—I would have to set him
free and go with him to *his* tower. However he might torment me, I would submit wholly to his will. Yet I have
good reason to thank God that he has not taken me prisoner
since his wrath would not cease until he laid siege to me
here. Now give me good counsel," he said to the townspeople, "in this very difficult matter."

Then many a wise man spoke up. "If innocence could
have availed you anything, we would not have come to this
pass." With one voice they counseled him to open his gates
and ask the ablest men to ride out to the jousting. "We would
rather fight that way," they said, "than defend   356
ourselves from the ramparts against both of Meljanz' armies.
After all, most of those who have come with the king are
nothing but youngsters. It will be an easy matter for us to
seize one as a hostage—such a thing has often caused wrath
to subside. And perhaps if the king can show his knightly
prowess here, he may be of a mind to release us from these
straits and moderate his anger. And better battle on the
open field than for them to take us out from the walls as
captives. We could certainly hope to drive them back to their
tent ropes if it weren't for the strength of Poydiconjunz.
He leads a rough and ready band of knights, among them
our greatest danger, the captive Britons. Their leader is
Duke Astor, and he is sure to be out in front in the battle.
Also among them is Meljacanz, the son of Poydiconjunz.
If Gurnemanz had been his teacher he would have a better
name, yet he too belongs among the fighters. But now aid

has arrived to help us against these men." You have heard the counsel of the townspeople.

The prince did as they advised. He broke open the walled-up gates. The townsmen, not lacking courage, set out for the field, and here and there a joust began.   357 The army[10] now began to move toward the town, its spirits high. Their vesper tourney was a fine one; on both sides were countless troops and the battle cries of the pages rang out in a medley of Scotch and Romance tongues. No quarter was given in the fight; mightily did the heroes swing their arms, though most of them who came with that army were little more than youngsters. They performed great deeds there and took the townsmen captive as one holds strangers in a cornfield for ransom.[11] Knights who had not yet won a token of favor from a lady wore their most splendid armor.

I am told that Meljanz also had adorned himself richly for battle. His courage too was high, and he rode a handsome Castilian which Meljacanz had won from Keie when he flung him so high with his thrust that Keie was caught on the branch of a tree and hung there.[12] The horse which Meljacanz had won then in battle, Meljanz of Liz was riding here. His deeds outshone the rest, and Obie saw all his jousts from above in the great hall where she had gone to watch.

"Now see, sister," she said, "my knight and   358 yours behave quite differently. Yours thinks for sure that we shall lose both hill and castle. We shall have to look elsewhere for protection."

The younger sister had to endure her mockery. Then she said, "He will make amends for this. I still have faith in his courage. It will set him free of your scorn. He shall serve me and I shall give him happiness as a reward. Since

[10] I.e., the enemy or "outer" army.

[11] It is a custom still today to secure any stranger who enters a harvest field and hold him fast until he redeems himself by paying a ransom or tip.

[12] The allusion is to an episode in Hartmann von Aue's *Iwein*. Meljacanz had abducted Queen Ginover, and Keie was among the knights who pursued him.

you say he is a merchant, he shall buy my reward for a price."

Gawan heard their dispute quite clearly, but, as seemed to him proper, he ignored it as far as possible, for if a pure heart does not feel shame, it is because death has already stilled its beating.

The great army of Poydiconjunz lay quiet, save for one brave youth who had joined the battle with all his men, the Duke of Lanverunz. Then came Poydiconjunz, the old and seasoned warrior, and fetched them all back to the camp. The vesper tourney was ended, and the battle had been well fought for the sake of fair ladies.

Then Poydiconjunz said to the Duke of Lan-   359
verunz, "Didn't it suit you to wait for me? When you ride out to battle, lusting for fame, you think you have done the right thing. Yet here is the noble Laheduman and also my son Meljacanz. If these two and I myself should join in the battle, you would see what real fighting means, that is, if you know what a fight should be. I shall not leave this city until we have all had our fill of combat, unless all of them, man and woman, come out as my prisoners."

"Sir," Duke Astor[13] said, "your nephew, the king, started the attack with all his army of Liz. What was your army to do? Sleep soundly in the meantime? Did you teach us that? If so, I'll sleep when there's fighting to be done. I can sleep very well during battle. But believe me, if I had not intervened, the townsmen would have gained the advantage and fame. I saved you there from disgrace. In God's name, moderate your wrath. We have won more than we have lost of your forces. Even Lady Obie would have to admit that."

Now all the wrath of Poydiconjunz was turned   360
against his nephew Meljanz. Yet the noble young man brought away on his shield so many marks of battle that his fresh young fame had nothing to complain of.

Now listen as I tell about Obie. She vented her anger on Gawan, who endured it, though innocent of blame. In-

[13] Duke Astor is the Duke of Lanverunz.

tending to humiliate him, she sent a page to where Gawan
was sitting. "Now ask him," she said, "if the horses are for
sale and if he has any fine cloth goods in his boxes. If so,
we women will buy it all immediately."

The page came up and met with an angry reception. The
flash of Gawan's eyes sent terror to his heart. So frightened
was the lad that he neither asked nor gave the message
which his mistress had bidden him deliver.

Gawan, however, did not remain silent. "Off with you,
you rascal!" he said. "You'll get slaps in the face free of
cost if you show yourself here again." The page went running away, gradually slowing down to a walk.

Now hear what Obie did then. She asked a   361
young noble man to speak to the burgrave of the city—
Scherules was his name. "Ask him," she said, "to do this
for my sake and take it in hand like a man. Under the olive
trees by the moat are seven horses. Those he shall have and
other riches as well. There is a merchant here who is trying
to cheat us. Ask him to put a stop to this. I trust in his
power to seize those goods without payment, and no one
will blame him for that."

The squire went down and reported his lady's complaint.
"I am to protect us from fraud?" said Scherules. "I shall
come at once." He rode up to the place where Gawan was
sitting. And he found in this man who rarely missed a
battle no trace of weakness, but a face that was fair, a chest
well-developed—in short, a comely knight. Scherules observed him well, his arms and hands, his whole bearing.
And then he spoke, "Sir, you are a stranger. We have indeed been lacking in courtesy since you do not have a lodging. Consider this an oversight on our part. I shall   362
now act as marshal myself. All my people and all that I
possess are at your service. Never has a guest been welcomed by a host who was more devoted to him."

"Sir," said Gawan, "I thank you for your favor. I have
not earned it yet, but I shall follow you gladly."

The distinguished Scherules spoke as his loyal heart
bade him: "Since it has fallen to me, I shall be your pro-
tector against harm unless the outer army should take you

prisoner. And then I shall fight at your side." With a friendly smile he turned to all the squires whom he saw there and said, "Load up your harness again. We are going down to the valley." And Gawan rode off with his host.

Obie did not give up her efforts. She sent a minstrel woman, whom her father knew well, to carry the message to him that a counterfeiter was passing that way. "He has with him rich and goodly treasures. Ask my father by his honor as a knight, since he has many mercenaries serving him for horses, silver, and clothing, to let them have these treasures as their first pay. There is enough to fit out seven men for the field."

The minstrel woman told the prince all that his   363 daughter had said. Anyone who has engaged in battle knows how great is the need to win rich booty. The mercenaries were a burden on Lippaut's mind, the loyal man, so that his first thought was, "I must get these treasures, either peacefully or by force." And he set out to follow Gawan. Scherules came riding toward him and asked him why he was in such haste. "I am pursuing a swindler. They tell me he is a counterfeiter."

Sir Gawan was innocent. Only his horses and the other treasures he carried with him were to blame.

Scherules had to laugh, and he said, "Sir, you have been misled. Whoever told you that, maid, man, or woman, told a lie. My guest is innocent. You must change your opinion of him. If you want to hear the truth, he has never possessed a matrix nor ever carried a money changer's purse. Observe his bearing, listen to him speak—I just left him in my house—and if you know how to judge   364 knightly ways, you will have to admit he is an honorable man. *He* was never bent on deception. Anyone who tries to lay hands on him for this, even if it were my father or my own child, anyone who is hostile to him, a kinsman of mine or my own brother, would have to direct the rudder of strife against me, for I shall defend him and protect him from unjust attacks as far as is possible, Sir, without losing your favor. I would sooner renounce my knightly calling, clothe myself in sackcloth, and flee from my own land to where no one knows me than let you do something to him which would bring you shame, my lord. It would be better to welcome kindly all those who have come here and have heard about your misfortune than to rob them. This intent you should abandon."

The prince answered, "Well, let me see him. That can do no harm." So he rode to where he saw Gawan. The two eyes and the heart which Lippaut brought with him confessed that the stranger was fair to look upon and that his bearing revealed true manly virtue.

Whoever, constrained by true love, has suffered   365
the pain of love, knows full well that the heart is forfeit to Love, is so wholly pawned and surrendered, that no mouth can ever complete the tale of the miracles Love can fulfill. Whether woman or man, Love often lessens their wisdom. Obie and Meljanz loved each other so much and with such loyalty that you should feel pity for his rage. Because he rode away from her in wrath, her sorrow was so heavy that her composure quickly turned to anger. Gawan and others, though innocent, had to bear the brunt and suffer because of her. Often she forgot womanly manners, so much did anger disturb her composure. It was a thorn to her sight whenever she saw a man given honor, for her heart desired that Meljanz be the foremost of all the knights. "Though he may cause me pain," she thought, "I shall bear it gladly for his sake. I love him more than all the world, this young and sweet and noble man. It is to him that my heart drives me." Love is often the cause   366
of anger still. Make Obie no reproach for that.

Hear now what her father said and with what words he began when he saw the noble Gawan and welcomed him to his land. "Sir," he said, "your coming may well bring us good fortune. I have traveled many a journey, but never have my eyes beheld so fair a sight. In this, my present misfortune, the day of your arrival shall bring us comfort, for it can comfort us." He asked Gawan for his knightly assistance. "If you lack for weapons, let me provide you with all that you need. If it please you, Sir, join with me and my knights."

Then the noble Gawan spoke, "That I would gladly do, for I am strong of limb and armed for battle, but I must keep peace and avoid all strife until an appointed time. Whether you win or lose, I would gladly share your fate, but I must forego that, Sir, until my own battle has been fought, for my honor is so much at stake that to keep the respect of all honorable men I must redeem my honor in combat or lose my life upon the field. It is to this   367 encounter that I am now on my way."

Lippaut was very distressed at this and said, "Sir, by your honor and your friendly courtesy hear the proof of my innocence. I have two daughters, and I love them, for they are my children. The gift that God gave me in them I want to enjoy all my life. I am even glad for the sorrow which I have because of them. One of them shares this sorrow with me, though the sharing is not the same. My lord causes *her* sorrow with his love and *me* with his hatred. If I understand this rightly, my lord intends to do me harm because I have no son. But I would rather have daughters. What does it matter if I suffer because of it? That too I shall count as a blessing. If a man, of one mind with his daughter, chooses a husband for her, though she may not bear a sword, she has a weapon quite different but just as valuable—by her purity she may win him a valiant son. That is what I hope for."

"May God grant you your wish," said Gawan.

Prince Lippaut pleaded with him earnestly.   368

"Sir, in God's name, cease your pleading," said the son of King Lot. "Do this for the sake of your own courtesy, and do not make me betray my word of honor. Yet one thing I will grant you—I will tell you before it is night what I have decided."

Lippaut thanked him and rode away. In the courtyard he found his daughter with the burgrave's little girl. The two were playing the game of tossing rings. "Daughter, how does it happen you are here?" he said to Obilot.

"Father, I came down from the castle. I think he will grant me my request. I want to ask the strange knight to serve me for reward."

"Daughter, I regret to say that he gave me neither yes nor no. Try to gain his consent to my entreaty."

Away she ran to the stranger. When she entered the room, Gawan sprang up. He bade her welcome and, sitting down beside the sweet child, he thanked her for having defended him when he had been maligned. "If ever a knight suffered distress for such a little lady," he said, "then I should suffer it for you."

The sweet, innocent child spoke out without any   369 shyness, "Sir, as God is my witness, you are the very first man with whom I have talked in private. If I do keep my good breeding and my woman's modesty, this talk will make me very happy, for my teacher told me that speech is the housing of the mind. Sir, I beg for your sake and for mine. It is real distress that prompts me to do this. I will tell you about it if you will permit me. And if you think the worse of me for it, I know nonetheless that I walk the path of decorum, for when I was pleading with you, I was pleading to myself. In reality you are me, even if our names are different. You shall now bear *my* name and be both maid and man. Of you and of myself I have made this request. If you allow me to leave you now, ashamed, my plea refused, your repute must stand before the judgment of your own honor, since I, as a maid, sought refuge in your kindness. Sir, if you wish it, I will give you my love with all my heart. If you have a manly heart, I am sure you will not   370 fail to serve me. I am worthy of being served. It is true, my father wishes help from friends and kinsmen, but do not be deceived by that. For my reward alone you will serve us both."

"Lady," said Gawan, "the words you speak would have me break faith, yet such disloyalty should be abhorrent to you. My loyalty is pledged, and if it is not redeemed, I am ruined. Even if I turned my thoughts and my service to winning your love, you would have to be five years older before you can give a man love. That will be the right number of years for your love."

Then he thought of how Parzival once said it was better to trust women than God, and this counsel was a messenger of the maiden to Gawan's heart. So he gave the little lady his promise that he would bear arms in her honor and added, "Into your hands I give my sword. If anyone challenges me to a joust, it is you who must ride to meet him and do the fighting for me. Others may think they see *me* in the battle, but I shall know it was you who did it."

"That will not be too much for me," she said.   371 "I shall be your protection and your shield, your solace and your heart. Since you have freed me from uncertainty, I shall be your comrade and your guard against mischance, a roof against misfortune's storm and a tranquil retreat. My love shall bring you peace and protect your good fortune against all perils so that your courage will not flag even though, defending yourself, you have to fall back as far as your host. I am host and hostess too, and I shall be with you in battle. If you trust in this, fortune and courage will not desert you."

Then the noble Gawan spoke, "Lady, now that I live at your command, I shall have both, your love and the favor of your comfort." And all the while her little hands lay clasped between his own.

Then she said, "Sir, let me leave you now. I have something to see to, for how could you ride out without a gift from me? You are far too dear to me for that. I must take great pains and prepare my token for you. If you wear it, no other knight will ever surpass you in fame."

Obilot and her playmate took their leave and   372 assured Gawan the stranger of their deep devotion. He bowed and thanked them warmly for their favor and said, "Once you have grown to womanhood, even if the forest grew nothing but spears, as it now grows only wood, the crop would not be enough for you two. If you, so young, have such power over men, how will it be when you are grown? Your love will teach many a knight how spears can shatter shields."

Away went the two girls, happy and free from grief. "Now tell me, my lady," said the burgrave's little daughter, "what do you mean to give him since we have nothing but dolls? If mine are any nicer than yours, then give them to him. I don't mind. We won't quarrel over that."

Prince Lippaut then came riding up and overtook them halfway up the hill. He saw Obilot and Clauditte climbing up ahead of him and called to them both to stop.

"Father," little Obilot said, "I have never needed your help so much. You must give me your advice. The knight said yes to me."

"Whatever you wish, my daughter, if I have it,   373
I will give it to you. Blessed is the fruit which was in you. The day of your birth was a happy day."

"Then I'll tell you, Father, but I want to tell you my troubles in secret. And then be so good and tell me what you think." He bade them set her in front of him on the horse. "But what about my playmate?" she said. Then many of the knights with him gathered round and vied with each other as to who should take her. Any one of them would have liked to do so, but finally she was handed to one. Clauditte was pretty too.

As they rode along her father said, "Obilot, now tell me something about your trouble."

"I promised the strange knight a token. I think I must have been out of my mind. If I have nothing to give him, what is the use of living? Since he has offered me his service, then I must blush in shame if I have nothing to give him. Never was a man so dear to a maid."

"Trust to me, my daughter," he said. "I shall provide you with that. Since you desire his service, I shall give you something with which to requite him if your mother is also willing. God grant that I profit from it! O that   374
gallant, noble man, what hopes I have of him! Never a word had I spoken with him, yet I saw him last night in a dream."

Lippaut went to the duchess, and his daughter Obilot with him. "Lady, help us," he said. "My heart cried out for joy when God gave me this maid and freed me from affliction."

"What is it you would have of me?" the old duchess asked.

"Lady, if you permit, Obilot would like a better dress. She thinks she deserves it now that so noble a man de-

sires her love and offers her great service and even wishes
a token from her."

Then the girl's mother said, "What a gallant man and
good! You mean, I think, the stranger knight. His glance is
like the radiance of May."

Wisely she ordered samite of Ethnise to be brought. With
it they brought an uncut piece of pfellel-silk from Tabronit
in the land of Tribalibot. The gold of Caucasus is red,
and from it, weaving the gold artfully onto silk,   375
the heathen make magnificent fabrics. Lippaut gave orders
to cut dresses for his daughter immediately. Gladly he
gave her both, the simplest and the richest. Of pfellel-silk
interwoven with gold they cut out a dress for the little lady.
Her one arm had to be left bare, for they took away that
sleeve to give to Gawan. This was her present for him, of
pfellel-silk from Nouriente,[14] brought from far-off heathendom. It had rested upon her right arm[15] but was not sewed
to the dress, nor was any thread twisted for the sewing.
Clauditte carried the sleeve to the handsome Gawan, and
at the sight he felt himself free from care. He had three
shields, and on the one he straightway nailed the sleeve.[16]
All his sadness vanished, and he did not fail to give his
great thanks. More than once he bowed toward the road by
which the young maid had come[17] when she bade him such
kindly welcome and with her sweetness brought him such a
wealth of joy.

Day was over and night came. On both sides   376
great armies were encamped, valiant knights and good.
Had there not been such a flood of besiegers, the inner army
would have made the attack. Under the bright moon they

---

[14] Von Nouriente is almost certainly a distortion of "from the
Orient."

[15] Ordinarily a sleeve from a dress that had already been worn was
selected as token to be given a knight, for the token derived its mysterious power from having touched the body of the lady.

[16] A lady's token was fastened either to the knight's shield, as here,
or on the spear point, in which case it was rammed through the opponent's shield.

[17] Thus blessing the path on which she had walked.

now measured out the lines of their outer defense. No fear
or cowardice oppressed them. Before daybreak they had
prepared twelve wide breastworks, separated from the battlefield by moats, each breastwork with three gates for the
horsemen's sorties.

The marshal of Kardefablet of Jamor took charge of
four gates, and when morning came Kardefablet's army
was seen prepared for brave defense. This rich duke,
brother of Lyppaut's wife, fought there with knightly
valor. He was firmer of courage than many other fighting
men who yet bear up well in battle, and hence he enjoyed
the stress of combat. His army had moved into the city
during the night. He had come from far away, for a rare
thing it was if he ever turned away from a hard fight.
Four gates he guarded well.

The army encamped on the other side of the   377
bridge crossed over before the day came and, as Prince
Lippaut requested, entered the city of Bearosche. The
men of Jamor had already crossed the bridge before. Each
gate was so assigned that when daylight came they were
manned for the defense. Scherules took one gate which
he and my lord Gawan would not leave undefended.

From the stranger knights one could hear laments—and
I think it was the best of them who spoke thus—that
knightly action had already taken place without their seeing
it, and that this vesper tourney had ended without any joust
of theirs. Their complaint was unnecessary, for countless
jousts were there for all who wanted them and sought
them out on the battlefield.

In the streets many hoof tracks could be seen, and now
here and now there many banners moving in, all by the
light of the moon, and many a costly helmet too, to be worn
in the joust, and many a bright-colored spear. Regensburg
sendal-silk would not have counted for much   378
there, for on the field before Bearosche many a surcoat
could be seen more costly still by far.

Night did as was her custom of old; at its close she drew
a day along behind her. Not by the song of the lark did
they mark its coming, but by the loud clash of many a

charge. This was the voice of battle, with the cracking of spears like the splitting of a thundercloud. The army of young knights from Liz joined battle with the men of Lirivoyn and with the King of Avendroyn. Many a fierce and valiant joust resounded, as if whole chestnut trees were cast into a glowing fire. *Ah vois,* how bravely the strangers rode to the charge upon the field and with what valor the townspeople fought!

To protect their souls from the hazards of battle and assure them of salvation, Gawan and the *châtelain* had a priest sing a Mass for them. He sang it for God and for them. Their renown was soon to be increased—that was their destiny. Then they rode to their post. Their rampart was guarded by many noble and valiant knights, the   379
followers of Scherules, and they fought a brave fight there.

What further shall I tell you? Save perhaps that Poydiconjunz shone in splendor. He came riding up with such a host that, if every bush in the Black Forest were a spear shaft, you could see there no greater forest. He rode up with six banners, in front of which fighting began in early dawn. Trumpeters sounded ringing blasts, like thunder rousing fear and dread, and drummers beat a lively accompaniment to the noise of the trumpets. If any blade of grass was left untrampled there, it was no fault of mine. The Erfurt vineyards still show today such signs of trampling—from the feet of many norses.[18]

Now Duke Astor came face to face in battle with the men from Jamor. The jousts were sharpened there, and many a noble knight was thrust backward from his horse upon the field. They proved themselves brave in battle. Many strange battle cries were to be heard. Many a battle horse ran about without its master, while the master went on foot. He had learned, I guess, what falling means.

Then my lord Gawan saw that the field was a   380
tangle of friend and foe, and he spurred on so swiftly to the attack that the eye could scarcely follow him. Scherules

---

[18] In 1203 King Philip of Swabia, son of Frederick Barbarossa, was besieged in Erfurt by Wolfram's patron, Landgrave Herman of Thuringia.

and his men did not spare their horses, yet they could not
keep pace with Gawan. How many knights he thrust
from their steeds and how many strong spears he broke,
this noble representative from the Table Round! Had he not
been given this strength by God, one would have attributed
the renown to *him*. There was many a clang of sword
against sword. To him the two armies were all the same, the
one from Liz and the one from Gors—against both of them
he set his hand. From both he took many a horse and
brought them straightway to his host's banner. He asked
if anyone wanted them, and there were many who answered yes. They all became rich through his comradeship.

Then a knight came riding up who also did not spare the
spur. It was the burgrave of Beauvais,[19] and he and the
courtly Gawan charged each other with such force that the
young Lisavander came to lie behind his horse   381
among the flowers as if he had practiced falling in the
joust. I am grieved at this for his squire's sake, who the
day before rode along so courteously and told Gawan how
all this had come about. He dismounted beside his master.
Gawan recognized him and gave him back the horse he had
just won in battle. The squire bowed his thanks, I was told.

But look! There stands Kardefablet himself on the field,
struck in a joust by a thrust from the hand of Meljacanz.
But his men snatched him up on his horse again, and amid
the hard clash of swords resounded again and again the
battle cry "Jamor." Then the fight closed in on him till
scarcely a space was left as onslaught pressed against onslaught. The blows on their helmets rang in their ears.
Gawan went to his aid, speeding mightily to the charge.
Flying the banner of his host he defended the noble Duke
of Jamor. Many a knight was felled then. Believe this if
you like—I have no witnesses. I know only what the adventure says.

Le comte de Muntane rode against Gawan, and   382
so excellent was the joust that the mighty Laheduman soon
lay behind his horse upon the field. Then the proud and

[19] Lisavander, burgrave (*châtelain*) of Beauvais, was mentioned in
348.

worthy warrior gave Gawan his pledge of security. Nearest
the ramparts fought Duke Astor at the head of his troop,
and many a sharp combat took place there. The cry of
"Nantes" was often heard, Arthur's battle cry, for many
Britons, far from home, were there, rugged men, not soft,
and the mercenaries from Destrigleis in Erec's land.[20] They
made their appearance there with their leader, *le duc de*
Lanverunz. Poydiconjunz might well have set the Britons
free, since they fought so bravely for him. In the storming
of the Muntane Cluse they were taken captive from
Arthur, and here, as was their custom wherever they might
fight, they shouted "Nantes!" That was their regular battle
cry. There were many whose beards were already grey.
As emblem each of the Britons wore a gampilun[21]   383
either on his helmet or on his shield, for that was Ilinot's
coat of arms, who was Arthur's noble son. What was Gawan
to do? He sighed as he saw that coat of arms, and his heart
was filled with grief. The death of his uncle's son caused
Gawan deep distress. As he recognized that coat of arms,
his eyes overflowed with tears, and he left the Britons
battling away on the field. With them he did not want to
fight—such is the tribute one must pay friendship. He rode
over toward the army of Meljanz, which the townsmen
were opposing. They deserved full praise for this, yet they
could not hold the field against superior forces and had
fallen back to the moat.

One who challenged the townsmen in many a joust was a
knight completely in red. He was called "The Nameless
Knight," for no one knew him there. I tell this to you as I
heard it. He had joined Meljanz three days before, and the
townsmen had reason to lament that he came to   384
the aid of their foe. Meljanz gave him twelve squires from
Semblidac who attended him at the single jousting and at
the onsets in groups. Spear upon spear they handed him,
and he broke them all in the battle. Loud rang the clash of

[20] In Hartmann von Aue's *Erec* Destrigleis is the country of the
hero, not a city.

[21] A gampilun is probably a heraldic dragon in the form of a winged
lizard.

the jousts when he captured King Schirniel and his brother. And he did still more; he did not fail to exact an oath of surrender from Duke Marangliez.[22] These three were the core of the army. Their followers, however, fought bravely on.

King Meljanz himself was also there in the battle, and whether he had been to them friend or foe, all had to own that seldom had greater deeds of valor been done by a man so young. His hand split many a sturdy shield, and strong spears splintered at his thrust as onslaught clashed with onslaught. His young heart swelled with the lust for battle, and no one there could give him his fill of it—that vexed him greatly—until he challenged Gawan.

Gawan took from his squire one of the twelve spears from Angram which he had won at the 385 Plimizoel. The war cry of Meljanz was "Barbigoel," the splendid capital of Liz. Gawan spurred on hard to the joust, and then the strong reed shaft from Oraste Gentesin dealt Meljanz a painful blow, piercing his shield and breaking off in his arm. It was indeed a fine joust. Gawan thrust Meljanz from his horse as he galloped by, but from the force of the thrust the back bow of his own saddle broke so that both heroes landed on the ground behind their horses. There they kept up the fight with their swords. Such threshing would have been more than enough for two peasants. Each one bore the sheaf which the other threshed, and they beat those sheaves to shreds. Meljanz still had to carry the spear which had pierced his arm and stuck fast there, and he grew hot from the streaming blood. Then my lord Gawan jerked him into the gate of the Brevigariez rampart, and forced him to pledge security. Meljanz was ready for that, yet had the young man not been wounded, the news would not have got around so fast that he had been vanquished. One would have had to wait longer for that.

Lippaut, the prince and lord of the land, did 386 not spare his courage in battle. Against him fought the King of Gors, and men and horses alike had perforce to suffer from missiles, for the Turks of Kaheti and the foot soldiers

22 Duke Marangliez is Lippaut's brother.

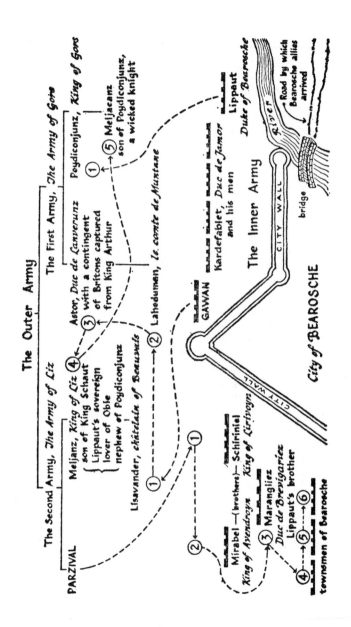

of Semblidac exercised their skills and knew how to evade
counterblows. The townsmen bent all their efforts to holding the enemy from their defenses. They too had *sergeants
à pied,* and their ramparts were as well protected as they
could possibly be. The brave men who lost their lives there
paid cruelly for Obie's wrath; her foolish arrogance brought
many a man to grief. For what was Prince Lippaut being
punished? His lord, the old King Schaut, would surely have
spared him this.

Now the troops began to grow tired, but Meljacanz
fought bravely on. Was his shield still whole? Not a hand-
breadth remained of it. Duke Kardefablet had driven him
far afield. On a flowery meadow the tourney reached a
deadlock. Then my lord Gawan rode up, so that   387
Meljacanz was sorely pressed. Not even the noble Lanzilot
had charged against him so violently when he came from
the Sword Bridge and later did battle with him. Lanzilot
was angry that Lady Ginover was suffering captivity, and in
that fight he delivered her.[23]

Lot's son rode straight to the attack. What could
Meljacanz do now but spur on his horse in turn? Many
were there who watched the joust. Who was that lying behind his horse? He whom the knight from Norway had
thrown upon the meadow. Many a knight and lady looked
on at this joust and spoke praise of Gawan. The ladies
could easily see it, looking down from the great hall.
Meljacanz was trampled underfoot. Over his gambeson
waded horses which never again would taste the juicy green
of a plant, and their bloody sweat rained down on him. For
the horses it was a day of doom; they were soon to be prey
for the vultures. Duke Astor rescued Meljacanz from the
knights of Jamor, who had all but captured him. And thus
the tourney was ended.

Now who won the prize there and earned the   388
reward of the ladies? I should not like to be the judge, for
if I should name them all, I would have small leisure indeed. Among the inner army the best deeds were done for
the sake of young Obilot, and with the outer army it was a

[23] See note to 357.

Red Knight who excelled. These two outshone the rest, and none outdid them.

When the stranger knight in the outer army learned that he would receive no thanks from the master he had served, for Meljanz had been taken captive into the city, he rode to where his squires were waiting, and spoke to his prisoners: "You, Sirs, pledged security to me. Misfortune has come upon me here. The King of Liz has been captured. Now try what your efforts will avail to see whether he can go free. This much I still may do for him." This he said to the King of Avendroyn and to Schirniel of Lirivoyn and to Duke Marangliez. He allowed them to ride away to the town only after they had sworn him a carefully worded oath, that they would either free Meljanz or win the Grail for him, their captor. But they could not even tell 389
him where it was; they knew only that a king named Anfortas had it in his keeping.

When they said this, the Red Knight answered, "If my request is not fulfilled, then ride to Pelrapeire and take your oath to the queen. And tell her that he who once fought for her sake with Kingrun and with Clamidê now yearns for the Grail and yet also for her love. Both are always in my thoughts. Tell her that I sent you, and may God keep you safe, you heroes."

They took their leave and rode into the town. Then he said to his squires, "We are not at a loss for booty. Take whatever you want of these captured horses. Just leave me one to ride now, for you can see that mine is badly wounded."

"Sir," the trusty squires answered, "you are very gracious to give us your aid so generously. You have made us rich forever."

Then he chose a horse for his journey, Ingliart with the short-cropped ears, which had escaped from Gawan when he took Meljanz prisoner. The Red Knight caught it now himself, the horse from whose back he was to shatter many a shield.

With a farewell greeting he rode away. Fifteen 390
horses or more, all unwounded, he left for the squires, and

they thanked him and begged him to stay with them. But the goal he had set lay far away, and the good knight turned his course to where great ease was rare; strife was all he sought. In the times when he lived no man, I think, ever fought so much as he.

The outer army rode in orderly line to the camp to take their rest, while inside the town Prince Lippaut spoke and asked what had happened out there, for he had heard that Meljanz had been captured. This was welcome news to him and was soon to bring him great relief. Gawan loosened the sleeve gently from his shield so as not to tear it—he thought it too precious for that—and gave it to Clauditte. At the edges and in the center too it had been pierced and slashed. He bade her take it to Obilot, and the little maid was overjoyed. Over her bare white arm she drew it on,   391 and walking back and forth in front of her sister, she asked each time as she passed, "Who was the knight who did this for me?" Obie met this mischievous mockery with fury.

The knights, compelled by great weariness, all needed rest. Scherules took Gawan with him as his guest, and also Count Laheduman and other knights he found there whom Gawan had captured that day on the field where so many valiant battles had been fought. Politely the noble burgrave showed them to their seats, yet he and all his weary band remained standing before their king till Meljanz had eaten. With such courtesy did they treat him.

For Gawan this was too much and he spoke out openly, "If the king will permit, Sir Host, you should take your seat." His sense of true courtesy led him to speak thus.

His host refused and said, "My lord is the king's vassal, and he would have done the same if it pleased the king to accept this service from him. Only out of respect for his king does my lord absent himself now since he is no longer in favor. If God ever joins them again in friendship, we shall all obey his command."

Then young Meljanz spoke, "Your courtesy   392 was always so complete all the while I lived here among you that your counsel never failed me. If I had followed it better, I would be happy today. Now come to my aid,

Count Scherules, for I can count on you for that, with my captor who holds me as prisoner here—both will listen to your counsel—and with Lippaut, my second father. Ask him to grant me his courtesy as a knight. I would never have lost his favor if his daughter had not made mock of me and treated me like a fool. That was unwomanly behavior."

Then the noble Gawan said, "Here bonds must be joined anew which nothing but death can sever."

Then came those whom the Red Knight had captured out on the field, having climbed to the castle to find the king, and they told what had happened to them. When Gawan heard what coat of arms he who had fought with them bore, and to whom they had pledged security, and when they told him about the Grail, he thought to himself, the one who had done these things could be none other than Parzival. He bowed his head in thanks toward heaven that God had kept them apart that day in the   393 ardor of their strife. The discreet courtesy of both was a guarantee that neither name would be revealed. And no one knew them there, though elsewhere they were famous.

Scherules said to Meljanz, "Sir, if I may make a request, consent to see my master. The counsel friends on both sides give you, you should follow gladly. And do not be angry with him." This seemed to them all well said.

At that moment the inner army came riding up from the town to the king's hall. The prince's marshal had asked them to come. Then my lord Gawan took Count Laheduman and his other prisoners who now gathered around him, and he asked them to transfer to Scherules his host the pledge he had won from them that day in battle. Not a man was loath to do this, and they rode, as they had promised, up to Bearosche to the great hall. The burgrave's wife gave Meljanz rich garments and a veil for a sling in which he hung his wounded arm which Gawan's thrust had pierced.

Gawan sent a message by Scherules to his lady   394 Obilot that he would like to see her and assure her of his devoted service, and at the same time take leave of her.

"And tell her I shall leave the king here in her care. Ask her to take thought how she should entertain him so that her conduct may be praised."

Meljanz heard these words and said, "Obilot will be a crown of all womanly goodness. If I must give *her* my pledge of security, it sets my mind at ease that I shall live here under her protection."

"You must know," said the noble Gawan, "that only by her hand you were taken captive and she alone must have the fame called mine."

Scherules rode on ahead. Now at the court not a maid nor man nor woman but was so richly dressed that on that day one had little use for poor and shabby garments. With Meljanz there rode to court all those who had given their pledge of security out on the field. The new ar-   395
rivals ascended to the hall, where sat all four, Lippaut, his wife, and his children, and the host sprang up and hastened toward his lord. A great crowd thronged the hall as he greeted his foe and his friends. Meljanz walked by Gawan's side.

"If it would not displease you, your old friend would like to greet you with a kiss, I mean my wife, the duchess."

Meljanz answered his host, "I see *two* ladies here from whom I'll gladly take kiss and greeting, but to the third I'll grant no reconciliation."

At that the parents wept, but Obilot was overjoyed. The king was greeted with a kiss, and two other kings, still beardless, and Duke Marangliez as well. Nor did Gawan fail to receive a kiss, and they asked him to take his lady in his arms. He pressed the pretty child like a doll to his breast as affectionate delight impelled him.

He called to Meljanz, "Your hand pledged me your surety. Of that you are now set free; pledge it instead to her. The prize of all my joys I hold here in my arm, and *her* prisoner you now shall be."

As Meljanz stepped closer to her, the maid   396
clung to Gawan. Yet to Obilot the pledge was given while many noble knights looked on.

"Sir King, you did wrongly, if my knight is indeed a

merchant as my sister insisted, to give your oath of surrender to him." Thus spoke the maiden Obilot, and then she commanded Meljanz to offer to her sister Obie the pledge he had sworn in her hand. "For your knightly renown you shall have her as your *amie,* and she shall have you for always as her lord and her *ami.* I shall not let either of you off."

God spoke from her young mouth, and both did as she had asked. Then with her mighty skill and loving loyalty Lady Love created their love anew. Obie's hand crept out of her cloak and took hold of Meljanz' arm. Weeping, her red mouth kissed the wound he had received in the joust, and many a tear that flowed from her bright eyes dropped upon his arm. Who made her so bold before the crowd   397 of people? It was Love who did it, so young and yet so old. Lippaut saw his wish fulfilled, and never had anything pleased him more, since God now gave him the honor of calling his daughter his queen.

As to how the wedding was, ask those who received gifts there. And neither can I tell you where the knights all rode, nor whether they fought or rested. I was told that in the great hall where he had come to say farewell, Gawan now took his leave. Obilot wept bitterly. "Take me with you," she said, but Gawan refused this plea of the sweet young maid. Her mother could scarcely get her away from him. Gawan said farewell to all, and Lippaut proffered his services for the fondness he felt for him. Proud Scherules, his host, did not neglect to give him escort. With all his men he rode out with the bold warrior. Gawan's path led upward to a forest. There Scherules gave him food and sent a huntsman with him as guide, and then the noble hero said farewell. Gawan's heart was heavy with grief.

BOOK VIII

No matter who had come to Bearosche, Gawan   398
alone had still won the prize on both sides, except that there
appeared there a knight, unrecognized despite his red weapons, whose praise was unfurled like a signal banner aloft.
Gawan had honor and good fortune, both in full share. But
now his battle hour approaches.[1]

Long and broad was the forest through which he had to
make his way if he was not to shun the battle to which,
through no fault of his, he had been summoned. Moreover, Ingliart was lost, his horse with the short ears—never
was a better horse jumped by Moors in Tabronit. Now the
forest became intermittent, with here a wooded stretch and
there an open field, some of the latter of a breadth that a
tent would scarcely stand on them. Gazing, he perceived
cultivated land, and that was Ascalun. From people he encountered he inquired for Schanpfanzun. High mountains
and many a marshy moor he had traversed on his way
there, but now he caught sight of a castle, and oh! how
nobly it shone! Toward it the stranger to that country made
his way.

---

[1] The time is apparently near the end of the forty-day interval stipulated in 321, 18; this, by Professor Weigand's calculation, would be
very close to October 29.

Now listen to adventures, and amid them help   399
me lament Gawan's great distress. My wise man and my
foolish man, by your friendliness, do so and grieve with me
for him.

Alas! I should now be silent. No, let him sink lower yet,
who often enough had his luck to thank and who was now
sinking toward misery.

This castle was so splendid that never did Aeneas find
Carthage so magnificent when Lady Dido's death was the
pledge of love.[2] How many halls did it have? And how many
towers were there? There were enough of them for Acraton, which, aside from Babylon, encompassed the greatest
breadth according to the arguments of the heathens. All
around, it was so high—and moreover it fronted on the sea
—that it feared no assault nor any great violent hostility.
Before it lay a mile-wide plain, across which Sir Gawan
rode. Five hundred knights or more, with a commander
over them, came riding toward him attired in colored garments of trim cut. As the adventure told me,   400
their trained fowl were hunting there for cranes or for
whatever they could start. On a tall Arabian horse from
Spain rode King Vergulaht, and his splendor was like day,
even in the midst of night. His family issued from Mazadan
out of the mountain in Famorgan, and his race was of the
fairy. To see this king's beauty, you would think you were
seeing the Maytime adorned at proper season with flowers.
Gawan thought, as the king's brightness flashed toward
him, that it was a second Parzival and that he had the
features of Gahmuret the way this story portrayed him as
he rode into Kanvoleis.[3]

A heron in flight escaped to a swamp-like pond, brought

---

[2] The reference is not to Vergil's *Aeneid* but to Heinrich von Veldeke's chivalric romance, the *Eneit*, adapted from the ancient poem.

[3] Vergulaht, King of Ascalun, and Parzival are first cousins. See
the genealogical chart of characters and also Gahmuret's statement of
his ancestry in Book I, 56. Gawan notices the family resemblance and
even seems to recall from his boyhood how Gahmuret looked at the
time of the Kanvoleis tournament in Book II.

down by falcon swoops. To help the falcons,[4] the king got into a deceptive fording place and was drenched, losing his horse thereby and his clothes as well—but he rescued the falcons from their distress. Horse and garments were taken by the falconers. Did they have any right to them? Yes, they did have a right, they properly claimed them, and they had to be allowed their rightful claims. Another horse was furnished him and he relinquished his own. Dif-   401 ferent garments were placed upon him, for the others now belonged to the falconers.

At this point up rode Gawan. Ah! then it could not be otherwise but that he was better received than Erec was at Karidoel when he came to Arthur after his battle, and when Lady Enite was safe-conduct to his joy, after the time when the dwarf Maliclisier rudely slashed his skin with the whip in the sight of Ginover, and after the fight took place in the broad ring at Tulmeyn for the prize of the sparrow hawk. Ider, *le fils de* Noyt, famed in story, gave him his oath of surrender there, forced to do so or face death.[5]—But let us leave that topic and listen to this: never, I think, have you heard of so noble a reception and greeting as here. Alas! this child of noble Lot will pay most unkindly for it.

If you would rather, I will stop here and tell you no more about it. For very grief I will turn back. And yet, by your kindness, hear how a pure nature[6] was troubled   402 by the falsity of others. If I carry this story on for you with true report, you will come to sadness from it, along with me.

Then said King Vergulaht, "Sir, I have considered, and you shall ride inside over there. If it may be with your gracious pleasure, I shall not bear you company. If, how-

[4] On seizing its prey, the falcon locks its claws within the flesh of its captive so that the huntsmen are obliged to release the grip. Hence the falcons here were being dragged down with the wounded herons into the pond waters and were drowning.

[5] The events mentioned are, in reversed order, those of the first sequence in Hartmann's *Erec*.

[6] I.e., Vergulaht's.

ever, my continuing my ride offends you, I shall leave whatever I have to do."

Then the noble Gawan said, "Sir, whatever you bid, you do so properly. It is quite without offense to me and readily pardoned."

To which the King of Ascalun replied, "Sir, you see Schanpfanzun: up there is my sister, a maiden, and whatever lips may have said about beauty, she has her full share of it. If you would consider it any pleasure, she will take pains to entertain you till I return. I will come to you sooner than I was planning to. But you will gladly wait for me once you have seen my sister, and you won't be sorry if I am away still longer."

"I shall be glad to see you, as I shall her. How- 403 ever, grown ladies have always spared me their hospitality." So spoke proud Gawan.[7]

The king despatched a knight and instructed the maiden that she was to entertain him in such a way that he would think a long stay was a hastening away. Gawan rode to where the king had indicated.

If you want me to, I can still keep silent about the great unhappiness. —No, I will go on with the story.

The road and a horse took Gawan to the gateway at one end of the great hall. Anyone who has ever built anything can tell you better than I can about the solidity of this building. There stood a castle, the best that was ever called an earthly construction, and immensely vast was its expanse.

Praise of the castle we shall pass over here, because I have a great deal to tell you about the king's sister, a maiden —enough has been said here about buildings—and I shall describe her as I properly should. If she was beautiful, it became her well; and if she had a good disposition besides, that was a help in her nobleness. Thus her manners and her nature were like those of the Margravine who radiated beauty down from the Heitstein across all the 404

[7] Gawan alludes to *little* Obilot's love for him and to *big* Obie's hostility to him.

marches.[8] A lucky fellow is he who might privately know her charms! Believe me, he found better entertainment there than elsewhere. —Of women I can speak what my eyes are able to see, and wherever I bestow a good word it must have the guarantee of good breeding.

Now let the true-hearted and the well-wishing listen to this adventure! About the untrue-hearted I do not care. With their contrition full of holes, they have all lost their salvation anyway, and their souls will certainly suffer wrath on that account.

To the courtyard there before the great hall rode Gawan in search of entertainment just as he had been sent to do by the king—who presently behaved dishonorably toward him. If womanly honor may be considered a commodity, she had driven a good bargain in it, rejecting all that was not genuine, and thus her purity had won renown. A pity that the wise gentleman from Veldeke should have died so young! He could better have sung her praises.

As Gawan came in sight of the maiden, the   405
messenger approached her and delivered all that the king had bidden him to say.

Whereupon the queen without hesitation said, "Come nearer, Sir. You are the preceptor of my behavior. Command me and instruct me. If entertainment is to be provided for you, such must be indicated in your orders. Since my brother has recommended you so warmly to me, I shall kiss you—if you wish me to. Command me, according to your standard of propriety, what I am to do and not to do."

Very graciously she stood there before him, and Gawan answered, "Lady, your mouth is so kissable that I shall have your kiss of greeting." Her mouth was hot, full, and red; upon it Gawan pressed his own, and there ensued a nongreeting-like kiss. Beside the maiden rich in courtesy the highborn guest sat down.

[8] Elizabeth, wife of Berthold von Vohburg and sister of Ludwig I of Wittelsbach, lived on the Heitstein near Cham in southern Bavaria and died in 1204.

Sweet converse did not fail either party, and they spoke openly to each other. They could only reiterate, he his plea, she her refusal. Whereat he complained bitterly. Yet he kept right on asking for her favor.

Then the maiden replied as I am about to tell you: "Sir, if you are otherwise discreet, you will consider   406 that you have gone far enough. At my brother's request I am treating you no less kindly than Ampflise treated my uncle Gahmuret, without going to bed together. My kindness would in the long run outweigh hers, if anyone were to weigh us properly. And besides, Sir, I don't know who you are, and yet in such a short space of time you want to have my love."

Then the noble Gawan said, "Knowledge of my kin informs me, and I can inform you, Lady, that I am my aunt's brother's son. If you want to do me a favor, don't let my ancestry keep you from it. Compared to yours, it is well enough vouched for that they can both stand on a par and keep step with one another."

A serving maid poured them drink and immediately disappeared again. Other ladies were, however, sitting there, but they too did not forget to go and find something to do. The knight who had escorted him was also out of the way. Now that they had all gone out, Gawan reflected that a weak eaglet will often catch the large ostrich.   407 He slipped his hand under her mantle, and I think he touched her thigh. This only increased his anguish. Love drove both maid and man to such distress that something came very near happening, if malevolent eyes had not caught sight of it. They were both eager for it.

But see, their hearts' sorrow now approaches. In through the door came a white knight, that is to say a grey-haired one. On recognizing Gawan he named his name in a call to arms and set up a loud shouting: "Alas! and hey-hey! for my master whom you murdered, and, as if that weren't enough, here you are about to rape his daughter!"

At a call to arms men always come, and so did it happen here.

To the maiden Gawan said, "Lady, let's have your advice, for neither of us has much in the way of weapons of defense." And he added, "If I only had my sword!"

Then said the noble maiden, "Let's go to some place of defense, let's flee up into that tower over there, the one that stands next to my chambers. Maybe it will all turn out favorably."

Here a knight, there a merchant, came run-   408
ning, and then the maiden heard the rabble coming up from the city. She ran with Gawan for the tower, but her friend came in for trouble. She kept begging them to hold off, but such was their noise and tumult that no one noticed her. Fighting, they pressed on toward the door, while Gawan struck a position of defense in front of it and prevented their getting in. A bolt used to lock the tower he pulled out of the wall, and in the face of it his menacing neighbors repeatedly fell back before him with their supporters. The queen kept running back and forth to see if there wasn't something in the tower that would serve as a defense against the rebellious mob. Then that maiden pure found a set of chess pieces and a chessboard, broad and beautifully inlaid, and this she brought to Gawan in the battle. It had been hanging by an iron ring, with which Gawan grasped it now. On this square board a great deal of chess had been played, but now it was sorely riddled.

But hear now about the lady. Kings and rooks and all she hurled down on the enemy. The pieces were large and heavy, and of her the story says that whoever   409
was hit by the swing of her missiles went down in spite of himself. Like a knight that mighty queen fought there, and at Gawan's side showed herself so warlike that the huckster-women in Dollnstein never fought better on Carnival —only they do it for sport and work themselves up over nothing.[9] When a woman is soiled with armor rust she has forgotten what is seemly, if we are judging her manners, unless she does such a thing out of faithfulness. Antikonie's grief was demonstrated at Schanpfanzun and her proud

[9] Dollnstein (the Tolenstein of the text) is a hamlet near Wolfram's Eschenbach.

spirit was bowed. All through the fight she was weeping, and thus she showed that lovers' love is true.

And what was Gawan doing meanwhile? Whenever he had a free moment so that he could catch a glimpse of the girl, her lips, her eyes, her nose—a better shape I doubt you ever saw on a spitted rabbit than she had here and there between her hips and her bosom; well might her body rouse love's desire! You never saw an ant with 410 a slimmer waist than she had where her belt went around —all these things put manly courage in her friend Gawan.[10] And she stuck it out with him through the peril. The hostage specified in this battle was—death; there was no other pact. But each time he sighted the girl, enemies' hatred counted for nothing with Gawan, and for that reason a good many of them lost their lives.

Then came King Vergulaht and saw the forces battling against Gawan. If I am not to mislead you, I must not gloss over the fact that he disgraced himself by what he did to his noble guest. The latter was standing firm and fighting in self-defense, and now his host did something that grieves me for Gandin's sake, the King of Anjou, to think that so noble a lady as his daughter should ever have borne a son who would have ordered his people to fight hard as a treacherous band. Gawan had to wait until the king had put on his armor, for he was going to start in fighting. Then Gawan had to fall back, but with no dis- 411 honor, and he was forced into the tower entryway.

But look! Now came along that very man who once had challenged him in Arthur's presence, the Landgrave Kingrimursel. He tore his hair and his face and wrung his hands over Gawan's distress, because he had guaranteed him on his honor that he should have peace until *one* man's strength had overcome him in battle. Old and young he drove away from the tower.

The king ordered it torn down.

Whereupon Kingrimursel shouted up to where he could see Gawan: "Hero, grant me a truce to come in to you! I

[10] We have imitated as far as possible the structure of this tortured sentence.

want to share your troubles with you as a comrade in this pass. Either the king will strike me dead or I shall save your life!"

Gawan granted the truce and in ran the Landgrave to where he was. This gave the outer forces pause, for he was also castle warden there, and now both youths and greybeards wavered in their fighting. Gawan escaped to the open, and so did Kingrimursel—they were both   412 swift when it came to courage.

The king urged his men on: "How long are we to endure the tormentations from these two men? My father's brother's son has taken it upon himself to rescue the man who has inflicted this harm on me when he should more properly be taking revenge on him, unless his bravery is failing."

Many men, prompted by their loyalty, selected one of their number to speak to the king: "Sir, if we may be so bold, there are many here who will not kill the Landgrave. May God turn your intentions to something we can better accept! The world's praise will heap hatred upon you if you murder your guest and you will take upon yourself the burden of disgrace. Besides, the other man, against whom you have started this abuse, is your kinsman, and he is in his safekeeping. You should call this off. You will be outlawed because of it. Proclaim us an armistice now for as long as this day lasts. Let there be an armistice tonight too. Whatever you then decide will still be as your hand may dispose, whether it is to your credit or to your shame. My lady Antikonie, of falsehood free, is with him and   413 all in tears. If that fact does not touch your heart, when one mother bore you both, consider, Sir, if you are wise, that you sent him up to see the girl in the first place. Even if no one were guaranteeing his safety, he should still be spared for her sake."

The king proclaimed an armistice until he had time to think out more clearly how his father was to be avenged. Sir Gawan was innocent; the hand of another had done the deed: the proud Ehcunat had cleared a lance's track through him when he was taking Jofreit, *le fils d'*Idoel, to Barbigoel after capturing the latter at Gawan's side, and through fault of *his* this sorrow had come about. Once the armistice was proclaimed, the men left the battle at once and went to their separate homes. Antikonie the Queen embraced her cousin and pressed many a kiss upon his lips for having rescued Gawan and preserved himself from an evil deed. "You are my uncle's son," she said, "and you could not do anything bad for anyone's sake."

If you are willing to listen, I will tell you about   414
what my lips previously mentioned, of how a pure nature became troubled. Dishonor fall upon that attack that Vergulaht made at Schanpfanzun! It was certainly nothing born in him from either his father or his mother. The young man, who had much good in him, felt profound shame when his sister the queen began to upbraid him, and he was earnestly begging her forgiveness.

Then that noble maiden said, "Sir Vergulaht, if I wore a sword, and if by God's command I were a man so that I could ply the knightly trade, there would have been no more of this fighting of yours here. There I was, defenseless, and a maiden, except that I did have one shield on which honor was emblazoned. I shall name that coat of arms to you if you will deign to hear about it: proper bearing and upright conduct. These two are always constant. That shield I used to protect the knight whom you had sent up to see me. I had no other protection to offer him. Even if you mend the matter now, you still have done me wrong, if womanly honor is to be paid its just due. I have always heard it said that, whenever it befell that a man   415
fled to a woman for protection, brave pursuit should give up the fight, if the pursuer had manly virtue. Sir Vergulaht, the flight that your guest made to me in order to escape death will yet teach your reputation the pain of disgrace."

Then Kingrimursel spoke: "Sir, relying on you, it so happens that on the plain of the Plimizoel I gave Sir Gawan guarantee of safe-conduct into your territory. Your word of honor was pledged, in case he was brave enough to come here, and I guaranteed him in your name that only *one* man would challenge him to combat here. On this score, Sir, I have suffered an affront. My fellow princes shall look into

this. This heinous act has happened all too soon for our taste. If you cannot treat princes decently, we, in turn, will not respect the crown. If you have any chivalry about you, your chivalry will tell you that your kindred extends so far as to include me. Even if no more connection were involved in my case than through a concubine, you would still have presumed too far, because I am, after all, a knight, and one in whom no one has found any disloyalty yet. And I shall die without any either. I trust to God for   416
that, and may my salvation so plead before Him. Wherever this story is heard, that Arthur's sister's son came to Schanpfanzun under my escort—Frenchman or Briton, Provençal or Burgundian, Galician[11] or men of Punturtois—once they hear of Gawan's discomfiture, if I have any reputation, it will be dead. His perilous fight reflects narrow credit on me, but my broad blame is going to drive my joy away and put my honor in pawn."

When this speech was done, there stood there one of the King's vassals, Liddamus by name. Kyot himself so names him. —Kyot was called *le chanteur*[12] and his skill would not allow him to do other than sing and recite so that many are still made glad thereby. Kyot is a Provençal who saw this tale of Parzival written in heathen language.[13] Whatever he told of it in French, I, if I am not weak in my wits, am telling further in German. —Then Prince Liddamus said, "What is that one doing in my master's   417
house when he slew his father and brought shame so close to him? If my lord is acknowledged worthy, his own hand will avenge it and thus one death will make up for the other death. I think this misery would equal the other one."

Now you see how Gawan stood. Not until now did he know serious anxiety.

[11] Galicia is the northwestern province of Spain. Punturtois is un-identified.
[12] Wolfram's words are: *"Kyot laschantiure hiez."* On the analogy of *lampriure,* "L'Empereur" in 712, 9, the word *laschantiure* might be construed as *"l'enchanteur,"* "magician," but *le chanteur,* "singer," fits the context better.
[13] I.e., Arabic.

Then Kingrimursel remarked that anyone so quick to threaten should also be swift to combat. "Whether you fight in close quarters or in wide, it's easy to defend oneself against you. Sir Liddamus, I fancy I can save this man from you. If he had done you any harm, you would leave it unavenged. You have overstated yourself. Are we expected to believe that any man's eyes ever saw you out in front when fighting was going on? Fighting has always been so disagreeable to you that you led the retreat. You could do even better than that: whenever there was a thronging toward a battle, you did a womanish about-face. Any king that relies on your advice has his crown on mighty crooked. For *my* part, I would gladly have faced Gawan, 418 the noble knight, in the combat circle. I had pledged my word that the encounter was to take place here, provided my master had permitted it. *He* bears both the sin and my hatred. I looked for better things from him. —Sir Gawan, swear to me here between my hands that one year from to-day you will face me in combat, and if things so turn out here that my master spares your life, then you will have combat from me. I challenged you at the Plimizoel: now let the encounter take place at Barbigoel before King Meljanz. Sorrows enough to make a crown I shall wear until that day of judgment when I come into the ring against you. Then your manly hand can acquaint me with sorrow."

Gawan the rich in valor graciously offered his oath in accordance with this request.

Duke Liddamus was at once ready with talk and he began his talk with artful words within the hearing of every-one. He spoke because it was high time for him to speak: "Whenever I enter battle, whether I stand 419 up to the fighting or with bad luck retreat, whether I am a coward among cowards or whether I win renown there, Sir Landgrave, these things you may praise in me as you see fit, and if I never win any reward out of it from you, I am nevertheless perfectly satisfied with myself." And the rich Liddamus went on to say: "If you want to be Sir

Turnus, then let me be Sir Tranzes.[14] Abuse me if you
know why you are doing it, and don't act so high and
mighty! Even if you are the noblest and most powerful of
the princes of my rank, I am also lord and master of a
country. In Galicia I have numerous castles in various
places, even as far as Vedrun. And any harm that you—or
any other Briton[15]—may do me, I wouldn't hurry so much
as a chicken to safety when you attack. The man from
whom you accepted a challenge has come here from Britain.
Well, avenge your lord and kinsman, but spare me your
harangue. Whoever it was that took your uncle's life—you
were his vassal—go ahead and take revenge on him. I didn't
do anything to him. And I don't think anyone   420
will claim that I did. I can easily get over your uncle's
death. His son is to wear the crown in his stead and he is
high enough to be my lord. Queen Flurdamurs gave him
birth, his father was Kingrisin, and his grandfather was
King Gandin. I will explain it even more clearly for you:
Gahmuret and Galoes were his uncles. Unless I maligned
him, I can with honor receive my land with bestowal of
banners from his hand. If anyone wants to fight, let him
fight! If I am slow to battle, I do manage to learn how the
battle comes out. Whoever wins praise in battle, let proud
women thank him for it. I won't let myself be misled to
too great suffering, not for anybody. Why should I be a
second Wolfhart?[16] My road to battle is cut off by moats;
my lust for fighting wears a hood, as falcons do.[17] Though
you might never love me for it, I would do as Rumolt did,
who advised King Gunther when that monarch was leaving
Worms to go to the Huns: he urged him to stay at home[18]
and said he would stew him some nice big pieces of bread

---

[14] Turnus and Tranzes are characters in Veldeke's *Eneit*, but see also
Virgil's *Aeneid*, Book XI, and the characters of Turnus and Drances.

[15] By "any other Briton" Gawan, of course, is meant.

[16] A warrior in the *Nibelungenlied*. See Note 1, p. 433.

[17] Hoods are placed over falcons' heads until the falconer has selected a prey.

[18] To clarify the allusion, the translators have supplied the words:
"he urged him to stay at home."

and swirl them around for him in his stewing kettle." [19]

The Landgrave, rich in valor, said, "You talk   421
just like the person you have been known to be this many
a day and year. You advise me to do just what I wanted
to do anyway, and you say you would do just what a certain cook advised the brave Nibelungs to do when they
were starting out undismayed for the place where vengeance was taken on them for what they had previously done
to Siegfried. Sir Gawan will have to kill me or I shall
teach him the pain of revenge."

"I agree," said Liddamus. "Even if someone gave me all
his Uncle Arthur has, and all those people in India have,
and brought it to me just as it is, without any conditions
attached to it, I would pass it up before I would fight. Keep
the renown that people now credit you with. I am not
Segramors, whom they had to tie up to keep him from
fighting. I get the king's greetings without that. Sibeche
never drew a sword, he was always with those that fled,
and yet people had to pay him deference. And he received
plenty of rich gifts and big fiefs from Ermenrich, yet he
never brought a sword down through a helmet.[20] My skin
is never going to be flayed by you, Sir Kingrimursel. I've
thought that out quite carefully in your case."   422

Then King Vergulaht intervened: "Stop this arguing! It
annoys me to have you both so free with words. My presence makes this sort of wrangle unseemly. It doesn't become
either me or you."

This all took place in the great hall, where his sister had
now arrived. With her stood Gawan and many another
worthy man besides.

To his sister the king said, "Well, take your friend with
you, and the Landgrave too. Those who side with me, come
along with me and weigh what is best for me to do."

She said, "Put your sense of loyalty on the scales too."

Now the king goes to his council, while the queen has
taken her cousin and her guest along with her. Her third

[19] Further reference to the *Nibelungenlied*, see Note 2, p. 433.

[20] King Ermenrich and his vassal Sibeche are characters from Germanic saga. See Note 3, p. 434.

companion was the burden of care. With all graciousness she took Gawan by the hand and led him where she wanted to be.

To him she said, "If you had not survived, it would have been a loss for all countries."

Led by the queen's hand, the son of noble Lot walked along, and he went quite willingly too. To the women's quarters then went the queen and the two men,   423 and chamberlains saw to it that the quarters remained vacant except for lovely young ladies, of whom there were many there. Graciously the queen tended Gawan, who was dear to her heart. With them was the Landgrave, but he in no way interfered, for the noble maiden took great pains with Gawan—so I was told. Thus they were both there with the queen until the day gave up its struggle and night came on. Then it was time to eat. Mulberry wine, regular wine, and spiced wine were brought in by slim-waisted maidens, and other good foods besides—pheasant, partridge, good fish, and white bread. Gawan and Kingrimursel had escaped from great peril, and since the queen so bade them, they ate with a will, as did others who wished for anything. Antikonie herself carved for them, which, in their courtly training, they found excessive. Of all the cupbearers that knelt before them, not one had a garter break—for they were maidens, and of the age which is still said   424 to be the best years. I wouldn't be surprised if their plumage had molted, as falcons do—and I have no objections on that score.

Now listen to what the council, before it adjourned, advised the country's king. He had assembled his wise men and they had come to his council. Each one spoke his mind as his best understanding prompted. They weighed the matter on several sides, and then the king bade them hear what *he* had to say.

He said, "I had an encounter in battle recently. I had ridden at adventure into the *Forêt* of Laehtamris,[21] and in that week a knight gained all too great renown from me,

---

[21] Laehtamris—Old French: *les tamreis*—"near the tamarisk" (?).

for with no delay he sent me flying backwards off my horse. He forced me to take an oath to get the Grail for him. Even if I were to die in the attempt, I must fulfill the vow which his hand won from me. Give me your advice in this matter: I need it! My best protection from death was to pledge my hand to that, as I have just explained to you. He was a master of manhood and valor, and   425 that hero laid a further charge on me, namely, that if, without sly evasion, and within the space of a year, I had not won the Grail, I was to go to her who wears the crown in Pelrapeire—her father's name was Tampenteire; and when I beheld her, I was to pronounce my oath of surrender to her; his word to her then was: if she was thinking of him, that was his joy's reward, and he was the man who once delivered her from King Clamidê."

When they had heard this speech, Liddamus spoke again: "With these lords' permission I shall now speak. They may also give their advice. For the thing into which you were forced by that lone man, let Sir Gawan here be the hostage —he's flapping his wings in *your* trap. Ask him to take an oath here before us all that he will get the Grail for you. Let him ride out of here in all friendliness and go fight for the Grail. We would all be disgraced if he were killed *in your house*. So forgive him his guilt for the sake of your sister's favor. He has suffered grave peril here,   426 and now he has to go to his death. In lands as far as the sea encloses, never was a house so well defended as Munsalvaesche; where it stands, the road goes rough with fighting. Leave him in peace tonight; in the morning inform him of the decision."

All the councilors concurred, and thus Sir Gawan was left alive.

Such tending was accorded the hero undismayed that night—so I was told—that his rest was mighty good. When mid-morning came and Mass had been sung, there was a great crowd at the palace, both commoners and noble folk. The king did as he had been advised and had Gawan brought in. He wasn't going to force him to anything except what you yourselves have heard. See now how the fair

Antikonie brought him in. Her uncle's son came with her, and many more of the king's men. With her own hand the queen led Gawan before the king. A wreath of flowers was her headdress, but her mouth robbed the flowers of their praise, for in that wreath not a single one was that red. Whoever received her gracious kiss could not help   427 but go out and waste whole forests in many jousts untold.

With praise let us greet the sweet and gracious Antikonie, of falsehood free, for she lived in such a way that nowhere could her reputation be ridden over roughshod with carping remarks. All who heard her praises, every mouth wished that her praises might so remain, protected from false and dark talk, clear-eyed as a falcon's sight. If fragrant steadfastness was hers, it came from her desire for noble conduct. And now this sweet and lovely girl graciously spoke: "Brother, I bring you here this knight, whom you yourself bade me entertain. Let him now have the advantage of my intercession. Do not be annoyed at this. Think of your loyalty as a brother and do this without reluctance. Manly loyalty becomes you better than suffering the world's hatred and mine—if I could hate. Teach me how to temper it in regard to you."

Then that sweet and worthy man replied,   428 "That I shall do, sister, if I can. Let us hear your own advice besides. You think that wrongdoing has undercut the worthiness in me and driven me away from honor. What good would I then be to you as a brother? If all crowns were subject to me, I would still renounce them at your command, for your hatred would be my supreme sorrow. Joy and honor repel me except as you judge them good— Sir Gawan, I should like to ask you a favor. You rode here for honor's sake; now for honor's sake help me to get my sister to overlook my guilt. Before I lose her love, I will forgive you my heart's sorrow, provided you give me your oath of surety that, without delay, and in all good faith, you will seek the Grail for me."

With that, the reconciliation was concluded, and Gawan was at the same time sent to fight his way to the Grail. Kingrimursel likewise forgave the king, who had lost his friendship by breaking his guarantee of safe-conduct. In the presence of all the princes this took place in the hall where the swords of Gawan's pages had been hung up. The weapons had been taken from them at   429 the time of the battle, with the result that none of them had been wounded. A man so empowered by the city had obtained custody of them safe from their opponents and had taken them and put them in prison. Frenchman or Briton, sturdy squires and little lads, from whatever country they came, they were all brought out now, free, to Gawan the rich in valor. When those lads caught sight of him there was a great embracing. They all clung to him and wept, but their weeping was for loving joy. From Cornwall there was there with him *le comte* Laiz, *le fils de* Tinas. Another noble lad in his retinue was *le duc* Gandiluz, *le fils de* Gurzgri, who lost his life for Schoydelakurt, whereat many a lady found her grief. Liaze was the youth's aunt. His mouth, his eyes, his nose, were the very core of love; the whole world loved to look at him. Six other lads were there besides. These eight youths were, by birth, assured to be of noble stock. They were devoted to him by virtue of kinship and served in his pay.   430 He gave them distinction as reward and treated them well in other respects.

To these lads Gawan said, "Well done, sweet kinsmen of mine! I understand you would have mourned for me if I had been killed here." —Well might they have been trusted to mourn, they were in a state of misery anyway. —He went on to say: "I was worried about you. Where were you when they were fighting with me?"

They told him, and not one of them was lying: "A sparrow-hawk hen got away from us while you were sitting with the queen, and we all ran after it."

All who were standing or sitting there did not fail to take notice, and they saw the evidence that Sir Gawan was a manly and courteous gentleman.

Now he asked permission to leave, which the king granted and all the people there—only the Landgrave remained with him. Then the queen took the two lords with her, and Gawan's pages as well. She took them where maidens tended them without ado, and many a lovely maiden waited on them courteously.

When Gawan finished breakfast—I am telling   431 you what Kyot read—great sorrow rose out of heartfelt sincerity. To the queen he said, "Lady, if I have my senses and if God keeps me alive, I must journey in your service and ever devote my knightly spirit to serving your womanly kindness. The fact that you have triumphed over deceit can only bring you blessedness, for your renown outweighs all other renown. Good fortune keep your soul's salvation. Lady, I must ask your permission to leave. Grant it and let me be on my way. May your gracious breeding preserve your renown."

His departure grieved her, and many a lovely maiden of hers wept with her out of friendship. Without guile the queen said, "If I had been more help to you, my joy would be exalted over my sorrow, but you could not have obtained better terms of peace. Believe me, when you suffer pain, or if knightly life casts you into the power of grievous sorrow, be assured, Sir Gawan, that my heart shall be concerned, whether it be for loss or for gain." The noble   432 queen kissed Gawan's mouth. He was joyless enough at having to leave her so soon. —I think they were both sad.

His pages had thought to have his horses brought up in front of the great hall, where there was shade from a linden tree. The Landgrave's men had also come up—so I heard— and he rode out a way with him from the town. Courteously Gawan asked him if he would be so kind as to escort his retinue back to Bearosche. "Scherules is there, and they can ask him themselves for escort to Dianazdrun. There many a Briton lives who will take them to my lord or to Ginover the Queen."

Kingrimursel promised to do so, and then the brave knight took leave of him.

Armor was immediately placed on Gringuljete, the horse, and on my lord Gawan. He kissed the lads his kinsmen, and also his noble squires. His oath of surety bade him seek the Grail, and he rode off alone toward great peril.

BOOK·IX

"Open up!"

To whom? Who are you?

"I want to come into your heart to you."

Then it is a small space you wish.

"What does that matter? Though I scarcely find room, you will have no need to complain of crowding. I will tell you now of wondrous things."

Oh, is it *you*, Lady Adventure? How fares that lovable knight? I mean the noble Parzival whom Cundrie with harsh words drove forth to seek the Grail. Many a lady there did lament that he could not be spared that journey. From Arthur, the Briton, he rode away then—how is he faring now?

Take up that tale again and say whether he despairs of joy, or whether he has won great honor, or whether his unmarred renown has grown in length and breadth, or has it grown short and scant? Tell us all that his hands have done. Has he seen Munsalvaesche since that time, and the gentle Anfortas whose heart was then so full of sighs? For your mercy's sake give us comfort and say if he be released from suffering. Let us hear if Parzival was there, your lord and also mine. Reveal to me how he has fared, sweet Herzeloyde's child and son of Gahmuret, since he rode away from Arthur. Has he won joy or affliction in battle since then? Does he ride out to the open field, or has he tarried at his ease since then? Tell me how he lives and all that he does.

The adventure tells us now that he had wandered through many lands, on horseback and in ships on the sea, and that no one save a fellow countryman or kinsman ever vied with him in a joust and kept his seat. Thus the weight of his scale can sink and cause his own fame to rise, but the fame of the others to fall.[1] In many hard fights he had guarded himself against defeat, exerting himself so unsparingly in combat that he who wished to borrow fame from him tried it to his sorrow. The sword that Anfortas had given him when he was with the Grail snapped later when he was attacked, but the power of the spring of Karnant, called Lac, made it whole again. This sword helped him win fame. Whoever does not believe   435 this, commits a sin.

The adventure tells us now that Parzival the bold warrior came riding into a forest, I do not know at what time, where his eyes found a hermit's cell, newly built, with a swift stream flowing through it. One side of it jutted out over the water. The dauntless young warrior was riding in search of adventure. Then God took thought for his guidance, and Parzival found a hermitess, who for love of God had dedicated to Him her maidenhood and renounced her joy. From its roots in her woman's heart sorrow put forth fresh flowers each day, yet the troth from which it sprang was old.

Schianatulander and Sigune he found there. Inside the cell the hero lay buried and dead, and she, bowed down upon his coffin, suffered a life of anguish. Sigune *la duchesse* heard no Mass, yet her whole life was a kneeling in prayer. Her lips, once so full and warm and red, were

---

[1] This is not as obscure as it seems. Parzival represents one side of the scales, those he defeats, the other. With every combat won, Parzival's scale goes down, tipped in his favor. The other side of the scales, representing his foes, goes up, for their defeats make their scale lighter. The paradox that *falling* scales equal *rising* fame, and vice versa, obviously appealed to Wolfram.

blanched and pale since the day when worldly joy entirely
forsook her. Never did a maid suffer such cruel pain. It
was to cry out her grief that she lived alone.

For the sake of the love which had died with   436
him—for the prince had had no pleasure from it—she
loved and cherished his dead body. Had she become his
wife, Lady Lunete would have been slow to offer such
speedy counsel as she gave her own mistress.[2] We still often
see today Lady Lunetes come riding up with all too hasty
advice. The woman who, joined with her husband in true
companionship and ruled by the power of self-restraint, re-
fuses alien love, if as long as he lives she shuns such love,
that man, to my mind, has received in her the crown of
his desires. Such constancy becomes a woman as nothing
else. —To that I shall gladly bear witness if I am asked.
—After his death let her do as she pleases. Yet if she still
preserves his honor, she wears a garland brighter than if
she went, wreathed and merry, to the dance.

How can I speak of joy in the presence of such suffering
as Sigune's faithfulness imposed on her? Let me say no
more about it.

Over fallen tree trunks, where there was no path, Parzival
rode up to the window—too near, he was sorry for that
later. He wanted to ask about the forest and the direction
he should take.

Hoping for an answer, he asked, "Is anyone   437
within?"

She answered, "Yes."

When he heard that it was a woman's voice, he quickly
wheeled the horse aside upon untrodden grass. Yet he felt
that even in this he was too slow, and he smarted with
shame that he had not dismounted before.

He tethered his horse to the branch of a fallen tree and
hung his hole-ridden shield there too. When for courtesy's
sake the bold yet gentle man had also removed his sword,
he went to the window in the wall to ask what he wished

[2] Another reference to Hartmann's *Iwein*. See Book V, 253. The
implication here is that Lady Lunete would not have dared to give such
counsel to Sigune.

to know. The cell was empty of joy, bare of all gaiety. He
found nothing there but great sorrow. He asked her to
come to the window, and the pale maiden rose courteously
from her knees. Even then he did not know who she was
nor who she might possibly be. She wore a hair shirt next
to her skin, under her gown of grey. Great sorrow was her
dearest companion; it had crushed her high spirits and
had pressed from her heart many sighs.

Politely the maid came to the window and greeted him
with friendly words. She carried a psalter in her   438
hand, and Parzival the warrior noticed a little ring which
in all her misery she had never taken off, but wore it still,
as true love counseled her. The stone in it was a garnet
which gleamed out through the darkness like a little spark
of fire. The band that held her hair was proof of her sorrowing love.[3]

"Out there by the wall, Sir," she said, "there is a bench.
Have a seat there if you like and if your affairs permit. For
the greeting which you have given me may God reward
you, as He rewards all true courtesy."

The hero did as she advised him and sat down by the
window, asking her too to be seated inside.

"Seldom have I sat here with a man," she said.

The hero began to question her about what she did here
and how she lived. "It seems to me strange, Lady, that you
live so far from the road in this wilderness. What do you
live from when all around you there is not one human
dwelling?"

"My food comes here to me directly from the Grail," she
said. "Cundrie *la sorcière,* as she herself arranged,   439
brings me every Saturday night food enough for the whole
week." And she added, "If only all else were well with me,
I would take little thought for food—of that I have enough."

Then Parzival thought she was lying and that she wished
to mislead him in other ways too. So he said to her jokingly,
"For whom are you wearing that ring? I've always heard
it said that hermitess and hermit were not allowed to have
amours."

[3] This band was worn by widows.

She said, "If your words had the power, you would like to dishonor me. If I ever learn to deal falsely, reproach me with it if you are present. God willing, I am free from all dishonor, and far from any ill will." And she added, "This betrothal ring I wear for the sake of a beloved man, whose love in the *human* sense I never possessed. It is my virgin heart that bids me love him so." And again she spoke, "I have him here within, whose token I have worn ever since Orilus' spear struck him down. All the years 440 of my life of mourning I will dedicate to my love for him. True love will I give to him, who with shield and spear and with knightly hand wooed me until he died in my service. I am a maid, and unmarried, yet in the sight of God he is my husband. If thoughts are the same as deeds, then I have nothing to conceal which would sever my marriage bond. His death brought grief to my life. This true marriage ring shall go with me into God's presence. The tears that stream from my heart are the bolts and bars of my fidelity. Here within I am not alone. Schianatulander is the one, and I am the other."

Then Parzival understood that it was Sigune, and her grief weighed heavy on him. Before he spoke to her again, he went to the trouble of removing his coif of mail, leaving his head uncovered.

The maiden, perceiving how his skin shone fair through the grime of the iron, at once recognized the sturdy warrior. "Is it you, Sir Parzival?" she said. "How fares it with your search for the Grail? Have you at last dis- 441 covered its true nature? How has your journey been?"

He said to the highborn maiden, "Great joy I lost there, and sorrow enough does the Grail bring me. I left a land where I wore the crown, and the loveliest wife as well— never on this earth was one more beautiful born of human kind. I long for her gentle courtesy, and for her love I sorely mourn—yet even more for the high goal, to behold Munsalvaesche and the Grail. That has not yet come to pass. Cousin Sigune, it is cruel of you to bear me such ill will when you know how many are my cares."

The maid replied, "All my censure of you, cousin, I

shall withdraw. You have indeed lost much joy through being so slow and not asking the precious question when the sweet Anfortas was your host and your happiness. Your question then would have gained you the supreme reward. Now your joy must languish and your noble spirit go lame. Your heart has tamed care, which would be wild and alien to you, had you but asked your question then."

"I did as one who is bound to be the loser," he   442 said. "Dear cousin, give me counsel. Remember how close we are of kin, and tell me too how things stand with you. I would lament for your sorrow, save that I bear a grief greater than any man has ever borne. My misery is beyond all measure."

She said, "Now may help come to you from the hand of Him who knows all sorrow. You may perhaps succeed in finding a track which will lead you to Munsalvaesche, where, as you say, your joy abides. Cundrie *la sorcière* just now rode away from here. I am sorry I did not ask whether she meant to return there or to some other place. Always when she comes, her mule stands there where the spring flows out of the rock. I advise you to ride after her. She may not be so far ahead but that you could soon overtake her."

Then there was no tarrying more. The hero bade farewell, and turned to the fresh hoof track, the way Cundrie's mule had gone. But misfortune and the pathless woods[4] prevented him from pursuing the track he had seen. And so, once more, the Grail was lost to him, and his   443 joy was then forgot. I think, if he had come then to Munsalvaesche, he would have done better at questioning than you heard of him before. Well, let him ride, but where shall he go?

There came riding toward him a man, his head bare, wearing a rich and costly surcoat, and under it armor shining bright. Except for his head he was fully armed. He rode straight toward Parzival and said, "Sir, I do not like

---

[4] The word *ungeverte* has the double meaning of "misfortune" and "pathlessness."

it that you thus invade my lord's forest. You will speedily get a rebuke you will feel very painfully. Munsalvaesche is not accustomed to let anyone come so near unless he were ready to face perilous strife or make the atonement which outside this forest is known as Death."

In his hand he carried a helmet with ties of silken cord and a sharp spearhead on a fresh shaft. Angrily the hero bound the helmet on his head. His threats and his fighting too were soon to cost him dear. No matter, he readied himself for the joust.   444

But Parzival too had splintered many a spear just as costly. He thought to himself, "It would be my death if I rode over this man's crops. What could avail me then against his wrath? But here, after all, I am trampling down only wild fern. If my hands and both arms do not fail me, I'll pay him a price for my journey so that his hand will not stop me."

Both set their horses at a gallop, spurring them on to full career, and neither joust missed its aim. But many a thrust of spear had Parzival's sturdy chest confronted, and training and impulse both taught him to aim his thrust straight at the knot in the helmet cords—he struck him just where one holds the shield in knightly sport.[5] The templar from Munsalvaesche fell from his horse and rolled far down into a ravine so steep that he scarce found place for sleeping.

Parzival rushed ahead. His horse was going too fast to stop. It plunged into the chasm and was dashed to pieces. Parzival gripped the branch of a cedar tree with   445 his hands. Now please don't hold it against him that, lacking a hangman, he hanged himself. With his feet he caught hold of the hard rock beneath him. Down below, in the pathless waste, his horse lay dead.

The knight was hastily escaping up the opposite slope. Did he intend to share his winnings from the fight with Parzival? He would do better to get a donation at home from the Grail.

---

[5] The explanation usually given is that Parzival struck the templar at the spot just above the upper edge of the shield, namely, on the chin.

Parzival climbed back again. The templar's horse had caught its feet in the reins, which were dragging on the ground, and it stood there as if it had been ordered to wait, an order which that knight had quite forgotten to give. Parzival swung himself on its back. Nothing was missing but his spear, and the find of the horse outweighed that loss. I think that neither the strong Lehelin nor the proud Kingrisin, neither *le roi* Gramoflanz nor *le comte* Lascoyt, *le fils de* Gurnemanz, ever rode a better joust than the one in which this horse was won.

Then Parzival rode away, he knew not where, but he met with no further attack from the knights of Munsalvaesche. The Grail was far away, and that saddened him.

Whoever cares to listen, I will tell how he   446
fared after that. I cannot count the weeks nor reckon how long the time Parzival rode, seeking adventure as before. One morning a light snow had fallen, yet thick enough for people to feel the chill. It was in a great forest, and toward him came a knight, old and with beard all grey, but his skin was fair and bright. His wife had the same appearance, and both wore rough grey cloaks over their naked bodies for their pilgrimage of penance. His children, two young maidens, a joy to look upon, came after, dressed in the same manner. Following the counsel of their humble hearts, all four were walking barefoot. Parzival greeted the grey knight as he passed, whose counsel was later to bring him happiness. He looked like a man of noble birth. The ladies had little dogs which ran along beside. With modest mien and far from proud, other knights and squires walked with them reverently. They too were on this pilgrimage, many so young they were beardless yet.

Parzival the noble warrior was dressed with   447
great care in garments richly adorned and knightly. The armor in which he rode was very unlike those clothes which the grey man coming toward him wore. He immediately pulled on the horse's bridle, turning it off the path, and asked the good people what their journey meant. With friendly speech they answered him. Then the grey knight spoke out his regret that the holy days had not moved him

to cease riding armed or to go barefoot and thus to celebrate this day.

Parzival answered him, "Sir, I have no idea when the year began nor how many weeks have passed. Not even what day of the week it is—of all that I know nothing. I used to serve one whose name is God until He in His charity doomed me to shameful disgrace. My mind had never wavered from Him Who I was told would give me help. Yet now His help has failed me."

Then the grey knight said, "Do you mean 448 God, Whom the Virgin bore? If you believe He became a man and what He suffered for our sakes as on this day, wherefore we celebrate this season, then it is not right for you to wear armor thus. Today is Good Friday, when the whole world can rejoice, yet at the same time sigh in grief. Where was a love more faithful ever shown than that which God showed for us, Who for our sakes was hung on the Cross? Sir, if you have been baptized, you should lament that exchange. To redeem our guilt, He gave His precious life and paid the price of death because mankind was lost and for its guilt destined for hell. If you are not a heathen, Sir, be mindful of this day. Ride on, following our track. Not far ahead of you there lives a holy man. He will give you counsel and impose penance on you for your offense. And if you will confess to him and repent, he will absolve you from sin."

His daughters spoke up. "Why do you want to punish him, Father? With the bad weather we're having, how can you give him such advice? Why don't you take 449 him where he can get warm? His iron-clad arms, for all they look so knightly—we think they must be cold. Even if he had the strength of *three* men, he would freeze. You have tents near by and a store of pilgrims' cloaks. If King Arthur himself came to visit you, you would have enough food to entertain him well. Now do as a host should, and take this knight with you."

Then the grey man said, "Sir, what my daughters say is true. Every year I journey to this wild forest, to a place near here, whether it is warm or cold, and always at the time when He was martyred, Who gives for service sure reward. What food I brought with me, for His sake, I'll gladly share with you."

The maidens, kindly disposed toward him, begged him eagerly to stay. It would be to his honor, they said, and they meant it quite sincerely. Parzival looked at them and saw, though sweat there was none because of the frost, that their mouths were red and warm and full. They did not seem as sad as would have been fitting on this day. —If I had some little thing to avenge on them, I would be reluctant to give up my grudge unless I could get a kiss of atonement, that is, if they would say yes to that atonement. Women are always women. Even the strongest man they have conquered in a trice. In that they've often been successful.   450

All around him Parzival heard their friendly words and pleading, from father, mother, and daughters. "If I remain with them," he thought, "I shall feel ill at ease in this company. These maidens are so lovely, for me to ride beside them would be unfitting since men and women here go on foot. It is better that I part from them, for I hate Him Whom they love with all their hearts and from Whom they look for help. He has barred His help to me and has not spared me sorrow."

Parzival spoke to them then and said, "Sir, and Lady, let me take leave of you now. May good fortune bring you blessing and your full share of joy. Sweet maidens, let your own gracious courtesy be your reward that you were concerned for my comfort. And now I must bid you farewell." He bowed, and the others bowed. And they did   451 not restrain their laments.

Away rides Herzeloyde's son. His manly breeding inclined him to virtue and compassion. And since the young Herzeloyde had bequeathed to him true loyalty, repentance arose in his heart. Now for the first time he thought on his Creator, how He had made the whole world and how mighty was His power. "What if God will give help to overcome my sadness?" he said. "If ever He wished a knight well and if ever a knight earned His reward, if He deems shield and sword and true manly combat to be worthy enough of His help that His help may heal my sorrow, if today is His day for helping, then let Him help, if help He can!"

He turned and rode back the way he had come. They were still standing there, grieving to see him going from them. Their true hearts moved the maidens to follow him with their eyes, and his heart told him too that he liked to look upon them, for their radiance seemed to him so beautiful.

He said, "If God's power is so great that it   452 can guide both horse and beast, and men as well, then I will praise His power. If God's art possesses such help, then let it show this Castilian of mine the road that is best for me. Thus His kindness shall show its help. —Now go, whichever way God chooses!" And he let the reins fall loosely over his horse's ears and urged it on vigorously with his spurs.

It took the path toward Fontane la Salvatsche, where Orilus had received the oath.[6] Here lived the pious Trevrizent, who many a Monday had little to eat, and many a full week too. He had renounced wine, either mulberry or grape, and even bread. His piety demanded still more from him—he had no desire for food such as fish or flesh, in which there had been blood. Such was his holy life. God had turned his thoughts toward making ready to meet the heavenly host. He chastened himself with fasting, and his continence struggled with the Devil.

From him now Parzival will hear the mysteries of the Grail.

Anyone who asked me before about the Grail   453 and took me to task for not telling him was very much in the wrong. Kyot asked me not to reveal this, for Adventure commanded him to give it no thought until she herself, Adventure, should invite the telling, and then one *must* speak of it, of course.

Kyot, the well-known master, found in Toledo, discarded,

---

[6] Book V, 269.

set down in heathen writing, the first source of this adventure. He had first to learn the *abc*'s, but without the art of black magic. It helped him that he was baptized, else this story would still be unknown. No heathen art could be of use in revealing the nature of the Grail and how its mysteries were discovered.

A heathen, Flegetanis, had achieved high renown for his learning. This scholar of nature was descended from Solomon and born of a family which had long been Israelite until baptism became our shield against the fire of Hell. He wrote the adventure of the Grail. On his   454
father's side Flegetanis was a heathen, who worshipped a calf as if it were his god. —How can the Devil bring people so wise to such a shameful pass that they do not and did not distinguish between a calf and Him Whose hand is supreme and to Whom all wonders are known?

The heathen Flegetanis could tell us how all the stars set and rise again and how long each one revolves before it reaches its starting point once more. To the circling course of the stars man's affairs and destiny are linked. Flegetanis the heathen saw with his own eyes in the constellations things he was shy to talk about, hidden mysteries. He said there was a thing called the Grail whose name he had read clearly in the constellations. "A host of angels left it on the earth and then flew away up over the stars. Was it their innocence that drew them away? Since then baptized men have had the task of guarding it, and with such chaste discipline that those who are called to the service of the Grail are always noble men." Thus wrote Fle-   455
getanis of these things.

Kyot, the wise master, set about to trace this tale in Latin books, to see where there ever had been a people, dedicated to purity and worthy of caring for the Grail. He read the chronicles of the lands, in Britain and elsewhere, in France and in Ireland, and in Anjou he found the tale. There he read the true story of Mazadan, and the exact record of all his family was written there, and further how Titurel and his son Frimutel bequeathed the Grail to Anfortas, whose sister Herzeloyde was. By her Gahmuret had a child who is the hero of this story. He is riding now along the new path on which the grey knight met him.

He recognized a place, though snow lay there now, where bright flowers had grown before, just close by a mountain wall, the spot where his manly hand had won favor for Lady Jeschute and Orilus' wrath had vanished. But the path would not let him stop there.   456
Fontane la Salvatsche that place was called where his journey led him. There he found the host, who welcomed him.

The hermit said to him, "Alas, Sir, what ill fortune has been yours in this holy season? Did perilous strife force you into this armor? Or have you ridden unchallenged? If so, another garb would befit you better, did your pride but permit it. But now, Sir, please dismount—you will not find that unpleasant, I imagine—and warm yourself by a fire. Did Adventure send you out seeking love's reward? If your longing is for true love, then love with the love that belongs to this day. You can serve some other time for a lady's favor. But dismount, I pray you."

Parzival the warrior dismounted at once and standing with great modesty before him, he told of the people who had shown him the way and how they had praised the hermit's counsels. Then he said, "Sir, now give me counsel. I am a man who has sinned."

When Parzival finished speaking, the good man   457
answered him, "I promise you my counsel. But tell me first who it was that sent you here."

"Sir, in the forest I met a grey man who greeted me kindly, and so did all his company. That man free of falsity sent me here to you. I followed his track until I found you."

"That was Gabenis," said the host. "He knows how a noble man conducts himself. He is a prince from Punturtois, and the rich King of Kareis is wedded to his sister. Never were more excellent children born than those two maidens of his whom you encountered there. The prince is of royal lineage, yet every year he comes on pilgrimage to me."

Parzival said to his host, "When I saw you standing

there, and rode up to you, were you at all afraid? Weren't you apprehensive at my arrival?"

"Sir, believe me," the hermit answered, "bear or stag have frightened me more often than a man. One thing I can say truly, I fear nothing that is human. I know how to deal with humans. If you will not think me   458 boastful, I could say as to running away I am still a virgin. Never, in all my fighting days, did my heart grow so faint that I fled from battle. I was a knight as you are, and like you, I strove for noble love. Sometimes I mingled sinful thoughts with the good. I lived a life of pomp and show to gain a lady's favor. I have forgotten all that now. Give me your reins. There under the face of that cliff your horse can stand and rest. Later on we will both go and gather fern and young buds and twigs of fir for him; I have no other fodder. But we shall find enough for him to eat."

Parzival did not want him to take the reins. "Your courtesy will surely not permit you to oppose your host, if your courtesy be not marred with incivility," the good man said. Parzival yielded his host the reins, and the latter led the horse under that cliff, where the sun seldom shone in and a gushing spring flowed through. That was a wild stable.

Parzival stood on the snow. Even a weaker   459 man than he would have suffered, wearing armor in such a cutting frost. His host led him into a cave where the wind rarely penetrated. There were glowing coals, a welcome sight for the guest. The host lit a candle, and the warrior laid off his armor. For a seat he had straw and fern, and as his limbs grew warm, his skin shone with a rosy glow. Well might he be weary from the forest, for he had ridden where few roads were and last night, as many another night, had waited roofless for the day. Now he had found a kindly host.

A cloak lay there. His host gave it to him to put on and led him into another cave where were the books the good man read. An altar stone stood there, bare, as is the custom on this day, and on it a casket with holy relics. This Parzival knew at once for the one on which his hand had sworn an oath without deception, whereby Lady Jeschute's suffering had been turned to love and she had felt joy again.

Parzival said to his host, "Sir, I recognize this   460 casket, for I swore an oath on it once when I was passing by. I found here, beside it, a spear painted in bright colors. I took that away with me, Sir, and from what I was told later on, won some glory with it. I was lost so deep in thoughts of my wife that my senses left me. Two excellent jousts I rode with that spear, not knowing I was fighting. *Then* I still had honor. *Now* I have more cares than were ever seen in a man. Sir, by your courtesy tell me, how long ago is it since I took that spear away?"

The good man answered, "My friend Taurian forgot and left it here, and later lamented to me its loss. Four years and a half and three days it has been since you took it away with you. If you care to hear, I shall prove it to you." From the psalter he read him exactly the years and even the number of weeks that had passed meanwhile.[7]

"Only now do I perceive how long I have ridden unguided and bereft of joy," Parzival said. "To me   461 joy is a dream, and grief the heavy burden that I bear. Sir, I will tell you more. Wherever church or minster stood, wherever men spoke God's praise, there no eye, since that time, has ever seen me. I looked for nothing but fighting. And toward God I bear great hatred, for He stood godfather to my cares. He has heaped them up all too high, and my joy lies buried beneath them. If God's power could be of any help, what an anchor my joy would be! But now it sinks down through bottomless depths of grief. If my manly heart is wounded—and how could it remain whole where sorrow presses her thorny crown on the fame my knightly skill won for me in combat—then I say, shame upon Him Who has all power to help, if His help is swift to help and He is the lord of all help, as they say, that He does not then help me."

---

[7] A psalter is a collection of psalms bound as a small devotional book, to which there was sometimes added a calendar as a guide to church observances of the year

His host sighed and looked at him. Then he said, "Sir, if you are in your right mind, you ought to put your trust in God. He will help you, for He must. May God   462 help us both! Sir, explain to me—but first be seated—tell me calmly and soberly how that wrath began whereby God got your hatred.

"But before you accuse Him to me, have the patience of your courtesy and hear from me His innocence. His help has never failed. Though I was but a layman, I could read the Scriptures and set forth in writing how man should be steadfast in serving Him Whose help is great and Who never wearies in helping the soul that may be lost. Be loyal without any wavering, for God Himself is loyalty. Falseness was ever hateful to Him. We should be grateful to Him; He did much for us when His noble, lofty nature took on, for our sakes, the likeness of a man. God is called, and is, truth. False ways He has ever abhorred. Reflect carefully upon this. He cannot be untrue to any man. Now let your thought teach you to beware of wavering toward Him.

"You can wrest nothing from Him with   463 anger. Anyone seeing you defy Him in hate will think you are weak in your wits. Consider what befell Lucifer and his fellows. They once knew nothing of gall.[8] Now, Sir, where did they get that rancor, for which their endless strife now reaps its bitter reward in hell? Astiroth and Belcimon, Belet and Radamant, and others I know about—that shining heavenly host through rancor became the color of hell.

"When Lucifer with his host took his way to hell, man was created in his stead. God fashioned from earth the noble Adam. From Adam's living body He sundered Eve, who, not heeding her Creator, delivered us up to suffering and destroyed our happiness. From these two now came children, born.[9] *One,* driven by his discontent, in greedy arrogance robbed his grandmother of her virginity. There are some who do not wait till they hear the rest of this tale

[8] I.e., the gall of hate and anger.
[9] Born, not created as God had created Adam and Eve.

and understand it, but want to know straightway how such a thing could be. Yet that is clear—through sin."

Parzival said to him, "Sir, I do not think this 464 ever happened. Of whom was that man born who robbed his ancestress, as you say, of her virginity? You might better have kept silent about that."

But his host replied, "I shall take away your doubt. If I do not tell you the real truth, you may reproach me for my deception. The earth was Adam's mother; from the fruits of the earth Adam lived and nourished himself. And yet the earth was a virgin. But I have not told you yet who took her virginity from her. Adam was Cain's father. Cain slew Abel for the sake of paltry possessions. When blood then fell upon the pure earth, her virginity was forfeit, and it was Adam's son who took it from her. Then, for the first time, hatred sprang up among men, and so it has been ever since.

"In all the world there is truly nothing so pure as a maiden innocent of guile. Just think how pure maidens are. God Himself was the Maiden's child. Two men were born of maidens. God Himself took on human countenance like that of the first maiden's child. That was a gracious courtesy from Him Whose nature is so exalted.

"From Adam's race there sprang both sorrow 465 and bliss: bliss that He Whom all the angels see exalted above them did not deny His kinship with us, and sorrow that that race[10] is a wagonload of sin and that we must bear that sin. May the power of Him with Whom compassion dwells have pity upon us! Since He was once a man, and true, and fought faithfully against all that was false, you should make your peace with Him. If you do not wish to forfeit your salvation, make atonement for your sin. Do not be so free in word and deed. He who seeks to avenge his suffering by speaking insolently—I'll tell you what reward he will get—his own mouth will condemn him.

"Hear now age-old tales as if they were new, that they

---

[10] I.e., Adam's race.

may teach you to speak true. Plato foretold it in his day, and Sibyl, the prophetess, too. Long years ago they told us, with no fault or error, that to us there would surely come redemption for the greatest guilt. With divine love the hand of the Highest delivered us from hell, only the wicked did He leave there.

"Of this true Lover these sweet tidings tell. He   466
is a brightly shining light and does not waver from His love. The man to whom He gives His love finds bliss in that love.

"God shares two things with man, His love and His hate, and all the world can choose between them. Now consider which would help you more. The unrepentant sinner flees from God's true love, but he who atones for the guilt of his sins does service for the sake of noble grace. This grace is His Who penetrates our thoughts. Thoughts can be hidden from the light of the sun; thoughts are secure without a lock, proof against all creatures; thoughts are darkness without light. Only the Deity can be so pure and bright that it pierces this wall of darkness, like a rider running to the attack, but soundless and unseen. There is no thought so swift, as it springs from the heart, but that, before it can pass from the heart out through the skin, it is already judged by God. Pure thoughts He approves. Since God perceives our *thoughts* so clearly, alas that our feeble *works* grieve Him! When by works a man forfeits His   467
grace and the Deity must be ashamed of him, to whom can human guidance entrust this man? Where can the poor soul find refuge? If you would now do harm to God, Who is ready for both, for love or for wrath, then you are lost. Now turn your heart to Him, that He may acknowledge your goodness."

Parzival then replied, "Sir, I am very glad that you have told me of Him Who leaves nothing unrewarded, whether it be wickedness or virtue. But I have spent my youth in care, up to this very day, and for my faithfulness have received only sorrow."

His host spoke to him again. "If you have no reason to conceal it, I would gladly hear what is your sorrow and your sin. If you will place them before me, perhaps I can give you counsel which you yourself do not have."

Then Parzival said, "My greatest grief is for the Grail, after that, for my own wife. Never on earth did a fairer child suck at a mother's breast. I yearn for both with longing."

"Well spoken, Sir," said the host. "This sorrow   468 that you suffer is right and good if you yearn for your own wife. If you remain true in marriage, then though you suffer the pain of hell, that distress will soon come to an end, and with God's help you will straightway be freed from its bonds.

"You say you yearn for the Grail. You foolish man, I am grieved to hear that. For no man can ever win the Grail unless he is known in heaven and he be called by name to the Grail. This I must tell you about the Grail, for I know it to be so and have seen it for myself."

"Were you there?" asked Parzival.

His host replied, "Sir, I was."

Parzival did not reveal that he too had once been there, but asked the hermit to tell him about the Grail.

"Well I know," said his host, "that many brave knights dwell with the Grail at Munsalvaesche. Always when they ride out, as they often do, it is to seek adventure. They do so for their sins, these templars, whether their reward be defeat or victory. A valiant host lives there, and   469 I will tell you how they are sustained. They live from a stone of purest kind. If you do not know it, it shall here be named to you. It is called *lapsit exillis*.[11] By the power of that stone the phoenix burns to ashes, but the ashes give him life again. Thus does the phoenix molt and change its

---

[11] Many different explanations have been given for these two words, but the attempted derivations are not necessary in order to understand the story. The words are apparently a corruption of some Latin phrase, but no one knows for certain what that phrase was. Such interpretations have been made as: *lapis ex caelis*, "stone from the heavens"; *lapsit ex caelis*, "it fell from the heavens"; *lapis elixir*, which would correspond to the philosopher's stone. Stapel suggests that Wolfram, depending on memory only, ran two words together in *lapis*, the full phrase having been *lapis lapsus ex caelis*, "a stone fallen from heaven."

plumage, which afterward is bright and shining and as
lovely as before. There never was a human so ill but that,
if he one day sees that stone, he cannot die within the week
that follows. And in looks he will not fade. His appearance
will stay the same, be it maid or man, as on the day he saw
the stone, the same as when the best years of his life began,
and though he should see the stone for two hundred years,
it will never change, save that his hair might perhaps turn
grey. Such power does the stone give a man that flesh and
bones are at once made young again. The stone is also
called the Grail.

"This very day there comes to it a message wherein lies
its greatest power. Today is Good Friday, and   470
they await there a dove, winging down from Heaven. It
brings a small white wafer, and leaves it on the stone. Then,
shining white, the dove soars up to Heaven again. Always
on Good Friday it brings to the stone what I have just
told you, and from that the stone derives whatever good
fragrances of drink and food there are on earth, like to the
perfection of Paradise. I mean all things the earth may
bear. And further the stone provides whatever game lives
beneath the heavens, whether it flies or runs or swims. Thus,
to the knightly brotherhood, does the power of the Grail
give sustenance.

"Hear now how those called to the Grail are made
known. On the stone, around the edge, appear letters in-
scribed, giving the name and lineage of each one, maid or
boy, who is to take this blessed journey. No one needs to
rub out the inscription, for once he has read the name, it
fades away before his eyes. All those now grown   471
to maturity came there as children. Blessed is the mother
who bore a child destined to do service there. Poor and
rich alike rejoice if their child is summoned to join this
company. They are brought there from many lands. From
sinful shame they are more protected than others, and receive good reward in heaven. When life dies for them
here, they are given perfection *there.*

"Those who took neither side when Lucifer and the

Trinity fought—these angels, noble and worthy, were compelled to descend to earth, to this same stone. Yet the stone is always pure. I know not if God forgave them or condemned them still more. If it was His right to do so, He took them back again. Since then the stone has always been in the care of those God called to this task and to whom He sent His angel. Sir, such is the nature of the Grail."

Then Parzival spoke and said, "If knighthood 472
with shield and spear can win renown in this life and Paradise for the soul as well—for knighthood I have always striven. I fought wherever I found a battle, and in such way that my armed hand had highest honor within its reach. If God is a good judge of fighting, He should summon me by name to the Grail so that they may come to know me. My hand shall not fail me there in battle."

"But there," said his devout host, "a humble will would have to guard you against pride. Your youth could all too easily tempt you to violate the virtue of moderation. Pride has always sunk and fallen." So said the hermit, and tears welled up in his eyes as he thought of the things which he was about to tell.

Then he said, "Sir, a king was there who was called and is still called Anfortas. You, and I too, poor though I be, should never cease to feel compassion for his grief of heart, which pride gave him as reward. His youth and power brought grief to all around him, and his desire for love beyond all restraint and bounds.

"Such ways are not fitting for the Grail. There 473
both knight and squire must guard themselves against incontinence. Humility has conquered their pride. A noble brotherhood dwells there, who with valiant strength have warded off the people of all lands so that the Grail is unknown save to those who have been called by name to Munsalvaesche to the Grail's company. Only one came there unbidden. That was a foolish man who took sin away with him, since he said not a word to the king about the distress he could see in him. I make no reproach to anyone,

but he will have sin to atone for in not inquiring about his host's affliction. He was so heavily stricken with suffering that never was such great anguish known.

"Before that, *le roi* Lehelin had once come riding to the lake of Brumbane where Lybbeals, the noble hero from Prienlascors, was expecting him for a joust. But in that joust Lybbeals was destined to die, and Lehelin led the hero's horse away with him. This despoiling of a corpse was soon discovered.

"Sir, are you Lehelin? For in my stable stands   474 a horse that looks exactly like the horses belonging to the company of the Grail. On the saddle is a turtledove. That horse comes from Munsalvaesche. It was Anfortas who assigned his knights this emblem, which formerly only their shields had borne when he was still a man of joy. Titurel bequeathed this emblem to his son, *le roi* Frimutel, who, wearing it on his shield, lost his life in a joust. Frimutel loved his wife as never another man had loved a woman, I mean, in true faithfulness. You should renew this way of his and love your wife with all your heart. You should do as he did, for your looks resemble his. He too was once Lord of the Grail. Sir, tell me, where do you come from? And to what family do you belong?"

Each looked the other full in the face.

Parzival said to his host, "I am descended from a man who lost his life in a joust because of his love of knighthood. Sir, by your kindness, give him a place in   475 your prayers. My father's name was Gahmuret. He was by race an Angevin. Sir, I am not Lehelin. If I ever despoiled a corpse, it was when I still had no sense. Nevertheless I did it, and I must admit to that sin. Ither of Kukumerlant I slew with my sinful hand. I laid him dead upon the grass and took from him what there was to take."

"Alas, world, how can you be so?" said the host, troubled at these words. "You give people more grief of heart than joy, and more of care and sorrow. Such is your reward! Thus ends the melody of your tale."

Then he said, "Dear son of my sister, what counsel

can I give you now? You have slain your own flesh and
blood. If you bring your guilt before God, seeing that you
were both of one blood, then if God gives a judgment that
is just, you will pay for that with your life. What recompense can you make for him? In Ither of Gaheviez God
had revealed the fruits of true nobility by which the world
was purified. He grieved at all wrongdoing, he,   476
the spice of balsam upon good faith! All worldly shame fled
before him, and virtue entered his heart. Noble women
should hate you for the sake of this beloved man. So
devotedly did he serve them, women's eyes lighted up for
joy from his sweetness when they saw him. May God have
mercy on you for causing such distress! My sister, too,
died because of you, your mother Herzeloyde."

"No, oh no, good Sir! What are you saying?" said Parzival.
"Even were I Lord of the Grail, that could not compensate
for what your lips have told me. If I am your sister's child,
deal with me in good faith, and tell me honestly, are both
of these things true?"

The good man answered, "I am not one who can deceive.
Your mother, for her faithful love of you, died the instant
after you parted from her. You were the beast she suckled
and the dragon which flew away from her, as came to pass
in her dream before she, sweet one, gave birth to you.

"I have two other sisters besides. My sister   477
Schoysiane bore a child, but of that birth she died. Her
husband was Duke Kyot of Catalonia, who after that renounced all joy. Sigune, his little daughter, was given into
your mother's care. Schoysiane's death still cuts me to the
heart. Her woman's heart was so good, an ark against the
impure flood.

"A maiden, my other sister, lives so that purity is her
companion. Repanse de Schoye tends the Grail, which is so
heavy that all of sinful humanity cannot move it from its
place.

"Her brother and mine is Anfortas, who, by right of
birth, both was and is the Lord of the Grail. Alas, joy is far
from him. Only one hope does he have, that his suffer-

ing will one day bring him to eternal peace. It is a strange tale, how he came to such distress. I will tell it to you, nephew. If your heart is true, you will feel pity for his misfortune.

"When Frimutel, my father, lost his life, they   478 chose his eldest son to succeed him as king and Lord of the Grail and the Grail's company. That was my brother Anfortas, who was worthy of crown and power. We were still small. Then my brother reached the age when his beard began to grow—the time when Love wages battle with youth. Here Love does not act quite honorably, one must say, for she presses her friend so hard. But if any Lord of the Grail craves a love other than the writing on the Grail allows him, he will suffer distress and grievous misery.

"My lord and brother chose for himself a lady, of virtue, so he thought. Who she was does not matter. In her service he fought as one from whom cowardice has fled. Many a shield's rim was riddled for her by his good hand. With his adventures the sweet and valiant man won such fame that never in all the lands where chivalry held sway could any one question that his was the greatest of all. *Amor* was his battle cry. But that cry is not quite appropriate   479 for a spirit of humility.

"One day the king rode out alone—and sorely did his people rue it—in search of adventure, rejoicing in Love's assistance. Love's desire compelled him to it. With a poisoned spear he was wounded so in the jousting, your sweet uncle, that he never again was healed, pierced through the testicles.

"It was a heathen who fought him in that joust, born in Ethnise, where from Paradise the Tigris flows. This heathen was sure that his valor would win the Grail. Its name[12] was engraved on his spear, and only for the sake of the Grail's power did he seek knightly deeds far off, roaming over sea and land. In this battle our joy was lost to us.

"Your uncle's fighting was deserving of praise; with the iron spearhead in his body he rode away. When that gallant young man came home to his people, great indeed was their

[12] This could also mean his, the heathen's, name.

grief. The heathen lay dead where he had left   480
him. Let us make lament for him too—but sparingly.

"When the king returned to us so pale and all his strength
ebbed away, a physician probed the wound until he found
the iron spearhead and a splinter of the reed shaft, and removed them. I fell on my knees and prayed. I made a vow
to God Almighty that nevermore would I practice knighthood if only He, for the sake of His own great name,
would help my brother from that distress. And I renounced
flesh also, and wine and bread, and all things that have
blood in them, and swore nevermore to desire them. That
caused fresh sorrow for the people, dear nephew—and I
am speaking the truth—when I parted with my sword.
They said, 'Who shall be the guardian now of the mystery
of the Grail?' Bright eyes were weeping there.

"Straightway, hoping for God's help, they carried the king
to the Grail. When the king beheld the Grail, that brought
him further anguish, since now he could not die. Death was
not permitted him, seeing I had dedicated myself   481
to a life of poverty, and the lordship of that noble race hung
upon such weak strength.

"The king's wound had festered, and we found no
help in all the books of medicine we read. All cures that
are known for aspis, ecidemon, ehcontius and lisis, jecis
and meatris—these harmful snakes all bear a burning poison—and all that are known for the stings of other venom-
ous serpents, all the herbs wise physicians have found in
their study of the art of healing—but let me be brief—none
of these could help. God himself denied us their aid.

"We sought help from the Geon and the Fison, the
Euphrates and the Tigris,[13] the four streams flowing out of
Paradise, and to Paradise we came so near, where its
sweet fragrance has still not faded away, to see if perhaps
there might come drifting some herb that would take our
sorrow from us. It was labor lost. Our grieving began
afresh.

"Still we kept on trying various things. We obtained the

[13] Genesis 2, 11-14, in the Vulgate version. Luther and the King
James Bible give variant names.

very bough which the Sibyl had told Aeneas[14]   482
would protect him from Hell's pain and from the smoke of
the Phlegethon[15] and from the other rivers flowing there.
Long did we search till we found that healing bough,
thinking perhaps the dreadful spear, which was destroying
our joy, might itself have been poisoned and tempered in
the fire of hell. But that proved not to be so.

"There is a bird called the pelican. When it has young, it
loves them beyond all measure. Its loyal love impels it to
bite its own breast and let the blood run into the beaks of
the young ones. It dies in that very hour. We secured the
blood of this bird, to try if its loyal love would help us too,
and we rubbed it as best we could on the wound. That did
not help us.

"There is a beast called the unicorn, which is so attracted
by the purity of virgins that it falls asleep in their laps. We
took a portion of this animal's heart to heal the king's pain.
And we took the garnet from the same animal's   483
forehead where it grows beneath the horn. We rubbed the
edge of the wound and even inserted the stone into the
wound, which seemed to be full of venom. This was painful
to us and to the king.

"Then we got an herb called trachonte.[16] Of this herb we
hear it said that when a dragon is slain, it springs up from
the blood. This herb is inclined to have the characteristics of
air.[17] Perhaps the Scorpion's[18] orbit in the sky would help us
too in the time before the planets turn backward in their
course and the change of the moon begins—this was when
the wound pained most. But even this herb's high and noble
origin was of no avail.

"We fell on our knees in prayer before the Grail. All at

[14] An allusion to Aeneas' visit to the Lower World, probably suggested by Heinrich von Veldeke's *Eneit*.

[15] The flaming, smoking river of the Lower World.

[16] Greek *drakóntion*, "dragon-wort."

[17] I.e., it is dry and cold, antidotes for the wound that is moist and hot.

[18] This is the sign of the Zodiac, which relates to the genital organs. The scorpion is of course identical with the dragon, and a repetition of the dragon motif in the dragon-wort.

once we saw written upon it that a knight should come, and
if from him a question came, our sorrow would be ended,
but if anyone, child or maid or man, should prompt him in
any way to the question, his question would not help, but
the wound would remain as before and pain more violently.
The writing said, 'Have you understood? Any prompting
from you can do great harm. If he does not ask   484
the first night, the power of his question will vanish. But if
at the right time his question is asked, he shall be king of
the realm and an end shall be made of your sorrow by the
Hand of the Highest. Then Anfortas shall be healed, but he
shall no longer be king.'

"These words we read upon the Grail, that Anfortas'
anguish would cease once the question came. We spread his
wound with whatever we could to soothe it, with the good
salve nard and other salves mixed with theriac, and we
smoked it with *lign aloe*. Still he was always in pain.

"Then I withdrew to this place. Little joy do the years
bring me here. Since then, a knight did come—I told you
about him before. He would better have stayed away. Only
shame did he win there, for he saw the real sorrow and yet
did not say to his host, 'Sir, why is it you suffer so?' Since
his stupidity bade him *not* to ask, he lost, being slow, great
happiness."

They were both sad at heart. It was now get-   485
ting on toward noon, and the host said, "Let us go and
look for food. Your horse is not provided for. Nor do I have
any food for us unless God shows us where to find it. My
kitchen seldom sends forth smoke. You will be the loser for
that today and all the time you are with me. I would teach
you knowledge of herbs today if only the snow would permit. God grant that it will soon melt! Meanwhile, let us
break twigs of yew. Your horse, I think, often ate better at
Munsalvaesche than here. Yet neither you nor it ever had
a host who would serve you more gladly if only the means
were at hand."

They went out then to search for food. Parzival saw to
the fodder, and his host dug roots. No better food was to
be found. The host did not forget his rule; no matter how

many roots he dug, he ate none of them before the Nones.[19]
He carefully hung them on bushes and went to search for
more. For God's honor he went many a day unfed if he did
not find the bushes again where he had hung his food.

Patiently the two companions went to where   486
the stream was flowing, and there they washed their roots
and herbs, but no sound of laughter was heard from their
lips. They both washed their hands, and Parzival took a
bundle of yew twigs to his horse. Then they went back to
their seats of straw by the coal fire. There was no need to
bring them more to eat. There was nothing boiled or
roasted, and their kitchen was bare. Parzival, moved by the
true affection he bore for his host, felt that here he had
more abundant fare than when Gurnemanz had entertained
him, or in Munsalvaesche when so many ladies in their radiant beauty passed before him and he received the hospitality of the Grail.

The hermit wise and true now spoke, "Nephew, do not
disdain this food. You would not easily find a host who
would welcome you more gladly or more cordially."

"Sir," answered Parzival, "may God's favor be far from
me if ever I received from a host anything that tasted better."

Whatever dishes were served there, if they had   487
left their hands unwashed afterward, it would not have
hurt their eyes to rub them, as people say fishy hands will
do. —As for myself, I assure you, if I were used as a falcon,
and they went with me on the chase, I would soar up—
were my meal such scraps as these—hungrily from the hand
that held me and would show how I could fly.

But why do I make sport of these faithful souls? My
old boorishness makes me do this.[20] Still, you have heard
how they lost their riches and why they were deprived of
joy and were often cold and seldom warm. Only out of
true, unblemished loyalty did they suffer grief of heart.
From the Hand of the Highest they received reward for

---

[19] This is 3 P.M., the traditional hour of Christ's death on the Cross.
[20] In Book IV, 184, Wolfram made fun of the suffering townspeople
of besieged Pelrapeire and then apologized for it afterward.

their sorrow, and God gave both His favor, then and later.[21]

They rose and went out, Parzival and the holy man, to the stable to see to the horse. In tones that had little of joy, the host said to the steed, "I grieve that you must hunger so, since the saddle you wear bears the arms of Anfortas."

After they had cared for the horse, their talk   488 was of another sorrow. Parzival said to his host, "Sir, and dear uncle of mine, if I dared tell you, to my shame, I would lament my misery. By your kindness, I beg you, forgive me. My trust seeks refuge in you. My offense has been so great, if you make me pay for it, I shall lose all consolation, and from sorrow shall never more be redeemed. Bewail my stupidity, and give me counsel. He who rode to Munsalvaesche, he who saw true sorrow there and who put no question—that was I, misfortune's child. Thus, Sir, have I offended."

"Nephew, what are you saying?" said the host. "We should both grieve with all our hearts and let joy slip away, since you know so well the art of renouncing happiness. God gave you five senses, but they denied you their aid. How did they help you then, at the wound of Anfortas, to preserve your loyalty? Yet I will do my best to   489 give you counsel. And you must not grieve too much. You should in right measure grieve and abstain from grief. Mankind is by nature wild and strange. Sometimes it is youth that chooses the path of wisdom. Then if age decides to practice folly and roil the clear ways of youth, what is white becomes dirty, and verdant virtue faded, in which promise of noble worth might otherwise take root.

"If I could give you back your verdant freshness and make your heart so bold that you would strive and win renown and not despair of God, you might succeed in achieving such honor that it would be a recompense. God himself would not forsake you. I am surety for that, in God's name, and I shall give you counsel.

"Now tell me, did you see the spear in the house of Munsalvaesche? When the star Saturn had returned to the zenith, we knew it by the wound and by the summer snow.

[21] I.e., to Parzival and the hermit.

Never had the frost caused your sweet uncle such anguish. The spear had to be thrust into the wound; then   490 one pain helped the other, and from this the spear became blood-red.

"On days when certain stars appear, the people of Munsalvaesche have reason to lament their woe. These are the stars[22] whose courses run parallel, one high above the other, and which move irregularly, in contrast to the others. And the change of the moon also hurts the wound sorely. At the times I have named, the king can find no rest. A great chill torments him so that his flesh becomes colder than snow. At such times, since they know the poison on the iron spear point is hot, they lay it on the wound. That draws the frost out of the body, and it hardens to glass, like ice, around the spear. But no one was able in any way to break this ice off from the spear. Then Trebuchet, the wise man, forged of silver two knives which could cut right through it. A charm engraved on the king's sword had taught him this skill. There are many who claim that the wood aspindê[23] will not burn, but if a bit of this glass fell upon it, a flame of fire shot up, and the aspindê burned. What wondrous things this poison can do!

"The king cannot ride or walk; he cannot lie or   491 stand. He leans but cannot sit, and he sighs, well knowing why. At the change of the moon he suffers much. A lake is there, called Brumbane, and to it they carry him, for the sake of the sweet air and for the sake of his bitter, gaping wound. He calls that his hunting day, but what he can catch there, with a wound so painful—he needs more than that at his house. From this came the rumor that he was a fisherman. The rumor he cannot prevent, but of salmon or lampreys he has very few for sale, this sad and mournful man."

"On that lake," said Parzival quickly, "I saw the king anchored on the water, to catch some fish, I thought, or for other pastime. I had ridden many miles that day. I had left Pelrapeire about mid-morning, and that evening I was wor-

[22] These are the planets.
[23] Probably asbestos.

ried as to where I could find lodging for the night. It was
my uncle who counseled me where to go."

"You rode a perilous way," said his host, "well   492
guarded by outposts, each so manned with fighters that
seldom does anyone succeed in getting through. Any man
who rode there to them was riding into danger. They accept no man's surrender; they stake their life against the
other's. Thus they atone for their sins."

"Well, that time," said Parzival, "I rode without any
fighting to where the king was. That evening I saw the
great hall full of sorrow. Did they find grief so pleasant?
A squire rushed in at the door, and thereat the hall resounded with lamentation. He held in his hands a spear
shaft and bore it around the four walls. In the shaft was
a spear point—blood-red. It was that caused the people distress of sorrow.

"Nephew," said the host, "never before nor since has the
king suffered such pain as then, when with a hard frost,
the star Saturn heralded its coming. It did not help to lay
the spear on the wound as had been done before; they had
to thrust it right into the wound. Saturn climbs   493
so high aloft that the wound knew of its coming before the
other frost[24] arrived. The snow was in even less of a hurry.
It did not fall till the following night, but still during summer's reign. When in this way they warded off the king's
frost, the people were robbed of joy."

And the devout Trevrizent added, "From sorrow they received their wages, for the spear which pierced their hearts
to the core carried away their joy. Then in the constancy of
their grief they were baptized anew."

Parzival said to his host, "Five-and-twenty maidens I
saw there who with courteous decorum stood before the
king."

"Maidens are appointed to care for the Grail," said his
host. "That was God's decree, and these maidens performed their service before it. The Grail selects only noble
company. Knights, devout and good, are chosen to guard
it. The coming of the high stars brings this people great

24 I.e., the frost outside.

sorrow, young and old alike. God's anger at them has lasted all too long. When shall they ever say yes to joy?

"Nephew, I will tell you something more,   494 whose truth you may well believe. A twofold chance is often theirs: they both give and receive profit.[25] They receive young children there, of noble lineage and beautiful. And if anywhere a land loses its lord, if the people there acknowledge the Hand of God and seek a new lord, they are granted one from the company of the Grail. They must treat him with courtesy, for the blessing of God protects him.

The men God sends forth secretly; the maidens leave openly. You can be sure that when King Castis desired Herzeloyde, his wish was gladly granted, and they gave him your mother as his wife. But he was not to enjoy her love; death laid him in his grave too soon. To your mother he had given before that Waleis and Norgals with their cities Kanvoleis and Kingrivals, to hold in her own right. The king was not destined to live longer. It was on his homeward journey that he lay down to die. Then she wore the crown of two lands, and there Gahmuret won her hand.

"Thus the maids are sent out openly from the   495 Grail and the men in secret, that they may have children who will in turn one day enter the service of the Grail, and, serving, enhance its company. God can teach them how to do this.

"Any man who has pledged himself to serve the Grail must renounce the love of women. Only the king may have a wife, and she must be pure and his in lawful marriage, and those other knights whom God has sent as rulers to lands without a lord. This command I violated when I entered the service of Love. My high-spirited youth and the excellence of a noble woman moved me to ride out in her service. And many a hard battle did I fight. I liked these wild adventures so much that I seldom went to the tourneys.[26] Her love led joy into my heart, and for her sake I

[25] This is explained in what follows. They receive profit in the children. They benefit others by providing other lands with a lord.

[26] Organized tournaments in contrast to chance combats, "adventures," which might be dangerous.

often sought combat. The power of her love drove me to
seek out knightly adventures in places wild and remote.
Thus did I earn her love. Heathen or baptized were the
same to me in battle. She seemed to promise rich reward.

"And so I fought for the fair lady's sake in the   496
three parts of the earth, in Europe and in Asia and in far-
off Africa. When I wanted very sumptuous jousts, I rode
before Gauriuon. I also fought many jousts at the mountain
of Famorgan. And splendid jousting did I wage at the
mountain of Agremontin. If you seek combat on one side
of the mountain, fiery men come riding out; on the other
side they do not burn, the jousters that you see. And once,
when my adventures had led me to the Rohas,[27] a valiant
host of Wends came out to offer me combat.

"From Seville I had sailed all round the sea to Aquileia,
then to Cilli by way of Friuli. O alas and alas, that ever I
saw your father; it was then I came to know him, when
I arrived in Seville. The noble Angevin had taken lodgings
there before me. I still grieve that he went then to Baghdad,
where, in a joust, he died. Just as you told me. It   497
is still my heart's lament.

"My brother has great wealth, and often he sent me
forth secretly on knightly missions. Whenever I left Munsalvaesche, I took his seal with me and brought it to
Karcobra, where the Plimizoel forms a lake, in the bishopric
of Barbigoel. The burgrave there, before I parted from
him, provided me by the seal's authority with squires and
all else that was needed for my wild jousts and other knightly
travels, and he did not spare the cost. Since I had to return
alone, I would stop again on my homeward journey and
leave my retinue with him and ride back to Munsalvaesche.

"Now listen, dear nephew of mine. When your noble
father first saw me there in Seville, he said straightway that
I must be the brother of Herzeloyde, his wife. Yet he had
never seen my face before. At that time, it's true, and none
could deny it, there was no handsomer man than I. Then I
did not yet have a beard. He visited me at my   498

[27] For the geographical references in the next two pages, see Note 4,
p. 434.

lodgings. Contradicting what he said, I swore many an un-
sworn oath, but when he still disputed me, I admitted it then
in secret, and it made him very happy.

"He gave me a keepsake, and the present I gave him in
return pleased him very much. That casket of mine which
you saw before—greener even than clover—I had made from
the stone which this noble man gave to me. He also gave
me his kinsman as squire, Ither, the King of Kukumerlant,
whose heart was so true it knew no falsehood. But we did
not want to delay our journeys longer and we went our
separate ways. He returned to the Baruch, and I rode to
the Rohas.

"Riding out from Cilli I came to the Rohas, and for three
Mondays I fought hard and, I thought, very well. From
there I rode with all speed to vast Gandine, from which your
grandfather Gandin had his name. And there Ither was
well known. That city lies just where the Grajena flows in
to the Drave, a stream that has gold in it. And   499
there Ither was loved. Your father's sister was queen of
that land, and he saw her now again. Gandin of Anjou had
made her the ruler there. Lammire is her name, and the
kingdom is called Styria. He who follows the service of the
shield must range through many lands!

"Now I mourn for my red squire, for love of whom she
welcomed me with great honor. You are kin to Ither, yet
your hand denied the kinship. But God has not forgotten it,
and He may still call you to account. If you would live in
true loyalty to God, you must make atonement to Him for
this. I grieve to tell you this: you bear the burden of two
great sins. Ither you have slain, and your mother too you
must mourn. Her love and devotion to you were so great
that your going from her, as you did at the last, parted her
from life. Now follow my counsel. Do penance for your
sins, and so take thought for your end that your tribulation
here may be rewarded and your soul may there find peace!"

His host questioned him further, not making   500
any reproach, "Nephew, I have not yet learned how you
got this horse."

"Sir, I won it in combat after I left Sigune. I spoke with

her outside a hermitage. Then later I sent a knight flying from his horse and took it away with me. The man was from Munsalvaesche."

His host said, "Did he escape with his life, the man to whom it belongs by rights?"

"Sir, I saw him walk away, and I found the horse standing beside me."

"If you are going to rob the Grail's people thus and still fancy you can some day win their love, you are thinking two contradictory thoughts."

"Sir, I took it in a *battle*. If for that anyone accuses me of sin, let him first examine the facts. I had lost my own horse before." Then Parzival asked, "Who was that maiden who carried the Grail? They lent me her cloak."

"Nephew, she is your mother's sister," said his host, "but if the cloak was hers she did not lend it to you to boast of. She thought you were to be the Lord of the Grail, and her lord and mine as well. Your uncle also gave you a   501 sword, but in taking it you burdened yourself with sin, since your lips, which can speak so well, alas did not ask the question then. But now let this and your other sins be. It is time to rest for today."

No beds or covers were brought to them. They went and lay down on the dirty straw. That couch was not at all proper for men of so noble a race.

Thus Parzival was there for fifteen days, and his host entertained him as I have told you. Herbs and roots were the best food they had. Parzival endured the privation willingly for the sake of the gladdening words—for his host absolved him from sin and yet counseled him to live as a knight.

One day Parzival asked him, "Who was the man lying there before the Grail? He was quite grey, but his skin was bright and fresh."

"That was Titurel," answered his host. "He is your mother's grandfather. He was the first to be entrusted with the banner of the Grail and the charge of defending it. He has a sickness called podagra, a lameness for which there is no help. Yet he has never lost his fresh color, for he sees the

Grail so often that he cannot die. They cherish   502
him, bedridden though he is, for the sake of his counsel. In
his youth he crossed many a ford and meadow in search of
a joust.

"If you would enrich your life and live a life of true worth,
you must never treat a woman ill. Women and priests,
as is well known, bear no weapons in their hands. Yet
God's blessing watches over priests. Serve them with unswerving devotion, and if your life is to have a good end,
you must show good will toward priests. Nothing your eye
sees on earth is like unto a priest. His mouth proclaims that
martyrdom which cancels out our damnation. And his con-
secrated hand takes and holds the highest pledge that ever
was given for guilt. A priest who lives in such manner that
in chastity he performs this office—how could he live a life
more holy?"

This was the day when those two parted. Trevrizent
made a decision and said, "Give your sins to me. In the
sight of God, I am the guaranty for your atonement. And
now do as I have bidden you, and follow that course undaunted."

So they parted from each other. If you like, you may
imagine how.

BOOK·X

We come now to fantastic tales that can drain our   503
joy away or bring delight: they strive toward both. The
appointed year had passed, and the quarrel had been settled which the Landgrave had provoked at the Plimizoel.
At Schanpfanzun the combat was set for Barbigoel, but
there King Kingrisin remained unavenged. His son Vergulaht appeared there against Gawan, but then people noted
their kinship and the power of kinship put an end to their
dispute. Besides, Count Ehcunat bore the grave guilt for the
deed of which Gawan was accused, and so Kingrimursel
forgave Gawan, the doughty warrior. Both Vergulaht and
Gawan then departed from there at the same time to go to
seek the Grail, and many a joust their hands had to deal on
that search. For whoever desires the Grail has to approach
that prize with the sword. So *should* a prize be striven for.

How Gawan, who was ever free of all miscon-   504
duct, had fared since leaving Schanpfanzun, and whether
his journey ran into any fighting, let them tell who witnessed it: he has to face fighting *now*.

One morning my lord Gawan came riding out onto a
green meadow. There he saw a shield flashing—it had been
pierced by a spear—and a horse carrying a lady's riding gear.
Bridle and saddle were precious enough. It was tied fast to
the bough of a tree, close by the shield. Then he thought,

"Who can this woman be who is so warlike as to use a shield? If she is inclined to do battle against me, how shall I defend myself? On foot I am sure I can hold my own, but if there is to be a joust on foot and she wants to wrestle with me for a while, she can throw me, for all I care, whether I win her anger or her favor. Even if it were the Lady Kamille who with knightly skill won fame before Laurente,[1] and if she were still alive as when she rode that time, I would still have to have a try at it with her if she offered me combat here."

The shield was badly scarred, Gawan noticed   505 as he came riding toward it, and the window in it had been cut wide with a lance. That's the way battle decorates them, but who would pay the shield painters if their colors were like this? The linden tree had a bulky trunk, and behind it on the green clover sat a lady bereft of joy. So grievous was her sorrow that she had completely forgotten joy. He rode around the tree nearer to her. In her lap lay a knight, and there was the reason why her grief was so great.

Gawan did not fail to greet her. The lady thanked him and nodded. He found her voice hoarse and faint with lamentation. Then my lord Gawan dismounted. There lay a man pierced through, with his blood rushing inward. He asked the hero's lady whether the knight were still alive or in the throes of death.

"Sir," she replied, "he is still alive, but I think it will not be for long. God has sent you here for my comfort. Now advise me as your good faith bids you. You have witnessed more dreadful things than I. Let your comfort be   506 shown to me so I may see your help."

"That I shall do, Lady," said he. "I could keep this knight from dying and I feel sure I could save him if I had a reed. You would soon see and hear him in health, because he is not mortally wounded. The blood is only pressing on his heart."

He grasped a branch of the linden tree, slipped the bark off like a tube—he was no fool in the matter of wounds—

[1] The warrior maiden in Veldeke's *Eneit*. (See also Virgil's *Aeneid*, Book XI.)

and inserted it into the body through the wound. Then he bade the woman suck on it until the blood flowed toward her. The hero's strength revived so that he could speak and talk again. When he saw Gawan bending over him he thanked him profusely and said it was to his honor to have saved him from his faint. He asked him if he had come here to Logrois in search of knightly action. "I, too, rode from far-off Punturtois," he said, "to hunt for adventure here. I shall always regret from my heart that I rode so close. You will keep clear of it too, if you have good sense. I never thought it would turn out this way. Li-   507 schois Gwelljus injured me badly and threw me off my horse with a superb thrust. It struck with a terrific impact through my shield and through me. But this good lady helped me onto her horse and to this place." He urgently begged Gawan to stay with them.

Gawan said he would like to ride to where the injury had befallen him. "If Logrois is so close by, and if I can overtake him before he gets there, he will have to answer to me. I'll ask him what he was avenging on you."

"Do not do that!" said the wounded man. "I can tell you the truth of the matter. It is no child's journey; it can well be called a disaster."

Gawan bandaged the wound with the lady's kerchief, and over the wound he pronounced a healing spell, asking God to care for both the man and the woman.

He found the trail all bloody, as if a stag had been shot there, and this kept him from riding astray. In a short time he saw Logrois, the far famed, for many people have honored it with praise. The structure of the citadel merited praise indeed. The mountain approach wound   508 like a top, and when a simple fellow saw the fortress from the distance he thought it spun like a top around the hill. Even today people say of that citadel that attack against it is futile. It little feared the distress that hatred might offer against it. All around the hill was a hedge of noble trees. Fig and pomegranate trees, olives, grapevines, and other fruit grew there in great profusion. Gawan rode up the whole length of the road and saw below him both his heart's joy and his heart's sorrow. A spring welled from the rock, and there he found something that did not displease him, a lady so lovely that he could not help but gaze at her, a *belle fleur* of womanly beauty. Save for Condwiramurs, was never such a beauty born. The woman was sweet with loveliness, gently bred and courteous. Her name was Orgeluse de Logrois. Of her the adventure says that she was the very bait of love, to eyes a sweetness without pain and a bowstring to stretch your heart.

Gawan gave her greeting and said, "If by your   509 leave I may dismount, Lady, and if you are willing to have my company, great sadness will depart and leave me with joy. Never was knight more glad. May I die if ever a woman pleased me so."

"That is all very well, and I am aware of that too." Such were her words as she glanced at him, but her sweet mouth went on to say, "Don't praise me too much! It might perhaps bring you dishonor. I don't like to have everyone pronouncing opinions of me. If my praise were common to wise and foolish, straight and crooked, it would not be much of an honor. How would it then excel in worth? I want to keep my praise such that *wise* men will uphold it. I don't know, Sir, who you are. It is time you were riding on. But not without hearing *my* opinion first: you are close to my heart—when you are far away, not inside it. You desire my love? How do you come to lay claim to my love? Many cast their eyes, but they would   510 cast them more gently with a sling if they don't refrain from looking at what cuts their hearts. Turn your hopeless desires toward some other love than mine, if your hand must serve love. If adventure has sent you out on knightly quest for love, you won't get any reward for it from me. But you could get disgrace out of it, if you want to know the truth."

Then he replied, "Lady, you are right. My eyes *are* a peril to my heart. They have beheld you, so that I have to admit in all honesty that I am your captive. Show me womanly sentiment. Much as it annoys you, you have me locked in your heart. Now loose or bind, you will find me of the same will: if I had you where I'd like to have you, I would be glad to put up with the enjoyment."

"Well, take me along with you then," she answered. "If you want to share what you win out of love for me, you will rue it later with shame. I should like to know whether you are the man to brave the pangs of combat for   511 my sake. If so, give it up, if you want honor! If I may advise you further, and if you agree to the proposal, you will look elsewhere for love. If you seek *my* love, you will lose both love and joy. If you take me away with you, great disaster will strike you later."

Then my lord Gawan said, "Who wants to have love unearned? Do I have to tell you that such a person takes it sinfully? Anyone eager for noble love must serve for it, both before and after."

She said, "If you want to do me service, you must live warlike, yet you might achieve disgrace from it after all. My service will tolerate no cowards. —Go down that path —it's not a road—and over that high bridge into that orchard and look after my horse. There you will see a great crowd of people dancing and singing songs, beating tambourines and playing flutes. Even if they try to escort you, walk right on through their midst to where my horse is standing, and untie it. It will follow you."

Gawan leaped down from his horse. He pon-   512 dered various notions of how to get the horse to wait for him, for there was nothing there by the spring that he could tie it to. He wondered whether it would be proper of him to ask the lady to hold it.

"I see what is bothering you," said she. "Leave this horse here with me. I will keep it till you come back. —But you will have little profit from my service."

Then my lord Gawan took the reins down from the horse and said, "Now hold them for me, Lady."

"I see you are pretty simple," said she. "My hand is not going to take hold of them where your hand has touched them."

Then the man who was looking for love replied, "Lady, I never take hold of them in front."

"Well, then I will take hold of them there," said she. "And now hurry up and bring me my horse. I am now ready to go traveling with you."

That seemed to him a happy gain, and so he hurried away from her across the footbridge and in through the gate. There he saw many resplendent ladies and many young cavaliers, all dancing and singing.

Now my lord Gawan was so handsomely at-   513
tired that it made them sad for his sake, for those people who tended the orchard were loyal-hearted. Whether they were standing about or lying down or sitting in tents, they did not cease to bewail his great misfortune. Men and women alike did not hesitate to speak up, and many who felt sorry for him said, "My lady's treachery is going to lead this man astray into great hardships. Alas, that he means to follow her to such regrettable outcome!" Many a worthy man there went up to him and put his arm around him in friendly greeting. Then he came to an olive tree, and there stood the horse. Its bridle and gear were worth many a mark. Standing near by and leaning on a crutch was a knight with a full beard that was grey and braided, and he wept to see Gawan come up to that horse. Yet he greeted him with gentle speech.

He said, "If you will accept advice, you will   514
leave that horse alone. Of course, no one here will stop you. All the same, the wisest thing on your part would be to leave the horse here. A curse on my lady, that she can part so many worthy men from their lives!"

Gawan said he wasn't *going* to leave the horse there.

"Alas for what will happen hereafter!" said the knight grey and noble, and, removing the halter from the horse, he added, "No need for you to stand here any longer. Let the horse follow after you. He Whose hand salted the sea, may He give you counsel in your distress! See to it that my lady's beauty does not bring you to grief. For she is sour along with sweet, just like a sun shower."

"Well, as God wills!" said Gawan, and took his leave of the grey-headed man. He did the same to all, right and left, and they all spoke words of lamentation. The horse walked the narrow path out through the gate and followed him over the footbridge. There he found the ruler of his heart.

She was the mistress of this country. Though his heart flew toward her, she caused him much pain therein. She had untied the ribbons of her headdress from un-   515 der her chin and put them up on her head. —Any woman a man finds that way is all set for battle, for she would very likely enjoy a good fight. —What other clothes was she wearing? Should I mention them? Her radiant glance absolves me from making an inventory of her apparel.

As Gawan came up to the lady her sweet lips received him thus: "Welcome, you goose! No man ever lugged such stupidity around as you do, wanting to do service for me. O, but you would do well to give it up!"

He said, "If you are so ready with bad temper now, then graciousness must come afterward. Since you abuse me so badly, you will have the honor of making up for it later. Meanwhile my hand will perform your service until you get into the rewarding mood. If you like, I'll lift you onto this horse."

"I didn't ask you to," said she. "Your unproven hand may well reach out for a lesser prize." And away from him she turned and leaped from among the flowers onto the horse. Then she told him to ride after her. "It would be a shame if I lost such an esteemed companion," she said,   516 and added, "May God throw you from that horse!"

Anyone wishing to follow me further should refrain from abusive talk about her. No one should talk out of turn unless he knows what it is he is damning and until he is informed how things stood with her heart. I, too, could say a lot against that lady of lovely hue, but whatever wrong she has done Gawan in her ill temper, or that she may do to him hereafter, I absolve her from all condemnation. The mighty Orgeluse behaved in unfriendly fashion. She came riding up to Gawan in such bad temper that I would hardly be confident that she will banish my cares.

They both rode out onto a heath bright with flowers, and there Gawan noticed an herb growing, the root of which he said was good for wounds. The noble man got down onto

the ground, dug it up, and mounted again. The lady did
not forget to put in her word: "If my companion can be
both doctor and knight, he can earn a good living, provided he learns how to sell ointment jars."   517

To the lady Gawan said, "I rode past a wounded knight,
who has a linden tree for a roof. If I can still find him, this
herb will cure him and restore all his lost strength."

"I'm glad to see this," she said. "Maybe I'll learn something."

Presently there came a squire up behind them with some
urgent message he was to deliver. Gawan decided to wait
for him. He seemed to be a monster. Malcreatiure was the
proud lad's name, and Cundrie *la sorcière* was his handsome sister. He had her face exactly, except that he was a
man. He, too, had a tusk sticking out either side of his
mouth like a wild boar, unlike the human countenance. He
did not have hair quite so long as Cundrie's—hers hung
down over her mule—but short hair, and sharp as a hedge-
hog's bristles it was. By the waters of the Ganges in the
land of Tribalibot people grow like that and cannot help it.

Our father Adam received from God the art of   518
giving names to all things, both the wild and the tame. He
knew the nature of each, and the revolutions of the stars
as well, and what forces the seven planets had; and he also
knew the virtues of all herbs and what the nature of each
one was. When his daughters had acquired the power of
years and might bear human offspring, he counseled them
against intemperance. Whenever one of his daughters bore a
child, he warned her repeatedly and rarely spared the ad-
monition, to avoid eating many herbs which would spoil the
human fruit and bring shame on his race: "Other than God
appointed when He sat at work over me," as he said, "my
beloved daughters, be not blinded as to your salvation."

The women did just what women do: their frailty
brought several of them to perpetrate the deed craved by
their hearts. And thus the human race was perverted. Now
Adam grieved at this. But *his* will never faltered.   519

Queen Secundille, whom Feirefiz won with knightly
hand, both her person and her land, had in her kingdom,

quite undeniably, and from time out of mind, a great many of these people with distorted faces, and they bore strange, wild marks. One time they were telling her about the Grail, saying there was nothing on earth so precious, and how it was kept by a king named Anfortas. To her that seemed wondrous enough, for many rivers in her country ran precious gems instead of silt, big ones too, and by no means small, and she had mountains all of gold. Then the noble queen thought, "How shall I find out about this man to whom the Grail is subject?" So she sent him her precious jewels, these two human creatures of strange shape, Cundrie and her lovely brother. She sent him more than that, to be sure, things that no one could repay her for and that are hardly for sale. Then the sweet Anfortas, generous as he always was, sent this courteous squire to Orgeluse de Logrois. A difference originating in woman's intemperance set him off from the human race.   520

This kinsman of the herb and the stars launched into a loud tirade against Gawan, who was waiting for him on the road. Malcreatiure came riding on a miserable little nag, lame in all fours and stumbling as it went. Why, Lady Jeschute, the noble, rode a better horse the day Parzival forced Orilus to restore her to the favor she had lost through no fault of hers.

The squire Malcreatiure looked at Gawan and said angrily, "Sir, if you are of knightly sort, you will wish you hadn't done this. I think you are a fool to carry my lady off. And you will be shown what praise you will get by it. I wonder if you can cope with it. But if you are a soldier, you will get such a beating with sticks that you will wish you had something else."

"My knighthood will never suffer any such chastisement," Gawan said. "They may beat up cheap trash that way, that have no manly defense, but I am still free from such punishment. If you and my lady here want to in-   521
dulge in abusive talk to me, *you* will have to enjoy alone something that you may well take for anger. Repulsive as you are, I'm not worried about your threats."

Whereupon Gawan grabbed him by the hair and flung

him under his horse. The wise and noble youth looked
back up at him in terror. But his hedgehog-bristles of hair
got him his revenge: they cut Gawan's hand so badly that it
was all covered with blood. The lady laughed at that and
said, "I love to see you both in such a fury!"

They went on their way, the squire's horse following
along, and came to where they found the wounded knight
lying. Gawan's hand bound the herb to the wound.

"How have things fared with you since you left me here?"
asked the wounded man. "You have brought a lady with
you who wishes you ill. It is through fault of hers that I
am here in such pain. In *Av' estroit mavoie* she helped me
to a sharp joust at the peril of my life and my possessions.
If you want to keep your life, have this treacher-   522
ous woman ride on and leave her. Judge her counsels by
me! Yet I might still recover if I had rest and quiet. Help
me to those, true-hearted man!"

Then my lord Gawan said, "Accept any help I am able to
offer."

"There is a hospital near here," said the wounded knight.
"If I could get there quickly, I could rest there for a long
time. We have my lady friend's horse still standing here,
quite strong enough. Lift her onto it, and me behind her."

Then the high-born stranger untied the lady's mount
from the branch and started to lead it over to her.

"Get away from me!" cried the wounded man. "Are you
in such a hurry to trample on me?"

He led the horse further off. The lady followed him de-
murely and yet in no haste, all in keeping with her lord's
instructions. Gawan swung her up onto the horse. Meanwhile the wounded knight had leaped onto Gawan's Castilian—I call that a nasty trick!—and off he rode, he and the
lady. That was a sinful gain.

At this Gawan complained bitterly, but the   523
lady laughed more at it than he felt the joke warranted.
After his horse was stolen her sweet mouth said to him,
"First I took you for a knight; a few hours after that you
turned surgeon for wounds; now you have to be a page. If

anyone has to live by his skill, you can fall back on your numerous aptitudes. —Do you still want my love?"

"Yes, Lady," said Sir Gawan. "If I could have your love it would be dearer to me than anything. There isn't a living soul on earth beneath a crown, nor any that wear crowns and pursue joyous fame, who could offer me their winnings in place of you, but that my heart's sense would bid me reject it. I would still want your love. If I can't win that, then a bitter death must soon be mine. You are destroying your own property, for even if I ever gained my freedom, you would still have me for your vassal. I think that much is your absolute right. So call me knight or groom, page or peasant. Whatever mockery you have perpetrated 524 upon me, you commit sin in so doing when you scorn my service. If I had any profit from your service, mockery would reflect on *you,* and though it did me no harm at all, it will still impair your dignity."

Back now came the wounded man riding. "Is it you, Gawan?" said he. "If you ever loaned me anything, I've paid you back now. When your manly courage overcame me in hard combat and you took me to your Uncle Arthur's house, four weeks on end he kept me eating with the dogs."

Then he said, "Is it you, Urians? You may wish me harm, but I bear it in all innocence. I sought the king's favor for you, but your base mind helped and made it advisable to expel you from the profession of knighthood and pronounce you an outcast from the law, because on your account a maiden lost her right and her peace under the laws of the land. King Arthur would have avenged it with a rope if I hadn't pleaded in your behalf."

"Whatever happened there, *you* are standing 525 *here* now. You've heard it said before this that any man that helps another to save his life will have the other for an enemy ever after. I am doing what clever men always do. It is more becoming for a child to weep than for a bearded man. I mean to keep this horse myself." And with a dig of the spurs he swiftly rode away.

That irked Gawan, and he said to the lady, "It happened this way: King Arthur was in the city of Dianazdrun and many Britons with him. A lady had been sent there to him on a messenger's errand, and this rascal had gone out in search of adventure. He was a stranger and she was a stranger. Then he took it into his stupid head to force the lady to his will without her consent. Her cry for help was heard as far as the court, and the king cried out, 'Hey, hey! What's this?' It happened near a forest, and we all rushed out there. I had ridden way out ahead of the others and picked up the guilty man's trail, and I brought him back a prisoner to the king.

"The lady rode back with us, woebegone at the   526
fact that someone who had never entered her service had taken her chaste maidenhood. Against her helpless hands he had won but small credit. She found my master, Arthur the true, in high dudgeon. 'The world,' he said, 'shall rue this accursed crime. Alas that the day ever shone by whose light this misery occurred, and I was called upon for judgment and to be the judge this day!' To the lady he said, 'If you are sensible, choose an advocate and present your charges.' The lady, quite undismayed, did as the king suggested. A great throng of knights was standing there.

"There stood Urians, Prince from Punturtois, before the Briton, with honor and life at stake. The woman came forward and made her complaint so that rich and poor heard her, and with words of accusation begged the king for the sake of all womankind to be moved by her disgrace, and for the sake of her virginal honor. She conjured him further by the usage of the Round Table and by the   527
journey she had come on to him in the capacity of a messenger: if he was acknowledged as a judge, he should adjudicate her complaint according to the rules of the court. She begged all those of the company of the Round Table to take note of her cause, since she had been robbed of something that could not be restored, namely, her maidenhood chaste and pure, and urged them all to beg the king for judgment and to support her plea.

"Counsel was also retained by the guilty man, by whose honor I set little store by now. He defended him as best he could, but the defense did him little good. He was condemned to loss of life and honor and to have a rope twisted by which he would meet death without shedding of blood. Compelled by his distress, he called on me and reminded me that he had given me his oath of surrender in order to save his life. I was afraid I would lose all my honor if he lost his life. I begged the accusing woman, since she had seen with her own eyes how I had avenged her like a man, to show clemency for the sake of womanly kind-   528 ness, for, after all, she had to attribute what had happened to her loveliness and her beauty of person; if ever a man came to grief through service to a woman, and if she thereafter offered him her help—'from respect for that kind of help,' said I, 'desist from your anger.'

"I begged the king and his men, if I had ever done him any service, to be mindful of it now and to avert the threat of dishonor from me by pardoning the knight. His wife the queen I implored from love of kinship—for the king had brought me up from a little child—and also because my fidelity always took refuge with her, to help me also. And so it was done. She spoke privately with the lady, and thus he was saved by the queen, though he had to endure serious punishment. This is how he was purified and this is the penance that was assigned to him: with lead dog and leash hound he had to eat from the same trough for four weeks. In that manner the lady was avenged. —And this, Lady, is his revenge on me."   529

She replied, "His revenge has missed its mark. I shall never grow well disposed toward *you,* but *he* shall be repaid for this, before he leaves my country, in such a way that he will call it shame. Since the king did not avenge it *there*, where the mischance befell the lady, and since it has devolved upon me, I am now the judge over both of you —even though I don't know who either one of you is. He will have to do combat for the lady's sake alone, but precious little for your sake.

Mischief shall be set aright   6 1-2
By thrust and parry of a fight.

Gawan went over to Malcreatiure's nag and with an easy
jump caught it. The squire himself came back at this point,
and to him the lady spoke in heathen and issued all her
commands for those at home.

Now trouble looms for Gawan also. Malcreatiure set off
on foot. My lord Gawan surveyed the young gentleman's
nag. It was too feeble for combat. The squire had taken it
from a peasant before coming down the hill, and now it fell
to Gawan to have this instead of his own horse.   530
There was nothing to do but accept the exchange.

The lady said to him—out of malice, I fancy—"Tell me,
do you intend to go on like this?"

And my lord Gawan said, "My journey will proceed at
your orders."

"Those you might find slow in coming," said she.

"I'll serve you for them all the same."

"I find you pretty stupid for that. If you don't give this
up, you are going to leave the happy and join the sad. Your
misadventures will begin afresh."

Then the man seeking love said, "I am always at your
service whether I get joy or sorrow from it, ever since your
love commanded that I must wait upon your command,
whether I ride or walk."

Still standing there by the lady, he began to inspect his
battle steed. It was mighty scant on equipment for a swift
onslaught. The stirrup leathers were ropes, and this noble
stranger was used to better saddles. He chose not to mount
for fear he would pull the saddle gear to pieces. The horse
had a sway-back; if he had jumped onto him the   531
back would have caved in. All these things he had to
watch out for, and it annoyed him not a little. So he led the
beast and carried his shield and one spear himself. At his
acute discomfiture, the lady who was causing him so much
trouble laughed and laughed.

Then he tied his shield onto the animal. Whereat she
said, "Are you bringing clothgoods for sale in my country?

Who ever gave me a doctor and then a tradesman for a companion? Watch out for tollgates along the way: some of my customs officials will take your joy right out of you."

Her peppery remarks he found so pleasant that he didn't care what she said, for whenever he looked at her his forfeit to sorrow was redeemed. She was sheer Maytime to him, a blossoming beyond all radiance, to eyes a sweetness and at the same time a sourness to the heart. Since she was both loss and gain and the thing that made sick joy well, she made him free, yet wholly captive, with every hour.

Many a master of mine says that Amor and   532
Cupid, and Venus the mother of these two, put love into people with darts and torches. Such love is unwholesome.

> One who has heart's sincerity,
> Of love will never be quite free.
> Now with joy and now with rue,
> Real love is devotion true.

Cupid, your arrow misses me every time, and so does Lord Amor's spear. The pair of you may be masters over love, and Venus with her flaming torch, but I know nothing of such tribulations. If I am to talk about true love, it must come to me out of loyalty. If my powers could help anyone in any way against love, I am so fond of Sir Gawan that I could help him gratis. Yet he is in no disgrace for lying in the bonds of love. If love is attacking him now and undoing his strong defense, yet he was always so good at defense, so equal to the defense of noble men, that a *woman* should not overcome his defenses.

Ride nearer, Lord Press-of-Love! You so   533
trample joy that the road of joy is stomped full of holes and a path is made for sorrow. Thus the trail of sorrow stretches afar. If it led elsewhere than to the heart's high spirits, I would think it a good thing for joy. If Love is quick to mischief, I should expect she was too old for that. Or does she put it down to her childishness when she causes sorrow to the heart? I would sooner put mischief down to her youth than have her do mischief to her old age. Many things have happened on her account, and from which of

these two things shall I say it comes? If she wants to make her old age giddy with youthful notions, she will soon be short of honor. She should be taught better.

Pure love I will praise, and all who are wise, be they men or women, will agree with me on that. When love answers love, pure and unsullied, and neither is vexed at having love lock their hearts with love that never alters—that love is over all others high.

Much as I would like to get him out of it, my   534 lord Gawan cannot give love the slip without her lessening his happiness. So what good is my stepping in, whatever I may say about it? A noble man must not resist love, for love will help to make him well.[2]

On love's account Gawan encountered difficulties. His lady rode, he walked on foot, and thus Orgeluse and the warrior bold came into a great forest. That was as far as he walked. Then he led the horse up to a log. His shield, which was tied on the animal and which he used in his knightly trade, he raised to his throat and bestrode the horse. It could hardly support him out through the other side of the woods to cultivated land. Then his eyes spotted a castle. Both his heart and his eyes assured him they had never yet known or seen any castle like this one. It was knightly in every particular, and many a tower and many a hall it had. Moreover, he saw many ladies at the windows, some four hundred or more of them; four of them were of noble lineage.

A road badly rutted from *passages* led up to a   535 river that flowed there, navigable, swift, and broad, and toward it he and the lady traveled. By the quay lay a meadow where jousts were held, while beyond the water stood the ford warden's keep. Gawan, the warrior bold, saw a knight coming up from behind, eager not to spare shield or spear.

Orgeluse the mighty then said with arrogance, "If you will admit it, I do not break my word. I told you before

---

[2] The digression, which, as in other instances, serves to indicate the lapse of time and to separate episodes, terminates in one of Wolfram's favorite puns: wert *man sol sich niht minne* wern, where *wert* means "noble, worthy" and *wern* means "to resist," "to put up defense."

that you would get into plenty of disgrace. Now defend
yourself if you can, you cannot be saved otherwise. That
man coming there, his hand will knock you off your horse,
and if your breeches split it will embarrass you before the
ladies sitting up there and looking on. What if they witness
your shame?"

At Orgeluse's behest the ferryman came across and she
got into his boat, much to Gawan's sorrow. From the boat
the mighty princess, nobly born, called back in anger, "You
shan't get in over here with me. You have to stay   536
there as hostage."

Sorrowfully he shouted back to her, "Lady, why are you
in such a hurry to get away from me? Shall I ever see you
again?"

"You *may* have the honor of my allowing you to see me
again, but I think it will be a long time."

And so the lady left him.

Now came Lischois Gwelljus. If I told you he was flying,
I would be fooling you with my words; but he was coming
on very fast just the same, so that it was a credit to his
horse, which did put on a show of speed across that broad,
green meadow. Then my lord Gawan thought, "How shall
I wait for this man? Which would be wiser, on foot or on
this pony? If he rides against me full tilt so that he can't
stop his charge, he will ride me down. But what's to keep
him from stumbling over my nag, either? Then if he wants
to offer me combat when we are both on foot, even though
I never win her favor who offered me this fight, I'll give
him combat, if that's what he wants."

That was now inevitable. The oncomer was a   537
determined fellow, and so was the one who was waiting.
The latter made ready for the joust by planting his lance
forward on the saddle felt. Both their jousts went off just as
Gawan had foreseen. The onslaught broke both spears and
both heroes were seen lying on the ground. The better-
mounted man had stumbled and he and my lord Gawan
lay among the flowers. And what did they do then? Up they
jumped and challenged each other with swords. Their
shields were not spared; so badly were they hacked that not

much was left of them. The shield always bears the brunt
of any fight. Flashes and sparks from helmets were seen,
and you can put it down to luck, whichever one God grants
victory to; but he has to win much renown first.

And so they persisted in their battle there on that
meadow wide. Two smiths would be weary from so many
mighty blows, strong as they might be of limb. Thus they
struggled for the prize. But who was going to praise
them, when these foolish men were fighting   538
without a reason, except for the sake of fame itself? They
had no issue to settle, they were risking their lives for nothing. Each reproached the other for having no cause to fight.

Gawan knew how to wrestle and he knew how to force
a man by throwing him. Once he had got past his sword
and grabbed him in his arms, he could make him do just
as he wished. As long as he had to defend himself he put
up a good defense, but then that worthy man, rich in
courage, seized the brave youth, who also had manly
strength. He quickly threw him down under him and
said, "Hero, if you want to live, give me your oath of
surrender!"

Lischois, as he lay there underneath, was not ready to
give in to that command, for he had never yet given an oath
of surrender. He found it amazing enough that any man
had a hand that could overpower him and force him to do
what had never before been exacted of him, an oath of surrender. *His* hand had up to now forced a good many of
them. However he was faring here, he had re-   539
ceived plenty of them that he would not pass on to anybody
else. Instead of surrender he offered his life and said that,
no matter what happened to him, he would never give an
oath of surrender under duress. He preferred to barter his
death.

Then the defeated man said, "Are *you* the victor? *I* used
to be, when God willed I should win the prize. Now my
fame has come to an end at your noble hands. When men
and women find out that I have been conquered, whose
fame flew so high aloft before, it will be better for me to
die before this news makes my friends empty of joy."

Gawan kept on demanding his oath of surrender, but his desire and his whole mind were set on nothing but losing his life and a quick death.

Then my lord Gawan thought, "Why should I kill this man? If he would take orders from me otherwise, I would let him go free." He said as much to him directly, but there was no compliance at all.

And so he let that warrior up without any   540 guarantee. They both sat down among the flowers. Gawan had not forgotten his annoyance over the fact that his horse was so feeble. In his cleverness he thought of how he could spur the other steed until he could test what kind of an animal it was. It was well armored for battle, and pfellel-silk and samite were its outer covering. Since he had won it in this adventure, why shouldn't he ride it now, as long as it was there ready to ride? He got on. Off it went so that he was delighted with its broad leaps.

Then he said, "Is it you, Gringuljete, that Urians stole from me with his lying plea? He's good at that, but he ruined his honor by it just the same. Who has put such armor on you since then? If it is really you, God has sent you back to me already, as He often averts distress."

He dismounted again, and then he noticed a mark: on its hock it was branded with a turtledove, the coat of arms of the Grail. Off this horse's back he of Prienlascors had been thrown by Lehelin in a joust; from him it had passed to Orilus, who gave it to Gawan on the plain of the   541 Plimizoel.

Now his sad spirits revived again, except that he felt sorrow and loyalty of service for his lady. Though she had given him abuse enough, his thoughts still raced toward her.

Meanwhile the proud Lischois had run over to where he saw his own sword lying, which Gawan, that worthy warrior, had twisted out of his hand in the fight. Many a lady saw them as they now fought a second time. Their shields had got to the point where they both left them lying where they were and rushed to the encounter without them. They both came on directly with stout-hearted manly defense.

Up in the windows of the great hall sat a host of ladies watching the battle down in front of them. New fury was displayed. Both were so nobly born that their pride could not let the other one out-fight him. Their helmets and swords, they took punishment; they were their shields against death. Whoever saw those heroes fighting there, I think he admitted they were both in trouble.

Lischois Gwelljus, that sweet young man,   542 fought thus: daring and feats of bravery were his high heart's prompting. He dealt many a swift blow, often he sprang back away from Gawan, and then again pressed hard upon him. Gawan held his ground. He thought, "If I can once grab you, I'll pay you back plenty!" Flashes of fire were seen as the swords came swinging again and again in doughty hands. They began to force each other to one side, forward, backward. Still they had no quarrel to be fighting over. They could have given it all up without a battle. Then my lord Gawan grabbed him and threw him down with violence underneath him. —I would avoid friendship that embraced like that! I certainly would not want to put up with it.

Again Gawan asked for surrender, but Lischois, lying there underneath, was just as unwilling as he had been after the first fight. "You delay needlessly," he said. "I offer death in place of surrender. Let your worthy hand put an end to whatever fame was acknowledged in me. I am accursed before God, who does not permit my re-   543 nown. For love of Orgeluse, the noble duchess, many a worthy man has had to leave his fame in *my* hands. You will inherit much fame if you can kill me."

Then King Lot's son thought, "Truly, I must not do that. I would lose Fame's favor if I slew this brave hero undaunted. It was her love that set him on me, and her love also drives me on and brings me much grief. Why don't I let him live for her sake? If she becomes mine, he cannot prevent it, if Fortune grants it to me. If our fight had been witnessed by her, I think she would have to acknowledge that I know how to serve for love." And then my lord Gawan said, "I will leave you alive for the duchess' sake."

Great weariness did not fail them now. He let him up, and they sat down a considerable distance apart.

Now up came the ferryman from the water to the land, carrying a hen sparrow hawk all grey on   544 his wrist as he walked. It was his legal right to claim the horse of any man defeated in a joust on that field and to bow before the one who had gained the victory, and not to stint his praise. Such was the toll exacted on this flowery meadow. This was his best income from that tract of land, unless his sparrow hawk brought a crested lark to grief. He did no plowing otherwise—he considered that income enough. He was born of knightly stock and had good breeding. Going up to Gawan, he politely asked for his tribute from the field, and Gawan, rich in valor, said, "Sir, I have never been a merchant, so you will kindly exempt me from your toll."

The ferryman replied, "Sir, so many ladies saw how the prize fell to you here, you should allow me my rights. Acknowledge my claim, Sir. In proper joust your hand won this horse for me with praise unimpaired, for   545 your hand overthrew this man to whom the whole world gave praise indeed until today. Your praise was a blow from God to him and has taken all his joy away. Great good fortune has come your way."

"*He* overcame *me*," replied Gawan, "but I made up for it afterwards. If you collect tolls on jousts, he is the one who should pay the toll. Sir, there stands a nag that he won from me in this fight. Take that, if you like, but *I* am the one who is going to claim this horse. It is going to carry me away from here if you *never* get a horse. You speak of claims: if you claim that, you will surely not want to have me leave here on foot. I should be very sorry if this horse became yours, for it was still mine, uncontestably, this morning. If you want to have peace, you will sooner get yourself a hobbyhorse to ride. This horse was given to me outright by Orilus the Burgundian, and Urians, the prince from Punturtois, stole it from me for a time.   546 You'll more easily get a mule's foal than this.[3] But I can

---

[3] Mules are sterile and have no foal.

give you something else. Since you think so highly of the man, instead of the horse you are asking for, take the man that rode it against me. Whether he likes it or dislikes it is of little concern to me."

The ferryman was glad and laughingly said, "I have never seen so costly a gift, if it is proper to accept it. But, Sir, if you are guarantee for it, my expectations are overpaid. Indeed his fame was always so brilliant that I would not take five hundred strong, swift horses for him. Since it wouldn't do for me—if you want to make me rich, act like a knight—and if you are strong enough, deliver him to me onto my boat there. That would be very noble of you."

Then King Lot's son said, "Onto your boat and off again and inside your very door I will deliver him as a prisoner."

"Then you will be well received," said the skipper, whose great thanks were profusely bowed. Then he   547 added, "My dear Sir, be so kind as to come to my house to rest tonight yourself. Greater honor was never done to any ferryman the like of me. It will be taken as a great stroke of luck if I put up such a noble man."

Then my lord Gawan said, "I was just about to ask you for what you have requested. Great weariness has overtaken me so that I am in need of rest. The lady that ordered me into this discomfort, she can well turn sweet things sour, and make the heart's joys dear, and make its sorrows rich. She bestows incommensurately. Alas, you find of a loss! You weigh down the left side of my bosom that used to swell so high when God granted me joys! A heart used to be underneath there, but I think it has disappeared. Where am I to find comfort now? Must I helplessly suffer such grief for love? If she is womanly true, she who can hurt me so should also multiply my joy."

The skipper heard how he wrestled with sor-   548 row and how love compelled him, and he said, "Sir, that is the way here, in the open and in the forest, and everywhere Clinschor is lord, and neither cowardice nor manly subtlety will make it otherwise: today sad, tomorrow glad. —It is perhaps unknown to you that this whole country here is a land of fantastic adventure. So it goes by night

and by day as well. With manliness, luck can always help.
—But the sun is getting lower. Sir, you should come
aboard." So spoke the skipper.

Gawan led Lischois with him onto the water, and patiently and without protest that hero obeyed. The ferryman
led the horse behind him.

Thus they passed to the further shore.

The ferryman bade Gawan, "Be the master in my house."
The house was such that Arthur would not have needed to
build a better one at Nantes, where he often resided. There
he led Lischois inside. The host and his household looked
after him.

Forthwith to his daughter the host said, "See to   549
it that my lord here is made comfortable. The two of you
go together. Serve him kindly, we have much to thank
him for." To his son he entrusted Gringuljete.

The maiden performed with great courtesy the service
she had been commanded to do. Accompanied by the girl,
Gawan went up to a warm room. Fresh rushes covered
the floor and flowers of pretty colors were strewn on top of
them. Then the sweet girl removed his armor.

"God thank you for that!" said Gawan. "Lady, I need
this relief. But if the master of the house had not so commanded you, you would be doing me too much service."

"I serve you, Sir, more for your favor," she said, "than
for the sake of others."

The host's son, a young boy, brought in plenty of soft
cushions and placed them along the wall opposite the door.
A carpet was spread in front of them, and there Gawan
was to sit. The boy skillfully laid a quilt of red sendal-silk
over this seat. A seat was also placed for the host,   550
and then another lad brought in the tablecloth and bread.
The host had so instructed the boys. Then the housewife
came in, and when she saw Gawan she greeted him cordially and said, "You have made us rich as never before, Sir.
Our good fortune watches."[4]

The host entered and water was brought. After Gawan

[4] *Unser saelde wachet,* an ancient formula meaning "Our good fortune is awake and not sleeping."

had washed his hands he did not fail to request the host for
company: "Allow this maiden to eat with me."

"Sir, she has never been taught how to eat with gentlemen or how to sit so near them. She would get too proud
for me. But we have much to thank you for. Daughter, do
as he desires, I have consented to it."

The sweet girl turned red with embarrassment, but she
did as the master commanded. Down beside Gawan sat
the maid Bene.

Two sturdy sons the host had also reared, and that evening their sparrow hawk had outflown three crested
larks. These he bade them serve to Gawan, all three
of them, and a sauce to go with them. The   551
maiden did not neglect to cut up sweet morsels for Gawan
with fine courtesy, and with her lovely hands she laid them
on white bread.

Then she said, "You should send one of these roasted
birds, Sir, to my mother, for she doesn't have any."

He told the lovely maiden that he would be glad to do as
she suggested, or anything else she might ask. And so one
lark was sent over to the hostess. Courteously she bowed
to Gawan's hand. Nor did the host omit his thanks.

Then one of the host's sons brought in purslane and let-
tuce cut up in vinegar. That kind of food is no good for
keeping up strength in the long run, nor will it give you a
good complexion either. Your complexion shows the truth
of what you put into your mouth. Color painted on the face
has seldom won much praise—but if a woman's heart is
true, I think *she* has the best beauty.

If Gawan could have eaten good will, he would   552
have dined well there, for never did any mother wish her
child better than the host whose bread he ate. After the
table had been removed and after the housewife had with-
drawn, many cushions were brought in and laid out for
Gawan. One was made of down and had a cover of green
samite—not the real article but an imitation samite. Over
the cushions, for Gawan's comfort, a coverlet was spread,
together with a pfellel-silk quilted on palmat-silk, without
gold, however—*that* is fetched from distant heathendom.

Over these were spread two snow-white sheets of soft material. A head pillow was added, and one of the girl's mantles, of fresh, clean ermine.

The host politely took his leave before going off to bed himself. Gawan remained alone there, I was told, with the girl. If he had wanted anything from her, I think she would have granted it.

But now he shall sleep if he can. God keep him!

And so day came.

BOOK·XI

A great weariness had closed his eyes and so he   553
slept till early morning. Then the warrior awoke. One wall
of his chamber had many windows, closed on the outside
by glass.[1] One of these was open and looked out on the orchard. He walked over to this window bay to have a look
outside, and also for the sake of the air and the birdsong,
but he did not sit there very long. He could see a castle
which he had seen the evening before when the adventure
had befallen him, and numbers of ladies in the great hall,
many of them very beautiful. It struck him as extremely
odd that the ladies had not grown tired of staying awake
and that they were not sleeping, for the day was still not
very bright. Thought he: "I'll honor them by going back to
sleep."

Back to his bed he went. The girl's mantle covered him
—that was his blanket. And did they wake him then? No,
the host would not have liked that. To keep him company
the maiden broke her own sleep, where she had been lying
at her mother's feet, and went over to the guest; but he
was still sleeping soundly. The girl did not neglect her service; on the carpet in front of the bed the lovely   554

[1] Glass was still rare and expensive enough in 1200 to be note-
worthy.

maiden sat down. —*I* rarely have an adventure like that steal up on me, morning *or* evening.

After a time Gawan awoke. He saw her and laughed, and said, "God keep you, little lady, for breaking your sleep for my sake and punishing yourself so, which I have not deserved."

Then the lovely maiden said, "I do not claim your service, I only seek your favor. Command me, Sir, and whatever you command I will do. All my father's household, and my mother and their children as well, should have you as our lord for good, you have been so nice to us."

"Have you been here long?" he said. "If I had heard you come in sooner, I would have liked to ask you a question, if it does not embarrass you to answer it. In these two days I have noticed many ladies up there above me. Would you be so kind as to tell me who they are?"   555

The girl started with alarm. "Sir, do not ask!" she said. "I will not be the one to tell you. I cannot tell you anything about them. I may know, but I must remain silent. Do not be offended at me. Ask me something else. That is what I suggest, if you will do as I wish."

But Gawan insisted and with his questioning pursued the matter of all those ladies that he had seen sitting up there in the great hall. The girl was so kindly that she wept from her heart and made great lament.

It was still very early, but meanwhile her father had come in. He would not have cared if the lovely maiden had been forced to anything, and if there had been any tumbling— and she looked as if there had, this decorous maiden sitting there so close to the bed—it would not have made her father angry. Then he said, "Daughter, don't cry! When a thing like this happens in fun, it may make you angry at first, but you will soon get over it."

Gawan said, "Nothing has gone on here but   556 what we are willing to tell you about. I was asking the girl a couple of things which she thought were not for my good to know and she asked me to abandon the subject. If it does not offend you, let my service impose on you, my host, and be so kind as to tell me about the ladies above us here. I never heard anywhere that so many lovely ladies were to be seen with such beautiful headdresses."

The host wrung his hands. "For God's sake! do not ask!" he said. "Sir, *there* is misery beyond all misery!"

"Then I must lament their sorrow," said Gawan. "Host, you must tell me why my question distresses you so."

"Sir, for your bravery's sake. If you won't forego your questioning, you will presently want to go further, and that will bring heaviness to your heart and make us empty of joy, me and all my children, who were born to serve you."

"You must tell me," said Gawan. "And if you keep it from me so that your story leaves me out of things, I will find out anyway how things stand up there."

In all honesty the host said, "Sir, I regret that   557 you will not let your question pass. I will lend you a shield, so arm yourself for battle! You are in the Land of Wonders.[2] The Wonder Bed is here.[3] Sir, never yet was distress put to the test in the Castle of Wonders.[4] Your life is bound for death. If you are familiar with adventure, anything your hand has ever fought was mere child's play: you are now nearing a goal of disaster."

Gawan said, "I should be sorry to have my comfort ride away from these ladies without some labor and without investigating their plight more carefully. I have heard about them before anyway, and since I have got this near, I shall not let myself be frightened off from venturing something in their behalf."

The host was genuinely distressed, and to his guest he said, "All troubles are nothing beside what comes to one to whom this adventure befalls. It is sharp and terrible indeed, no mistake about that. And I am not deceiving you, Sir!"

Gawan, famed in valor, paid no heed to the   558 man's fear. "Give me advice for battle," he said. "With your permission I shall do a knightly deed here, if God wills. I shall cherish your counsel and your suggestion. It would

2 *Terre marveile.*
3 *Lit marveile.*
4 *Schastel marveil.*

be a misdeed, my host, if I were to leave here like this: friend and foe would take me for a coward."

Now the host began to lament in earnest; never had anything grieved him so. Turning to his guest he said, "If God makes manifest that you are not doomed, you will become the lord of this land. All the ladies there held hostage and brought here by mighty enchantment, if your power can deliver them—which no knight's fame has ever achieved—and many a squire and noble knight as well, then you will be high acclaimed and God will have honored you well. You can be the joyous master over many a glorious beauty, ladies from many lands. But who would cry shame upon you if you left here just as you are, since Lischois Gwelljus lost his fame to you here? Many was   559 the knightly deed that he did, that sweet man, and rightly do I greet him as such; his chivalry has valor. God's strength never put so many virtues in any man's heart, except Ither of Gaheviez. Yesterday my boat ferried across the water the man who slew Ither before Nantes. He gave me five horses, may God give him life with blessing!—horses that dukes and kings once rode. Whatever he won from *them* is reported to Pelrapeire. He forced their oaths of surrender. His shield bears the mark of many a joust, and he came riding here in search of the Grail."

Gawan said, "Where has he gone? Tell me, my host, since he was so close by, did he learn what this adventure here was?"

"Sir, he did not find out about that. I certainly took good care not to mention it to him. I would be responsible for an impropriety if I had, and if you hadn't thought of asking, you would never have heard from me the story of what is here, namely, a strong magic, sharp with terror. If you don't leave it alone, such great sorrow will never   560 have befallen me and my children, if you lose your life there. But if you win out and come to rule over this land, my poverty will have an end. I will trust your hand to make my riches great. Here you can win love with happiness and without sorrow, if you do not perish.—Now arm yourself against great peril."

Gawan was still without his weapons, so he said, "Bring me my armor." The host did his bidding, and from the feet up, the sweet and lovely girl dressed him in his armor. The host went to fetch the horse. On his wall hung a shield so thick and hard that Gawan later preserved his life with it. Shield and horse were brought to him.

The host had also bethought him of something, and, standing there before him, he said, "Sir, I shall now tell you what you are to do in the face of your life's perils. You must carry my shield; it is neither pierced nor hacked for I fight rarely, so how could it be damaged?   561 Then, Sir, when you arrive up there, there is one thing that will be good for your horse: there will be a trader sitting in front of the gate; leave the horse outside there with him. Buy something from him, anything at all. He will watch your horse all the better if you leave it with him as a guarantee. If you come out unscathed you will have no trouble getting the horse back."

Then my lord Gawan said, "I am not to ride the horse inside?"

"No, Sir. All the ladies' beauty will be hidden from you. Then you will come to the dangers. You will find the great hall deserted, you won't find a living thing there, great or small. May God's grace prevail when you go into the room where the Wonder Bed stands. If that bed and its bedposts were weighed against the crown and all the wealth of the Mahmumelin[5] of Morocco, it could not be equaled. On it such pains will befall you as God purposes; may He turn it to your joy! Remember, Sir, if you are worthy,   562 never to let this shield or your sword get away from you, for when you think your troubles have come to an end, then you will really be just beginning to fight."

When Gawan mounted his horse the maiden was all woebegone. Everyone there wept, and little did they restrain themselves.

To the host he said, "If God permits, I shall not fail to repay you for the hospitality you have shown me." Then he

[5] A garble of Arabic *emir al muminim,* "Prince of the Believers."

took leave of the girl, who had cause for great sorrow. He rode away; they remained here grieving.

If you would be pleased to hear now what happened to Gawan there, I would be more pleased to tell you, and I will tell you just as I heard it.

When he arrived at the gate, he found the trader and did not find his booth empty. Inside there were things for sale —I would be mighty glad to have such precious things. Gawan got down from his horse in front of him. Such a rich market he had never seen as he saw there. The booth was made of samite, and it was square, high, and 563 spacious. What was for sale there? If it were weighed against gold, the Baruch of Baghdad could not pay for what was in there. Nor could the Katoliko[6] of Ranculat.[7] When Greece was the way it was when the treasure was found there,[8] the Emperor could not have paid for it, even with the added contributions of the other two: these wares were precious.

Gawan greeted the trader, and when he saw what wondrous things were for sale, Gawan asked him to show him some girdles or brooches that were within his means.

The trader said, "I have been sitting here for many a year and no one—except noble ladies—has dared look over what is in my booth. If you have manliness in your heart, then you will be master of all of it. It has been brought from afar. If you have come on adventure and undertaken to win the prize here, Sir, and if you succeed, you can easily deal with me: everything I have on sale will 564 all belong to you then. Proceed and let God dispose! Did the ferryman Plippalinot direct you here? Many a lady will praise your coming to this land if your hand delivers them here. If you mean to go into this adventure, leave your horse standing quietly here. I'll watch it if you're willing to trust me."

Then my lord Gawan said, "If it is in keeping with your

---

[6] The Katholikos, or Patriarch, of the Armenian church.
[7] See Book I, 9, and note.
[8] The allusion is to the capture of Constantinople by the crusaders in 1204.

station, I would like to leave it here. I am overwhelmed
with your wealth, and this horse has never known such
a rich groom since I have been riding it."

Without any displeasure the trader said, "Sir, I myself
and all I own—need I speak further about it?—are yours if
you survive. To whom should I belong with any better
right?"

Gawan's courage told him to proceed on foot manfully
and unafraid. As I told you before, he found the citadel
broad and such that every side of it was built up with defenses. For all sieges, not a berry would it give in thirty
years if men came against it. In the center of it   565
lay a field—the Lech Field is longer[9]—and many towers
rose high over the ramparts. The adventure informs us that
when Gawan saw the great hall, its roof was just like pea-
cocks' plumes, bright-hued and of a color that neither rain
nor snow could damage the roof's brilliance at all.

Inside, it was adorned and handsomely decorated, the
window posts were fluted, and high vaulted arches closed
over it. On this side and on that side lay[10] a marvelous
number of beds, each by itself, with all sorts of rich coverlets thrown over them. There the ladies had been sitting,
but they had been prudent and gone away. Hence they were
not there to receive their joy's arrival, their day of blessings,
which were embodied in Gawan. If they could but have
seen him, what more pleasant thing could have befallen
them? But none of them was permitted to do so, though
he came in their service. All this was no fault of theirs.
My lord Gawan walked around this way and that   566
way inspecting the hall. On one wall, I don't know on which
side, he saw a door standing wide open, beyond which he
was to win great renown or die in pursuit of renown.

He entered the chamber—its pavement shone bright and
smooth as glass—and there was the *Lit marveile,* the Wonder Bed. Four wheels, round and made of bright rubies,
rolled underneath it, and never was the wind so swift as
they. The bedposts were forked and attached to them. I

[9] The Lechfeld is in Bavaria between Landsberg and Augsburg.
[10] Lay, i.e., consisted of piles of cushions divan-fashion.

must particularly praise the pavement to you: it was of jasper and chrysolite and sard, whatever Clinschor, who invented it, desired. From many lands his cunning wisdom had brought the work that was expended here.

The pavement was so smooth that Gawan could hardly keep his footing. He moved as best he could, but as often as he took a step, the bed swerved from the spot 567 where it stood before. Gawan found it burdensome to carry the heavy shield that his host had so urgently pressed upon him. He thought, "How am I going to catch you if you dodge me this way? I'll show you if I can jump to you!" At this point the bed was standing in front of him: he made a leap and landed squarely in the middle of it.

Never has anybody known the speed with which that bed bumped back and forth. It didn't miss one of the four walls and slammed into each one with such a jolt that the whole fortress resounded. In this fashion he rode the bed to joust after joust, and all the thunder that ever thundered, and all the trumpeters, from the first to the last, if they had been there and blowing for pay, there couldn't have been a louder din. Gawan had to stay awake though he was lying in bed.

And what did the hero do then? The racket was so fierce that he pulled the shield up over him. He lay there and let Him take charge of it Who has help to bestow, 568 and Who never failed to grant help to one who in great need seeks help from Him. A shrewd and stout-hearted man, when trouble comes, will call upon the Hand Supreme, for It brings abundant help and helps him helpfully. And thus it was with Gawan. He prayed to Him to Whom he always attributed his renown and to His mighty goodness to protect him.

Now the din subsided. The four walls were an equal distance away and the bed of handsome colors stood right in the middle of the floor. Then greater terror came upon him. Five hundred slings[11] were ready by magic powers for the throw, and their throws took the direction of the bed where he was lying. His shield had such hardness, however, that he felt it very little. It was gravel stones they

[11] A medieval weapon called in Latin a *fustibalus.*

were hurling, round and hard, and in some places they went through the shield.

The stones had all been hurled. Seldom had he   569
endured such violent blows upon him. But now there were five hundred crossbows or more drawn for the shot, and all of them had the same target, right at the bed where he was lying. Anyone who has ever undergone such distress knows what arrows are. This went on for a short time until they were all whizzed out.

Anybody who wants to have rest had better not come to this bed, because no one will give him any peace there. Youth would turn grey from the rest that Gawan found on that bed. But his heart and hand were still free from dismay. Neither arrows nor stones had missed him entirely, and through his chain armor he had been bruised and slashed. Now he had hopes that his misery was over, but he still had to strive with his hand for the prize.

Just then a door opposite him opened and in came a stocky churl frightful to behold. He wore a   570
surcot and a *bonnet* of fishskin[12] and wide trousers of the same material. In his hand he carried a club with a knob at the end of it thicker than a jug. He started toward Gawan, who by no means wanted him; his arrival, in fact, irritated him. Gawan thought, "This fellow is not in armor, his weapons are poor compared to mine." He straightened up and sat there as if his limbs didn't pain him at all. The fellow took a step backward as if to flee, but he spoke angrily, "You need not be afraid of me, but I am going to see to it that something happens to you that will make you forfeit your life. It's by the devil's powers that you're still alive, but if he has saved you so far, you are still not protected from death. That's what I'll show you now as I go out." And the churl went out again. With his sword Gawan swept the arrow shafts from his shield; the arrowheads had gone through so that they rattled in his chain mail.

Then he heard a rumbling sound as if twenty   571
drums were beating out a dance. His firm courage unim-

12 Sharkskin, undoubtedly.

paired, which real dismay had never nicked or notched, he thought: "What is going to happen to me now? I should know what trouble is by this time: are my troubles to increase? But defend myself I shall!" He glanced toward the churl's door, and just then in rushed a husky lion as tall as a horse. Gawan, who never liked to retreat, took his shield by the handle straps and did what defense required: he sprang to the pavement. Hunger had made this big, husky lion ravenous, but that did him little good. Furiously he rushed at the man, but Sir Gawan was on guard. He all but tore the shield away, for his first lunge ripped through the shield with all his claws. Animals have rarely gone through such a thickness as this one's blow did. Gawan warded off any snatching away, and in turn sliced off a leg, so that the lion was running around on three feet—the fourth foot was caught fast on the shield. Such   572 a gush of blood did he let forth that Gawan was now able to stand fast on the slippery floor. Back and forth went the fight. The lion leaped time and time again at the stranger, and many a snort did he snuffle through his nose as he bared his teeth.—If he had been trained on a diet of good people, I wouldn't like to sit next to him!—Gawan didn't like it either, fighting with him, as he was, for his very life. He had wounded him so badly that the whole chamber was drenched in blood. In fury the lion lunged toward him and tried to pull him underneath him, but Gawan dealt him such a thrust through the breast, right up to the hilt, that the lion's fury quite disappeared and he fell down dead.

Gawan had now fought and overcome the supreme danger. At the same time he wondered, "What had I best do now? I don't like sitting in this blood. On the other hand, this bed can roll about so, that I must beware of sitting or lying on it, if I am really wise."

His head was now so dazed from blows, and   573 since his wounds were beginning to bleed, his brave strength parted company with him and he staggered from dizziness. His head was propped on the lion and his shield had fallen so that it was underneath him. All the strength and sense he had were taken away. He had been so ungently dealt with that all his senses failed. His pillow was not much like the one that Gymele of Monte Rybele, the sweet and wise, put under the head of Kahenis so that on it he slept away his chance for fame.[13] Fame came hurrying toward *this* man, for you have heard how he came to lose consciousness so that he lay there senseless.

It had been secretly observed that the chamber pavement was bedewed with blood and that both Gawan and the lion seemed to be dead. A comely maiden had timidly peeped in from above and her lovely color had gone pale   574 at the sight. This young girl was so upset that the aged and wise Arnive broke forth in lamentation. But I must praise her, for she cared for the knight and kept him from dying. She, too, went to have a look, but from glancing in through the window above, the lady could not make out whether she was seeing the days of her joy to come or her heart's everlasting grief. She was afraid the knight was dead, and the thought filled her with dismay, for he was lying there propped up on the lion and had no other bed.

"It grieves my heart," she said, "that your loyal manhood has cost you your noble life. If you have found death here for the sake of us wretched folk, and since it was your loyalheartedness that brought you to it, I am moved to pity for your virtue, whether you are old or young." And having seen the hero lying there like that, she turned to all the ladies and said, "All you ladies who have been baptized, call upon God to implore His favor."

She sent two maidens down and bade them   575 take good care to tread softly until they were out of the chamber, and told them to bring her word if he were alive or if he had expired. This command she gave to both of them. Those sweet maidens pure, did either of them weep? Yes, both of them did, grievously, out of true sorrow, when they found him lying there with his shield floating in the blood from his wounds. They looked to see if he were alive. With her lovely hand one of them untied his helmet

---

[13] In Eilhart's *Tristan*, Kahenis had a pillow placed under his head that made him sleep too soundly to be concerned with Isalde, who was lying beside him.

from his head and undid the ventail. The faintest trace of
foam lay on his red mouth. She waited to see whether he
drew breath or whether he was deceiving her with the appearance of life. Still the matter was in doubt. On his
gambeson he was wearing two gampiluns made of sable fur,
such as Ilinot the Briton once wore with great renown on
his coat of arms; [14] nobility did he show indeed in his youth
until his death. The maiden tore off a bit of the   576
sable fur and held it to his nose; then she watched to see
whether his breath, as it moved, would stir the hair. There
was breath there!

Immediately she bade her companion hurry after clean
water, and her lovely companion quickly brought it to her.
The girl forced her ring between his teeth and managed it
very skillfully. Then she poured water into his mouth, just
a little, and then more—but she didn't pour too much—until he opened his eyes. He greeted **them** both and thanked
them, those two sweet girls.

"To think you should find me lying in such an unman-
nerly position! I would take it as a kindness on your part
if you would not mention it to anyone. May your good
breeding keep you from doing so!"

They said, "You were lying and you are still lying
now as one who has gained the highest renown. You have
won the prize here, with which you can grow old in joy.
The victory is yours today. Now give us poor folk   577
assurance that your wounds are such that we may rejoice with you."

"If you want me to live," he said, "you must help me."
Then he begged the ladies, "Have someone examine my
wounds who has knowledge of such things. But if I am to
fight some more, tie my helmet on and go away. I am
eager to fight for my life."

"You are through fighting!" they said. "Sir, let us stay
with you. But one of us must earn messenger's reward
from the four queens with the news that you are still alive.
And a bed must be made ready for you, and pure medicines,

[14] See Book VII, 383, and note concerning Ilinot, the son of King
Arthur, and his heraldic "gampiluns."

and wholesome salves must be applied with care, that are
a cure for bruises and for wounds and that soothe and
help."

One of the maidens ran off so fast that it was clear she
had no limp. To court she brought the report that he was
alive "and so life-like that he will be glad to make us
glad, if God wills. But he has need of good care."   578

They all said, *"Dieu merci!"*

The wise old queen bade them make up a bed and
spread out a carpet in front of it, by a good fire. Salves
most precious and well prepared with skill the queen then
fetched for the bruises and the wounds. At the same time
she commanded four maidens to go and get his armor, and
to remove it from him gently, and to take care not to occasion him any embarrassment. "You must hold up a
pfellel-silk around you and remove his armor from within
its shadow. If he is able to walk, allow him to do so; otherwise carry him to where I will have the bed ready and I
will be waiting where the hero is to lie. If his battle has
turned out so that he is not mortally wounded, I will soon
have him well. But if one of his wounds is fatal, that would
cut right across our joy. Then we, too, would be defeated
and we would have to bear a living death."

Well, this was done. Sir Gawan's armor was re-   579
moved and he was led away and attended with the help of
those who knew how to help. He had fifty wounds or more,
but the arrowheads had not penetrated his chain mail very
far; the shield had protected it. Then the old queen took
dittany[15] and warm wine and a piece of blue sendal-silk
and wiped away the stain of blood from his wounds
wherever there was any, and bandaged him so that he recovered. Wherever the helmet was dented there were swell-
ings on his head, so that you could judge the blows he had
sustained. By the virtue of her salves and her mastery she
made these bruises disappear.

"I will quickly bring you relief," she said. "Cundrie *la
sorcière* is kind enough to come and see me frequently, and

15 Dittany (Wolfram's *dictam*) is an herb reported from classical
antiquity as being good for drawing arrows out of wounds.

whatever may be done with medicines she imparts to me. Ever since Anfortas has been in such wretched pain so that he was in need of help, this salve has aided in keeping him from death; it came from Munsalvaesche." 580

When Gawan heard the name of Munsalvaesche his heart skipped for joy, because he thought it was near by. Then he who was ever free from deceit, Gawan, said to the queen, "Lady, you have brought back to my heart my senses that had fled from me, and my pain is easing. Whatever strength or sense I now have, your servant owes to your efforts."

"Sir," she said, "we must all seek to come to your favor and try to win it. But now do as I say and do not talk too much. I am going to give you an herb that will make you sleep; it will do you good. You must not ask for food or drink until nightfall. That way your strength will return; then I will come to you with food so that you can be comfortable until morning."

She placed an herb in his mouth and directly he fell asleep. She covered him carefully, and thus he slept the whole day through, he who was rich in honor and poor in shame. Comfortable he lay, and warm. From time 581 to time he suffered a chill during his sleep so that he choked or sneezed; that was the effect of the salve. A great company of ladies kept coming in and others kept going out, and they all wore a noble beauty. The aged Arnive by her authority commanded that none of them should speak aloud while the hero was sleeping. She also ordered the great hall to be locked. Any knights who were there, or squires or castle folk, none of them learned of this news until the following day. Then to the ladies came fresh sorrow.

Thus the hero slept until nightfall. The queen bethought herself to remove the herb from his mouth, and then he awoke and craved drink. Whereat the wise queen had good food and drink carried in to him. He raised himself and sat upright to eat with a good relish. Many noble ladies were standing about, so that never had he known more gracious attendance, and their service was performed with fine

courtesy. My lord Gawan scrutinized now this one, now
that one, and now another, for he was feeling   582
once again the old yearning in love for Orgeluse the fair.
Never in all his life had any woman touched him so deeply,
either when he had received love or when love had been
refused him.

Then the hero undismayed said to his preceptress, the
aged queen, "Lady, it offends my sense of propriety, and
you may consider me too demanding, to have these ladies go
on standing in my presence. Either bid them go and sit
down or else have them eat with me."

"None of them may sit down here except me. Sir, they
would be ashamed if they did not serve you zealously, for
you are the midpoint of our joys. But, Sir, whatever you
command them, that they must do, if we are sensible."

The noble ladies of high lineage refrained in their courtesy from sitting down. They were glad to stand, and their
sweet lips begged him that they be allowed to go on standing until he had finished eating, and that none of them
should be seated. When he had finished, they withdrew.
Then Gawan lay down and slept.

BOOK·XII

He who would now disturb his rest, when rest   583
was what he needed, would, I think, be committing a sin.
As the adventure bears witness, he had toiled and, enduring
great perils, had heightened and broadened his fame.

What the noble Lanzilot[1] suffered on the Sword Bridge
and later when he fought with Meljacanz, that was nothing
to the peril Gawan knew now. Likewise what they tell of
Garel,[2] the proud and mighty king, who so valiantly threw
the lion out of the great hall of Nantes. And Garel secured
the knife too, and for that endured distress inside the marble pillar. If the arrows which Gawan, in his bravery, following the bidding of his manly heart, suffered to speed
against his own life—if all these were laid onto a mule, it
would collapse under the load.

The danger Gawan himself knew later at the ford *Li
gweiz prelljus*[3] and Erec too when he won Schoydelakurt
away from Mabonagrin[4]—neither could be compared with

---

[1] See Book VII, 387, note.
[2] The source of this reference is not known.
[3] Li gweiz prelljus, Old French *li guez perilleus*, "the Ford Perilous."
[4] A reference to Hartmann's *Erec*. See Book III, 178, note. In *Erec*
Schoydelakurt is the name of the adventure, but Wolfram apparently
thinks it is the name of the garden.

Gawan's torment now.[5] Not even when the proud Iwein[6] could not resist pouring the water on the stone of   584 the adventure. —If all these woes were joined into one, and the suffering weighed on the scales, Gawan's distress would outbalance the rest.

But what distress do I mean? If you do not think it is too soon, I shall tell you now. It was Orgeluse, who had come into Gawan's heart and thoughts—he who had always been lacking in cowardice and mighty in true courage.

How could it happen that a woman so large could find shelter in a place so small? She trod a narrow path straight into Gawan's heart, so that all his other pains vanished before this distress. These *were* small quarters for such a tall woman to sit in, this woman in whose service the faithful Gawan never slept.

Let no one laugh that such a valorous man can be vanquished by a woman. Alas and alas, how can that be?

Here Lady Love is displaying her anger at one who has won renown. Always before she found him courageous and unafraid, and now that he is sick and wounded she should not use force against him. She should   585 surely count it in his favor that before, when he had his strength, she conquered him against his will.

Lady Love, if you wish to gain praise and honor, then let me tell you, *this* battle does you no honor. Gawan has lived all his life according to your bidding that he might gain your favor, and so did his father Lot. And all his kin on his mother's side have given you loyal service since the days of Mazadan, who was touched by your power when Terdelaschoye carried him off to Famorgan. Of Mazadan's descendants it has often been reported that not one ever forsook you. Ither of Gaheviez bore your seal. Wherever

---

[5] Wolfram's style is so elliptical here that the phrase referring to Gawan's adventure at the ford has been expanded slightly beyond the original.

[6] A reference to Hartmann's *Iwein*. When water was poured on the stone, a great thunder ensued, and the lord of the castle appeared to fight against any knight who challenged him thus.

he was mentioned before women, if only to speak his name, no one of them was ashamed to yield to the power of love. Now imagine how it was when they *saw* him. Then they learned what love really meant. In him you lost a devoted servant.

Now kill Gawan too, as you killed his cousin Ilinot, when, compelled to it by your power, the sweet   586 youth sought to woo a noble *amie,* Florie of Kanadic. As a child he had left his father's land, and Queen Florie herself had reared him. In Britain he was a stranger. Florie so burdened him with her love that she drove him from the land. In her service he was found dead, as you, I suppose, have heard.

For love's sake Gawan's kin have often come to heart-rending torment. I shall name you other kinsmen of his who have also suffered because of love. To what did the blood-colored snow compel the faithful Parzival? The cause of that was his wife, the queen. Galoes and Gahmuret— you rode them both down and so trampled them that you delivered them up to death. The noble Itonje, Gawan's fair young sister, cherished for *le roi* Gramoflanz a true and constant love.[7] And to Surdamur too, Lady Love, you brought distress for her love of Alexander.[8] These and all the others of Gawan's kin, Lady Love, you never would set free—they had to do you service. And now you   587 want to win honor through him! Pit your strength against strength. Let the weak and wounded Gawan live, and harass those who are well.

There are many who sing of love, whom love never pressed so hard as this. Perhaps *I* ought to keep silent. It is lovers who should lament what happened to him of Norway after he had escaped alive from that adventure, when, helpless as he was, love's tempest struck him all too bitterly.

He said, "Alas that I ever saw these two restless beds.

[7] See Books XIII and XIV.

[8] A reference to *Cliges,* an Arthurian romance. Chrétien's version is still preserved; a German *Cliges,* attributed by Konrad von Ems to Konrad Fleck, has been lost.

One wounded me, and the other has heightened my yearning for love. Orgeluse, the duchess, must grant me her favor if joy is to remain my companion."

In his impatience he so turned and tossed that some of the bandaging tore loose from his wounds. And so, in great distress, he lay there.

But see, there the day shone in on him, whose coming he had awaited in such discomfort. Many a hard sword fight he had fought before seemed more peaceful to him than his night of rest. Should any lover claim his mis-   588
ery to be equal to Gawan's, just let him be so sorely wounded by darts and then healed—that will hurt him quite as much as his pangs of love before. Gawan suffered love and other pains as well.

It began to grow bright from the day, so that his tall candles did not cast their light very far. The warrior arose, and there lay his linen garments stained from his wounds and his armor. But shirt and breeches of buckram had been placed there for him—and he was glad for the change —and a gambeson and an outer robe, both of marten fur and both with girdles[9] brought from Arras. A pair of boots stood there too, not too narrow for comfort.

Sir Gawan put on the new clothes and left the room, walking this way and that until he found the sumptuous castle hall. Never had his eyes seen richness which could compare with this. At the one end of the hall   589
rose a narrow tower high above the castle roof, a winding staircase leading up to it. Up there stood a shining pillar, not made of rotten wood, but bright and firm, and so large that Lady Kamille's coffin[10] could well have rested upon it. From the lands of Feirefiz the wise Clinschor had brought this structure that towered up here. It was circular like a tent. If the master Jeometras had had to fashion this, his skill would not have sufficed, for it had been wrought by sorcery.

[9] This word *schürbrant,* occurs only here, and its meaning cannot be determined with absolute certainty. Some scholars believe it to mean "girdle," others think it is a fabric of some sort.

[10] See Book X, 504, note.

Of diamond and amethyst—the adventure tells us so—of topaz and garnet, of chrysolite, ruby, emerald, and sard were the costly windows, as wide as they were tall. And as the window columns, so was the roof above. But among these columns was none that could compare with the great pillar which stood in the center. The adventure tells us what wondrous properties it had.   590

Wanting to look at the many precious stones, Gawan climbed alone to the watchtower. There he found a marvel so great that he could not take his eyes from it. It seemed to him he could see in the great pillar all the lands round about, and it seemed the lands were circling the column and the mighty mountains collided with a clash. In the pillar he saw people riding and walking, others running or standing still. He seated himself at a window to observe the marvel better.

Just then the aged Arnive and her daughter Sangive came in, and with them Sangive's two daughters, and all four approached him. Gawan sprang up when he saw them.

Queen Arnive said, "Sir, you should still be sleeping. Have you given up your rest? You are too sorely wounded to take any other trials upon yourself now."

"Lady and mistress mine," answered he, "your help has restored my strength and wits, and I shall serve you as long as I live."

The queen said, "If I have heard rightly, that   591 you, Sir, acknowledged me your mistress, then I command you, kiss these ladies, all three. This will bring you no disgrace for they are descended from royalty."

This command Gawan was glad to obey. He kissed the fair ladies, Sangive and Itonje and the sweet Cundrie, and the five sat down together. He looked at the two fair maids, now at one and now at the other, but so strong was the power of one woman who had found a place in his heart, that the radiance of these maidens was a misty day beside Orgeluse. So lovely did she seem to him, the Duchess of Logrois, that his heart compelled him to her.

Now this was done and Gawan had been greeted by the three ladies. Their beauty was so bright and lovely it could easily have wounded a heart that had never suffered the pangs of love before. To his mistress he spoke and asked her to tell him about the pillar he saw there, of what nature it was.

She answered, "Sir, this stone has cast its glow,   592 by day and all the nights since it was first known to me, for six miles round the countryside. Whatever happens within this space, in water or on meadow, may be seen in this pillar. Of everything it gives a true report. Bird or beast, guest or exile, stranger or friend, one finds them here. Its light gleams for six miles around and it is so strong and solid that neither hammer nor smith could harm it even with the greatest skill. It was stolen in Tabronit from Queen Secundille—against her will, I think."

At this moment Gawan perceived riders in the pillar, and he saw it was a knight and a lady together. The lady seemed to him beautiful. Man and horse were fully armed, and the knight's helmet richly adorned. They were coming on swiftly through the path toward the meadow. This was clearly their goal. They followed the same path   593 across the marsh which Lischois had ridden, the proud knight Gawan had vanquished. The lady was leading the knight by the bridle. A joust was his intention.

Gawan turned away, yet this only increased his sorrow. He thought the pillar had deceived him, but there he saw, beyond a doubt, Orgeluse de Logrois and a courteous knight on the grassy plain by the quay. As swiftly and sharply as hellabore[11] enters the nose, did the duchess pass through Gawan's eyes down into his narrow heart. A man quite helpless against love—that, alas, is Sir Gawan!

When he saw the knight coming there, he said to his mistress, "Lady, there comes a knight riding this way with spear erect. He will not give up seeking, and seeking, he shall find. If knightly adventure is his desire, combat he shall get from me. Tell me, who is the lady?"

"That is the beautiful Duchess of Logrois," she   594

[11] In German this is called "sneezing herb," and this name gives the passage its humorous touch, impossible to convey in the translation.

said. "Whom does she have it in for now? The Turkoite
has come with her. His courage is said to be dauntless,
and he has won with the spear honor enough for three
lands. Against his valiant hand you should abstain from
fighting now. It is much too soon for you to fight. You
are too badly wounded for that. Even if you were well,
you would do better not to fight with him."

Then Sir Gawan answered, "You said I should be master
here. If then anyone approaches so near in search of knightly
action, it reflects upon my honor, and since he desires
combat, Lady, I must have my armor."

At this many tears were shed by the ladies, all four of
them, and they said, "If you wish to enhance your honor
and your happiness, then on no account fight with him. If
you should fall before him, our misery would grow all
the more. Even should you come out of this battle alive, if
you put your armor on, your earlier wounds will take your
life. And thus we shall be delivered up to death."

Gawan wrestled with anxiety, and you shall   595
hear what oppressed him. The coming of the noble Turkoite he had counted as a threat to his honor. Yet his wounds
pained him sorely, and love even more, and the grief of
the four ladies, for he saw they bore him good will.

He asked them to cease their weeping, and called for
armor, horse, and sword. The fair and noble ladies led
Gawan back to the hall. He bade them descend the steps
before him, to where the other sweet and lovely ladies
were. There, while bright eyes wept, Gawan was speedily
armed for his ride to battle. They did this so secretly that
no one learned of it except the chamberlain who had his
horse curried. Gawan stole out to where Gringuljete stood,
but he was so sorely wounded he could scarcely carry his
shield. And it was riddled with holes.

Gawan mounted his horse and rode from the castle down
to his faithful host, who denied him nothing and   596
gave him all that his will desired. A spear he furnished him.
It was sturdy and unpolished. He had picked up many a
spear upon his meadow out there across the river.

Sir Gawan asked him to take him over, and he ferried
Gawan to the shore, where he found the noble, high-
spirited Turkoite.

This man disgrace could not touch, nor could any evil
stain him. So great was his fame that all knew whoever
jousted with him would be thrown from the horse, felled
by the thrust of his spear. Thus he had vanquished in
jousting all those who, seeking fame, had ever ridden
against him. And the noble warrior had declared that only
with the spear, not with the sword, would he become heir
to a rival's fame, or, failing that, hold his own fame lost.
If anyone should win honor by felling him with his spear,
he would not defend himself further, but would yield his
pledge of security.

Gawan learned this from Plippalinot, who took   597
the pledges for the joust. And this was the way he took
pledges: If a joust took place there, and the one fell and the
other stayed in the saddle, he received, with no ill will from
them, what the loser lost and the victor won, I mean the
horse. That he took away. He cared little whether they
fought with zeal. And as to who reaped fame and who disgrace, that he left to the ladies to say. They could often
look on at such battles.

Plippalinot asked him to take a firm seat in the saddle.
Then he led the horse to the shore and handed Gawan
his shield and spear.

The Turkoite came galloping up like a man who knows
how to aim his thrust, neither too high nor too low.
Gawan rode to meet him. Gringuljete from Munsalvaesche
followed Gawan's bidding, as the bridle directed, toward
the battle plain.

Now onward, let the joust be done! Here came the son
of King Lot, manly and with heart undaunted. Where is
the knot of the helmet cord? The thrust of the Turkoite
hit him there. Gawan's blow struck a different spot,
right through the Turkoite's visor. It was plain   598
to see who gave the other a fall. On the tip of his short,
sturdy spear Sir Gawan caught the Turkoite's helmet—off
rode the helmet, here lay the man. He who had ever been a

flower of knighthood until, with his fall in the joust, he spread himself over the grass—his costly finery now lay in the dew, vying in splendor with the flowers.

Gawan rode over him until he pledged security. The ferryman claimed the horse, and that was his right. Who would deny it?

"You would gladly rejoice if you knew what for," said the fair Orgeluse, to provoke Gawan once more. "Just because the strong lion's paw must accompany you in your shield, you think you have won fame. Since the ladies up there have seen this joust you fought, we must allow you this pleasure—if it makes you happy. Though the Wonder Bed took small revenge on you, yet your shield is splintered, as if you had really seen fighting. No doubt you are also too badly wounded to join in the fracas of battle. 599 That would hurt you and add to the pain I caused you when I called you a goose. Yet you like to boast of your shield, as full of holes as a sieve from the many darts that have pierced it. And now you would like to run away from any discomfort. I thumb my nose at you! Ride up again to the ladies. You would not dare seek the combat which I would have to demand if your heart desired to serve me for love."

He answered the duchess, "Lady, if I have wounds, they have found help here from you. If it pleases you so to help me that you will accept my service, then there was never peril so great but that I was destined to serve you in this danger."

"Then I shall let you ride with me," she said, "and in my company continue to fight for fame."

At this the proud and noble Gawan was filled with joy. He bade the Turkoite go with his host Plippalinot to the castle and sent a message that the fair ladies there should receive him with honor.

Gawan's spear had remained whole, though 600 both horses had been driven hard with the spurs to the clash of the joust. He bore it away in his hand from the bright meadow. Many of the ladies wept that he was leaving them, and Queen Arnive said, "He who was our comfort has chosen a pleasing sight for his eyes, but a thorn for his heart. Alas that he is following the Duchess Orgeluse to Li gweiz prelljus! That will not help his wounds."

Four hundred ladies mourned for him, but he rode from them to seek for fame. Painful as his wounds were, Orgeluse's radiant beauty had put an end to this distress. She said, "You must get me a wreath from the branch of a tree. For this deed I will praise you, and if you grant my wish, you may ask my love in return."

"Lady," he answered, "wherever this branch may be which can bring me happiness and the great reward that I may pour out to you my grief and my deed for your favor, I shall pluck it if Death does not prevent."

All the bright flowers blooming there were as   601
nothing to the radiance of Orgeluse. Gawan's thoughts were so constantly of her that his former pain troubled him no longer. So she rode with her companion a journey-stage or so from the castle on a road wide and straight that led to a beautiful *forêt*. Tamarisk and prisin[12] trees grew there. That was Clinschor's forest.

The bold warrior Gawan said, "Lady, where can I break the wreath which shall restore my joy, now riddled with holes?" He should have thrown her to the ground and taken his will of her, as has often happened since then to many a beautiful woman.

She said, "I'll show you where you can win this prize." Cross country they rode up to a ravine, so close that they could see the tree from which the wreath should come. Then she said, "Sir, that tree is guarded by the man who robbed me of my joy. If you bring me a branch from it, never will a knight have received such a rich reward for love's service." So said the duchess and continued, "*I* shall stop here. May God watch over your for-   602
tunes! If you wish to ride on, then you must not delay. You will have to force your horse to a mighty leap across Li gweiz prelljus."

So she remained there motionless on the field, and Sir Gawan rode on. He heard the roar of a waterfall; it had

[12] This is probably the redwood tree.

worn away a ravine, wide and deep and impassable. The valiant Gawan dug in his spurs and urged the horse on to the leap. It reached the other side only with the two front feet, and the leap had to end with a fall. Seeing that, the duchess burst into tears.

The current was swift and strong. Gawan exerted all his strength, but he was hampered by the weight of his armor. A branch of a tree hung down into the stream, and this the strong man seized, for he wanted very much to live. His spear was floating beside him, and laying hold of it, the warrior climbed up onto land.

Gringuljete was drifting, at one moment with head above water, in the next, completely submerged. Gawan set about to help it, but the horse had floated so far   603 downstream that he had little desire to run after it in the heavy armor he was wearing and with his many wounds. Then a whirlpool swept it toward the shore, to where torrents of rain had washed out a wide opening in a steeply sloping bank, so that he could reach the horse with his spear. This split in the shore saved Gringuljete. With the spear my lord Gawan guided it so close inshore that he could catch the bridle in his hand, and thus he pulled the horse out and onto the plain. It shook itself when it was safe. The shield had not been lost in the water. He set the saddle girth right and took the shield.

Whoever thinks these difficulties slight, well, I will let that pass—but he *was* in straits, for Love ruled over him. The shining Orgeluse drove him to seek the wreath, and that ride demanded courage.

The tree was so well guarded that, had Gawan been *two* men, not just one, they would have paid with their lives for the wreath, for King Gramoflanz defended it. Yet Gawan picked the wreath.

The river was called Sabins. Gawan collected   604 a strenuous interest when he and his horse splashed around in that water. —No matter how radiantly Orgeluse shone, I would not have cared to woo her love in such fashion. I know very well what I like and what I don't like.

When Gawan had plucked the branch and decked his

helmet with the wreath, there came riding toward him a
handsome knight. The years he had lived were neither too
few nor too many. His pride was so great that no matter
what injury *one* man might do him, he would never fight
with him alone, but only with two or more. So haughty
was his heart that if *one* man did harm to him, he let him
go unscathed.

Le fils du roi Irot bade Gawan good morning; that was
King Gramoflanz. Then he said, "Sir, I have not yielded my
claim to this wreath. I would not even have spoken a
greeting if there were *two* of you, who, to win great fame,
were bent on taking such a branch from my tree. They
would have had to face me in battle; as it is, that would be
a disgrace for me."

Gawan, too, was loath to fight with him, for   605
the king rode unarmed. The renowned warrior carried only
a falcon, which perched on his white hand. Itonje had sent
it to him, Gawan's sweet sister. The hat on his head was of
peacock plumes from Sinzester. The king wore a cloak of
grass-green samite, trimmed in white ermine, and so long
that on both sides it trailed on the ground. The horse he
rode was not very large, but strong enough and beautiful.
It had been brought from Denmark, either by land or by
sea. The king rode completely unarmed; he did not even
carry a sword.

"Your shield shows evidence of fighting," said King
Gramoflanz, "and so little of it is still whole that I see the
Wonder Bed must have fallen to you. You have withstood
the adventure which should have waited for me if the wise
Clinschor were not so friendly to me and if I   606
were not at war with her who by her beauty has gained the
true victory of love. She may still be angry with me, and she
has cause to be. I killed Cidegast, her noble husband, and
his three companions. Orgeluse I took captive and offered
her my crown and all my lands. But whatever service my
hand could give her, her heart responded with hatred for
me. For a year I held her prisoner and pled with her, but I
could never win her love. I must tell you of this, my sorrow,
for I know well she has promised you her love, since you

are here to seek my death. Had you come with a companion, you might have taken my life or you would both have perished, and that would have been your reward.

"But now my heart yearns for another love, and it lies with you and your good will to help me, since you have become lord of *Terre marveile.* You were victor in the battle. If you would be kind, help me to win a maid for whom my heart is longing in sorrow. She is the daughter of King Lot, and of all the women in the world no other   607 enslaved me so completely.

"I bear her token here, and I ask you to bring the fair maid my vow of service in return. I think she holds me dear. For I have endured peril for her sake ever since the haughty Orgeluse with passionate words denied me *her* love. What fame I have won since then, whether I fared well or ill—the noble Itonje was the cause. But alas, I have never seen her. If you would give me help and consolation, take to my fair, sweet lady this little ring. Here you are exempt from strife unless your company were larger, two of you or more. What honor would it bring me to kill you or force you to pledge security? Such combat my hand has always shunned."

Then Sir Gawan said, "But I am a man and armed. If you think you would win small fame, were I to be slain by your hand, I gain no fame either by plucking this branch. For who would count it to my great honor if I killed you, defenseless as you are? I will be your   608 messenger. Give me the ring. I will give the lady your pledge of service, and your sorrow of heart I will not keep from her."

The king thanked him warmly, and Gawan continued, "Since you disdain to fight with me, tell me, Sir, who you are."

"Do not count it an insult, I beg you," said the king. "And I shall not conceal my name. Irot was my father, and he was killed by King Lot. I am King Gramoflanz. My heart has always been so full of courage that I will never fight if a single man does me injury, save with one and his name is Gawan. I have heard of his fame and would gladly meet him in combat to seek vengeance upon him. His father broke faith and slew my father while greeting him. I have right enough to claim revenge. Now Lot has died, and Gawan has won such surpassing fame that no other knight of the Round Table can compare with him. I shall yet live to see the day when I do combat with him."

Then the noble Lot's son spoke, "If you think   609 to please your lady, if indeed she *is* that, by accusing her father of such faithlessness, and still more by seeking to kill her brother, then she must be a vicious maid if she does not reprove you for such behavior. If she were a true daughter and sister, she would defend them both so that you would forego this hate. How would this please your father-in-law if he had really broken faith? And *you* have not avenged him for *your* accusing him, the dead, of falsity? Then his *son* will not fear to do so. He will not hesitate, though his fair sister's love for you will profit him nothing. He will give himself as pledge. Sir, my name is Gawan. If my father did anything to you, take your revenge on *me*. *He* is dead. I shall defend him from slander, that I may live in honor, by giving security for him in combat."

Then the king said, "Are you he whom I hate with a hatred still unappeased? Then I am both glad and sorry that you are so noble a knight. One thing about   610 you pleases me, that I shall do battle with you. For you it is a great honor that I am willing to meet you, alone, in combat. Since our fame will be increased if we invite noble ladies to look on at the battle, I shall bring fifteen hundred with me, and you too have a fair company at the Castle of Wonders. Arthur your uncle will send you from a land called Löver—do you know the town, Bems on the Korca? —his court which is all assembled there. He can reach here by eight days from today with great *joie*. On the sixteenth day from today I shall come to the plain of Joflanze to avenge the old wrong done me and get recompense for this wreath."

The king asked Gawan to ride with him to the city of Rosche Sabins and said, "You will not find a bridge anywhere else."

But Sir Gawan answered, "I wish to go back the way I came. In all else I will do what you wish."

Both gave their word that they would come   611
to Joflanze on the appointed day, with a host of knights and ladies, to meet each other in battle, they two alone in the tilting ring.

So my lord Gawan parted from the noble man. Joyful, he galloped away, the wreath adorning his helmet. He did not hold back the horse but spurred it on hard to the ravine, and this time Grinuljete took the jump wide enough so that Gawan did not fall.

As the hero had sprung from his horse to the grass and was tightening the saddle girth, the duchess came riding toward him. The proud duchess quickly dismounted before him and cast herself at his feet. "Sir," she said, "such risk as I demanded of you—my worth was never worthy of this. Your peril and distress do indeed cause me such anguish of heart as a loving woman must feel for her beloved lover."

"Lady," he said, "if it is true that you greet me   612
in good faith, then you do yourself honor. This much I know: the shield should have its due, and you have sinned against it. Knighthood is so noble a pursuit that a true knight has always been exempt from mockery. Lady, if I may say so, anyone who has seen me fight must admit my knightly qualities. You once said otherwise, when you first saw me. That I shall say no more about. Accept this wreath, but never again use your shining beauty to bring such dishonor on any knight. If I must endure your mockery, I would rather be without love."

The lady so fair and so proud wept bitterly as she said, "Sir, when I tell you of the distress I bear in my heart, you will grant that my suffering is greater than yours. If I behave badly toward anyone, he will, I hope, in true kindness forgive me. Never can I lose more joy than I lost in Cidegast, that peerless knight. My sweet and noble   613
bel ami—so bright was his fame and his striving for true nobility that every man a mother gave birth to in the years when he was alive had to own that to him honor was due,

which no man's fame surpassed. He was a fountainhead of
virtue, and his youth bore such noble fruits it had no part in
falsity. Out of the darkness he had emerged, growing toward
the light, the goal for his honor set so high that no one
weakened by falseness could reach it. Out of the core of
his heart his honor grew so tall that all others remained far
beneath him. How high above all the stars swift Saturn
runs its course! A unicorn of good faith—since now I can
speak the truth—such was the man of my desire. For that
beast maidens should make lament; it must die for its
purity. I was his heart, he was my life. Him I lost, and was
forlorn. He was slain by King Gramoflanz, from whom
you took this wreath.

"Sir, if I have offended you, it was only that I   614
wished to try you, to see if you were worthy that I should
give you my love. I know well, Sir, my words did wound
you, but they were simply meant to test you. And now I
beg you, lay aside your wrath and forgive me. You are
the truly gallant one. I would compare you with gold. As it
is refined in the glowing fire, so your courage has been refined. The man whom I brought you here to harm, as I desired then and still desire—that man has caused me grief
of heart."

Then Sir Gawan said, "Lady, unless death prevents me,
I shall teach the king such distress as will put an end to his
arrogance. I have pledged my faith to ride against him
soon in combat. There we shall show our manhood. Lady,
I have forgiven you. If you in your kindness will not disdain my foolish counsel, I would advise you to act as does
honor to a woman and indeed as true womanly worth prescribes—you see, there is no one here but us—   615
lady, grant me your favor."

She answered, "In an ironclad arm I have seldom gotten
warm. But if, at some other time you wish to demand
my reward for your service, I shall not resist. I will share
with you in your suffering until your wounds are healed
and you are well again. I will go with you to the Castle of
Wonders."

"You make me very happy," said the man aflame with

love, and holding her close in his arms, he lifted the fair
lady onto her horse. She did not think him worthy of such
a favor when he saw her by the spring and she spoke so
crossly to him.

Gawan rode away happy, but she could not restrain her
tears and wept until he too became sad. He asked her to
tell him why she was weeping and begged her in God's
name to cease.

"Sir," she said, "I must make complaint to you about
him who slew my noble Cidegast. With that sorrow groped
its way into my heart, where once joy had its   616
place when I loved Cidegast. But I am not so completely
vanquished but that I have since sought to injure the king,
cost what it may, and many a fierce joust have I sent as
threat to his life. Perhaps from you will come the help
which will avenge me and make recompense for the grief
that whets at my heart.

"To accomplish the death of Gramoflanz, I accepted the
service of a king who was lord of what all men most desire. Sir, his name is Anfortas. As token of his love I received from him that booth full of wares from Tabronit
which still stands before your gate. For them great sums
are paid. The king won in my service what destroyed all
my joy. Just as I was of a mind to give him love, I found
fresh grief instead. In my service he won suffering. A sorrow as great or greater than Cidegast had caused me, I
endured from the wounding of Anfortas. Now tell me,
how could I, wretched as I was, since I am true of heart,
keep my senses in the face of such distress? Sometimes I
am truly beside myself when I think that he now   617
lies so helpless whom I chose after Cidegast's death to compensate and avenge me.

"Sir, now hear how Clinschor came to possess those rich
wares before your gate. When the noble Anfortas, who
had sent me the gift, was bereft of love and joy, I feared
some outrage from Clinschor. For he practiced the art of
black magic, and with sorcery he can compel both women
and men. Whenever he sees good people, he never lets them
go unharmed. To have peace with him, I gave Clinschor

my rich treasure. But if anyone should withstand the adventure and win the prize, then I was to seek his love. If I did not please him, the treasure would be mine once more. Now it shall belong to both of us. To this agreement all those present swore an oath. I hoped to lure Gramoflanz with the treasure, but the plan did not succeed. If he had undertaken the adventure, he would have suffered death.

"Clinschor is courtly and clever. To bring   618 honor to himself, he permitted my renowned followers knightly combat throughout his land, with many a thrust and blow. All the days of the week, all the weeks of the year, I send out special bands to set upon Gramoflanz, some by day and others by night. At great cost I plotted harm to the arrogant Gramoflanz. He often fights with my people. What is it that has always saved him from them? For I knew well how to threaten his life. Many of the knights who were too rich to serve me for pay, I allowed to serve for love of me, if they would not aid me otherwise, but I did not assure them of any reward.

"No man has ever beheld me but that I could have had his service, save for one who wore red armor. He put my men in peril. He came riding up before Logrois, and there, between Logrois and your ferry dock, his hand vanquished them and strewed them over the ground, so that I was not very happy. Five of my knights pursued him, and those he defeated on the meadow and gave their horses to the boatman.

"Since he had conquered my men, I rode after   619 the hero myself and offered him my land and myself. He said he had a more beautiful wife whom he preferred to me. I was hurt by these words and asked him who she was.

" 'The Queen of Pelrapeire she is called, that radiant and lovely lady, and my own name is Parzival. I do not want your love. The Grail causes me grief enough.' Impatiently he spoke, and then the peerless hero rode away. Did I do anything amiss—please tell me if I have—when in my heart's distress I offered the noble knight my love? Do you think less of my love for that?"

Gawan answered the duchess, "Lady, I know the man

whose love you desired, and I know him to be so noble that had he chosen you to love, your honor would have lost nothing by that."

Their eyes met and held for a moment as they rode, Gawan the courteous and the Duchess of Logrois. They had now come so near that they could be seen from the castle where he had had the adventure.

Then he said, "Lady, be so kind, if I may ask   620 you this favor, and do not give my name, which the knight who rode off with Gringuljete knew and called me by. Do me this favor I've asked of you, and if anyone should inquire about it, then say, 'I do not know who my companion is; his name was never spoken.'"

"I shall be glad to keep it secret," she said, "if you do not wish me to tell them." He and the lovely lady rode on toward the castle.

The knights there had heard of his coming, the knight who endured the adventure, overcame the lion, and later, in fair joust, struck the Turkoite down. Now Gawan came riding onto the plain toward the ferry, so that they could see him from the parapets, and with great clash and din they hurried from the castle. All of them bore rich banners, and came out so fast on their swift battle horses that he thought they were seeking combat.

When he saw them coming from afar, he said   621 to the duchess, "Are these men coming to attack us?"

"That is Clinschor's host," she said. "They have been waiting for you and now come riding to welcome you with joy. Do not reject their welcome. Their happiness moved them to come."

Plippalinot, too, had come on his ferry, and with him his beautiful daughter. The maid went to meet Gawan far out on the meadow and welcomed him joyfully. Gawan greeted her, and she kissed his stirrup and foot and also welcomed the duchess. Then she took his horse by the bridle and asked him to dismount. The lady and Gawan went to the boat's prow, where a carpet and coverlet lay spread. At Gawan's request, the duchess sat down there beside him. The ferryman's daughter saw to removing his armor, and I

heard it said that she had brought along her cloak, which
had covered him in the night when he found lodging at
her house. Sir Gawan was glad for it now, and he   622
put on her cloak and his own gambeson. The armor she took
away.

Now for the first time, as they sat there beside each
other, the fair duchess could look upon his face. Two
roasted larks, with a flask of wine and two white rolls, the
sweet maid brought to them on a fine, white cloth. A
sparrow hawk had caught the birds. Gawan and the duchess could easily get water from the river for themselves,
if they wanted to wash their hands, and this they both did.

Gawan was filled with joy that he was to eat with her
for whose sake he was willing to bear both happiness and
suffering. Each time she offered him the flask, which her
mouth had touched, his joy sprang up afresh that he could
drink after her. His sadness began to go lame, and his high
spirits sped on ahead. Her sweet mouth and fair skin drove
all distress away, so that his wounds no longer pained him.

From the castle the ladies looked down upon   623
this meal, and many noble knights came riding up to the
landing place across the river and displayed their skill at
the jousting in groups.

Gawan thanked the ferryman and his daughter, as did
the duchess too, for their kind hospitality. Then the clever
duchess asked, "What has become of the knight who was
jousting here yesterday when I rode away? He was vanquished by someone. How did it end, with life or death?"

Then Plippalinot replied, "Lady, I saw him alive today.
Instead of his horse, *he* was given to me. If you want to
ransom the man, I would like the harp[18] that once belonged
to Queen Secundille and which Anfortas sent to you. If I
can have that harp, *le duc de* Gowerzin shall go free."

"The harp and all the other wares," she said, "he who
sits here beside me may keep or give away, as he likes. Let
him decide. If he was ever fond of me, he will ransom

[18] The word here is *swalwe,* which means either a swallow or a
kind of English harp, resembling in shape a swallow's wing. The next
two sentences use the word *härpfe.*

Lischois, the Duke of Gowerzin, and also my   624
other prince, Florant of Itolac,[14] who used to watch over
me by night. He was my Turkoite, and if he is unhappy, I
can never be glad."

Gawan said to the lady, "Before the night comes on, you
shall see them both free."

Just then, as they had finished talking of these things,
they came to the other shore. Gawan lifted the lovely duchess upon her horse again, and many noble, valiant knights
welcomed the two of them. They turned their course toward the castle, and the knights tilted joyfully, with such
skill that it was a splendid bohourt.

What more can I say? Save this perhaps—the noble Gawan and the beautiful duchess were welcomed so warmly
by the ladies at the Castle of Wonders that they were both
very pleased. It was his good fortune, you must admit, that
such happiness was his. Then Arnive led him to his room,
where people skilled in healing attended to his wounds.

Gawan said to Arnive, "Lady, I must have a   625
messenger."

A maiden was sent to fetch one, and she brought a
squire, valiant and well-reared, as good as a squire can be.
The squire swore an oath that he would disclose his message to no one, whether it bring him joy or sorrow, either
here or elsewhere, save at the place where he should deliver
it.

Gawan asked for ink and parchment, and he, the son of
King Lot, wrote the message skillfully with his own hand.
He sent to the land of Löver, to Arthur and his wife, assurance of his service and his unwavering loyalty. The fame
he had won, he wrote, would lose all its worth if they did
not help him in his need, keep their faith with him, and
bring to Joflanze their retinue of knights and ladies. He
would meet them there himself and defend his honor in
combat. He wrote further that it had been agreed the King
should appear at the combat with all pomp and splendor.
And Sir Gawan asked the whole court, ladies and   626
vassals, to remain true to him and urge the King to come.

[14] Only at this point do we learn that this is the Turkoite's name.

This would enhance their honor. To all the noble company he pledged his service and told them of the peril of his combat. The letter bore no seal, for he wrote it clearly and with unmistakable signs of identification.

"Now wait no longer," said Gawan to his squire. "The King and Queen are in Bems on the Korca. Go speak to the Queen in the early morning and do as she counsels you. But let me give you one word of wisdom: do not reveal that I am the lord here. And do not tell anyone at all that you belong to this retinue."

The squire hurried away, but Arnive stole softly after him. She asked him where he was going and what his mission was.

He answered, "Lady, I cannot tell you if I am to keep my oath. May God protect you! I must be on my way." And he rode to meet a noble company.

BOOK·XIII

Arnive was angry that the squire would not tell   627
her where he was being sent, and she said to the watchman
at the gate, "When the squire returns, be it night or day,
make him wait until I speak to him. You can do that. You
are clever enough."

Nevertheless she was still angry with the squire, and she
went in again to the duchess to question her. But the duchess was also quick-witted, and her lips did not reveal the
name that Gawan bore. His request made her keep silent
about his name and family.

Then the sound of trumpets and other instruments rang
joyfully through the great hall. Tapestries were hung up in
the hall, and on the floor one trod only on beautifully woven
carpets. It would have been enough to frighten a *poor* host.
Around all sides of the hall they set couches with soft
cushions of down, and over them they spread rich coverings.

Wearied from his labors, Gawan had gone to   628
sleep in the middle of the day. His wounds were bandaged
so skillfully that if his beloved had lain with him and he
had made love to her, it would have seemed to him pleasant
and good. Moreover, he slept much more soundly than that
night when the duchess disturbed him so sorely. Toward
the hour of vespers he awoke. Yet once again in his sleep

he had fought love's battle with the duchess. One of his
valets brought him clothing of shining pfellel-silk heavy
with costly gold embroidery, as I heard said. Then my lord
Gawan said, "We need more clothes as rich as these, for
the Duke of Gowerzin and for the handsome Florant, who
has won fame in many lands. See that these clothes are
made ready."

Through a squire he requested his host Plippalinot to
send Lischois to him, and the boatman's fair   629
daughter Bene led Lischois by the hand up to the castle.
This she did in fondness for Gawan, but also for the good
things he had promised her father on the day when he
rode away and left her crying bitterly. It was then his
courage won him the prize.

The Turkoite too had come, and Gawan gave both a
friendly greeting. They sat down with him there until
clothes were brought for all three of them. These were
costly indeed and could not have been better. There was
once a master called Sarant, from whom the land of Seres[1]
got its name. He was from Triande. In Secundille's land
there is a city called Thasme, larger still than Niniveh or
the vast city of Acraton. There Sarant, to win the rewards
of fame, invented with artful skill a pfellel-silk. They call
it saranthasme. Do you suppose it looks magnificent? You
can spare yourselves that question, for it can be gotten only
at great cost.

Gawan and the other two put on these gar-   630
ments and went to the great hall where on the one side
stood many knights and on the other the lovely ladies. A
man of judgment would have named the Duchess of Logrois the fairest of them all. The host and his guests
stepped up to the radiant Orgeluse, and for the sake of the
Duchess of Logrois, the Turkoite Florant and the handsome Lischois, those two courteous princes, were set free
without condition. She thanked Gawan for this, she, so
ignorant of falsity, yet so wise of heart, in all that would
bring a woman honor.

---

[1] China.

As she was speaking, Gawan saw four queens[2] standing near the duchess. Courteous as he was, he asked his two guests to come nearer and bade the three youngest to give them a kiss of greeting. The maid Bene had come to the hall with Gawan, and she too was welcomed warmly.

The host did not wish to stand any longer and asked his two guests to go and sit with the ladies wherever they liked. A request such as this did not displease them at all.   631

Then the noble Gawan asked Bene softly, "Which of these maids is Itonje? I want to ask her if she will permit me to sit beside her."

Since he wished it, she pointed out to him the fair maiden. "The one there with the bright eyes and red lips— with the brown hair—if you wish to speak to her in secret, be kind and considerate," said the gentle-mannered maid Bene. For she knew of Itonje's sorrow in love and that the noble King Gramoflanz had offered her heart his service and knightly devotion.

Gawan sat down beside the maid—I am telling ⸱⸱ only what was told to me—and began to speak with the courtesy in which he was so skilled. Young Itonje too knew how to behave, and though her years were few she showed great courtesy and decorum.

Gawan had asked her if she knew yet what it meant to love. Cautiously the maiden answered, "Sir, whom should I love? Since the day I first saw the light, I have never spoken with any knight save the words you have heard just now."   632

"But perhaps tales have reached you of some knight who has won fame with his courage and knightly skill and who with all his heart offers his service in return for love," said Sir Gawan.

"No one has said anything to *me* about service for love," answered the pretty maiden. "Many gallant knights serve the Duchess of Logrois, some for love and others for pay.

[2] These are Arnive, Arthur's mother and Gawan's grandmother; Sangive, Gawan's mother; and Sangive's two daughters, Gawan's sisters, Cundrie and Itonje.

For her many a man has fought a joust here where we could see it, but no one of them ever came so close to us as you have. Your battle here has raised your fame high."

"Who is it the followers of the duchess are fighting, these many splendid knights?" he asked the pretty maid. "Who is it who has fallen out of favor with her?"

"It is King Gramoflanz," she said, "who wears the wreath of glory, so everyone says, at least. Sir, I know nothing more of him than that."

"Then you shall hear more about him," Sir Ga-   633
wan said, "for he is striving eagerly for the prize. I have it from his own lips that with all his heart he offers you service, that he may, if it please you, seek help and comfort in your love. It befits a king to feel the torment of love only for the sake of a queen. Lady, if your father's name was Lot, then you are the one he means, for whom his heart is weeping, and if your name is Itonje, then you are the one who is causing him anguish of heart. If you are true, you will take his sorrow from him. I will gladly serve as messenger for you both. Lady, accept this ring. The noble knight sent it to you. I shall see that there is no difficulty about the messages. Lady, that you can leave to me."

She blushed, and her whole face became as red as her mouth had been before. Then suddenly she changed color. Shyly she reached for the ring, which she recognized at a glance, and in her white hand she took and held it.

"Sir," she said, "I see now, if I may speak   634
freely to you, that you have come from him toward whom my heart strives. If you give knightly courtesy its due, Sir, it will now teach you to keep a secret. This gift has been sent me before by the hand of the noble king. This ring is a token from him. It was I who first gave it to him. Of any sorrow he has ever known I am quite innocent, for in my thoughts I have granted him all he desires of me. He would have learned that long since, could I only escape from this castle. I kissed Orgeluse, who seeks to have him killed. That was the kiss of Judas which people still talk

of today. And all loyalty vanished from me when I kissed the Turkoite Florant and the Duke of Gowerzin as you bade me. Yet I can never forgive them completely that in hatred they constantly pursue King Gramoflanz. Say nothing of this to my mother or to my sister Cundrie."

And Itonje appealed to Gawan, "Sir, you asked   635 me to suffer their kiss on my lips, though I did it without forgiveness, and for this I am sick at heart. If we two are ever to know joy, it can only be through your help. The king does truly love me more than all other women, and I want him to enjoy my love, for I hold him dear above all other men. May God give you help and counsel, so that you may at last see us happy."

"Lady," he said, "tell me *how!* You are his, and he is yours, and yet you are apart, he there, you here. If I knew what counsel to give you that you might live in joy and honor, I would gladly give it, and I would spare no pains."

She said, "We place ourselves in your hands, the noble king and I. May your help and God's blessing come to the defense of our love, so that I, an exile here from my land, can take away his sorrow, since in me rests all his joy. As sure as I am true and cannot be otherwise, my heart yearns unceasingly to grant him my love."

Gawan saw that the little lady was very ready   636 for love and that her hatred for the duchess was anything but spent. Thus she bore both love and hate. Yet he sinned a greater sin against the simple maid who had poured out to him her trouble, for he did not tell her that *one* mother had carried him and her and that Lot was father to them both. He offered the maiden his help, and she bent her head, but so slightly that no one else could see, in gratitude that he had not refused her comfort.

Now the time had come, and into the great hall, where many fair ladies were, they brought bread and cloths of gleaming white for the tables. The knights, as was the custom, sat along one wall, separate from the ladies. Gawan arranged the order of seating. The Turkoite ate at his table. Lischois dined with Gawan's mother, the beautiful Sangive, and the fair duchess with Queen Arnive. His two lovely sisters Gawan bade sit down beside him, and they did as he requested.

My knowledge is not large enough by half—no   637
such master chef am I—that I could name you the dishes so ceremoniously set before them there. Pretty maidens served the host and the ladies; the knights sitting along their wall were served by many squires. A strict discipline kept these squires from crowding the maidens as they served. Squires and maidens walked separate, whether they were carrying food or wine. Thus the serving was done with great decorum.

They could well praise this hospitality, for seldom had these knights and ladies seen the like. Since Clinschor's power had overcome them with his arts, they had remained unknown to each other, though a single gate closed them in, and had never exchanged a word with each other, the ladies and the men. My lord Gawan gave the order that this company should meet, and they were very pleased. Gawan too was in gay spirits, yet he secretly watched the lovely duchess who had so completely captured his heart.

Now Day began to falter, and its light was   638
close to falling, so that through the clouds could be seen many a star, messenger of the Night, hurrying on its way to reserve for Night a lodging. Upon the banners of the night Night herself swiftly followed.

All round the great hall hung crown-shaped chandeliers set full with candles, and on every table separately they set a host of candles. Moreover, the adventure says so radiant was the duchess that had no candles been brought at all, there would yet have been no night where she was. Her glance alone could shed the light of day. So I was told of that lovely lady.

You would do him injustice if you did not admit that seldom have you seen such a joyous host. Everyone there was filled with gladness. And with joyous desire the knights from the one side, the ladies from the other, gazed eagerly at each other. At first they were frightened by these glances, being strangers to one another, but now they are feeling more and more at ease, and that I do not begrudge them.

If it meets with your approval, they have now   639
eaten quite enough, unless perchance there is a glutton
among them. The tables were carried away again, and
Gawan called for good fiddlers, asking if there were any
there. Many of the noble squires were well trained in playing string instruments, but their mastery did not go beyond
playing old-fashioned dances. Of the many new dances
which came to us from Thuringia none were heard at all.

Now give your thanks to the host that he did not restrain
them in their joy. Many a fair lady danced there in his
presence. The knights mingled freely with the host of
ladies, pairing off now with one, now with another, and
the dance was a lovely sight. Together they advanced to
the attack on sorrow. Often a handsome knight was seen
dancing with two ladies, one on either hand. Everywhere
one looked one saw gaiety. If any knight was of a mind to
offer service for love, his request was gladly granted. Poor
in cares, rich in joy, they passed the hours in talk, sweet
lips conversing with other lips as sweet.

Gawan and Sangive, with Queen Arnive, sat   640
quietly by as the company danced. The fair duchess went
over and took a seat beside Gawan. He held her hand in
his, and they spoke of this and that. He was happy at her
coming. His sorrow shrank and his joy increased, and all
his suffering vanished from him. If the others found pleasure in dancing, Gawan's joy was by no means less.

Then Queen Arnive spoke. "Sir, remember that you need
rest. For the sake of your wounds you should be resting at
this hour. Has the duchess decided to keep you company
tonight and see that you are covered? She can give you
help and comfort."

"Ask *her* that," said Gawan. "I am entirely at your command and hers."

Then the duchess said, "He shall be in my care. Let these
people go to their sleep. I shall watch over him tonight as
no lover ever tended him before. Have the knights see that
Florant of Itolac and the Duke of Gowerzin are made comfortable."

Shortly afterward the dance came to an end.   641

The maidens in their bright beauty sat here and there, and the knights took seats at their side. He who pleaded for noble love and received a gracious answer, his joy took revenge on sorrow. Then the host was heard to ask that drink be brought to him, and the wooers heard this with regret.

The host, like his guests, was a wooer, and on him too love weighed heavy. They sat there, he thought, far too long, for his heart too was oppressed by noble love. The drink gave the sign for departure, and squires then carried clusters of candles before the knights. To all present my lord Gawan commended his two guests, Lischois and Florant, and they were pleased at this. The duchess wished them good night, and they went to seek their rest. Then the whole host of ladies also retired to their rooms, bowing as they parted, with the courtesy of their gentle breeding. Sangive and Itonje left, and Cundrie too.

Bene and Arnive set about to see that their host   642 found comfort, and the duchess lent a willing hand. The three of them led Gawan to find his rest. In a chamber he saw two separate couches. I shall not tell you how these were decorated; there are other things to relate.

Arnive said to the duchess, "Now take care that this knight finds rest, since you were the cause of his coming here. If he desires help from you, you will have honor from your help. I shall say no more to you, save that his wounds are bandaged with such skill that he could now wear armor. Yet you should pity his grief, and if you can soften it, that is good. If you can raise his spirits, we shall all gain by that. So spare no pains to help him." With her lord's consent, Queen Arnive took her leave, and Bene carried a light before her. Sir Gawan made fast the door.

That these two could now steal love, I am re-   643 luctant to conceal. It would be easier for me to tell you what happened there, but people have always accused of impropriety anyone who makes public things that are secret. Even today the courteous disapprove of this, and he who does so is censured. Let courtesy be the lock that conceals the ways of love.

The rigors of love and the beautiful duchess had once caused Gawan's joy to vanish. Yet without a beloved he would have been lost forever. Wise men and all who had ever sat and pondered the hard questions of knowledge, Kancor and Thebit, and Trebuchet the smith, who did the engraving on Frimutel's sword, thereby giving it such miraculous strength, and the skill of all physicians—if they had all meant him well and given him healing herbs well blended, without a woman beside him Gawan would have borne that sharp distress until his bitter death.

I shall make the story short. He found the proper herb. With its help he recovered completely and suffered no more pain. This herb was brown beside the white. On his mother's side a Briton, Gawan, *le fils du roi* Lot, exchanged bitter need for sweet delight and pursued the healing, helpful task, with loving help, until the dawn of day. But the help which he received was kept secret from the people. After that he devoted himself with such joy to all the knights and ladies that their sadness all but vanished. 644

Now hear how the squire gave the message, the one Gawan had sent to the land of Löver, to Bems on the Korca. King Arthur was there, and his wife the Queen, and the brilliance of many ladies, and a flood of noble vassals.

Now hear what the squire is doing. It was early of a morning when he undertook to deliver his message. The Queen had gone to the chapel and was on her knees, reading the psalter. The squire knelt down before her and presented the gift that was to make her glad. From his hand she took a letter in writing she recognized before even the squire there on his knees spoke the name of his lord. 645

The Queen spoke to the letter, "O blessed the hand that wrote you! I have not been free of care since the day I last saw the hand which wrote this writing." She wept, and yet she was happy too. To the squire she said, "You are Gawan's servant?"

"Yes, Lady, I am, and he sends you what is your due, loyal, unwavering service. But he also says that his happiness will grow faint unless you raise his spirits, for his honor has never been in such peril as now. Lady, he says further he would live in perfect joy if he could have the favor of your comfort. You can probably learn more from the letter than I can tell you."

She said, "It is true, I see why you were sent to me, and I shall do him worthy service and come to him with a host of lovely ladies who are now without doubt praised as the most beautiful. Except for Parzival's wife and Orgeluse I know of none on earth of those baptized who are so noble. Since Gawan rode away from Arthur I have felt   646 the fierce crash of care and sorrow upon me. Meljanz of Liz told me he had seen him since in Barbigoel. Alas," she said, "that my eyes ever beheld you, Plimizoel! What suffering befell me there! Never since then have I seen Cunneware de Lalant again, my sweet and dear companion. The power of the Table Round was broken there with angry words. It was four years and a half and six weeks ago[3] that the noble Parzival left the Plimizoel to seek the Grail. It was then that Gawan too, the worthy man, rode away toward Ascalun. And Jeschute and Eckuba parted from me there. Great yearning for these dear friends has kept me since then from any lasting joy."

The Queen spoke much of her sadness. Then she turned again to the squire and said, "Now follow my instructions. Go from me in secret, and wait till the day has reached its height and the people are all at court, knights and squires and all the retinue. Then come trotting fast to the   647 court. Give no thought to whether anyone holds your horse. Leave it and go quickly to where the noble knights are standing. They will ask you for news, and you behave, in words and actions, as if you were running from a fire. They can scarcely wait to hear what news you bring, but that doesn't matter. You press on through the crowd to the rightful lord. He will give you greeting. Put this letter in his hand, and from it he will quickly learn your news and your lord's desire. He will surely grant the request. One more thing I want to tell you. Address me openly, where I and the other ladies can hear and see you. There make your

[3] By Professor Weigand's calculation the present date is April 30.

plea to us as well as you know how, if you would further the cause of your lord. And now tell me, where is Gawan?"

"That I cannot do," said the squire. "I shall not tell you where my master is. But it lies in your power to make him happy." The squire was glad for her counsel. He parted from the Queen in the way you have heard and came again as she bade him.

Just at mid-morning, openly and not in secret,   648 the squire rode to court. The court squires eyed his clothing critically, as squires are wont to do. On both flanks the horse was badly cut with the spurs. Following the Queen's instructions, he sprang quickly from his horse, and immediately a great crowd thronged around him. He threw off cloak, sword, and spurs, caring little if they, or even his horse, were lost, and pressed through the throng to where the noble knights were standing. They asked him for news of adventures. It is said the rule of the court was that no one, neither man nor woman, could eat till the court had had its due, the news of some knightly adventure worthy of the name.

The squire answered, "I don't have time to tell you. Please do not be offended, but be so kind as to tell me where I can find the King. I would like to speak to him first. I regret that I am in such haste. You will soon hear the news I bring. May God move you to aid me in this distress!"

So urgent was his message that the squire   649 pressed on regardless of the crowd till the King himself caught sight of him and gave him greeting. The squire gave him the letter, and in Arthur's heart, as he read it, it awakened two feelings; one was joy, the other sorrow.

"Blessed be this fair day," he said, "by whose light I have read the true tidings of my noble sister's son. If I can do him knightly service as kinsman or as friend, then if loyalty ever had power over me, I shall do what Gawan has asked if I can."

Then he turned to the squire and said, "Now tell me, is all well with Gawan?"

"Sir, if you help him, yes," said the clever squire. "Then

joy will be his companion. But he would lose his honor if
you deserted him now. Who *could* be happy then? Your
solace will lift up his spirits again when through the gate of
sorrow your loyalty to him sends grief flying from his heart.
To the Queen my lord sent assurance of his serv-   650
ice, and it is also his desire that all the knights of the Table
Round keep faith with him and help him and not spoil his
joy, but counsel you to come to his aid."

All the noble knights joined in this request.

Then Arthur said, "Dear friend, take this letter to the
Queen and let her read it and say what it is that brings
us both joy and sadness. To think that King Gramoflanz
should dare display to a kinsman of mine such brazen arrogance! He must fancy my nephew Gawan is another
Cidegast. He slew *him,* and that has given him trouble
enough. I shall add to his trouble and teach him better
manners."

The squire went to where he was warmly welcomed. He
gave the Queen the letter, and many an eye overflowed
with tears as her sweet mouth read all that was written in
it, Gawan's distress and plea. And the squire used all the
skill he knew to win the ladies to Gawan's cause.

Gawan's kinsman, the mighty Arthur, urged   651
his vassals to undertake this journey. Nor did the courteous
Ginover delay, but urged the ladies to join in this trip,
clad in their finest robes.

But Keie said sourly, "Was there ever such a gallant man
as Gawan of Norway? If I believed that, I would say—
Go and get him! Bring him here! He'll be someplace else in
a moment. He frisks about like a squirrel and is gone before you can catch him."

The squire said to the Queen, "Lady, I must return to my
lord at once. Work for his cause and to your own honor."

To one of her chamberlains she said, "See that this squire
gets some rest and look at his horse. If it is too much cut
from the spurs, find him another, the best that is here to
be had. And if there is anything else he needs, money to
redeem something pawned, or clothing perhaps, see that he
has everything."

To the squire she said, "Say to Gawan, he has my devoted service. I shall say good-bye to the King for you. Assure your lord of *his* service too."

Now the King made ready for his journey. 652 And so on that day the custom of the Table Round was fulfilled.[4] Great joy had awakened in them when they heard that the noble Gawan was still alive, and without discord the order of seating at the Table Round was done. The King ate at the Table, and the others who had their allotted places, who had won fame in strife. And all members of the Table Round rejoiced at the news they had heard.

Now permit the squire, whose errand you have heard, to return again to his lord. When the time had come, he set forth. The Queen's chamberlain gave him money for redeeming his pledge, a horse, and fresh garments. The squire then rode away, happy that he had won from Arthur what would destroy the cares of his lord. He came back— in how many days I cannot say for sure—to the Castle of Wonders.

Arnive rejoiced when the porter sent her word that the squire had returned, his horse exhausted from the ride. Just as he was being let into the castle, she stole 653 up to him and asked him about his journey and why he had ridden out.

The squire answered, "That is forbidden, Lady. I dare not tell you. Because of my oath I must keep silent, and my lord would be angry with me if I broke my oath by talking too much. You would think me a fool yourself. Lady, ask *him* about it."

She kept on with her questions, now in this direction, now in that. But the squire only repeated, "Lady, you are delaying me here without reason. I shall do what my oath commands."

He went to see his master. The Turkoite Florant and the Duke of Gowerzin and the Duchess of Logrois were sitting with him in the company of a host of ladies. The squire approached them, and my lord Gawan stood up. He took

[4] I.e., an adventure had befallen, and the meal could be served. See 648.

the squire aside, bade him welcome, and said, "Now tell me, my friend, what message you have for me from the court. Does it mean joy or sorrow? Did you find the King there?"

"Sir, I did," said the squire. "I found the King and his wife and many gallant knights. They pledge you 654 their service and promise to come. Your message was received with such honor that poor and rich alike rejoiced when I told them you were alive and well. I found there a fabulously vast host. And the Table Round was set because of your message. If ever any knight's fame had power, I mean the power to win respect and honor, then your fame wears the crown far and wide above the fame of all others."

He also told Gawan how it chanced that he spoke to the Queen and how she graciously counseled him. And he told him of the company of knights and ladies, and that he would see them in Joflanze *before* the time set for the combat.

Gawan's cares vanished completely, and nothing but joy was left in his heart. He stepped out of care and into gladness. The squire he pledged to secrecy. All of his cares quite forgotten, he returned to the group and sat down. And with joy he waited there in the castle until King Arthur should come riding with his host to bring him aid. 655

Now hear of joy and sorrow! Gawan was always in high spirits. One morning it so chanced that many knights and ladies were together in the resplendent great hall. At a window facing the river Gawan had taken a seat apart from the others, and with him sat Arnive, who knew strange tales. Gawan said to the queen, "Dear Lady mine, if it does not displease you, I would like to ask you about certain things which till now have been kept from me. I know only that I owe it to the gift of your help that I am alive and in such rich joy. If I ever had in my heart a man's will, the noble duchess had taken it captive with her power. But now with your help this distress has been relieved. I would have died of love *and* wounds, had you not given help and comfort and freed me from their bonds. I owe my life to you. Now tell me, Lady of Healing, about the marvel that

was here and still is, and by what means the wise　　656
Clinschor acquired such potent magic. Save for you I would
have lost my life from it."

Then said the kind, wise woman—never did youth reach
old age with such womanly honor—"Sir, his marvels here
are but small by the side of the mighty marvels he still has
in many lands. But he sins who thinks that is *our* disgrace.
Sir, I will tell you what he is like: he has become bitter toward many people. His land is called Terre de Labur,[5] and
he is descended from one who had also learned how to
work great marvels, from Virgil of Naples.

"I shall tell you what Clinschor, his kinsman, did. His
capital was Caps.[6] He took the high path to fame and did
not go unrewarded. Clinschor the Duke was in the mouths
of all, both men and women, until he fell into disgrace.
Sicily had a noble king called Ibert, and Iblis was his wife,
the loveliest woman ever weaned from a mother's breast.
Clinschor served her until she rewarded him with　　657
love. For this the king robbed him of his honor. If I am
to tell you his secret, I must ask your forgiveness, for it is
unseemly for me to say such things. One cut of the knife,
and Clinschor became a eunuch."

Gawan burst out laughing. Then she told him still more,
"In the famous castle of Kalot enbolot[7] he became the
mock of the world. The king found Clinschor with his
wife, sleeping in her arms. If he found a warm bed there,
he had to pay the heavy price that by the hand of the king
he was made smooth between his legs. The king thought
that was his right. He clipped him in such a way that he
can never more give pleasure to any woman. But that has
meant suffering for many people.

"It is not in the land of Persia, but in a city called Persida,
that magic was first invented. To that place Clinschor
traveled, and brought from there the magic art of

---

[5] Terra di Lavoro, a region near Naples.

[6] Capua.

[7] Kalot enbolot—Saracen Qal'at al-ballut (Fortress of the Oaks),
modern Caltabellotta, a town inland from Sciacca, in western Sicily, and
dominated by the peak of Monte Castello.

how to do whatever he will. For the shame done   658
to his body he never again bore good will toward anyone,
man or woman, and when he can rob them of any joy,
especially those who are honored and respected, that does
his heart good.

"In Rosche Sabins there was a king, Irot by name, who
feared such threat for himself. He offered Clinschor whatever of his possessions he desired if he would leave him in
peace. From his hand Clinschor received this castle, famous
for its inaccessibility, together with the land for eight miles
around. Here on this mountain Clinschor wrought the
strange structure which you see. There are here great
marvels of all kinds of wealth. If the castle should be besieged, there would be ample food here to last for thirty
years. And he has power over all *les mauvaises* and *les belles
gens*[8] dwelling between the firmament and the earth, save
those whom God desires to protect.

"Sir, since your great peril has passed without   659
your dying, the gift he once received, this castle and the
land around it, belong to you. He will leave them alone, for
he declared openly—and he is a man of his word—that
he who withstood the adventure would be left in peace by
him and have all this for his own. All the noble people
Clinschor caught sight of on Christian soil, be they maid,
woman, or man, are now subject to you, and many
heathen men and women must dwell up here with us too.
Now let these people return home, where everyone is anxious about them.

"To live in exile chills my heart. May He who has counted
the stars teach you to give us help and turn our grief to
joy. A mother bears her fruit; the fruit becomes the mother
of its mother. From water comes ice; that is not the end
by any means, for in due course the ice becomes water
again. If I think of myself and that I was born of joy—if
joy should appear again in me, then one fruit thus   660
gives birth to the other. This you shall accomplish if you
have true courtesy. It was long ago that joy forsook me.

---

[8] Meaning all spirits, good and evil.

With its sail the keel speeds fast, but faster still the man who is on it. If you understand this riddle, your fame will grow high and fleet. You can make our joy so bright that we shall bring joy to many a land where they were anxious about us.

"Once I had joy in abundance. I was a woman who wore a crown. My daughter too wore a crown regally before the princes of her land. We were both honored and respected. Sir, I never counseled harm to any man, but with all, women or men, I knew how to deal fairly. The folk saw and knew that I was a fit mistress for a people, for, with God's help, I never mistreated anyone.

"Every happy woman, if she makes any claim to nobility, should treat all decent people well. It can easily happen that such sorrow and grief will befall her that some poor lad can open up a broad space for her close-pent joy. Sir, I have waited here a long time, and never, on foot or on horseback, has anyone come here who knew me and could   661 take away my grief."

Then Sir Gawan said, "Lady, if my life is spared, you shall be happy once more."

That very day it chanced that Arthur the Briton, son of the sorrowing Arnive, came with his host, out of loyalty to his kinsman. Gawan saw many new banners moving toward him, and he saw how the troops, with many a shining, brightly colored spear, covered the field along the road from Logrois. Gawan was glad at their coming. When one has to wait for an army, delay brings the frightening thought that the help may fail to come. Arthur freed Gawan from this doubt.

Oh, look at how they watched him coming! Gawan tried to conceal that his bright eyes were learning to weep. They would have been no good as cisterns, for they could not hold water. It was for love he wept, and Arthur was the cause. Arthur had reared him from childhood, and their loyalty to one another was true and steadfast,   662 with never a falsehood coming between them.

Arnive saw the tears and said, "Sir, you should greet joy with sounds of joy. Sir, that would comfort us all. Guard yourself against sorrow, for the army approaching belongs to the duchess. That will console you soon enough."

Arnive and Gawan saw many tents and banners being carried onto the plain, and everywhere they saw shields alike, with a coat of arms which Arnive knew at once. "Isaies," she said, thinking of the marshal of Utepandragun. But now another Briton carried the shield, Maurin of the handsome legs, the Queen's marshal. Arnive did not know that Utepandragun and Isaies were both dead and that Maurin had taken over his father's office, as was right.

Onto the flat plain by the landing place rode the great retinue. The Queen's squires chose a camp site suitable for the ladies by a clear, fast-running brook, and soon   663 one saw many beautiful tents set up there. Further off many a great circle of tents was prepared for the King and the knights who had come with him. They had indeed left behind them on their ride a broad trail of hoof prints.

Gawan sent Bene down from the castle to his host Plippalinot, to ask him to tie fast the boats and the barges so that the army would be prevented from crossing over that day. The maid Bene received from Gawan's hands the first gift from his rich treasure, a "swallow," [9] which is still known in England as a costly harp, and Bene went away happy.

Then Sir Gawan gave orders to close the outer gate. Old and young listened as he spoke to them courteously. "Over there on the further bank is encamped an army so large that never on land or sea have I ever seen such a mighty host. If they should attack us, help me, for I shall show them knightly action." With one accord they gave   664 their word.

They asked the mighty duchess if that army were hers, but she said, "You must believe me, I know no shield nor man among them. Perhaps the one who did me injury before has ridden into my land and fought before Logrois. But he found it well defended, I'm sure, for my people could have withstood this army from the ramparts and the battlements. If the wrathful King Gramoflanz fought

[9] See Book XII, 623, and note.

there, he was seeking revenge for his wreath. But whoever they may be, they must have seen at Logrois spears upright and ready for the joust."

What she said was scarcely a lie, for Arthur had suffered great injury before he had got past Logrois. Many a Briton was felled in knightly joust. Arthur's host repaid these wares in kind, and both sides were sorely pressed.

Battle-weary they came, and those watching could see them of whom it is heard so often that they sold their lives dearly. They were hard fighters.

On both sides there had been losses. Garel and Gaherjet, and *le roi* Meljanz de Barbigoel and Jofreit, *le fils* 665 *d'*Idoel, were sent up captive to the castle before the group jousting was ended. And Arthur's men took from Logrois *le duc* Friam de Vermendois and *le comte* Ritschart de Nevers, who never used but one spear. Any man who felt its thrust from his hand always fell in the joust. It was Arthur who with his own hand captured this famed and noble warrior. Then dauntlessly the two hosts so clashed and mingled that a forest of spears was spent. In untold jousts the splinters flew and fell. Manfully did the noble Britons also defend themselves against the army of the duchess. Arthur's rear guard had to keep poised for battle, for they were attacked the whole day long up to the place where the mass of the army lay camped.

My lord Gawan should have told the duchess that someone was passing through her land to help him. Then no battle would have taken place. But he did not want to tell her, nor anyone, until she should see it for her- 666 self. He did as seemed right to him and, ordering rich tents made ready, he prepared to march toward Arthur the Briton. No one of his men was neglected for being a stranger to him. Gawan's generous hand showered gifts upon all, as if he were about to die. Foot soldiers, knights, and ladies received his gifts, and seeing how rich they were, they all said that true help had now come to them. You could see how happy they were. Then the noble warrior ordered strong pack horses, beautiful mounts for the ladies, and armor for all the knights to be brought. Great numbers of foot soldiers in coats of mail stood ready. And this is what my lord did—he chose four noble knights, one to be his chamberlain, the second his cupbearer, the third his steward, and the fourth his marshal. Thus he did and the four obeyed his command.

Let Arthur rest peacefully now. Gawan sent   667 him no greeting the whole day long, though that grieved him. In the morning early, Arthur's army rode amid clamor toward Joflanze. He bade his rear guard be alert for attack, but when they found no enemy there, they followed upon his track.

Then my lord Gawan, not wanting to wait longer, took his office bearers aside and made the marshal ride to the plain of Joflanze. "I wish to have there a camp apart. You will see the great army camped there. The time has come for me to tell you the name of its lord that you may recognize him. It is Arthur, my uncle, in whose court and whose household I was reared from childhood. Now see to it without fail that my march there shall proceed so sumptuously that all will see how rich I am. And let no one up here at the castle know that Arthur's host has come here for my sake."

They did as he bade them, and Plippalinot now had never an idle moment. Ships and barges, boats and   668 skiffs, with troops of stalwart men, on horseback and on foot, crossed over the river with the marshal. And squires and pages ran this way and that, following on the track of the Britons.

With them they took—you may be sure—a tent which Iblis had once sent Clinschor as a token of her love and from which their secret first became known, that they were lovers, one of the other. No cost had been spared to make this tent, and no scissors had ever cut a better, save for one that belonged to Isenhart. Not far from Arthur, but apart, the tent was set up on a grassy spot, and round it in a wide wing, so I was told, many other tents were placed. This was a magnificent sight.

The news was brought to Arthur that Gawan's marshal had come and set up a camp on the plain, and that the noble Gawan himself would come that very day. And this tale spread to all his retinue.

Gawan, the man free of falseness, marshaled   669 his companies from the castle, and so splendid was this train that I could tell you marvels about it. There were pack horses laden with reliquaries and clothing, and others bore rich suits of armor and sturdy shields with helmets tied fast on top of the load. Many a handsome Castilian charger one could see being led along by the bridle, and behind came knights and ladies riding close side by side. The train must have measured a journey-stage or more in length.

Gawan did not neglect to see that by the side of every fair lady there rode a handsome knight. And they were indeed lacking in wit if they did not speak of love. The Turkoite Florant was given as companion to Sangive of Norway, and the far from laggard Lischois rode by sweet Cundrie's side. Gawan asked his sister Itonje to ride with him, and Arnive and the duchess chose to keep each other company.

Now it chanced that to reach Gawan's tent   670 ring they had to pass through Arthur's camp. What a sight that was to behold before this train of folk had finished passing through! Out of courtesy and to do honor to the King, Gawan bade the first lady halt at Arthur's ring. His marshal then took care that a second lady rode up close beside her. All the others joined them and formed a circle, here the old and there the young, and beside each a knight in attendance to do her service. And so one could see Arthur's broad ring of tents completely encircled by ladies. Then Gawan, rich in happiness, was welcomed, and warmly, I think.

Arnive and her daughter and granddaughters dismounted with Gawan, as did the Duchess of Logrois, the Duke of Gowerzin, and the Turkoite Florant. To greet this noble and famous company Arthur stepped from his pavilion and welcomed them cordially. His wife the Queen   671 did likewise and welcomed Gawan and his companions with warm and true affection. And many a kiss was given there by many a lady fair.

Arthur asked his nephew, "Who are these companions of yours?"

"I would ask that my lady give them a kiss of greeting," said Gawan. "It would be discourteous for her to refuse. They are both of noble race."

Then the Turkoite Florant and the Duke of Gowerzin were kissed by Ginover the Queen, and they went back into the tent.

To many it seemed that the whole wide field was full of ladies. Then Arthur, not heavy of foot, leaped upon a Castilian charger and rode all round the ring of ladies fair with knights beside them. Graciously he greeted them. It was Gawan's will that they should all stay until he led them away, for this was a courtly custom.

Arthur dismounted, entered the tent, and tak-   672
ing a seat beside his nephew, besought him to tell who the five ladies were.

My lord Gawan spoke first of the eldest and said to the Briton, "Did you know Utepandragun? This is Arnive, his wife, and from those two you had your origin. There is my mother, the Queen of Norway, and these are my sisters. Look what pretty maids they are!"

Then they kissed one another again, and those looking on could see the joy and the sorrow they suffered for love's sake. Laughing and weeping, their lips spoke the greeting. This came from their great love.

Arthur said to Gawan, "Nephew, I still do not know who the fifth beautiful lady is."

Gawan the courteous answered, "It is the Duchess of Logrois. I am here in her service. You were looking for her, I am told. You need not hesitate to tell me how you profited from that. You could be a kind of widow   673
yourself." [10]

"She has your sister's son, Gaherjet, captive there at Logrois," said Arthur, "and Garel, who braved many a charge with knightly deeds. The fearless man was captured right at my side. One of our onslaughts had pushed to their very bulwarks. Ah, how the noble Meljanz de Liz

[10] Because he has lost so many of his men.

fought there! Under a white banner he was seized and
taken up to the castle. On the banner was a black arrow of
sable piercing a splash of crimson, a bleeding heart, the sign
of sorrow for a man.[11] 'Lirivoyn!' was the battle cry of the
host that rode to battle beneath it, and their hands gained
the victory. My nephew Jofreit was captured too, and I am
grieved at that. I myself led the rear guard yesterday, and
this distress was what I reaped." The King thus admitted
how great had been his losses.

Courteously the duchess said to him, "Sir, I absolve you
of any dishonor, else you would have gotten no greeting
from me. You may have done me injury which I did not
deserve when you rode through my land. Now   674
may God counsel you how to make me recompense! He,
to whose aid you have ridden here, did battle with me, and
I was defenseless when he stormed me on my unprotected
side. If he desires further strife with me, it will be an encounter without swords."

Gawan then said to Arthur, "What do you advise? Shall
we fill this plain with more knights still? That we can
easily do, for I can persuade the duchess to let your men
go free and bid her own knights to join us here with fresh
spears."

"I agree to that," said Arthur.

The duchess summoned the noble knights from Logrois,
and I think that never on earth was there such a splendid
assembly. Gawan begged leave to continue the journey to
his camp, and this the King granted him. All those who
had accompanied him rode away with him to their resting
place. Gawan's tent stood out there, so knightly in its
splendor and costliness, lacking any sign of poverty.

Many a knight, grieved that Gawan had been so   675
long away, rode to his tent. Now Keie too had recovered
from his joust by the Plimizoel. He observed Gawan's display of wealth and said, "Lot, my lord's brother-in-law, never
tried to shame us, vying with us and setting up a camp of
his own." Then he remembered when his right arm was
broken and Gawan had not avenged him. "God does won-

[11] Sorrow for Cidegast.

ders for some people," Keie said mockingly. "Where did Gawan get this swarm of women?"

This was not very kindly behavior toward a friend. A true friend always rejoices at the honor a friend receives, but the faithless man cries bloody murder when good fortune comes to his friend and he is a witness of it. Gawan possessed happiness and honor. If anyone wishes more, what *can* he be thinking of? Ignoble men are full of greed and hate, but the gallant are glad when their friend's honor stands fast and shame flees from him. Gawan was without falseness and malice and never failed in knightly loyalty. So it was only fitting that one should see him   676 happy.

How did the knight from Norway care for his folk, the knights and the ladies? Arthur and his company could marvel there at the wealth of the noble Lot's son. But now that they have eaten, they must go to sleep. I don't begrudge them their rest.

In the morning, before daylight, an armed host came riding, all the knights of the duchess. By the light of the moon one could see the glittering ornaments on their armor. Through the camp they passed, where Arthur and his host lay, and came on the other side to Gawan's wide ring of tents. He who wins such aid by the might of his hand can well be hailed as a man of renown. Gawan bade his marshal show them a camp site, and the noble folk of Logrois, as the duchess' marshal directed, set up their many tent rings apart from the rest. Mid-morning was past before they were lodged.

New cares were now approaching. Arthur, the   677 far-famed, sent his messengers to the city of Rosche Sabins to deliver to King Gramoflanz a message: "If it cannot be otherwise and he will not renounce his combat with my nephew, my nephew will do as he wishes. If this sturdy knight tells you he will not give up the contest, bid him come to us quickly. No other man would dare this." And Arthur's messengers rode away.

Then my lord Gawan took Lischois and Florant aside and asked them to show him those soldiers of love who had come from many lands to fight for the duchess in love's high service. He rode over to them and gave them such greeting that all were agreed the noble Gawan was a gallant and courtly knight.

With that he left them and went secretly to his room where he armed himself to see if his wounds were 678 healed enough so that the scars would not pain him. He wanted exercise, since so many men and women were to watch his combat and experienced knights would know when they saw him whether his dauntless hand would gain the victory that day. He had asked a squire to bring him Gringuljete, and he gave the horse free rein. A practice run was his aim, so that he and the horse should be in good form. Never did a ride of his so grieve me. All alone my lord Gawan rode far from the army out onto the plain. May Fortune watch over him!

By the river Sabins he saw a knight draw rein whom we can well call a rock of manly strength. A hailstorm, he, in knightly combat! Never did falsehood conquer his heart. So sensitive was he to all dishonor, that he could bear not a hand's breadth of it, not even a finger's length.

You have heard of this noble man before. And now my tale has returned again to its main stalk.

BOOK·XIV

If now in his bravery the noble Gawan under-   679
takes a joust, I have never so feared for his honor in battle
as now. I ought perhaps to fear for the other too, but about
him I need not worry. In combat against one man he always
had the strength of an army.

From heathendòm far over the sea his gleaming armor
had come. Redder far than a ruby were his gambeson and
the trappings of his horse. The hero was riding in search of
adventure, for his shield was pierced through and through.
And from the tree which Gramoflanz guarded he too had
plucked so fair a wreath for his helmet that Gawan knew
it at once. If the king[1] had ridden out to seek combat with
him and was waiting for him there, then he would be disgraced if battle were not done at once, though not a single
lady should see it.

From Munsalvaesche they came, the two horses galloping
hard to the attack, urged on by the spurs. Green clover,
not dusty sand, stood dewy where the joust was fought. I
grieve for what these two must suffer.

They made the charge in proper form, for both   680
were born of a race of jousters. Whoever gains the victory
here has won little and lost much. He will never cease to
rue it if he is wise. Their loyalty to each other stood firm,

[1] Gawan thinks his opponent is Gramoflanz.

and now when it was old, as at first when it was new, it had
never a nick or puncture.

Now hear how the joust proceeded. Both galloped hard to
the charge, yet neither had cause to rejoice, for here with
the force of courage renowned kin and noble friendship
closed in a sharp struggle. Whoever wins the prize must
forfeit his joy to sorrow. Each dealt such a powerful thrust
with his hand that the two kinsmen and comrades brought
each other down, horses and all. Then with their swords
they slashed and hacked until all around the green grass and
splinters of shields were a blended froth. All too long they
had to wait for an arbiter to separate them, for it was early
when they began to fight, and no one came to part them.
They were all alone; no one else was there.   681

Would you like to hear now how at the very same
time Arthur's messengers came upon King Gramoflanz
and his host? It was on a plain by the sea. On one side
flowed the Sabins, on the other the Poynzaclins, both rivers
broadening here to lakes. On the fourth side the plain was
fortified. There stood Rosche Sabins, the capital, with
walls and moats and many a lofty tower. The camp
stretched out along the plain about a mile in length and
perhaps half a mile in width. As Arthur's messengers approached, many strange knights came riding to meet them
and Turkish archers and many foot soldiers clad in mail and
bearing spears. Behind them great bands of troops came
swinging along with banners flying above them. The whole
army was on the move, to start on the ride to Joflanze. There
was the blast of trumpets, and the bells on the ladies' bridles
rang out cling-a-ling, as they circled round King   682
Gramoflanz' tent ring.

If I am master of my tale, I must tell you now who had
answered the king's call for aid and was encamped there
on the grass. If you have not heard before, let me tell you
who they were. From the water-buttressed city of Punt his
noble uncle, King Brandelidelin, had brought him six
hundred beautiful ladies, and each had her *ami,* armed for
knightly action and eager for victory. The noble knights of
Punturtois were happy at this journey. And there was, if

you will believe me, the handsome Bernout de Riviers. His wealthy father Narant had bequeathed Uckerlant to him. He had brought, in ships upon the sea, a host of ladies so lovely that everyone praised their radiant beauty, and there was no one who would gainsay it. Of these, two hundred were maidens, and two hundred came with their husbands. If I have counted rightly, there had come with Bernout, *le fils du comte* Narant, five hundred renowned and noble knights who could be a threat to any foe.   683

Thus King Gramoflanz meant to take revenge for his wreath in battle where many onlookers should see who would win the prize. The princes from his own realm were there with valiant knights and a host of ladies too. It was a handsome company.

Arthur's messengers arrived. Now listen to how they found the king. He was sitting on a couch with a thick mattress of palmat-silk, and on it a broad piece of pfellel-silk was quilted. Gay and pretty maidens knelt before the proud king and drew on his iron greaves. To shade him there swung high above his head, supported by twelve spear shafts, a costly silken covering, both broad and long, woven in Ecidemonis.

Arthur's messengers had now come before him, and to him who was swollen with pride they spoke these words, "Sir, we have been sent here by Arthur, who, as everyone knows, has won a measure of fame and enjoys no small respect. This you wish to diminish. How could   684 you think of being so ungracious to his sister's son? Even had the noble Gawan done you serious harm, the knights of the Round Table would always protect him, for all those who belong to it are sworn to him in brotherhood."

The king answered, "The combat has been agreed upon, and my dauntless hand shall wage it so that this very day I shall lift Gawan to fame or drive him to disaster. I have been informed that Arthur has come with his warriors and with his wife the Queen. She shall be welcome here. If the spiteful duchess counsels him to hate me, lads, then you must speak for me. No one can prevent me from fighting this battle. I have so many knights that no display of force can frighten me. Whatever peril the hand of *one* knight can bring me, that I will gladly endure. If I were now to shy away from what I have sworn to do, I would give up service for love. I have devoted all   685 my life to gain love's favor, and God knows Gawan now profits from that, for I have always disdained to fight with one man alone. Only the noble Gawan is so brave a man that I am glad to fight with him. My manhood has sunk to this! Such an easy fight I have never fought! I have fought, as anyone will tell you—ask them about it, if you like— with men who had to admit my hand had won the prize. But never have I fought against a single man. The ladies are not to praise me if I am the victor today.

"I am told, and my heart rejoices, that she for whose sake this battle will be fought, has been released from her bonds. Arthur the far-famed who, they say, has power over so many strange *terres*—perhaps she has come with him at whose bidding I shall serve in joy or in sorrow until I die. What better fortune could be mine than that I should know this bliss, that she deign to watch me as I serve her?"

Close by the king sat Bene. The coming battle   686 did not perturb her, for she had so often seen the king's valor in combat that she had no fears for his safety. Had she but known that Gawan was her lady's brother and that these harsh words concerned her own master, she would not have been so cheerful. She had brought the king a ring, sent him as token of her love by Itonje, the young queen, the very ring that her gallant brother had taken across the Sabins.[2]

Bene had come down the Poynzaclins in a small boat, and this is the message she bore: "My mistress has ridden from the Castle of Wonders with the other ladies." And as her lady had bidden her, she begged him, with entreaties more than a maid had ever sent a man, to be mindful of constancy and honor and remember her distress since, forsaking all other good, she sought to serve him for his love. This raised the king's spirits, but he is still being unfair to

[2] See 607f.

Gawan.—If *I* had to suffer thus for my sister's sake, I would rather not have any sister.

They brought him his armor, so costly and fine   687 that no man compelled by love to fight for reward from a lady, be it Gahmuret or Galoes or King Killicrates, had ever adorned himself more splendidly to appear before the ladies. No richer pfellel-silk was ever brought from Ipopotiticon or from the vast Acraton or from Kalomidente or from Agatyrsjente than the silk that was used for his adornment.

Then he kissed the ring which the young Queen Itonje had sent him as token of her love. He knew so well how true she was that whenever sorrow was about to overcome him, her love was a shield against it.

The king was armed now, and twelve maidens on sturdy horses, a fair company, seized, each of them, one of the spear shafts bearing the costly silk canopy beneath which the king wished to ride. They carried it over his head for shade as he set forth for the battle he craved. And   688 two little maids, yet not too frail, the fairest of all who were there, rode beside the king and supported his arms as they rode.[8]

Arthur's messengers tarried no longer but rode away and on their homeward journey came to the place where Gawan was fighting. Never had these lads been so frightened, and moved by their devotion to him, they cried out aloud at his peril.

The battle had very nearly reached the point where Gawan's foe was the victor. So surpassing great was his strength that Gawan the noble warrior had all but given up victory for lost. When the squires, recognizing him, called him by name in their grief, he who till then had pressed on hard in the struggle lost his zest for battle and cast his sword far from him.

"Accursed and dishonored am I," cried the stranger, and wept. "Fortune completely deserted me when my degraded hand engaged in this combat. Too great was this sacrilege for her. I own myself guilty. My evil fortune came to the fore and deprived me of happiness.

[8] An Oriental custom.

And so, as often before, this old escutcheon of   689
mine has once again appeared.[4] Alas that I fought with the
noble Gawan! It is myself I have vanquished, and misfortune met me here. At my first blow against him happiness fled from me."

Gawan heard and saw his lamenting and said to the man
who had fought with him, "Alas, Sir, who are you? You
speak so graciously to me. If you had only said these
words before while I still had strength left in me! Then I
would not have lost the honor which you have won here. I
beg you to tell me your name, that I may know from whom
I might later seek to regain my fame if I should wish. As
long as Fortune favored me, I always withstood a single foe."

"Kinsman, I shall tell you who I am and shall be at your
service now and ever more. I am your kinsman Parzival."

Gawan said, "It was fitting so. Here devious Folly has
gone straight to her mark. Here two simple hearts have in
hatred done violence to each other. Your hand gained
the victory over us both, now may you grieve for the sake
of us both. It is yourself you have vanquished—   690
if your heart knows true faith."

Having spoken so, my lord Gawan for weakness could no
longer stand. He felt a roaring in his head, and with steps
that stumbled, he sank down upon the grass. One of
Arthur's squires ran up and held his head, and the sweet
youth undid his helmet and with a hat of white peacock
feathers he fanned the air before his eyes. Through the
lad's efforts Gawan's strength was renewed.

From both armies knights came riding with their troops,
on this side and on that, and each army went to its assigned place, where the lists were set with huge posts as
smooth as mirror glass. Gramoflanz bore the cost, since he
was the challenger to the combat. There were a hundred
of these posts, shining bright and fair, and no one was to
enter the space between. They stood, so I was told, forty
horse-charge lengths apart, fifty on either side, gleaming
with bright colors. Between them the battle was to take
place, and the army was to remain outside, as if   691

---

4 Parzival means the escutcheon of misfortune.

separated by walls or deep moats. So Gramoflanz and Gawan had agreed, giving a handclasp as pledge.

Many men from both armies had already ridden out to the combat which had *not* been agreed upon, to see to whom they would grant the prize. They were curious to know who fought there with such knightly skill or who had been challenged to this combat. Neither army had escorted its fighter to the ring,[5] and this seemed to them very strange.

As this battle came to an end on the field bright with flowers, Gramoflanz rode up, intent on avenging his wreath. He was told a fight had taken place there, and never had fiercer strife with swords been seen. Those who battled each other had done so without any cause. Gramoflanz rode away from his company to the battle-weary men, and warmly did he lament their labors. Gawan had sprung to his feet, though his limbs were still heavy from strife, and the two, Parzival and Gawan, stood there together.

Now the maid Bene had also ridden with the   692 king to the ring where the battle had been fought. She saw Gawan drained of his strength whom she had chosen above all the world as the crown of her fairest joy. Crying out with heartfelt grief she sprang from her horse and threw her arms tight about him. "Cursed be the hand," she said, "that did injury to one so fair as you. Truly, to all men you were a mirror of manly beauty." She made him lie down upon the grass, and weeping openly, the sweet maid wiped away the blood and sweat from his eyes, for he was hot in his armor.

Then King Gramoflanz said, "Gawan, I am sorry for your misfortune since my hand did not cause it. If you wish to come to the field again tomorrow to meet me there in battle, I will gladly wait that long. *Now* I would rather fight with a woman than with you, weak as you are. What fame could I win against you until I hear you have gained some strength? Rest now for tonight. You will need it if you are to take the place of King Lot as my opponent."

[5] It was the custom for a combatant to be accompanied to the tilting ring by his own men.

The strong Parzival felt no weariness in his 693 limbs and showed no sign of pallor. He had already removed his helmet when the noble king saw him, and Parzival said to him courteously, "Sir, if my kinsman Gawan has done anything to forfeit your favor, let me be security for him. My hand is still ready for battle. And if you turn your wrath against him, I shall restrain you with my sword."

The Lord of Rosche Sabins said, "Sir, tomorrow he will bring me the tribute he owes me for my wreath, that its fame may be restored, or he will drive me to such a pass that I must tread the path of disgrace. You may well be a hero, but this battle is not destined for you."

Then Bene's sweet lips said to the king, "You faithless dog! Your heart is in the hands of the man whom your heart hates. To whom have you pledged yourself for love's sake? To her who is dependent on his favor. Your own words doom you to defeat. Love has lost its claim on you, for if ever you felt love, it was joined with falsity."

As Bene gave vent to her great anger thus, the 694 king took her aside and pleaded with her, "Lady, do not be angry that I demand this battle. Stay here with your master, and say to Itonje, his sister, that I am her true servant and will serve her in any way I can."

When Bene heard the truth, that her master was brother to her lady and must fight upon the grass, the oars of grief drew into her heart a heavy load of sorrow, for she had a heart that was true. "Be gone, accursed man," she said. "You have never known what true loyalty is."

The king rode off with all his retinue, and Arthur's squires caught the horses of the two combatants. They too showed the strain of the battle. Gawan and Parzival and the fair Bene rode away to join their army. Parzival had in manly strife so clearly won the prize that all rejoiced at his coming. When they saw him riding toward them, they all acclaimed his great renown. I shall tell you more, 695 as best I can. The best-skilled knights in both the hosts spoke of nothing but this one man and praised his knightly prowess. "He who won the prize there, if you please—that was Parzival." Never was a knight more warmly received, for he was so fair to look upon, and women and men both said so when Gawan escorted him there. Gawan ordered fresh clothing for him, and rich garments, each as costly as the other, were brought for both of them. Everywhere the news spread that Parzival had come. They had all heard so often of the great fame he had won, and many there were who declared that these reports were true.

Gawan said, "If you would like to see four ladies kin to you and other fair ladies too, I will gladly lead you to them."

The son of Gahmuret answered, "If noble ladies are gathered here, spare them the unwelcome sight of my face. No lady who was there by the Plimizoel and heard the words accusing me of falsehood will want to meet me again. May God watch over their womanly honor, for I   696 will always wish women happiness. My shame is still so very great that I am loath to appear among them."

"But you must," said Gawan and led him to the four queens, who greeted him with a kiss. For the duchess it was painful that she must kiss the man who once had refused her greeting and her offer of love and a kingdom—she suffered now in her shame—when he fought before Logrois and she rode so far in pursuit of him. But the others chatted without constraint in the fair Parzival's presence, and before long all shame was driven from his heart, and he became joyful again without embarrassment.

Gawan, for very good reasons, bade the maid Bene, if she wished to retain his favor, not to reveal to Itonje "that King Gramoflanz bears such anger toward me because of his wreath and that we are to meet in battle tomorrow at the appointed time. Say nothing of this to my sister, and do conceal your tears."

"I have cause to weep and make lament," she   697 said, "for whoever falls in the combat, my lady will mourn for him. The death of either of you will be the death of her. For my lady and for me I must grieve. What does it help that you are her brother? It is against her heart you intend to fight."

The army had now all arrived at the camp, and a meal was ready for Gawan and his companions. The charming duchess was to sit by Parzival at table, and Gawan bade her take good care of him.

She said, "Do you mean to give into my care a man who mocks at women? How am I to attend to such a man? Yet if this is your bidding, I shall serve him, and little do I care if he takes that for mockery."

Then Gahmuret's son said, "Lady, you do me great injustice. I know myself well enough to know that never do I mock at a woman."

Of whatever food was there, enough was provided, and with great courtesy it was set before them, so that maid, woman, or man, ate with enjoyment.

Itonje, observing Bene, saw that her eyes were weeping secretly, and she turned pale from anguish, and   698 her sweet mouth could eat no more. "What is Bene doing here?" she thought. "I sent her to him who bears my heart with him there, though it pounds here within me so painfully. What am I being punished for? Has the king renounced my service and my love? His true and manly heart may accomplish nothing more than that I, poor maid, must die for grief and love of him."

It was past midday when the meal was ended. Arthur and his wife, Lady Ginover the Queen, came riding with a host of knights and ladies to where the fair Parzival was sitting in the company of noble ladies. He was welcomed joyfully, and many a lovely lady gave him a kiss of greeting. Arthur did him honor and thanked him for his high renown which had spread so far and wide that he was rightly praised above all other men.

The Waleis said to Arthur, "Sir, when I last   699 saw you, my honor was attacked, and I had to pay such a high forfeit in honor that I well nigh lost it entirely. Now, Sir, I hear you say, if you are speaking candidly, that I still merit some share of praise. Hard though it is for me to believe, I gladly trust your word. Would that others might also believe it, from whom I parted there in shame!"

Then all who sat there assured him that his hand had

won the prize in many lands and gained so high a fame that his fame was without blemish.

Then the knights of the duchess also came up to where the fair Parzival sat beside Arthur. The noble King did not neglect to welcome them in the house of their host.[6] Large though Gawan's tent was, the wise and courtly Arthur sat in front of it on the field, and the others took their places around him on the camp ground.

There many were assembled who were strangers to each other. If I were to tell you the names of this one or that one among the Christians and Saracens there, that would be a long tale. Which was Clinschor's army? Which   700 were those who had so often ridden out to battle from Logrois to fight for Orgeluse? Who were the men Arthur had led? If one were to name the land and home of all of them, it would still be hard to remember them.

They all said that Parzival alone, beyond all other men, was so fair that any woman would gladly love him and that his nobility was lacking none of the signs of high renown.

Up stood Gahmuret's son and said, "All who are here remain seated and help me to win what I miss so painfully. An incomprehensible wonder banished me from the Round Table. All you who once pledged me fellowship, help me now again, as friends, to return to the Table Round."

What he desired Arthur granted him courteously. Then, stepping aside with a few of the knights, he made another request, that Gawan should leave to him the battle which he was to fight on the morrow at the appointed time. "I shall gladly wait there for him who is called King   701 Gramoflanz. Early this morning I plucked a wreath from his tree as a challenge to battle. I came to his land to fight, and to fight with no one but him. Kinsman, I could not expect to find you here. Nothing has ever grieved me so. I thought you were the king, who did not mean to spare me the combat. Kinsman, do allow me to fight him. If he must be defeated, my hand will do him such injury that he will

indeed have enough. My rights have been restored to me
here, and I can now live in fellowship with you, dear kinsman. Be mindful of our well-known kinship, and let this
fight be mine. I shall show I have the courage of a man."

Then my lord Gawan said, "I have many kinsmen and
comrades here with the King of Britain—and to none of
them will I grant that he should fight for me. I trust in my
good cause, and if good fortune prevails, I shall win the
prize. May God reward you for your offer to fight, but I
have not come to such a pass as yet."

Arthur had heard the request and now put an   702
end to the conversation. He took his place in the ring with
them again. Gawan's cupbearer did not fail to have pages
bring many costly goblets of gold, adorned with precious
stones. The cupbearer did not go about alone. When the
drink was done, the people went to their rest.

And then the night began to draw near. Parzival occu-
pied himself with examining all his armor. Any strap that
was broken he had repaired and beautifully adorned. And
he had a fresh shield brought, for his was battered and
slashed outside and in. A sturdy shield he ordered. The
squires who brought it he did not know; some of them
were French. His horse, which the templar had once ridden to the joust against him, was tended to by a squire,
and it was never so well groomed since. Now it was night
and time for sleep. Parzival too lay down to rest. His armor
lay ready before him.

But King Gramoflanz was vexed that another   703
man[7] had fought for his wreath that day. His men had not
ventured, nor were they able to separate the combatants. He
regretted bitterly that he had arrived too late. What did
this hero do now? Since he always strove to win the prize,
scarcely had it begun to grow light when his horse was
armed, and he himself as well. Do you suppose wealthy
ladies gave him some of his finery as gifts? But even apart
from that his trappings were costly enough. He adorned
himself for the sake of a maid in whose service he was con-

[7] I.e., Parzival.

stant. Alone, the king rode out to look for his opponent, and was very indignant that the noble Gawan did not immediately appear on the field.

Now Parzival too had secretly stolen out. From its wrappings[8] he took a sturdy spear from Angram. He too had all his armor on. Then the hero rode alone to the posts as smooth as mirror glass, marking the place where the battle was to take place. He saw the king waiting there. Without speaking a word to each other, they say, each   704 thrust his spear through the other's shield, so that the splinters whirled up from their hands through the air. Both were skilled in the joust, but also in other ways of fighting.

Over the wide meadow the dew splashed, and on the helmets beat sharp blades, keenly cutting. Undaunted they fought, these two. The meadow was trodden, and the dew in many a place trampled down. I grieve for the red flowers and still more for the heroes who suffered distress there, unfaltering. Who could rejoice in this and not grieve—if they had done nothing to harm him?

Now Sir Gawan also made himself ready for the hazards of his battle. It was already mid-morning before the news was heard that the bold Parzival was missing. Did he think to bring about a reconciliation? [9] He was not behaving as if he did; he was fighting bravely with him who was also holding his own in the combat. And now it was broad daylight.

A bishop sang Mass for Gawan. A throng of   705 warriors gathered there, and knights and ladies on horseback could be seen at Arthur's circle of tents. Before the singing began, King Arthur himself appeared where the priests perform their office.

When the benediction had been spoken, Sir Gawan put on his armor. Those present had already noticed that the proud man was wearing greaves of iron on his shapely legs. Then the ladies began to weep.

The whole army moved out, and there they heard the

---

[8] The word here is *banier* and may mean a bundle of spears wrapped in a pennant.

[9] I.e., between Gawan and Gramoflanz.

clang of swords and saw sparks flying from helmets and
blows dealt with mighty strength.

King Gramoflanz had been accustomed to scorn combat
with one man alone, but now it seemed to him as if six
men were attacking him. Yet it was only Parzival who
faced him there in battle and taught him a lesson men still
value today. Never again did he claim for himself the special honor that he would fight only with *two* men, for *one*
proved too much for him there.

The armies on both sides[10] had arrived at the   706
broad green meadow, each at its appointed place, and now
watched this battle game. The brave warriors had left their
horses standing and these worthy men fought now on foot
on the ground a battle hard and fierce. Again and again
these fighters threw their swords out of their hands and
high into the air, thus reversing the cutting blade.[11] So King
Gramoflanz received a bitter payment for his wreath, but
the kinsman of his beloved got from him, too, scanty pleasure. And so the noble Parzival suffered for the fair Itonje
when he should have had joy from her if right had received
its due.[12] These two, who had often ridden out in search of
fame, had to pay the penalty in combat; one fought for a
friend in need, the other at love's command, for he was the
vassal of love.

Then my lord Gawan came too, just as the proud bold
Waleis was almost at the point of winning the victory.
Brandelidelin of Punturtois and Bernout de Ri-   707
viers and Affinamus de Clitiers,[13] with heads bare these
three rode up closer to the battle. From the other side Arthur and Gawan rode onto the field to the battle-weary
pair. The five agreed to put an end to this combat. Gramoflanz too thought it time to stop and conceded the victory to
him they saw facing him there. And others admitted this
was so.

Then the son of King Lot said, "Sir King, I shall do for you today what you did yesterday for me when you bade me rest. Rest now for tonight. You will need it. He who forced you to this battle wanted to weaken your strength to resist my hand in combat. I could certainly withstand you now *alone*. But you never fight unless there are *two!* I will venture it tomorrow anyway, and may God show forth the right!"

The king rode away to his men, but first giving his pledge that on the morrow he would come to the field to meet Gawan in battle.

Arthur said to Parzival, "Kinsman, it so hap-   708 pened that, like a real man, you asked to fight this combat, but Gawan refused permission, whereat your lips made great lament. And yet you fought the battle, whether it pleased us or not, against him who had waited there for Gawan. You crept away from us like a thief, else we would have restrained your hand from this combat. But Gawan must not be angry if you are praised for this."

"My kinsman's high fame does not displease me," said Gawan. "Indeed, tomorrow is all too early for me if I am to do battle. If the king would release me from this, I would pay tribute to his reasonableness."

The army rode in many divisions back to camp. There lovely ladies could be seen and many a man richly adorned. Never did an army have such a wealth of adornment. The knights of the Round Table and the retinue of the duchess—their surcoats glistened with pfellel-silk from Cynidunte and from Pelpiunte. And the trappings of   709 their horses shone bright.

The valiant Parzival was praised in both armies so highly that his friends could well rejoice. In Gramoflanz' army they said never had the sun shone on a knight who fought so bravely in battle, and whatever feats had been done on either side, he alone should have the prize. But they did not know yet who it was whom every mouth there was praising.

They counseled Gramoflanz to ask Arthur that he should take care no other man from his host should come to fight against him, but that Arthur should send him the right one, Gawan, the son of King Lot, for it was with *him* he wanted to do battle.

The messengers were sent, two clever youths, distinguished for courtesy.

"Now observe," said the king, "to which of all the fair ladies you would give the prize. And look especially to see by whom Bene is sitting. Notice carefully how she acts. Observe secretly whether she is happy or sad. You   710 can see in her eyes if she is sorrowing for a friend. And see to it that you do not omit to give my friend Bene this letter and this ring. She knows to whom to give them. Perform your task skillfully, and you will do your duty."

Meanwhile, in the other camp, it happened that Itonje had heard that her brother and the dearest man a maid ever took to her heart were to fight with one another and were determined not to forego the combat. Then her grief burst the bonds of her modesty. Anyone who rejoices at her sorrow does so against my will, for she did not deserve it. Her mother and her grandmother then led the maiden aside to a small tent made of silk. Arnive reproached her for her grief and chided her for her misbehavior. But this did not prevent her from confessing openly what she had long kept secret from them. Then the noble maiden said, "Shall my brother's hand cut down my heart's beloved? That he surely would not do!"

Arnive said to a page, "Tell my son I wish to   711 speak to him immediately and only to him alone." The squire brought Arthur to her.

Arnive's intention was to tell Arthur for whose sake the fair Itonje suffered such anguish of heart—perhaps he could banish it.

Now the pages from King Gramoflanz arrived at Arthur's camp and dismounted on the field in front of the little tent. One of them saw Bene sitting beside her who was speaking to Arthur. "Does the duchess think it honorable if my brother, at her frivolous counsel, should slay my *ami?* He himself would confess that an outrage! What has the king done to him? Gawan should let him find happiness in

me. If my brother is sensible—he knows of the love between us two, how pure it is, without a flaw—and if he insists on fighting, he will rue it. If his hand kills the king, it
will deal me too a bitter death. Sir, that is my lament."
Thus the sweet maiden spoke to Arthur and added,
"Now remember that you are my uncle; keep   712
faith with me and prevent this battle."

Straightway Arthur answered with words of wisdom,
"Alas, dear niece of mine, that so young you should
know such great love! That will bring you sore distress.
Thus it was with your sister Surdamur for her love of the
empereur of the Greeks. Sweet and lovely maiden, I would
indeed prevent this battle if I knew from *both* of you that
his heart and yours are one. Gramoflanz, son of Irot, is a
man of such valor that the battle will be fought if your love
does not stay his hand. Did he ever, at any festive occasion,
see your bright beauty and your sweet red mouth?"

"No, that has never happened," she said. "We love each
other sight unseen. But for love's sake and the sake of true
friendship he has sent me many a present, and he has received from my hand what true love requires and what
banished doubt from us both. The king is true to me and
knows not the counsels of a faithless heart."

Then the maid Bene noticed the two squires   713
and recognized them, these lads from King Gramoflanz
who had come to Arthur. "No one should be standing
here," she said. "If you permit, I shall bid these people withdraw beyond the tent ropes. If my lady wishes to stir up such
trouble for the sake of her beloved, the tale will soon be
known everywhere."

The maid Bene was sent out of the tent, and one of the
lads secretly slipped the letter and the ring into her hand.
They too had heard her lady's great grief and said they had
come to speak to Arthur—could Bene arrange that?

She said, "Stand farther away to the side until I bid you
come to me."

Then Bene, the sweet maid, told them in the tent that
Gramoflanz' messengers were there, asking where Arthur

the King could be found. "It seemed to me improper to show them in here to this conference. Why should I do my lady such hurt by letting them see her weeping here?"

Arthur said, "Are they the lads I saw trotting 714 up to my tent ring? They are of noble birth, those two. What if they may be so excellent and so proof against impropriety that they might well take part in our counsels? *One* of them may be discerning enough to see the love my niece has for his master."

"That I do not know," said Bene, "but, Sir, if you will permit, the king has sent this ring and this letter. When I went out in front of the pavilion, one of the lads gave them to me. Here, Lady, these belong to you."

Then Itonje kissed the letter fervently and pressed it to her breast. And she said, "Sir, you can see from this whether the king desires my love."

Arthur took the letter in his hand, and in it he found written by one who knew the meaning of love what the faithful Gramoflanz had said with his own lips. In this letter Arthur perceived a love so true such as he had never known before in all his life. These were words with which love could well be pleased.

"I greet her to whom my greeting is due and 715 from whom I win a greeting with my service. Little lady, it is you I mean, for with solace you solace me.

"My love and yours are friends; that is the root of my happiness. The solace which you give me outweighs all other solace, for your heart is true to me.

"You are the lock keeping fast my faith, and the ruin of my heart's sorrow. Your love gives me so richly of help that never will anyone see me perform an evil deed.

"I may well call your goodness steadfast, without wavering. As the antarctic pole[14] faces the north star, and neither moves from its place, so my love and yours shall stand true and never leave each other.

[14] Wolfram means the polar star.

"Now think of me, noble maiden, of the sorrow I have lamented, and be not slow to help me. If for hatred of me any man should try to part us, remember that love can reward us both. Be mindful of what is honor for a woman, and let me be your servant. I will serve you in any way I can."

Arthur said, "Niece, you are right. The king   716 greets you without deception. This letter shows me a wondrous store of love such as I have never seen before. You shall turn his sorrow aside, and he shall do the same for you. Both of you leave it to me—I shall prevent the battle. Meanwhile cease your weeping. Now tell me—you were a prisoner—how did it happen that you became fond of each other? But you shall give him your love's reward, and for that he will do you service."

Itonje, Arthur's niece, answered, "She is here, she who brought that about. Neither of us ever said a word. If you permit, she will arrange for me to see him to whom I have given my heart."

"Show her to me," said Arthur. "If I can I shall see to it, for his sake and yours, that your will be done and your happiness be complete."

Itonje said, "It is Bene. And two of his squires are here. Do try, if my life is dear to you, to have the king see me, for all my joy depends on him."

Arthur, the wise and courtly lord, went out to   717 the lads at once and greeted them when he saw them. Then one of them said to him, "Sir, King Gramoflanz requests you for the sake of your own honor to see that the vow given by him and Gawan is fulfilled. Sir, he requests further that no other man should come to fight with him. Your host is so vast, if he had to vanquish them all, that would not be fair. He asks you to send Gawan, for it was with *him* the battle was agreed upon."

The King answered the lads, "I will free us from this reproach. My nephew never knew greater grief than that he himself did not fight there. He who fought with your master was born to victory; he is Gahmuret's son. In the three

armies that have come here from all sides[15] no man has ever known a hero so valiant in battle. His deeds equal his renown. He is my kinsman Parzival. You shall see him, that handsome knight. That Gawan's good faith may   718
not suffer, I shall do what the king has requested."

Arthur and Bene and the two squires rode back and forth through the camp. He let the lads observe the fair radiance of the many ladies, and they could also see the rustling crests of many helmets. Even today it would not harm a man of power to behave in so friendly a way. They remained on horseback, and Arthur showed the lads the best knights of all the armies. There they could see the greatest of splendor, many a beautiful figure, knights and maidens and ladies. The army was camped in three parts, with two spaces in between.

Arthur rode then with the lads away from the army far out onto the field. Then he said, "Bene, sweet maiden, you heard the complaint of Itonje, my sister's child. She cannot cease her weeping. My friends who pause here beside me will believe, if it pleases them so, that Gramoflanz has almost extinguished Itonje's shining beauty. Now   719
help me, you two, and you also, my friend Bene, and have the king come to me now, even though he may fight the battle tomorrow. I will see that my nephew Gawan goes to meet him on the field. If the king rides today to my army, he will be the better armed for tomorrow. Here love will give him a shield which will be too strong for his foe, I mean love's high courage which works enemies ill. Let him bring with him men of his court; I intend to negotiate here between him and the duchess. Now do this thing skillfully, dear friends; it will be to your own honor. I will tell you more that grieves me—what have I, unhappy man, done to King Gramoflanz, that he should behave toward my kin, which he surely does not regard very highly, alike with great love and great animosity?[16] Any other king, as my peer, would leave me unmolested. If he wants to repay with

---

[15] The three armies are the army of Arthur, the army of Gawan (and Orgeluse), and the army of Gramoflanz.

[16] I.e., love for Itonje, animosity for Gawan.

hatred the brother of her whom he loves, then he will see upon reflection that his heart is untrue to love if it teaches him such thoughts."

One of the lads said to the King, "Sir, what   720
you deem improper my lord should omit if he wishes to be courteous. But you know about that old dissension. My lord had better stay away than ride over here to you. The duchess still denies him her good will, and to many a man has made complaint about him."

"He shall come with but a small company," said Arthur. "Meanwhile I will have obtained from the noble duchess assurance of peace in that very conflict. I will send him a good escort. Beacurs, my sister's son, will meet him halfway, and he shall travel under the protection of my escort. He need not think that a disgrace, for he shall see worthy people here."

They took leave and rode away. Arthur remained alone upon the field. Bene and the two lads rode into Rosche Sabins and out by the other side to where the army lay camped. Never in his life had Gramoflanz known a day so happy as when Bene and the squires spoke with him. His heart told him the news he had received Fortune herself had devised for him. He said he would be glad   721
to come.

Then he chose his company. Three princes of his land rode with him, and his uncle, King Brandelidelin, took the same number. Bernout de Riviers and Affinamus of Clitiers each chose a companion who was suitable for this journey. In all there were twelve of them. Numerous pages and many a stout squire were also selected for this journey.

How were the knights dressed? In pfellel-silk which glittered brightly from the heavy gold. As if to hawking, the king's falconers rode with him.

Now Arthur had not forgotten his promise and sent the fair Beacurs to meet the king halfway and give him escort. Across the breadth of the fields, whether through ponds or streams, wherever he saw a ford, the king rode on a-hawking, or rather, on the hunt for love. Beacurs welcomed him graciously, to the rejoicing of all.

With Beacurs had come more than fifty hand-   722
some lads, whose fair radiance bespoke their lofty lineage,
dukes and counts, and several kings' sons were among them
too. And on both sides the youths greeted each other
warmly, without grudging.

Beacurs was possessed of such shining beauty that the
king immediately asked Bene to tell him who this fair
knight was. "It is Beacurs, Lot's son."

Then he thought to himself, "Now, my heart, find her
who resembles this man. He who rides here so winsomely—
she is his sister. If she who sent me the sparrow hawk and
the hat from Sinzester shows me further favor, then rather
than all earthly riches, though the earth were twice as wide,
I would take her and her alone. She is surely true to me.
Trusting in her favor I came here. She has always brought
me comfort, and I have faith in her that she will do what
will lift my spirits."

Her fair brother's hand clasped the hand of the king, no
less fair than his.

Now in the army it had come about that Ar-   723
thur had obtained a truce from the duchess. For Cidegast,
whom she had mourned so deeply before, she had received
consolation. Her wrath lay well nigh covered, and ever
weaker had her anger grown while Gawan's embraces had
awakened her.

Arthur the Briton summoned the fine and lovely ladies,
maidens and women both, all of them fair to look upon. A
hundred of these noble ladies he had placed in a tent apart.
Itonje sat there among them, and nothing could have
pleased her more than that she should see the king.[17] She
knew a steadfast joy, but in the glow of her eyes one could
see that Love had taught her suffering. Many a handsome
knight sat there, yet in beauty beyond all others the noble
Parzival bore the prize.

Gramoflanz came riding up to the tent ropes. The undaunted king wore a pfellel-silk from Gampfassasche with
woven threads of gold, and it cast a gleam afar.

17 I.e., Gramoflanz.

Those newly arrived dismounted, and many of   724
King Gramoflanz' pages ran ahead of him and pressed into
the pavilion. The chamberlains vied with each other to
clear a wide path for the Queen of the Britons. Brandelidelin, the uncle of Gramoflanz, preceded the king into the
pavilion. Ginover greeted him with a kiss, and the king
was also greeted thus. And likewise the Queen gave a kiss
of greeting to Bernout and to Affinamus.

Arthur said to Gramoflanz, "Before you are seated, look
about you and see whether there is one among these ladies
whom you love, and kiss her. You both have my permission
for this."

A letter he had read out on the field told him who his
beloved was. I mean, he had seen the brother of her who
had secretly sent him word that she loved him more than
all the world. Gramoflanz' eyes recognized her who loved
him. Great indeed was his joy that Arthur had given permission for them to greet each other openly. He kissed
Itonje on the mouth.

King Brandelidelin took a place by Ginover the   725
Queen, and King Gramoflanz seated himself beside her who
had drowned her fair radiance in tears. That was the only
pleasure she had had from him. If he did not wish to punish innocence, he perforce had to speak to her now and offer her his service for love's reward. She too knew what was
proper and thanked him for his coming. What they said
could be heard by no one—they only gazed fondly at each
other.—If I can learn that language, I shall know what they
said then, whether it was no or yes.

Arthur said to Brandelidelin, "You have spoken enough
with my wife," and led the dauntless hero to a smaller tent
a short way across the field.

Gramoflanz remained there with his other friends—that
was Arthur's intention. The knights were not displeased at
this, for the ladies glowed with beauty, and this diversion
was so pleasant that a man who wished to win joy after a
time of peril could very well put up with it. Drink   726
was brought and set before the Queen. And when they had

drunk enough, the knights and even the ladies, they looked all the better for it.

To Arthur and Brandelidelin in their tent drink was also taken, and the cupbearer withdrew again. Then Arthur began to speak, "Sir King, supposing they do this and supposing the king, your sister's son, had slain my sister's son. If he then wished to love my niece, the maiden who is making lament to him of all her sorrows, there where we left them sitting—if she were in her right senses, she would never be fond of him after that. She would reward him with such hatred as could be very unpleasant for the king if he desired any pleasure from her. When hatred overcomes love, joy is banished from true hearts."

Then said the King of Punturtois to Arthur the Briton, "Sir, it is our sisters' children who will face each other in hatred. We must prevent the battle. There can be only one outcome, that they love each other with true affection. Your niece Itonje should first bid my nephew   727 give up the battle for her sake, if he desires her love. Thus the battle, with all its strife, will be avoided completely. And do you also help my nephew to win the favor of the duchess."

"That I will do," said Arthur. "Gawan, my sister's son, has enough power over her that she, finely bred as she is, will leave to the two of us, to him and to me, the settlement of the issue. And you then make peace on your side."

"I shall," said Brandelidelin, and the two returned to the other tent.

There the King of Punturtois sat down by Ginover, that courteous lady. At her other side sat Parzival. So fair was he that never had any eye beheld a man so handsome.

Arthur left to go to his nephew Gawan. The latter had been informed that King Gramoflanz had arrived, and quickly he was brought the news that Arthur was dismounting before his tent. Gawan hastened out to the field to meet him.

They brought it about that the duchess agreed to a reconciliation, but only on one condition would she   728 grant it, if Gawan, her *ami,* was willing to renounce the battle for her sake. And further, she would make peace if the king would cease to accuse her father-in-law Lot.[18] By Arthur she sent this message, and Arthur, the wise and courtly man, delivered it.

Then King Gramoflanz had to renounce his wreath. And all the hatred he felt for Lot of Norway melted away completely and without bitterness before the lovely Itonje, like snow in the sun. This happened as he sat by her. He granted her every request.

Gawan was seen approaching, accompanied by handsome knights. I prefer not to tell you their names nor from what race they stemmed. Then for love's sake sorrow was forgiven. Orgeluse the proud and her noble warriors, and also Clinschor's company—of these last only a part, not all— were seen coming with Gawan. The tent walls   729 had been removed from Arthur's tent, leaving only the roof.

The good Arnive, Sangive, and Cundrie—these Arthur had bidden before to come to this meeting of reconciliation. Whoever thinks that a small thing may judge whatever he pleases to be greater. Jofreit, Gawan's friend, conducted the radiant duchess by the hand underneath the pavilion. In her courtesy she was mindful to let the three queens enter before her. Brandelidelin kissed her, and Orgeluse greeted him too with a kiss. Gramoflanz went up to her to be reconciled and receive her favor. In token of forgiveness her sweet red mouth kissed the king. She would have liked to weep, for she thought of Cidegast's death. Womanly grief compelled her even now to mourn for him. Admit, if you will: this is true loyalty.

Gawan and Gramoflanz completed their reconciliation with a kiss. Arthur gave Itonje to Gramoflanz in true marriage. He had done service a long time for that. Bene rejoiced when it happened.

To Lischois, the Duke of Gowerzin, Cundrie   730 was given to wife; her love had taught him suffering. His

---

[18] I.e., of murdering Gramoflanz' father.

life was without joy until he felt her noble love. To the Turkoite, Florant, Arthur offered Sangive for wife, she who had formerly been the wife of King Lot.[19] This was a gift well worthy of love, and the prince accepted it gladly. Arthur was lavish with ladies. He gave such gifts readily and had considered the matter well beforehand.

This discourse ended, the duchess spoke and said that Gawan had earned her love with deeds of high renown and that of right he was lord over her land and herself. These words were a heavy blow to her knights who had broken many a spear in their longing for her love.

Gawan and his friends, Arnive and the duchess, many a fair lady, and the noble Parzival as well, Sangive and Cundrie took their leave. Itonje remained there with Arthur.

No one can maintain that there was ever anywhere a more sumptuous marriage festival. Ginover   731 took into her care Itonje and her *ami*, the noble king, who, compelled by his love for Itonje, had often won many a prize in knightly deeds. To his lodgings rode many a man who from noble love suffered grief. We can well omit a description of their evening meal. Whoever pursued noble love there, wished for the night rather than the day.

King Gramoflanz sent a message to his men in Rosche Sabins—his pride impelled him to this—that they should spare no pains but break camp there by the sea and come with his army before daylight and that his marshal should choose a camp site suitable for the army. "Make my quarters as sumptuous as possible, and for every prince set up a special ring of tents." Such was the plan, to display a costly splendor. The messengers departed, and then it was night.

Many a man there was sad, taught this sadness by women. Whoever sees his service fading without finding any reward falls prey to sorrow if a woman does not offer him help.

Now Parzival thought of his fair wife and of   732 her pure sweetness. Should he not perhaps speak to another,

[19] Sangive is Arthur's sister and Gawan's mother, but that is not important. In such tales as this the women are ageless.

offer his service for love, and cultivate inconstancy? No, such love he avoids. Great loyalty had so guarded his manly heart and body that truly no other woman ever had power over his love save the Queen Condwiramurs, the lovely *belle fleur*.

He thought, "Ever since I learned how to love, how has Love treated me? Yet I was born of love. How did I lose Love thus? If I am to strive for the Grail, the thought of her pure embrace must drive me on. I parted from her—too long ago. If I must look with my eyes on joy, though my heart knows nothing but distress, these two things fit ill together. In such manner no one can become rich in courage. May Fortune show me what would be best for me to do."

His armor lay close beside him.

He thought, "Since I am lacking what those   733 who are happy can command—I mean love, which with the aid of joy makes many sad spirits joyful—since I am denied this, I care not what happens to me. God does not wish my joy. And she who compels me to long for love—if our love were thus, mine and hers, that parting were part of it and inconstancy disturbed us, I might well look to another love. But her love has robbed me of other love and the consolation of joy. I am still the captive of sorrow. To all who desire the fullness of joy, may Fortune grant it to them! May God bestow joy on all these hosts! From these joys I shall depart."

He reached for where his armor lay. He had often done this unaided, and speedily he was armed. Now he intends to seek distress anew. When this man fleeing from joy had all his armor on, he saddled his horse with his own hand. Shield and spear he found ready. When the morrow came, you could hear them lamenting his leaving. As he departed from there, it was just beginning to grow light.

BOOK·XV

Many people have been perturbed because this   734
story has been withheld from them and numbers of them
have not been able to find out—now I shall hold back no
longer and I will inform you with true report, for in my
mouth I bear the key to this adventure—how the sweet
and good Anfortas was made well.

The adventure informs us how the Queen of Pelrapeire
kept her womanly heart pure until she arrived at the place
of her reward, where she entered into high happiness.
This Parzival will bring about.

If my art does not fail me, I will first tell about his struggle, for whatever his hand had won hitherto was mere
child's work. —If I could turn this story backward, I would
not want to take a chance on my hero; nor would I enjoy
it myself. But now I present his happiness, his share of good
fortune, to his heart, where intrepidity dwelt side by side
with restraint, for it never entertained dismay. May that
give him assurance so that he may preserve his life, for it
befell him to face a master over all warfare on his fearless
journey. This courteous man was a heathen who   735
had never known baptism.

Parzival was riding smartly along toward a great forest
when in a bright glade he encountered a rich stranger. It
will be a wonder if a poor man like me can describe for

you the richness that the heathen displayed in his adornment. If I overstate it, I could still say more, unless I am to
pass over his richness in silence. All that lay within the
power of Arthur's hand in Britain and in England would
not match the worth of the jewels of noble water and pure
that studded this hero's surcoat. It was precious for a certainty. Rubies and chalcedony would not have paid for it.
This surcoat gave forth a blaze of light. In the mountain of
Agremuntin salamander worms had woven it in the hot
fire, and the genuine precious gems lay dark and bright
upon it. I cannot name their virtues.

His quest was for love and the winning of   736
fame, and it was chiefly women who had given him all
these things with which the heathen had adorned himself
so preciously. Love led high valor into his manly heart, as
she still does to those seeking love. In token of his fame's
reward he wore on his helmet an ecidemon; all serpents
that are poisonous have not long to live once this little beast
has caught their scent. Such pfellel-silks as his horse wore
for its caparison are unknown in Thopedissimonte and
Assigarzionte, in Thasme or in Arabi. This unbaptized and
gracious man was striving for ladies' rewards, and that is
why he adorned himself so splendidly. His high heart compelled him to strive for noble love.

Now this same valiant lad had cast anchor in a wild bay
of the sea near the *forêt*. He was leading five-and-twenty
armies, not one of which understood the language of the
others, and this was all in keeping with his power, for just
that many separate countries served his noble   737
hand—Moors and other Saracens of dissimilar appearance.
Many a wondrous weapon was to be found in his far-assembled army. And yet this lone man had ridden away
from his army and into the *forêt*, in search of adventure
and just to sport about. Since kings help themselves to that
prerogative, I allow them to ride alone to fight for fame.
Parzival was not riding alone: with him were himself and
his High Courage that does such manly fighting that
women have to praise it, unless they want to talk nonsense

out of sheer frivolousness. Here now are two men who are going to attack each other, lambs of gentleness and lions of valor. Alas that, wide as the earth was, they had to meet —and fight for no reason. I would be worried for the one I have guided here if I didn't recall the consolation that the Grail's power will sustain him. Love, too, will afford him protection. He served both of them unwaveringly with the strength of his service.

My art does not provide me with the capacity   738 to describe this battle exactly as it took place. The eyes of each lighted up when he saw the other coming, but if their hearts cried joy, a sorrow was standing close by. These pure men without a flaw each bore the heart of the other, and in their strangeness to one another they were still intimate enough. Well, I can't part this heathen from the baptized man if they are determined to show hatred. This should bend low the joy of good women. Each was risking death in hard combat for the sake of a beloved lady. May Fortune decide the outcome without a death!

The lion is born dead from its dam; its sire's roar brings it to life. These two men were born from battle din and marked for fame in many a joust. And they knew something about jousts and outlay of spears for consumption. From free rein they tightened bridles and as they rode a charge they kept a sharp eye out not to miss. They took care not to forget to sit firm in the saddle, and to face around toward the encounter, and to jab the   739 horse with the spurs. Here the joust was ridden so that both gorgets were ripped open by stout spears that did not bend. The splinters flew from that onset.

The heathen took it ill that this man still kept his seat; no one had ever done so before, against whom he had ridden in combat. Didn't they have swords with them? Yes, and they were sharp and ready at hand as the two closed in, and their skill and manhood were shown to advantage. The beast ecidemon was dealt several wounds—the helmet under him might well have complained. The horses became hot from weariness. Repeatedly they sought out new spots in which to fight, and finally both leaped down from their horses. Then the swords did clang.

The heathen pressed the baptized man hard. His war cry was "Thasme!"—but every time he cried "Tabronit!" he advanced one pace forward. The baptized man put up a good fight, too, in many a swift lunge they made against each other. Their battle had come to the point where I cannot refrain from speaking up: I must mourn   740 their fighting from loyalty of heart because one flesh and one blood are doing one another such harm. Both of them were, after all, sons of one man, the foundation stone of pure loyalty. The heathen never wearied of love, and from that fact his heart was mighty in combat. His will was bent on fame for the sake of Queen Secundille, who had given him the land of Tribalibot. She was his shield in danger.

The heathen was gaining now. What shall I do about the baptized man? Unless he thinks of love he will never escape, this fight will surely win him a death at the heathen's hand. Avert that, Grail of power! Avert it, Condwiramurs the beautiful! The servant of both of you stands here in the direst peril he ever knew.

The heathen swung his sword aloft, and many of his blows were so dealt that Parzival sank to his knees. One may say that "they" were fighting this way if one wants to speak of them as two, but they were indeed only one, for "my brother and I," that is one flesh, just as is good man and good wife.

The heathen pressed the baptized man hard.   741 His shield was made of a wood called aspindê, which neither rots nor burns. He was beloved by her who gave it to him, of that you may be sure! Turquoise, chrysoprase, emerald, ruby, and many a gem of startling brilliance was inlaid for the sake of rich glory all over the stud ribbings of his shield, and on the housing of the boss there was a gem the name of which I will tell you: in those regions it is called "antrax," but it is known here as a carbuncle. As a safe-conduct of love, ecidemon, that pure beast, had been given to him for his coat of arms by Queen Secundille, in

whose favor he wished to live. This device was her wish.
Purity of loyal-heartedness was now fighting here; great
loyalty was fighting with loyalty. For love's sake they both
had subjected their lives to God's decision in battle. Both
their hands had pledged it. The baptized man had faith in
God since departing from Trevrizent, who had so earnestly
counseled him to seek help from Him Who can confer joy
in the midst of trouble.

The heathen was sturdy of limb. Each time he   742
cried "Tabronit!," where Queen Secundille was, near the
mountain of Caucasus, he gained new high courage against
him who had always been spared from such superior force
of warfare; he had been a stranger to conquest from never
having suffered it, though many had learned it from him.
With skill they swung their weapons. Flashes of flame
leaped from their helmets and from their swords blew a
sour wind. God shield Gahmuret's son! That is my wish
for both of them, the baptized man and the heathen. I have
already termed them *one,* and they would think so too if
they were better acquainted; and they wouldn't fight for
such high stakes, for they were risking nothing more than
joy, salvation, and honor in that fight. Whichever one wins
here, if he loves loyalty, has lost worldly joy and found
heart's regret for ever more.

Why are you so slow, Parzival, to think of her who is
chaste and beautiful—I mean your wife—if you want to
save your life?

The heathen had two comrades-in-arms, and on   743
them rested most of his strength: one was the love that he
bore steadfastly in his heart, the other was the gems which
by their pure and noble kind taught him high spirits and
increased his power. It worries *me* that the baptized man is
so weary in thrust and in leap and in stout blows. If now
neither Condwiramurs nor the Grail can help him, then
there is one thing that has got to give you courage, brave
Parzival, and that is the sweet, fair boys, Kardeiz and
Loherangrin, who must not be orphaned young, the boys
that his wife bore after his last embrace.

Children chastely born, I ween,
Have many a man's salvation been.

The baptized man was gaining in strength. He was thinking—and none too soon!—of his wife the queen and of
her noble love, which he had won by the play of the sword
against Clamidê before Pelrapeire when fire had sprung
from helmets under blows. "Tabronit!" and "Thasme!"
were now answered with a countercry as Parzi-   744
val began to shout "Pelrapeire!" And just in time Condwiramurs came across four kingdoms with the sustaining
power of her love. Then chips, I fancy, flew from the heathen's shield, several hundred marks' worth. In one blow
the stout sword of Gaheviez broke over the heathen's helmet so that the brave stranger staggered down to a posture
of prayer on his knees. God would not allow corpse rob-
bing to thrive in Parzival's hand, for this was the sword he
had taken from Ither, as then befitted his simplicity. Then
he who had never sunk beneath a sword's blow before, the
heathen, jumped quickly up. —The battle is not decided
yet; the judgment still stands for both of them before the
Supreme Hand. May It avert their deaths!

The heathen rich in nobleness then said courteously with
his heathen lips, and in French, a language which he knew,
"I see, brave man, that your fighting would have to continue without a sword. But what renown would I win from
you that way? Stand still and tell me, brave hero,   745
who you are. You would certainly have had my fame that
has so long been vouchsafed to me, if your sword had not
broken. Now let there be a truce between us two until our
limbs are better rested."

They sat down on the grass. There was manliness and
breeding together in the two of them, and both were of an
age for battle, neither too old nor too young.

The heathen said to the baptized man, "Believe me now,
hero, that I have never seen in all my time any man that
might better win the prize men seek in fighting. Be so kind,
hero, as to tell me both your name and your race, and then
I will not have made this journey for nothing."

Then the son of Herzeloyde said, "If I am to do that out of fear and if I am expected to comply out of compulsion, then no one has the right to ask it of me."

The heathen from Thasme said, "I will give you my name first, and let the odium be mine![1] I am Feirefiz the Angevin, and powerful enough to have many countries pay tribute to my hand."

After these words were spoken, Parzival said to   746 the heathen, "How do you come to be an Angevin? Anjou is mine by right of inheritance—castles, land, and towns. At my request, Sir, you will have to choose a different name. If I am supposed to have lost my country and the noble city of Bealzenan, you would have had to overpower me. If one of us is an Angevin, *I* am of that race. —But I was told once that a hero undismayed is living in heathendom who has won love and praise by knightly valor so that he possesses both. He is called my brother, and he is known out there for renown." And then Parzival went on to say, "Sir, if I might see your face, I could tell at once if it is as it was described to me. If you will trust me that far, Sir, bare your head. If you will believe me, my hand will forbear any attack upon you until you have your helmet back on again."

Then the man from heathendom said, "I am   747 very little afraid of your fighting. If I had no armor on at all, as long as I had my sword, you should be kept from victory because your sword is broken. All your battle cunning could not save you from death if I didn't want to spare you anyway. Before you began to wrestle with me I would bring my sword clanging through iron and through skin."

The heathen strong and swift displayed his manly nature. "This sword," he said, "shall not belong to either one of us." And the bold warrior and brave hurled it far away from him into the woods. "Now if there is to be any fighting done," he said, "the chances must be equal."

Then the mighty Feirefiz said, "Hero, by your courteous breeding, if you do have a brother, tell me, what does he

[1] The loser was obliged to reveal his name.

look like? Describe his countenance as his complexion was described to you."

To which Herzeloyde's child replied, "It was like a parchment with writing all over it, black and white all mixed up. That is how Eckuba described it to me."

The heathen said, "I am the one."

Then neither lost any time, each immediately removed his helmet and coif of mail from his   748 head. Parzival found a precious find and the dearest one he ever found. The heathen was recognized at once, for he had the markings of the magpie. With kisses Feirefiz and Parzival concluded their enmity, and friendship beseemed them both better than heart's hatred against one another. Faith and love rendered that battle decision.

With joy the heathen said, "Blessed am I that I have seen the noble Gahmuret's child! Honor to all my gods for it! My goddess Juno may well rejoice at this praise. My mighty god Jupiter has warranted me this happiness. You gods and goddesses, I shall ever love your power! Honor to the planet's shining under which my journey at adventure brought me to you, you dreadly dear man, at whose hand I almost came to grief! Blessed be the air and the dew that fell upon me this morning! Courteous key of love, blessed are the women who shall behold you, for happiness   749 will come to them!"

"You speak well, and I would speak better still if I could, and without malice. Unfortunately, I am not learned enough to outdo in words your noble praise. But God knows my intention. All the skill of my heart and eyes will never fail to follow what your renown prescribes. Never have I been in greater peril from a knight's hand than from yours, that I know for sure," said he of Kanvoleis.

Then the mighty Feirefiz said, "Jupiter has bestowed his care upon you, noble hero. But you must not go on addressing me with *'ir'*; after all, we had the same father." In brotherly faith he begged him to drop the polite address and call him by the intimate *"du."*

His words embarrassed Parzival, and he said, "Brother, your power is well nigh equal to that of the Baruch, and what is more, you are older than I. My youth and my poverty must guard against such impudence as calling you *'du'* if I am to be concerned about proper conduct."

He of Tribalibot lauded his god Jupiter in   750
words of various kinds, and he gave much high praise to his goddess Juno also for having so disposed the weather that he and all his army had landed from the sea in the country where they met one another. Again they sat down, and neither omitted to do the other honor.

The heathen spoke again. "I will give you two rich countries that will ever serve your hand, which my father and yours obtained when King Isenhart died, Zazamanc and Azagouc. His manhood never practiced deceit upon anyone —though he did leave me orphaned. That reproach against my father I still have not forgiven. His wife, of whom I was born, found her death through love of him when she lost his love. But I should like to see that man. I have been given to understand that there was never a better knight. My costly journey was undertaken in search of him."

Whereat Parzival said to him, "I never saw him   751
either. They report good work of him, so I have heard in numerous places, that he knew how to broaden his fame in battle and how to exalt his noble worth. All wrongdoing fled from him. He was at the service of ladies, and if they were faithful, they rewarded him in all sincerity. He cultivated what is still held in honor in Christendom, loyalty without wavering. He well knew how to suppress all false deeds in himself; his steadfastness of heart guided him in that. Those who were acquainted with that same man whom you would so much like to see have been so kind as to tell me this. I think you would give him praise if he were still alive, for he strove for praise. That Reward of Ladies was compelled by his service to meet King Ipomidon, who rode in joust against him. The joust took place before Baghdad, and there his noble life was brought to an end for the sake of love. In proper joust we lost him, the man of whom both of us were born."

"Alas for the sorrow unavenged!" said the hea-   752
then. "Is my father dead?" I can rightly say I have seen

joy's loss and seen the finding of joy. In this hour I have both lost and found my joy. If I am to grasp the truth, my father and you and I, we were all one, but this one appeared in three parts. When you see a learned man, he doesn't reckon kinship as between father and son, if he wants to find the truth [but considers them as one].[2] You have fought here against yourself; against *my*self I rode into combat here and would gladly have killed my very self; you could not help but defend my own self in fighting me. Jupiter, write this miracle down! Your strength helped us so that it prevented our deaths!" —He laughed and wept, though he tried to conceal it, and his heathen eyes shed tears as in honor of baptism. Baptism must teach fidelity since our new covenant was named for Christ: in Christ may fidelity be seen.

The heathen said—and I'll tell you what: "We   753 mustn't sit here any longer. Ride with me not too far from here, and for you to look at, I'll have the mightiest army Juno ever gave sailing winds to, come off the sea onto the *terre* and take quarters. For a certainty and no mistake, I'll show you many a worthy man who is subject to my service. Come on and ride down there with me."

To him Parzival replied, "Do you have such control over your men that they will wait for you today and all the while you are away?"

"No question about it!" said the heathen. "If I were away for half a year, rich and poor would still wait for me. They wouldn't venture to go anywhere. Their ships are, to be sure, well provisioned in the harbor, as is proper. Neither horse nor man needs to get off, except for fresh water and to breathe the inland air."

To his brother Parzival said, "In that case you ought to see the beauty of women and great pleasure, many a courteous knight of your noble kindred. Arthur the Briton is camped close by with a noble retinue—I left them   754 just today—with many a host of lovely beauties. We'll see fair ladies there."

When the heathen heard ladies mentioned—they were

2 The words in brackets are not in the text.

life itself to him—he said, "Take me there with you! You can also answer questions I want to ask you. Will we be seeing relatives of ours when we get to Arthur's? I've heard a great deal about his way of living, how he is rich in fame and travels about in state."

"We shall see ladies of fair beauty," said Parzival, "and our trip won't be in vain; we'll find our own kindred, people of whose race we were born—and several heads among them marked with a crown."

Neither one sat there any longer. Parzival did not forget to go and get his brother's sword, which he thrust back into that noble warrior's sheath. Then they both dismissed all anger and enmity and rode off in comradely fashion.

Even before they arrived at Arthur's, news had been heard of them. That same day there had been a 755 general regret all through the army that the noble Parzival had left them. After taking counsel, Arthur had decided he would wait up to the eighth day for Parzival to come back, and not to stir from the spot. Gramoflanz' army had also arrived, for which many a broad circle was marked out and well furnished with tents. Lodgings were thus provided for the proud and noble folk. They could not have offered the four brides anything more delightful. At the same time a man had come riding from the Castle of Wonders, and he reported that a combat had been seen in the pillar on the lookout tower. All that had ever been done in swordplay, "that is nothing compared to *this* fight." This report was made to Gawan as he was sitting with Arthur. Several knights made guesses as to who had been doing the fighting, but Arthur spoke up and said, "One of the combatants I know perfectly well. It is my kinsman from Kanvoleis who left us this morning."

Just at that moment the two of them came riding in.

In keeping with battle's honor, their helmets 756 and shields were much dented with swords. The well practiced hands of both had sketched the battle design, for in battle too a skill is required. They rode along by Arthur's tent circle, and then there was much looking at the heathen as he rode—he displayed *that* degree of richness. The field was well supplied with tents, but the two of them turned in at the main tent in Gawan's circle. —Will they be led in and made welcome? I think they will. —Gawan quickly followed them, for he had seen them riding toward his tent from where he had been sitting with Arthur, and he received them with joy.

They still had their armor on, and Gawan, courteous as always, had servants remove the armor at once. The beast ecidemon had come in for his share in the battle, and the heathen was wearing a gambeson that was also the worse for blows. It was made of saranthasme, with many a precious gem inwoven into it. Under this was his surcoat, coarse, figured, and snowy white. This, too, had   757 precious stones inwoven into it symmetrically on either side. Salamander worms had wrought it in the fire. She had hazarded her love, her land, and her person, the woman who gave him this adornment, the Queen Secundille, and he gladly obeyed her command both in joy and in sorrow. It was her heart's will to give him her wealth, and his high renown won her love.

Gawan admonished the servants to take good care that this handsome adornment should not be taken from its place or any part of it removed, gambeson, helmet, or shield. A poor woman would have been made more than rich with the surcoat alone, so precious were the gems on all four articles. Noble love can well adorn handsomely when wealth is there along with the will, and noble craftsmanship besides. The proud, rich Feirefiz was most assiduous in his service for women's favor, and one of them had not forgotten to reward him for it.

His armor was removed from him. Then all   758 who knew anything about marvels gazed at this black-and-white-spotted man, for they could well perceive that Feirefiz bore strange markings.

To Parzival Gawan said, "Kinsman, present your companion to me. He has such a distinguished appearance that I have never seen the like."

And Parzival said to his host, "If I am your kinsman, then so is he. Gahmuret is your warranty for that. This is the King of Zazamanc. My father by his fame won the love of Belacane, who bore this knight."

Then Gawan cordially kissed the heathen. The rich Feirefiz was black and white all over his skin, except that half of his lips showed red. Garments were brought for both of them, and costly they were seen to be, too. They had been fetched from Gawan's chamber. And then came lovely ladies. The duchess had Cundrie and Sangive kiss the stranger first, then she herself and Arnive kissed him. Feirefiz was delighted to see such lovely ladies. I think he enjoyed that.

Gawan said to Parzival, "Kinsman, your latest 759 tribulation is clear to me from your helmet and shield. You have both had a go at combat, you and your brother. From whom did you meet that grief?"

"There was never a harder fight seen," said Parzival. "My brother's hand forced defense out of me at great peril. Defense is a charm against death. On this stranger in the family my strong sword broke, but then he displayed very little fear: he threw his own away. Even before we had figured out our kinship, he was afraid of committing a sin against me. But now I have his favor, which I shall gladly earn with my service."

Gawan said, "Report was brought to me of an undaunted battle. At the Castle of Wonders whatever takes place within six miles' distance can be seen in the pillar on my lookout tower. Then my uncle Arthur said that the one doing the fighting was you, kinsman from Kingrivals. You have brought us the actual story now, but the fight had already been attributed to you before that. Now believe me when I say that you were being awaited here for eight days' time and with high and splendid festivity. I 760 regret your encounter with one another, but you shall rest up from it here with me. Since combat did take place between you, you are the better acquainted with each other. So take friendship now in place of enmity!"

Gawan ate that evening all the earlier because his kinsman from Thasme, Feirefiz the Angevin, and his brother were still unfed. Mattresses thick and long were laid out in a broad circle, and coverlets of many sorts and made of silk, not thin at all, formed the mattress coverings. Long, broad strips of rich pfellel-silk were appliquéd on them. Clinschor's wealth was there spread out to view. Four silken tapestries with rich embroidery—so I heard it told—they hung up opposite each other on the four walls; below them were soft cushions of down covered over with spreads, and the tapestries were above. The camp circle extended over so wide a field that six tents could have stood there without the ropes getting tangled.

But I would be foolish to let the adventure go on like this. —Then my lord Gawan sent word to Ar-   761 thur at court of who it was that had arrived: this was the mighty heathen whom the heatheness Eckuba had so praised by the shores of the Plimizoel. Jofreit, *le fils d'*Idoel, took this news to Arthur, who was overjoyed at it.

Jofreit asked him to eat early and then come over in fine array with a host of knights and ladies in state to receive the proud son of Gahmuret in worthy fashion.

"I will bring along all the noble folk that are here," said the Briton.

And Jofreit said, "He is so courtly, you will all want to see him, for you will behold in him a wonder. He has come from great wealth. His battle garments nobody could buy: there is nobody who could afford it. Take all the *terres*—Löver, Britain, England, the land from Paris to Wissant[3]—and they would still fall far short of paying for this."

Jofreit had come back. From him Arthur had   762 learned how he should proceed if he wished to welcome his kinsman the heathen. The precedence of seating was arranged in Gawan's tent, observing courtly etiquette. The company of the duchess, friend by friend, sat at Gawan's right, while on the other side Clinschor's knights ate with pleasure. The ladies, too, were assigned seats. Along the opposite side of the table from Gawan sat Clinschor's ladies, of whom many a one was fair. Feirefiz and Parzival sat in the midst of the ladies, and there, there was beauty to be

[3] Wissant is a town on the English Channel between Boulogne and Calais.

seen. Florant, the Turkoite, sat opposite the noble Sangive, while the Duke of Gowerzin sat opposite Cundrie his wife. I don't think Gawan and Jofreit forgot any of their old comradeship; they ate together. Radiant in her glances, the duchess ate with Queen Arnive. Neither neg- 763 lected to wait on the other. Beside Gawan sat his grandmother, and on his other side Orgeluse. From that circle illbreeding fled. With proper courtesy the food was served to the knights and ladies.

The mighty Feirefiz said to his brother Parzival, "Jupiter conceived this journey of mine for my happiness, and his help brought me here where I see my noble kinsmen. With good reason I honor my father whom I have lost; he was indeed born out of renown."

The Waleis said, "You will *still* see people to whom you cannot deny fame, and with Arthur, our chief, many a knight of manly kind. As soon as the meal is over, it won't be long before you see the noble persons of whom so much praise is heard. Of all the strength of the Round Table only three knights are sitting here, our host, and Jofreit—though I, too, have won the honor of an 764 invitation to membership, with which I complied."

The tablecloths were removed from before all the ladies and all the vassals after they had eaten. Gawan, the host, remained seated no longer, and he urged the duchess and his grandmother to take Sangive and the sweet Cundrie and go over to where the parti-colored heathen was sitting and keep him company. Feirefiz the Angevin saw the ladies approaching and rose at once, as did his brother Parzival. The duchess of lovely hue gave Feirefiz her hand and bade all the ladies and knights who had stood up to be seated. Just then, amid music, Arthur and all his party rode up. A sound was heard of trumpets and drums and flutes and shawms, and the son of Arnive arrived with great fanfare. This merry business the heathen declared to be a splendid thing. In this way Arthur came riding to Gawan's 765 tent circle with his wife and many handsome persons, knights and ladies. The heathen could easily see that here too were young people, of such years as to have the radiance of youth about them. Among them was King Gramoflanz, who was still Arthur's guest, and with him came his beloved Itonje, that sweet lady free from falsity.

The throng from the Round Table dismounted with many a lovely lady. Ginover had Itonje kiss her cousin the heathen first, then she herself approached and welcomed Feirefiz with a kiss. Arthur and Gramoflanz also received this heathen with faithful love. Both of them honored him with offer of their service, and many more of his kindred expressed to him their good will. Feirefiz the Angevin had come among good friends; that he soon saw.

The men and women sat down, and many a   766 fair maiden. If he wished to try, any knight there could find sweet words from sweet lips; and if he could sue for love, his entreaty was not received hostilely by many a lovely lady who sat there. Good women have never been seen in anger if a worthy man bespoke their help; they are free to grant or deny. If joy may be considered a kind of terrain, true love must pay the tribute. That is how I always saw noble folk live. Here now sat Service and Reward. It is a helpful song when a beloved lady is heard saying what may come to be for a beloved man.

Arthur sat down by Feirefiz. Neither forgot to give questions and answers in gracious alternation. Arthur said, "I praise God for showing us this honor of seeing you here. Never has a man out of heathendom come traveling to baptism-practicing lands to whom I would more gladly grant the service of my serving hand in whatever your will desires."

Feirefiz said to Arthur, "All my misfortunes   767 ended when the goddess Juno furnished me sailing weather to bring me to these western lands. You behave indeed like a man whose nobility is famed far and wide. If you are called Arthur, then your name is known afar."

Arthur said, "He honored himself, whoever it was praised me to you and to other people. His fine courtesy inspired him more than I have deserved and he did so from politeness. I *am* called Arthur, but I should like to hear how you came to this country. If a lady sent you forth, she must be very kind for you to have come so far for the sake of adventure. If she has not spared her reward, that dignifies ladies' service still more. All women would win hatred from their servers if you were unrewarded."

"The report is quite different," said the heathen. "But let me tell you now about how I came here. —I am leading such a powerful army that the Trojan fortifica-   768 tions and the men that besieged them would have been forced to give way before me. If both were still alive and fought against me in combat, they could not win the victory but would have to suffer defeat before me and my men. I have fought in many a battle with knightly action so that Queen Secundille has accorded me her favor. Whatever she desires, that is my will. She has determined the manner of my life. She bade me give generously and assemble good knights about me, and that pleased me for her sake. And so it was done. Clad with his shield, many a knight of worthy note is numbered among my forces. Her love, in turn, is my reward. On my shield I wear an ecidemon, as she enjoined me to do. Whenever I have encountered peril since then, I have always thought immediately of her, and her love brought me aid. She has been a better warrant of comfort than my god Jupiter."

Arthur said, "From your father Gahmuret, my   769 kinsman, you fully inherit the habit of long journeys in the service of ladies. —But I would like to tell you about a service greater than any done on earth for any woman. For the sake of her lovely self—I mean the duchess who is sitting here—and for her love, many a forest has been squandered. Her love has held the pledge of joy for many a goodly knight and driven his high spirits away." And he went on to tell him about the warfare for her sake, and also about Clinschor's band, who were sitting all around, and about the two encounters that Parzival his brother had fought at Joflanze on the broad meadow—"and what else he has done, since he never spared himself—that he shall tell you for himself. He is searching for a noble find: he is striving for

the Grail. —From both of you it is now my wish that you
name for me the people and the countries that you have
come to know in your battles."

The heathen said, "I will name the ones who are now
leading my knights here:

> King Papiris of Trogodjente   770
> and Count Behantins of Kalomidente,
> Duke Farjelastis of Affrike
> and King Liddamus of Agrippe,
> King Tridanz of Tinodonte
> and King Amaspartins of Schipelpjonte,
> Duke Lippidins of Agremuntin
> and King Milon of Nomadjentesin,
> from Assigarzionte Count Gabarins
> and from Rivigitas King Translapins,
> from Hiberborticon Count Filones
> and from Centriun King Killicrates,
> Count Lysander of Ipopotiticon
> and Duke Tiride of Elixodjon,
> from Oraste Gentesin King Thoaris
> and from Satarchjonte Duke Alamis,
> King Amincas of Sotofeititon
> and the Duke of Duscontemedon,
> from Araby King Zaroaster
> and Count Possizonjus of Thiler,
> Duke Sennes of Narjoclin
> and Count Edisson of Lanzesardin,
> from Janfuse Count Fristines
> and from Atropfagente Duke Meiones,
> from Nouriente Duke Archeinor
> and from Panfatis Count Astor,
> those of Azagouc and of Zazamanc
> and from Ganpfassasche King Jetakranc,
> Count Jurans of Blemunzin
> and Duke Affinamus of Amantasin.

"One thing I took as a disgrace: in my coun-   771
try they said that never had there been a better knight than
Gahmuret the Angevin, ever to bestride a horse. It was my

will and also my way to travel forth until I found him. I have had experience of combat since then. From my two countries I led forth a mighty army upon the sea and far into foreign lands. I had a desire **for** knightly deeds, and whatever country was brave and good, I subdued it to my hand. At that time two powerful queens, Olimpia and Clauditte, granted me their love. Secundille is now the third. For ladies' sakes I have done much. Today for the first time I had knowledge that my father Gahmuret is dead.—Now let my brother recite *his* trials."

Then the noble Parzival said, "Since I left the Grail my hand has practiced much knighthood in combat, both in close and in open quarters, and forced down the fame of some who were not accustomed to it before. I will name them here:

> From Lirivoyn King Schirniel   772
> and from Avendroyn his brother Mirabel,
> King Serabil of Rozokarz
> and King Piblesun of Lorneparz,
> from Sirnegunz King Senilgorz
> and from Villegarunz Strangedorz,
> from Mirnetalle Count Rogedal
> and from Pleyedunze Laudunal,
> King Onipriz of Itolac
> and King Zyrolan of Semblidac,
> from Jeroplis Duke Jerneganz
> and from Zambron Count Plineschanz,
> from Tuteleunz Count Longefiez
> and from Privegarz Duke Marangliez,
> from Pictacon Duke Strennolas
> and from Lampregun Count Parfoyas,
> from Ascalun King Vergulaht
> and from Pranzile Count Bogudaht,
> Postefar of Laudundrehte
> and Duke Leidebron of Redunzehte,
> from Leterbe Colleval
> and Jovedast of Arl, a Provençal,
> from Tripparun Count Karfodyas.

All this was done in tourneys while I was riding in search of the Grail. If I were to name all those I *fought* against, many were unknown to me and I am forced to pass over them in silence. Such of them as I know, I think I have mentioned here."

The heathen was cordially delighted that his 773 brother's fame stood thus and that his hand had conquered so many a noble name. He congratulated him upon it and declared that he, too, was honored thereby.

Meanwhile Gawan—as though it were done without his knowledge—had the heathen's battle equipment brought in. Examination revealed what precious things these were. Knights and ladies all began to inspect the surcoat, the shield, and the gambeson. The helmet was neither too narrow nor too wide. They all praised the costly precious stones with which it was studded.—No one should ask *me* what kind they were, these light stones and these heavy ones. You would have been better informed on that score by Eraclius or Ercules, and Alexander the Greek, and also by another, the wise Pictagoras, who was an astronomer and without doubt so wise that no one since Adam's time can be compared to him: he could tell about gems.[4]

The ladies were whispering as to what woman 774 had given him all this array; if he were unfaithful to her, his fame would surely be damaged. Nevertheless several were so well disposed toward him that they would well have put up with his service—because of his strange marking, I suppose.

Gramoflanz, Arthur, and Parzival, and Gawan the host, these four withdrew to one side, while the rich heathen was left in the care of the ladies. Arthur proposed a festival to be held the next morning without fail out on the field for

[4] Eraclius—confused by Wolfram with (H)eraklis—was the hero of a French romance who was expert in gems. The romance, by Gautier d'Arras, had been translated by Master Otte into German.

Alexander the Great—not to be confused with the Alexander of 586, who married Gawan's sister Surdamur—was the hero of twelfth-century romances in French and in German; a fabulous jewel was brought him from Paradise.

Pictagoras is Pythagoras.

the reception of his kinsman Feirefiz. "Now give this matter your attention and your best minds, so that he may be seated with us at the Round Table." They all lauded the idea and they would look after the matter if Feirefiz was not unwilling. Feirefiz the rich promised them his membership.

After the farewell drink had been poured the people went one and all to their rest. The joy of many was to come next morning; if I may put it this way: then came the sweet day of fame.

Utepandragun's son, Arthur, then did thus: he   775
had a costly cloth, richly made out of drianthasme for the Round Table. You have already heard how, on the plain of the Plimizoel, a Round Table was arranged. This cloth was cut the same way, circular and with a show of richness. Around it the circle was laid out on a dewy green lawn, with an interval of distance sufficient for a horseback charge left from seats to Round Table. The Table stood in the middle by itself, not for actual use but just for the name's sake. Any base man could not help feeling ashamed if he sat there with those worthy folk; his mouth would sin in eating the food. The circle was measured out by bright moonlight and carefully planned for splendid effect. A poor king would have been hard put to it to pay for the magnificence that was to be seen there by mid-morning. The costs were met by Gramoflanz and Gawan, since Arthur was a guest in the land—though his contribution did not fail either.

Night has rarely come on without the sun's   776
bringing in a new day, as is the sun's habit. This very same thing happened here, and the day shone sweet and clear upon them. Then many a knight slicked down his hair and placed a wreath of flowers upon it, and many a lady's unpainted face was to be seen with red lips—if Kyot told the truth. Knights and ladies wore attire not tailored in any one country, and the women's headdresses were high or low depending on their country's fashion. It was a far-assembled throng and hence their fashions varied. Any lady without an *ami* did not venture in any case to come to the Round

Table, but if she had accepted service for reward and if she had given warranty of her reward, then she rode to the Round Table circle. The others had to forego it, and they sat behind in their tents.

After Arthur had heard Mass, people saw Gramoflanz coming, and also the Duke of Gowerzin and Florant his companion. These three were each seeking membership in the Round Table. This Arthur granted them at once. If man or woman asks you whose was the   777
richest hand that ever from any land sat at the Table Round, you cannot give an answer more correct than: it was Feirefiz the Angevin. And let it go at that.

Magnificently they moved toward the circle. Several ladies were run into in the throng, so that if their horses had not been tightly girthed they would have fallen off for sure. Many rich banners were seen approaching from all directions. Then all around the outside of the Round Table circle bohourts were run, but court etiquette required that none of them should ride into the circle itself. The field beyond was broad enough for them to gallop the horses and to throng headlong, group into group, and also to display feats of horsemanship so that the women were delighted to see it. Then they took their places where the noble guests were eating. Chamberlains, stewards, and cupbearers then had to bethink themselves how to serve them with propriety.—I imagine they were given enough to eat.—Each lady had honor who sat with her *ami,* and many a one   778
had been served with great deeds at the behest of a loving heart. Feirefiz and Parzival had the sweet choice of now this lady and now that one. Never on field or meadow were so many fair complexions seen, or so many red mouths, as were to be found now in this circle. That rejoiced the heathen's heart.

Hail to the day of her coming!

Honor to her words' sweet tidings that from her lips were heard!

A maiden was now seen approaching: her garments were sumptuous and of fine cut; costly and of the French style was her hooded mantle of rich velvet blacker than a civet

cat; Arabian gold gleamed thereon, wrought as many small
turtledoves, the emblem of the Grail. Much was she
gazed at in curiosity. Now let her hasten hither. Her headdress was tall and shining; with many a thick veil was her
countenance covered and not exposed to the view.

Quietly, yet at full amble-gait she came riding   779
across the field. Her bridle, her saddle, and her horse were
unmistakably rich and splendid. They admitted her immediately to the circle. The wise and by no means foolish
woman rode all around the ring. She was shown where Arthur was sitting, nor did she fail to give him greeting.
French was her speech, and she sued for vengeance to be
wreaked upon her and for people to harken to her tidings.
The King and the Queen she implored for assistance and to
give heed to her words. Then she turned away from them
directly to where she found Parzival sitting near Arthur
and leaped down from her horse onto the grass. With all
the courtesy at her command she fell at Parzival's feet and,
weeping, begged him for his greeting, so that he lost his anger toward her and forgave her—but without a kiss. Arthur
and Feirefiz lent support to her plea. Parzival bore her ill
will, but at the intercession of friends he dismissed it sincerely and ungrudgingly. Whereupon the noble,   780
if unlovely, lady quickly sprang to her feet again, bowed to
them, and expressed to them her thanks for assisting her to
favor after great guilt.

With her hand she undid her headdress and threw down
veil and fastenings in front of her in the ring. Cundrie *la
sorcière* was then recognized at once, and the Grail coat of
arms that she wore was gazed at curiously enough. She still
had the same appearance that so many men and women
had seen appear by the Plimizoel. You have heard her
countenance described: her eyes were still the same, yellow
as topazes, her teeth were long, her mouth shone blue as a
violet. Except to solicit compliments, there was no need of
her wearing her costly hat on Plimizoel meadow; the sun
did not hurt her any; it could not have gotten through her
hair with its dangerous radiance to tan her complexion.
With dignity she stood and proclaimed things that the hear-

ers found astonishing. Directly she began her   781
speech thus:

"Blessed are you, son of Gahmuret! God means to manifest His mercy in you—I mean the one whom Herzeloyde
bore. The speckled Feirefiz is welcome to me for the sake
of Secundille, my sovereign lady, and for the sake of many
a deed of lofty nobleness which his fame has achieved in battle since the years of his youth."

To Parzival then she said, "Show restraint now in your
joy! Blessed are you in your high lot, O crown of man's
salvation!—The inscription has been read: you shall be Lord
of the Grail. Condwiramurs, your wife, and your son Loherangrin have been named therein along with you. When
you departed from Brobarz the land, two sons she bore into
life. Kardeiz has his sufficient share there. But even if you
never again heard good tidings beyond this: that your
truthful lips shall now address greeting to that noble and
sweet man, and that now the question from your mouth
shall make King Anfortas well again and avert from him
his sighs and great misery—where would there ever be
your equal in blessedness?"

Seven stars then she named in the heathen   782
language. The names were familiar to the rich and noble
Feirefiz, who sat there before her, part black and part white.
She said: [5]

> *"Mark now, Parzival:*
> *The highest of the planets, Zval,*
> *And the swiftly moving Almustri,*
> *Almaret, and the bright Samsi,*
> *All show good fortune for you here.*
> *The fifth is named Alligafir.*
> *Under these the sixth is Alkiter,*
> *And nearest us is Alkamer.*

"I do not speak this out of any dream. These are the bridle
of the firmament and they check its speed; their opposition
has ever contended against its sweep.

"For you, Care is now an orphan. Whatever the planets'

[5] See Note 5, p. 435.

orbits bound, upon whatever their light is shed, that is
destined as your goal to reach and to achieve. Your sorrow
must now perish. Insatiety alone will exclude you from that
community, for the Grail and the Grail's power forbid false
friendship. When young, you fostered Sorrow; but Joy, approaching, has robbed her of you. You have achieved the
soul's peace and waited amid sorrow for the joys of the
flesh."

Parzival was not vexed by her tidings. From   783
joy, tears flowed from his eyes, the fountain springs of the
heart, and he said, "Lady, if I have been deemed worthy before God of such things as you have named to me here, so
that my sinful self, and my children if I have any, and my
wife, shall all have a share in them, then God has indeed
shown me favor. By this compensation that you do me your
own faithfulness is seen. Yet if I had not done wrong, you
would have spared me your previous anger. But then it was
still not time for my salvation, while now you grant me so
high a share of it that my sorrowing is brought to an end.
Your garments vouch for the truth of all this, for when I
was at Munsalvaesche with the grieving Anfortas, all the
shields I found hanging there were marked the same way
as your garments, with the same turtledoves that you are
now wearing. Now tell me, Lady, when and how I am to go
forward to my joy, and do not withhold this from me very
long!"

And she replied, "Dear lord of mine, a man must go
along as your companion. Choose him. To lead the way is
mine. For the sake of the help you bring, do not delay for
long."

All around the tent circle was heard: "Cundrie   784
la sorcière has come!" and what her tidings were. Orgeluse
wept for joy that Parzival's question was now going to turn
Anfortas' torments away.

Arthur, the bold to fame, said courteously to Cundrie,
"Lady, ride to a place of repose and allow yourself to be attended; issue commands yourself as to how."

But she said, "If Arnive is here, I will live in whatever
quarters she provides me for this present time until my

lord departs. If she is delivered from her imprisonment, allow me to see her and the other ladies upon whom Clinschor inflicted his torments in captivity these many years."

Two knights lifted her onto her horse and to Arnive rode the noble maiden.

Now it was time for them to eat. Parzival sat down beside his brother, and he it was whom he asked to be his companion. Feirefiz readily assented to ride to Munsalvaesche with him.

Now everyone was getting up all around the circle.

Feirefiz had a noble thought: he asked King Gramoflanz, if the love between him and his kinswoman   785 was perfect, to give proof now that such was the case: "Help her and my kinsman Gawan to see that all kings and princes present here, and all barons and poor knights as well, that not one of them rides away without receiving gifts from me. Disgrace would befall me if I left here without distributing gifts. And all the traveling minstrels here are all to expect gifts from me. Arthur, I ask you to look quickly to this matter and see that the noble ones do not scorn them. Assure them it is no shame for them to accept—they never knew so rich a hand—and appoint messengers to go to my harbor from where the presents are to come."

Everyone promised the heathen they would not leave this field before four days were up. At which the heathen was pleased—so I heard it said. Arthur assigned him reliable messengers to send down to the harbor. Feirefiz, the son of Gahmuret, then took ink and parchment, and he did not omit marks of identification in what he wrote.—I doubt that ever a letter sent for so much as this one.—Without delay the messengers set out.   786

Then Parzival began to talk, and he spoke to them all in French and related what Trevrizent had said on that former occasion, that no one could ever fight his way to the Grail "unless he has been summoned to it by God." This word traveled across all lands, that no fighting could win it, and thus many people desisted from searching for the Grail. For that reason it remains hidden still.

Parzival and Feirefiz gave the ladies cause for lamentation. They would have been reluctant not to do so, and therefore rode to the four sections of the army and said farewell to all the people. Then in joyous spirits, and well armed against battle, they set out.

On the third day there were brought to Joflanze from the heathen's army such quantities of gifts as were never dreamed of. Any king that received gifts there found his country forever improved thereby. To each man according to his station were given gifts more precious than he had ever seen, and to the ladies went costly presents from Triande and from Nouriente.

I don't know how the army broke up, but Cundrie and those two, they rode away.

BOOK·XVI

Anfortas and his people were still enduring the   787
pain of grief. Their fidelity caused him to continue in his
suffering. Often he begged them for death, and death would
surely have come to him, except that they frequently had
him view the Grail and the Grail's power.

To his knighthood he said, "I well know that if you were
truly loyal you would have pity on my suffering. How long
is this to go on with me? If you wish justice for yourselves
you will have to answer before God for me. I have always
stood ready to serve you ever since I first bore weapons. I
have sufficiently atoned for whatever dishonor befell me and
for what no one of you ever saw. If you are guiltless of in-
fidelity, then deliver me for the sake of the helmet's way
and the order of the shield! You have often witnessed, unless you held it in no esteem, how I turned both of them
dauntlessly to knightly work. Valley and hill I have over-
shot in many a joust and so wielded the sword that it dismayed the enemy—however little I have profited therefrom
with you. I, Joy's outcast, shall on Judgment Day   788
accuse you one and all, and so you are close to your own
hell-fall if you will not let me depart from you. You should
have pity on my distress. You have seen and heard how this
misfortune came to me. What good am I now as your lord?
It will unfortunately come too soon to suit you if you lose

your souls because of me. What manner of behavior is this that you have adopted!"

They *would* have released him from his misery, had it not been for the comforting comfort which Trevrizent had previously pronounced and which he had seen in writing on the Grail. They were awaiting the second coming of the man before whom all his joy had vanished previously and the hour of succor that would come with the question from his mouth. Often the king would keep his eyes closed, sometimes as long as four days. Then he was carried before the Grail whether he would or no. His sickness would force him to open his eyes, and thus against his will he would be forced to live and not to die. In this way they were able to keep him alive until the day when Parzival and   789 the speckled Feirefiz rode with joy up to Munsalvaesche.

Now the time had waited until Mars or Jupiter had once again come back all angry in their orbits to the point from which they had proceeded. Then he was lost. That caused such pain in Anfortas' wound, and he suffered so, that knights and maidens heard the sound of his repeated screams, and by his eyes he expressed to them his agony. He was wounded beyond help and they could not help him. Yet the adventure says that true help was coming to him now.

They set about easing his heart's agony. Whenever the sharp and bitter anguish brought the fierce distress upon him, they sweetened the air and ventilated the stench of his wound. On the carpet in front of him lay perfume and odor of turpentine, musk and aromatic. To purify the air there were there also theriaca and sandalwood, and the scent of them was sweet. Wherever one stepped on the carpet cardamom was trodden underfoot, and clove   790 and nutmeg, all to sweeten the air, and as these were ground under passing feet the foul stench was dispersed. His firewood was *lign aloe,* as I have informed you before, and the legs of his folding cot were of viper horn. For protection against the venom powdered herbs were strewn over the covers. Quilted, not merely sewn, was what he leaned against, and his mattress was of pfellel-silk from Nouriente and of palmat-silk. His cot was better still adorned with noble gems and with no other kind. It was held together by salamander strands which constituted the webbing underneath him. Of joys he had slim share. The bed was rich on every side: no one can claim he ever saw a better. Costly it was and resplendent from the various precious stones. Now hear these named aright: [1]

Carbuncle and moonstone,   791
balas and gagathromeus,
onyx and chalcedony,
coral and bestion,
pearl and ophthalmius,
ceraunius and hephaestites,
hierachites and heliotropia,
pantherus and androdragma,
prasius and sagda,
haematites and dionysia,
agate and celidon,
sardonyx and chalcophon,
carnelian and jasper,
aetites and iris,
gagates and lynx-eye,
asbesto and cegolitus,
galactites and jacinth,
orites and enhydrus,
apsyctus and alabandina,
chrysolectrus and hyaenia,
emerald and lodestone,
sapphire and pyrites.
Here and there stood also
turquoise and liparea,
chrysolite and ruby,
paleise and sard,
adamant and chrysoprase,

[1] English words have been used in this catalogue of jewels as far as possible; in several cases Latin and Greek spellings have been restored, e.g., *heliotropia* for *eljotropia*. The list occupies thirty lines, precisely one manuscript page.

melochites and diadochos,
peanites and medus,
beryl and topaz.

Several of these inspired high courage, while   792
the special virtue of many of these stones was good for healing and medication, and anyone with the knowledge to test
them properly found great potency in them. By means of
these they kept Anfortas alive, for he held their hearts
within him. He caused his people sorrow enough.

But joy will now be heard of him. Up from Joflanze into
Terre de Salvaesche has come one from whom his own sorrow has passed away, Parzival, accompanied by his brother
and a maiden. I was not told exactly how far the distance
was. They would have had to face attacks except that Cundrie, their guide, spared them that peril. They were riding
toward a lookout tower when a host of templars, armed
and well mounted, came pouring down against them. But
these behaved courteously because they could see by the
guide that joy was approaching. The leader of the troop
said, as soon as he saw the many turtledoves glittering on
Cundrie's garments, "Our grief has come to an end. With
the Grail's insignia there comes to us here he whom
we have ever desired since the rope of sorrow bound
us. Halt! Great joy approaches us!"   793

Feirefiz the Angevin urged on his brother Parzival and
at the same moment rushed to combat, but Cundrie seized
his bridle and his joust did not take place. Then the grace-
less maiden quickly said to her lord, Parzival, "These
shields and banners you should recognize. Yonder is nothing less than a Grail troop, and they are wholly in your
service."

Then the noble heathen said, "In that case let battle be
avoided."

Parzival bade Cundrie ride up the trail toward them,
and she did ride up and gave them news of what joy had
come to them. All the templars dismounted upon the grass
and many removed their helmets. They received Parzival

on foot and reckoned his greeting as a benediction. They also welcomed Feirefiz the black-and-white, and then up to Munsalvaesche they rode in tears, and yet with tokens of joy.

Untold throngs they found, many a winsome   794 aged knight, noble pages, many squires, and the whole sad household. Feirefiz the Angevin and Parzival could both rejoice in this arrival. They were handsomely received at the steps before the great hall. Then they stepped into the hall itself. There, as customarily, lay a hundred carpets broad and round, and upon each one a down cushion and a long samite spread. If the two were sensible they could sit down anywhere until their armor was removed. A chamberlain approached bringing them rich garments, identical for each of them. All the knights sat down. Many a precious goblet of gold—it was not glass—was brought to them. Feirefiz and Parzival drank and then betook themselves to Anfortas, the sorrowful man.

You have heard before how he leaned and did not sit, and how his bed was adorned. Now Anfortas received these two joyously, and yet with signs of suffering. He said,   795 "I have bided in misery for you to come and make me glad. You left me before in such a way that, if you are sincere about helping me, you must regret. If ever praise was spoken of you, then prevail upon the knights and maidens here to give me death and let my agony end! If your name is Parzival, keep me from the sight of the Grail for seven nights and eight days, and then all my lamentations will cease. I do not dare give you any further hint. Blessing upon you if help is reported of you!—Your companion is a stranger here: I cannot have him standing before me. Why do you not allow him to go and rest?"

All in tears then, Parzival said, "Tell me where the Grail is kept here. If God's goodness triumphs in me, this throng of people shall be witness to it."

Then, facing in that direction, he genuflected thrice in honor of the Trinity, praying that help might be vouchsafed for this sorrowful man's pain of heart. He rose to his feet again and said, *"Uncle, what is it that troubles you?"* [2]

He, Who for Saint Sylvester's sake brought a bullock
back to life from the dead, and Who bade Laza-   796
rus arise, the Same gave help that Anfortas was healed and
made well again. The luster which the French call *fleur*
came over his flesh. Parzival's beauty was now a mere
breath, and Absalom's the son of David, and Vergulaht's
of Ascalun, and all whose beauty was from birth, and all
that was reported of Gahmuret when he was seen entering
Kanvoleis so graciously; the beauty of none of these was
equal to that which Anfortas now bore as he emerged from
sickness. God has skills enough yet beyond these.

The election was made of none other than the writing
upon the Grail had named for its Lord, and Parzival was
forthwith proclaimed there King and Lord.—I doubt if anyone could find elsewhere two men as rich—if I can judge
of riches—as Parzival and Feirefiz. And zealously they were
served, this host and his guest.

I do not know how many stages Condwiramurs had
meanwhile ridden in joy toward Munsalvaesche.   797
She had already learned the truth—for the message to fetch
her had come—so that her mourning and grief were over.
Duke Kyot and many another worthy man had guided her
into the forest of Terre de Salvaesche, and at the point
where Segramors had been unhorsed and where the snow
and the blood had once borne her likeness, Parzival was to
fetch her. That was a journey he might well endure. A
templar brought him this report: "Many courteous knights
have graciously escorted the queen."

This was the thought that came to Parzival: he took a
part of the Grail company and rode to see Trevrizent. The
latter's heart rejoiced at the news that things so stood with
Anfortas that he had not died from the joust and that the
question had achieved his peace.

And he said, "God has many secrets. Who hath ever sat

---

[2] *"Oeheim, waz wirret dir?"* In Chrétien the question is a double
one: *Why does the lance bleed?* and *Whom does one serve with this
Grail?*

in His council or who knoweth the end of His power? [3] Not all the angels with their company of saints will ever come to know its limit. God is man and also His Father's Word, God is Father and Son, His Spirit can lend great aid."

And Trevrizent said to Parzival, "Greater mira-   798
cle has seldom come to pass, for you have forced God by defiance to make His infinite Trinity grant your will. From cunning, in order to divert you from the Grail, I told you a lie as to how things stood with it. Assign me penance for my sin! I now must obey you, my sister's son and my lord. To you I gave the information that the outcast spirits,[4] with God's assistance, were around the Grail in the expectation of His favor. But God is so changeless that He forever contends against them whom I named to you as recipient of His grace. Whoever desires to achieve his heavenly reward must renounce those same spirits. They are eternally lost, and they themselves elected their loss. I grieved for your trials, for it had never happened that anyone could ever fight his way to the Grail, and I would gladly have dissuaded you. Now it has turned out otherwise with you, and your gain has been increased. Now turn your mind to humility."

Parzival said to his uncle, "I wish to see her   799
whom I have never seen in all these five years. When we were together she was dear to me, as she still is dear to me. But I should like to have your advice nevertheless, as long as death does not part us, for you did give me your counsel once in time of great need. I want to go to meet my wife, who has arrived, I have heard, at a place on the Plimizoel." And he begged him for permission to depart.

The good man commended him to God and Parzival rode away that same night. The forest was thoroughly familiar to his companions. When daylight came, he came

[3] Jeremiah 23, 18.
[4] Trevrizent's statements in Book IX, 471, were contrary to church doctrine; he now asserts an orthodox position. (Compare the unequivocal damnation of the neutral angels in Dante's *Inferno*, Canto III, 37-42.)

upon a cherished find, a quantity of tents set up. From the land of Brobarz, I heard it told, was many a banner erected there, and many a shield had followed behind them. The princes of his country were encamped there. Parzival asked where the queen herself was lodged, and whether she had a separate tent circle. They showed him where she was camped in a splendidly adorned circle with tents all around.

Now Duke Kyot of Catalonia had risen early that morning, and up toward him rode these comers. The daylight was still grey, but Kyot immediately recognized   800 the coat of arms of the Grail on the troop—they were marked with turtledoves. The old man sighed, for Schoysiane, his gentle wife, had brought him happiness at Munsalvaesche until she died in giving birth to Sigune. Kyot advanced toward Parzival and welcomed him and his men with courtesy. He despatched a page for the queen's marshal and commanded him to look well after the comfort of all the knights he saw halted there. Parzival he took by the hand and led him to the queen's chambers, and in a small buckram tent had them remove his armor. The queen was still unaware of this. Parzival found Loherangrin and Kardeiz lying in bed with her—then joy could not help but triumph in him—in a high and spacious tent with lovely ladies lying asleep on all sides. Kyot slapped the covers and bade the queen wake up and laugh merrily. She glanced up and saw her husband. She was wearing nothing but her smock, but she flung the bedclothes around her   801 and leaped out of bed onto the carpet, Condwiramurs the fair, and Parzival clasped her in his arms.—I was told they kissed each other.

She said, "Fortune has sent you to me, joy of my heart!" and she bade him welcome. "I should be angry, but I cannot. Honored be this time and this day which have brought me this embrace, before which my sorrow fades away. Now I have what my heart desires, and Care is powerless against me."

Now the children, too, awoke, Kardeiz and Loherangrin, where they were lying quite naked in the bed. Parzival did not mind in the least, and he kissed them lovingly. Kyot, the rich in courtesy, had the boys carried away, and he told all the ladies in the tent to leave, which they did once they had greeted their lord after his long journey. Then Kyot the courteous commended her husband to the queen and led the maidens away. It was still very early, and the chamberlain closed the tent sides.

If blood and snow had once deprived him of   802
the company of his senses—he had found them lying on this very meadow—Condwiramurs now redeemed that pledge of sorrow, for she held the pledge. Never had he accepted love's assistance elsewhere for love's need, yet many a worthy woman had offered him love. I think he found diversion until mid-morning of the day. The army gathered from all around to see what was up. Then they noticed the templars, who were all in armor and whose spear-scarred shields were badly riddled from jousts and hacked with swords. Several wore gambesons of pfellel-silk or samite. They still had their iron greaves on but had removed their other armor.

Now there could be no more sleeping. The king and queen arose. A priest sang Mass. In the ring outside the tent circle gathered a great throng from that brave army that once had fought against Clamidê. When the benediction had been pronounced, Parzival was welcomed by his vassals with noble fidelity, many a knight of them rich in valor. The sidewalls of the tent were removed.   803

Then the king said, "Which one is the boy who is to be king over your country?" And to all the princes he proclaimed: "Waleis and Norgals, Kanvoleis and Kingrivals, this boy shall possess by right. In Anjou and in the city of Bealzenan, if he ever comes to man's estate, grant him your support there! Gahmuret was my father's name, and he left it to me in lawful heritage. With blessing *I* have received the heritage of the Grail. Accept therefore your fiefs from my son, if I am to find you loyal."

With good will that was done. Many a banner was then brought up, and two small hands bestowed many a broad territory in fief. And then Kardeiz was crowned. Later he

was to conquer Kanvoleis and much of what had been
Gahmuret's.[5]

On the grass beside the Plimizoel, seats were put out and
a wide circle cleared where they all might eat. Quickly
breakfast was served, and then the army set out on its
homeward journey. All the tents were struck, and they took
the young king back with them. Numerous maidens and
other persons said farewell to the queen and   804
showed their grief as they did so. Then the templars took
Loherangrin and his beautiful mother and rode briskly
away toward Munsalvaesche.

"Once in this forest," said Parzival, "I saw a hermitage
and through it a rapid brook, flowing clear. If any of you
knows it, show me the way there."

His companions said they knew of one: "A maiden dwells
there all in mourning upon her beloved's coffin. She is the
very ark of true goodness. Our way passes close by her.
She is seldom to be found free of grief."

The king said, "Let us see her."

They assented.

They rode swiftly on, and late that evening they found
Sigune in a posture of prayer, dead. Then the queen beheld
grief. They broke into the hermitage to reach her, and
for his cousin's sake Parzival bade them raise the stone
from the coffin. There, uncorrupted, shone Schianatulander,
embalmed in all his beauty. Beside him they placed her who
had given him a virginal love while she lived,   805
and closed the grave anew. Condwiramurs began to lament
for her uncle's daughter, so I heard it told, and lost much
of her joy, for Schoysiane, the dead maiden's mother, had
brought her up as a child, the same who was Parzival's
maternal aunt, and hence all joy fled from her—if the Provençal read the truth. Duke Kyot, the tutor of King Kardeiz, knew nothing of his daughter's death.

This tale is not bent like a bow, but true and straight: [6]
they did what the journey required and rode into Munsalvaesche by night.

---

[5] Lehelin had seized Waleis and Norgals. See Book III, 128.
[6] Wolfram alludes to the metaphor elaborated in Book V, 241.

There Feirefiz had waited up for them, having passed the time away meanwhile. Many candles were then lighted, until it looked as though the forest were on fire. A templar from Patrigalt rode under arms at the queen's side. The courtyard was broad and wide, and several separate groups were standing there, who received the queen and their lord and his son. They carried Loherangrin to his uncle Feirefiz, but since he was so black-and-white-speckled, the boy would not kiss him. Noble children feel fear 806 even today. The heathen laughed at this. Out in the courtyard they began to disperse, now that the queen had dismounted. Gain and joy had come to them in her. They led her to where there was a noble company of beautiful ladies, while Feirefiz and Anfortas both stood courteously on the steps near the ladies. Repanse de Schoye and Garschiloye of Greenland and Florie de Lunel all had bright eyes and fair complexions and the good name of virgins. There stood another one there, slender as a reed, who did not lack for goodness, the daughter of Jernis of Ryl, and this maiden's name was Ampflise. And there stood also, I was told, Clarischanze of Tenabroc, a sweet maiden of loveliness undiminished and slim-waisted as an ant.

Feirefiz advanced toward the queen, who bade him kiss her. She kissed Anfortas also, and was happy at his deliverance. Then with her hand she led Feirefiz 807 to where she saw the master's aunt, Repanse de Schoye, standing. Then many kisses followed. Her lips were so red already that they were weary of kisses by now, so that it makes *me* weary and I am sorry that I am not able to do the work for her—for *she* was weary when she arrived. Maidens escorted their lady in.

The knights remained in the great hall, which was well lighted with candles that brightly burned. Then in all solemnity preparation was begun for the Grail. This was brought forth, never merely for people to see, but only on festal occasions. That evening when they were all devoid of joy because of the bloody spear, the Grail had been brought forth for help, because they had hoped for consolation from it; but Parzival had left them in their plight. With joy it is brought forth now: their grief has been wholly overcome.

When the queen had removed her traveling dress and put on her coif, she made her appearance as befitted her. At the entrance door Feirefiz met her. Now it is beyond dispute that never has a man at any time heard or   808 spoken of a more beautiful woman. She was wearing pfellel-silk that a skillful hand had woven in Sarant, by a process previously invented in the city of Thasme. Feirefiz the Angevin escorted her, and her beauty shed a radiance. In the middle of the great hall three huge fires had been built; *lign aloe* was the firewood's scent. Forty more carpets and seats had now been placed there than at the time when Parzival beheld the Grail borne before him. One seat was adorned beyond all the others, and there Feirefiz and Anfortas were to sit with the host. Whichever one was to serve when the Grail came had to act with skill and courtesy.

You have heard previously how it was brought before Anfortas; likewise it was now brought before the son of noble Gahmuret, and for Tampenteire's child. The maidens tarry no longer. In order they came, five-and-twenty in number. The first one struck the heathen as beautiful, and   809 all curls was her hair. But the ones next following seemed even more beautiful, as he saw them come in directly, and all their garments were rich. Sweet, lovable, and gentle were the faces of all the maidens. Last of all came the lovely maiden, Repanse de Schoye. The Grail permitted, I was told, only her to carry it, no one else. In her heart there was much virtue, and her skin had the luster of flowers.

Shall I tell you the whole procedure of the service? How many cupbearers poured water? And how many tables were carried in to them? (There were more of them than I told you the other time.) And how Impropriety avoided that hall? And how many roller-carts were pulled in loaded with precious gold ware? And where the knights sat?— That would make too long a tale. I will be brief and quick. With all propriety there were taken from before the Grail meats wild and tame, for this one mead, for that one wine, just as each would have it, mulberry wine, spiced wine, and claret. *Le fils du roi* Gahmuret found Pelrapeire quite different the first time he was there.   810

The heathen wanted to know what it was that kept filling the empty gold dishes in front of the table. The marvel intrigued him.

Then the beautiful Anfortas, who had been seated next to him, said, "Sir, do you see the Grail lying there before you?"

The speckled heathen said, "I don't see anything but an achmardi. My young lady brought it to us, the one standing over there in front of us wearing a crown. Her glance goes right to my heart. I thought I was so strong that never could maiden or woman rob me of joy's strength, but now all the noble love I ever received is repugnant to me. Improper conduct undoes my proper conduct if I tell you of my distress, since I have never offered you my service; but what good are all my riches, or whatever I have won for women's sakes, or whatever my hand has bestowed in the way of gifts, if I must live in such discomfort? My mighty god Jupiter, why hast thou brought me here for such misery?"

Love's power and Joy's weakness made him turn pale in the white parts of his complexion. Condwiramurs the fair now very nearly found a rival in that lovely   811 maiden's radiance, and Feirefiz, the rich guest, became entangled in her love's snare. His first love died away in willed forgetfulness. What help was Secundille's love to her now? Or Tribalibot, her country? One maiden now caused him such acute distress that Clauditte and Olimpia, Secundille and women from many another place where they had rewarded his service and sounded his praises—all their loves seemed poor to Gahmuret's son from Zazamanc.

Then the beautiful Anfortas saw that his companion was in distress and that his white patches had turned pale, showing that his high courage had failed him. And he said, "Sir, I am sorry if my sister is causing you such pain. No man has suffered for her sake before; no knight has ever ridden in her service, and thus no one has received reward from her. With me she has been in great sorrow, and it has hurt her color a little to have been so seldom merry. Your brother is her sister's son: perhaps he can help you out there."

"If the girl is your sister," said Feirefiz the   812 Angevin, "the one over there with the crown on her loose-flowing hair, then give me advice about winning her love! All my heart's desire is for her. If I ever won fame by my spear, I only wish it had been done for her sake and that she would then grant me reward for it! There are five methods of tilting and my hand has performed them. One is 'at hand-thrust'; the second, which I also know, is 'broadside'; the third is 'at encounter'; and the good old 'regular joust' I have ridden also at top speed; and I have not shrunk from the 'by assent'.[7] Since the time when my shield first be-came my protection, today is my supreme unhappiness. Be-fore Agremuntin I rode against a knight of fire, and if my gambeson had not been of salamander and my second shield of aspindê, I would have been burned up in that joust. As often as I have won praise at the risk of my life—ah! if only *she* had sent me into the battle, your lovely sister! I would still be her messenger into combat. I will always hold it against my god Jupiter unless he preserves me from this great misery."

Frimutel was the name of the father of these two, and Anfortas and his sister were alike in face and com-   813 plexion. The heathen kept looking at her and then back again at him, and often as they carried dishes back and forth, his mouth did not eat of them. And yet he sat there like one about to eat.

Anfortas said to Parzival, "Sir, I do believe your brother has not yet seen the Grail."

Feirefiz agreed with the host: he did not see the Grail. All the knights found that odd indeed. Word of this also reached Titurel, the aged, crippled, bedridden man, and he said, "If he is a heathen man, then, without the power of baptism, he has no use wanting his eyes to join the company

---

[7] See Note 6, pp. 435-436.

of those who do see the Grail. There is a barrier raised around it." This message he sent out to the great hall.

Then the host and Anfortas said Feirefiz should observe what it was that all these people lived on: no heathen could behold it. They urged him to receive baptism and therewith purchase eternal reward.

"If I come to baptism for your sakes, will baptism   814 help me in love?" asked the heathen son of Gahmuret. "However battle or love ever compelled me, that was a mere breath up till now. Since my shield first protected me, for short time or for long, I have never known such distress. For courtesy's sake I should conceal my love, only my heart cannot conceal it."

"Whom do you mean?" asked Parzival.

"Why, that pretty girl over there, the sister of my companion here. If you will help me to her, I will show her such riches that vast lands will serve her."

"If you will allow yourself to be baptized," said the host, "you may sue for her love.—I can address you as *'du,'* now that our riches are roughly equal, in my case by the power of the Grail."

"Help me, brother," said Feirefiz the Angevin, "to the love of your aunt. If baptism can be gotten by combat, then lead me to it right away and let me serve for her reward! I have always loved the tune of splinters flying from a joust and swords ringing on helmets!"

The host laughed heartily at this, and Anfortas   815 laughed even more. "Can you receive baptism *that* way?" said the host. "*I* will bring her within your reach by means of *real* baptism. You will have to give up your god Jupiter for her sake, and renounce Secundille too. Tomorrow morning I will give you some advice that will serve your purposes."

Anfortas, before the time of his sickness, had spread his fame afar through knighthood for love's sake. Goodness and gentleness were the ways of his heart, and his hand had won many a prize. Thus there sat there in the presence of the Grail three of the very best knights that then bore shields, for they dared the risk.

If it is all right with you, they have now eaten enough. In proper form tables and tablecloths were now removed from before them all, and submissively the maidens made their bows. Feirefiz the Angevin watched them go away, and that made his sorrow greater. She who was his heart's prison carried the Grail away. Parzival gave them permission to withdraw.

How the hostess herself withdrew, and how   816 they set about making him comfortable who would lie uncomfortably anyway on account of love, and how all the company of the templars comfortably guarded them against all discomfort—that would be a long tale, and I want to tell you about the next day.

When bright daylight shone the next morning, Parzival came to an agreement with the good Anfortas, and they asked the man from Zazamanc, who was harried by Love, to come into the temple before the Grail. At the same time he summoned the wise templars. A great throng of squires and knights were standing there. Then the heathen came in. The baptismal font was a single ruby, and it stood on a circular step of jasper. Titurel, at some cost, had it erected that way.

Then Parzival said to his brother, "If you wish to have my aunt, you must renounce all your gods for her sake, and ever avenge gladly any insubordination to the Highest God, and with steadfastness keep His commandment."

"Whatever I have to do to have the girl," said   817 the heathen, "that I will do, and faithfully."

The baptismal font was tilted slightly in the direction of the Grail, and immediately it was full of water, neither too warm nor too cold. A grey and aged priest stood at hand, who had dipped many a child from heathendom in it.

He said, "You shall believe—and thereby rob the Devil of your soul—in the Highest God alone, whose Trinity is universal and everywhere of equal yield.[8] God is man and His Father's Word. As He is both Father and Son, Who are

---

[8] Wolfram's word here is *gurbort*, which has the dual meaning of land cultivated to yield crops and land yielding income from taxes. The statement signifies: "God helps everywhere."

held in equal honor, and of equal rank with His Spirit, may this water fend heathenry from you with the full power of all Three. By the power of the Trinity He also went into the water for baptism from Whom Adam received his features. From water trees derive their sap. Water fructifies all created things, which man calls creatures. From water man has his sight. Water gives many souls such radiance that angels cannot be more bright."

Feirefiz said to the priest, "If it is good against   818 distress, I will believe what you command, and if her love rewards me, I will gladly perform His commandment.— Brother, if your aunt has a god, I believe in him and in her, for never have I suffered like this. All *my* gods are abjured. Secundille shall also have lost whatever she may have done in my honor. For the sake of your aunt's god, bid them baptize me!"

They began to treat him as a Christian and pronounced the blessing of baptism over him. When the heathen had received baptism and his baptismal garment had been put on him, he waited impatiently for them to bring him the maiden. Then they bestowed Frimutel's child upon him. He who had been blind in seeing the Grail until the baptismal water had covered him had the Grail uncovered to his sight immediately after the event of baptism.

Upon the Grail it was now found written that any templar whom God's hand appointed master over foreign people should forbid the asking of his name or race, and that he should help them to their rights. If the question is asked of him they shall have his help no longer.   819 Because the sweet Anfortas was so long in bitter torment and went so long without the question, questioning is forever displeasing to them. All keepers of the Grail want no questions asked about them.

The baptized Feirefiz urgently besought his brother-in-law to come with him and not to shrink from availing himself of his riches, but Anfortas courteously dissuaded him from that proposal.

"I do not wish to spoil my submission to God. The Grail crown is just as rich. I lost it through pride, but now I have chosen humility. Wealth and the love of women are now receding from my mind. You are taking a noble wife away with you, and she will give you her chaste self in good women's way. Here I shall not shirk the duty of my Order. I shall ride many a joust and fight in the service of the Grail, but for women I shall never fight again: one woman brought me heart's grief. Nevertheless I am wholly without hatred toward women. High joy of men comes 820 from them, however small *my* gain there may have been."

Feirefiz continued to urge Anfortas to come with him for the sake of his sister's honor. Again he declined to go. Then Feirefiz the Angevin urged that Loherangrin should go with him. But his mother prevented that. And King Parzival said, "My son is destined for the Grail and there he must submissively devote his heart, if God permits him to achieve the proper spirit."

Feirefiz remained for joy and entertainment until the eleventh day, and on the twelfth day he departed. The rich man's intention was to take his wife to his army. Then a sadness came over Parzival for faithfulness' sake and he began to regret the journey. With his men he took counsel and sent a large company of horsemen with him out beyond the forest. Anfortas, that sweet warrior bold, rode with him as a guide. Many was the maiden who could not keep from tears.

They were obliged to make a new trail out 821 toward Carcobra. The sweet Anfortas sent word to the man who was burgrave there, reminding him that, if ever he had received rich gifts from his hand, he should now honor loyalty and show his brother-in-law the way "and his wife, my sister, through the *Forêt* of Laeprisin as far as the wild harbor wide."

Now it was time to part. They were to advance no further. Cundrie *la sorcière* was selected to deliver the message. All the templars took leave of the rich man, and the courteous knight rode on.

The burgrave did not fail to do as Cundrie bade him, and Feirefiz the rich was chivalrously received there with great pomp. Time did not hang heavy on his hands there; they

guided him immediately on his way with a noble *conduite*.
I don't know how many countries he covered until he
arrived at Joflanze on the meadow broad. He found a few
people left there yet, and at once Feirefiz inquired   822
where the army had gone. Each one had gone to his own
country as their ways took them. Arthur had gone to
Camelot.[9] Thus the man from Tribalibot could ride on
directly to his army. *They* lay there in the harbor all
sad for their lord's having gone off and left them. His
arrival now brought new high spirits to many a goodly
knight. The burgrave of Carcobra and all his men were then
dismissed to their homes with rich gifts. Cundrie learned
important news: messengers had reached the army saying
that death had overtaken Secundille. Then for the first time
Repanse de Schoye was able to be glad of her journey.

Later, in India, she gave birth to a son, whose name was
John. People called him Prester John. Ever since, people have
given that name to the kings there. Feirefiz ordered writings
to be sent all over the land of India about what Christian
life was like. It had not been so strong there previously. Here we call the land India; there it is   823
known as Tribalibot. Through Cundrie, Feirefiz sent back
word to his brother on Munsalvaesche of how things had
gone with him since, and of how Secundille had died. It
pleased Anfortas that his sister was now uncontested mistress of many lands so vast.

The true story has now come to you of the five children
of Frimutel, how they strove with goodness and how two of
them died. One was Schoysiane, without falsity before God.
The second was Herzeloyde, who thrust falseness out of
her heart. His sword and knightly life Trevrizent had renounced for the sweet love of God and for eternal reward.
The noble and beautiful Anfortas was manly with pure
heart. According to his rule, he rode many a joust for the
Grail's sake, but he did not fight for women.

❧§§❧

[9] Schamilot.

Loherangrin grew to manly strength; faint-heartedness was not to be found in him. When he reached understanding of knighthood he won praise in the service of the Grail.

Would you like to hear more?   824

Later on, over a land there ruled a lady who was free of all falsity. Wealth and nobility had both been inherited by her, and she knew how to act with true propriety. All human desires had perished in her. Noble men aplenty wooed her, some of whom wore crowns, and many a prince who was her equal in rank, but so great was her humility that she paid them no heed. Many counts of her country began to be annoyed with her. Why did she delay in taking a husband who would be suitable as her lord? She had put all her trust in God, whatever ill will was shown against her. Many tormented her for her innocence. She summoned a court of the lords of her land. Many a messenger traveled to her out of distant countries, but she forswore all these men, wishing only him whom God would indicate and whose love she would prize. She was the princess of Brabant.

From Munsalvaesche was sent he whom the swan brought and whom God had chosen for her. At Antwerp he was brought ashore. In him she was never de-   825
ceived, for he so acted that people declared him beautiful and manly in all the realms where he had ever been known. Courtly and wise in courtesy, he was a man sincerely generous without flinching, free from all wrongdoing.

The mistress of the land received him graciously. Now hear what he said. Rich and poor heard it as they stood about on all sides. He said, "My Lady Duchess, if I am to be the lord of this country, I must give up its equal. Now hear what I am about to ask of you. Never ask me who I am; then I shall be able to remain with you. But if I am subjected to your question you will lose my love. If you do not take this as a warning, God will give *me* warning: of *what,* He well knows."

She gave her pledge as a woman, which later on she broke because of love, that she would be at his command and that she would never transgress against whatever he bade her do, if God·left her in her right senses.

That night he received her love, and therewith   826
he became Prince over Brabant. The wedding took place
with splendor. Many a lord from his hand received the fief
that was rightfully his. This same man was also a righteous
judge, and he frequently performed feats of chivalry, so
that he won praise by his strength. Together, they acquired
lovely children. There are many people in Brabant even
now who know of these two, of her welcome, and of his departure, and how her question drove him away, and how
long he remained there. He left much against his will.

Then his friend the swan again brought him a dainty
little boat. As remembrances he left behind a sword, a horn,
and a ring. Then Loherangrin departed, for, if we are to
tell the story right, this was Parzival's son. Streams and
roads he traveled back to the tending of the Grail.

And why had the good woman lost her noble lover's love?
He had forbidden her to question when he had first appeared to her off the sea.—Here Erec should speak, for *he*
punished only with words.[10]

❧§❧

If Master Chrétien de Troyes did not do justice   827
to this story, that may well vex Kyot, who furnished us the
right story. The Provençal correctly[11] tells how Herzeloyde's child won the Grail, as he was destined to do, when
Anfortas had forfeited it. From Provence to Germany the
true facts were sent to us, as well as this adventure's final
conclusion. I, Wolfram of Eschenbach, shall tell no more of
it now than the master told there.

His children and his high race I have rightly named for
you, Parzival's I mean, whom I brought to the place which, in
spite of everything, his blessedness had destined for him. A

[10] In Hartmann's *Erec*, the loyal Enite humbly reported to her husband the popular reproach against him for neglecting chivalry amid the
delights of marriage. Stung by her words, Erec subjected her to protracted humiliations, but his chastisement was always *verbal.*

[11] The word *endehaft* may mean "correctly" or "through to the
end."

life so concluded that God is not robbed of the soul through fault of the body, and which can obtain the world's favor with dignity, *that* is a worthy work.

To good women, if they are sensible, I am all the more worthy—in case one of them wishes me well—now that I have completed this story. If it was done for a woman's sake, she will have to speak sweet words to me.

ADDITIONAL NOTES

Note 1 • Wolfhart is the warrior who, in the second-last *aventiure* of the *Nibelungenlied*, provokes by his truculence the last ferocious battle with King Gunther's men.

Note 2 • In citing the famous passage of "Rumolt's advice" from *aventiure* XXIV of the *Nibelungenlied*, Liddamus either paraphrases very freely or else quotes from a version unknown to us.

Kriemhilt, the murdered Siegfried's widow, has married the mighty King Etzel (Attila) of the Huns with a view to using his power to revenge herself on the murderers, who are her brother King Gunther, two other brothers, and their vassal Hagen. Amid the debate over whether or not to accept her invitation to come to Etzel's court, Rumolt, the outspoken cook (*kuchenmeister*), urges all parties to stay safely at home in Worms on the Rhine rather than to incur the unknown perils of the distant journey. "Besides," he says, "you will have the best food that any king ever got in this world."

It is a comment on Wolfram's audiences that Rumolt's better-safe-than-sorry advice could be quoted like a proverb. The same may be said of the opportunistic advice of Lunete, alluded to with disapproval in Book V, 253, and in 436 of

Book IX, who, in Hartmann's *Iwein* (Yvain), counseled her widowed mistress to marry her husband's murderer, Iwein, as the best possible guarantee of her crown and country.

NOTE 3 • Neither Ermenrich, the historical East Gothic King Ermanaricus who died in 375 A.D., nor his evil counselor Sibeche appears in the German version of the *Nibelungenlied*. They are figures from the lost mass of Germanic saga and are known to us through the Scandinavian *Thidrekssaga*, where they are associated with the story of Dietrich von Bern (Theodoric of Verona). Since part of that narrative was drawn into the latter sections of the *Nibelungenlied*, they may have figured in a version of that poem unknown to us.

NOTE 4 • The realistic itinerary of 496, continued in 498-499, has suggested to some scholars an actual journey of the author's, but it could quite as easily derive from some traveler's report.

Seville (Sibilje) on the tidal river Guadalquivir is still a Spanish port.

Aquileia (Aglei) was a Roman and then a medieval seaport at the northern end of the Adriatic Sea, and from the sixth to the fifteenth century the seat of a powerful patriarchate. After capture by Venice in 1420 it declined rapidly and is now a village of hardly more than a thousand inhabitants.

Friuli (Friul) is a province now divided between Italy and Yugoslavia, of which Aquileia was once the chief city.

Cilli (Zilje), founded as Claudia Celeia by the Emperor Claudius in the first century A.D., is now a city of 20,000 in the north Yugoslavian province of Slovenia and known by alternate names: Cilli (Italian) and Celje (Slavic).

"The Rohas," some twenty miles east of Cilli, is now known as Mount Rohitsch, its German name, or, in Slavic, as Rogatec.

"Gandin" or "Candin" is modern Haidin, in Styria.

The Grajena (Greian) is a stream flowing into the Drave (Tra), a tributary of the Danube.

Styria (Stire), also known by its German name of

Steiermark, is now a province of Austria. Its chief city is Gratz. No Queen Lammire is known.

This collocation of places represented in Wolfram's day the extreme southeastern corner of German language territory within the Holy Roman Empire. Immediately to the east lie Hungary and Slavic areas. In juxtaposition with the unidentified Celtic place names so matter-of-factly cited by Trevrizent in 497, there is the implication of "furthest east" and "furthest west" of "Europe."

NOTE 5 • In 782, Cundrie lists the seven planets, by their Arabic names, from farthest to nearest in relation to the earth according to the traditional concept of an earth-centered universe.

1. SATURN—"the highest of the planets, Zval" = Zuḥal —"Saturn."

2. JUPITER—"the swiftly moving Almustri" = Al Mushtori—"The Shining One."

3. MARS—"Almaret" = (?) Al Aḥmar—"The Red" (so listed in the eleventh-century *Glossarium Latino-Arabicum,* along with the Hebrew term "maadim," also signifying "The Red"); = (?) Al Marrekh— Spanish-Arabic for "He armed with the long spear."

4. The SUN—"the bright Samsi" = (ash-)shams—"the sun." (The Arabic word, however, may not stand without the article (ash-); the ending in -i is probably dictated by the rhyme.)

5. VENUS—"Alligafir." MS d has *aliasir;* MS g *Aligofir;* MS Gg *gofir.* The word is unexplained, and the proposal has been rejected that it represents the Arabic article *Al* plus Latin Lucifer.

6. MERCURY—"Alkiter" = (?) Al Kātib—"The Scribe" (*Glossarium Latino-Arabicum*); = (?) Al Kedr— "The Dark One"; = (?) Al Uṭarid—"Mercury."

7. The MOON—"And nearest us is Alkamer." = Al Qamar—"the moon."

See: C. F. Seybold's article in *Zeitschrift für deutsche Wortforschung,* Vol. 8, 147-151 (1906-07), who contradicts F. Schwally, *ibid.,* Vol. 3, 140-141 (1902).

NOTE 6 • Authorities quote the description of these five methods of tilting offered by Felix Niedner in his book *Das deutsche Tournier.*

1. "At hand-thrust" (MHG *puneiz,* OF *poigneis*)—a head-on charge by opposed groups of knights with lance lowered.

2. "Broadside" (MHG *ze triviers,* OF à *travers*)—a charge by one group of knights against the right side of the opposing group, again with lowered lance.

3. "At encounter"—an unusual method for which Wolfram apparently coined the term *zen muoten* for lack of a French term. It involved the head-on charge by one knight against an opposing group, with the added hazard of the single knight's attacking a particular member predesignated from among the opponents and eluding the attacks of the others.

4. "The regular joust" (MHG *ze rehter tjost*)—a charge by one knight against another, either head-on or from the right side with the objective of knocking the opponent off his horse.

5. "By assent" (MHG *zer volge*)—a rare type practiced only at the conclusion of a tournament by individual challenge and specific assent of two champions. It was a bravura performance in the presence of the ladies and hence known also as the "Damenstich."

INDEX OF PERSONS

(Persons easily recognizable, such as Adam or Jupiter, are not listed, nor are persons whose identity is explained in the notes. The long list of names recited by Feirefiz in 770 and by Parzival in 772 is also omitted.)

FLORIE DE LUNEL, a maiden in the service of the Grail.

FLURDAMURS, wife of Kingrisin, sister of Gahmuret, mother of Vergulaht and Antikonie.

FRIDEBRANT, King of Scotland, fights with Isenhart against Belacane.

FRIMUTEL, son of Titurel, father of Trevrizent, Anfortas, Herzeloyde, Schoysiane, and Repanse de Schoye, grandfather of Sigune and Parzival.

GABENIS, a prince.

GAHERJET, Gawan's cousin, one of Arthur's knights.

GAHMURET, son of King Gandin of Anjou, father of Parzival and Feirefiz.

GALOES, Gahmuret's older brother, King of Anjou.

GALOGANDRES, Duke of Gippones, a member of Clamidê's army before Pelrapeire.

GANDILUZ, son of Gurnemanz' son Gurzgri.

GANDIN, King of Anjou, Gahmuret's father.

GAREL, one of Arthur's knights.

GARSCHILOYE, of Greenland, a maiden in the service of the Grail.

GASCHIER, from Normandy, Kaylet's nephew, on Fridebrant's side in the battle of Patelamunt.

GINOVER, wife of King Arthur.

GRAMOFLANZ, King of Rosche Sabins, son of Irot.

GRIGORZ, King of Ipotente, related to Clamidê.

GUNTHER, King of the Burgundians.

GURNEMANZ, Prince of Graharz, uncle of Condwiramurs.

GURZGRI, son of Gurnemanz, father of Schianatulander.

GYMELE, a maiden in Isalde's following.

HARDIZ, King of Gascony.

HERLINDE, the woman for whose love Fridebrant killed Hernant.

HERNANT, a king killed by Vridebrant in the battle for Herlinde's love.

HERZELOYDE, Queen of Waleis and Norgals, Gahmuret's second wife, mother of Parzival.

HIUTEGER, Duke of Scotland in Fridebrant's service.

SCHAFILLOR, King of Aragon, defeated by Gahmuret before Kanvoleis.

SCHAUT, a king, brother of Poydiconjunz, father of Meljanz.

SCHENTAFLURS, son of Gurnemanz.

SCHERULES, burgrave of Bearosche.

SCHIANATULANDER, son of Gurzgri, beloved of Sigune.

SCHILTUNC, father-in-law of Fridebrant.

SCHIOLARZ, Count of Poitou, father of Liadarz.

SCHIRNIEL, King of Lirivoyn.

SCHOETTE, wife of Gandin, mother of Gahmuret.

SCHOYSIANE, daughter of Frimutel, mother of Sigune.

SECUNDILLE, Queen of India, wife of Feirefiz.

SEGRAMORS, a king, relative of Ginover.

SIEGFRIED, of the Nibelungen saga.

SIGUNE, daughter of Kyot of Catalonia and Schoysiane, beloved of Schianatulander.

SURDAMUR, daughter of King Lot and Sangive, sister of Gawan, wife of the Grecian emperor Alexander.

TAMPANIS, chief squire of Gahmuret.

TAMPENTEIRE, King of Brobarz, father of Condwiramurs.

TANKANIS, father of Isenhart.

TAURIAN, brother of Dodines, friend of Trevrizent.

TERDELASCHOYE, a fairy.

TINAS, father of Count Laiz.

TITUREL, father of Frimutel, grandfather of Anfortas.

TREBUCHET, a famous smith.

TREVRIZENT, son of Frimutel, brother of Anfortas, uncle of Sigune and Parzival.

TURKENTALS, vassal of Herzeloyde.

URIANS, a prince from Punturtois.

UTEPANDRAGUN, King of Britain, husband of Arnive, father of Arthur and Sangive.

VERGULAHT, King of Ascalun, son of Kingrisin, brother of Antikonie.

Grail and Arthurian circles

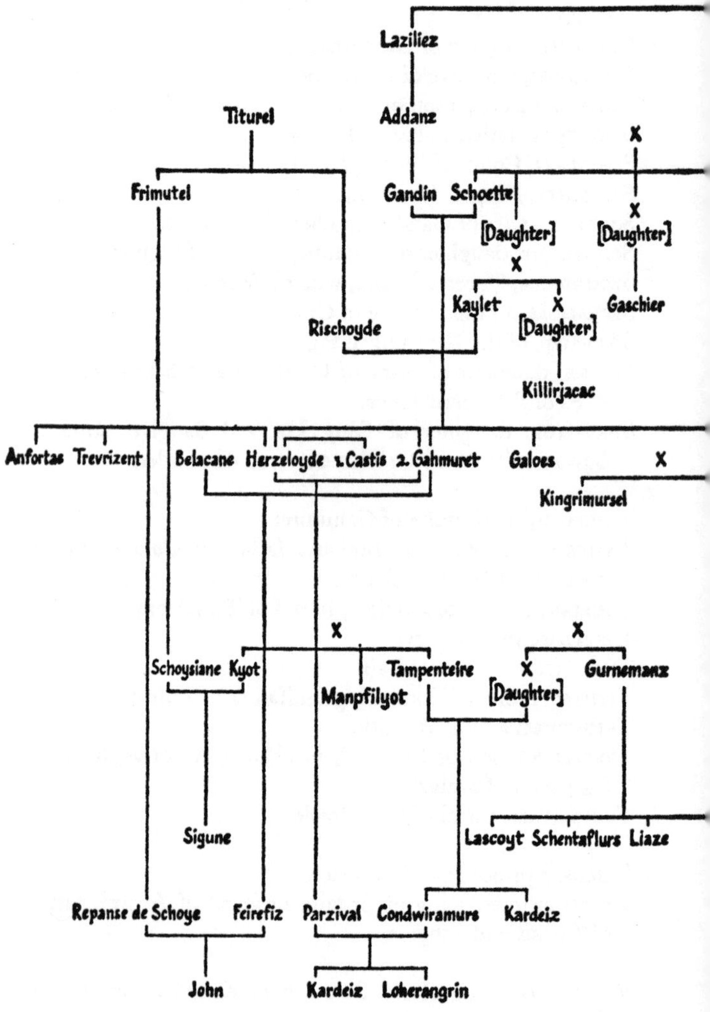

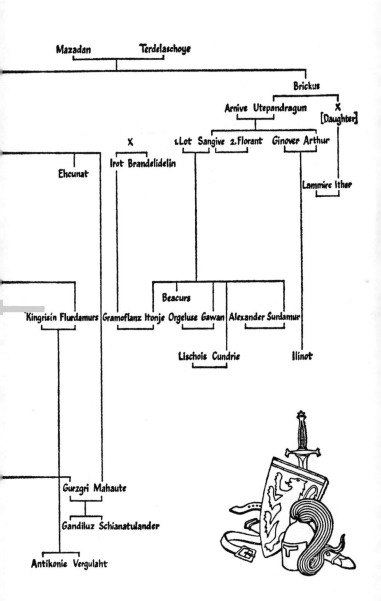

HELEN M. MUSTARD is Professor of German at the School of General Studies, Columbia University. Educated at Oberlin College (B.A.), the University of Leipzig, and Columbia University (M.A., Ph.D.), she has also taught at Randolph-Macon Woman's College and Wellesley College. Since 1959 she has been Chairman of the New York State Council on Foreign Language Teaching. Her previous publications include *The Lyric Cycle in German Literature* (1946).

CHARLES E. PASSAGE is Professor of Comparative Literature at Brooklyn College. Educated at the University of Rochester (B.A.) and Harvard University (M.A., Ph.D.), he has also taught at Harvard, Northwestern, and Columbia. During World War II he served for thirty months overseas as a cryptanalyst in the Signal Intelligence Service. His previous publications include *Dostoevski the Adapter* (1954), and translations of *The Prince of Homburg* (1956), *Wallenstein* (1958), *Don Carlos* (1959) and *Novalis: Hymns to the Night and Other Selected Writings* (1960).